Prai

"Using w... ...er's skill, Kasey Michaels aims for the heart and never misses."
—*New York Times* bestselling author
Nora Roberts

The Butler Did It

"Witty dialogue peppers a plot full of delectable details exposing the foibles and follies of the age… The heroine is appealingly independent minded; the hero is refreshingly free of any mean-spirited machismo; and supporting characters have charm to spare… [a] playfully perfect Regency-era romp."
— *Publishers Weekly*

"What fun, what pleasure, what a read!"
—*Romantic Times Bookclub*

Shall We Dance?

"Brimming with historical details and characters ranging from royalty to spies, greedy servants to a jealous woman, this tale is told with panache and wit."
— *Romantic Times Bookclub*

Kasey Michaels is a *New York Times* bestselling author of both historical and contemporary novels. She is also the winner of a number of prestigious awards.

Available from Mills & Boon® and Kasey Michaels

THE BUTLER DID IT

IN HIS LORDSHIP'S BED
(short story in *The Wedding Chase*)

SHALL WE DANCE?

IMPETUOUS
MISSES

Kasey Michaels

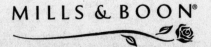

MILLS & BOON®

*First published in Great Britain 2006
by Harlequin Mills & Boon Limited,
Eton House, 18-24 Paradise Road, Richmond, Surrey TW9 1SR*

IMPETUOUS MISSES © Harlequin Books S.A. 2006

The publisher acknowledges the copyright holder of the individual works as follows:

The Questioning Miss Quinton © Kathie Seidick 1987
The Anonymous Miss Addams © Kathie Seidick 1989

ISBN 0 263 84432 3

153-0406

*Printed and bound in Spain
by Litografia Rosés S.A., Barcelona*

CONTENTS

THE QUESTIONING
MISS QUINTON

PROLOGUE

"How completely and utterly boring."

Victoria Quinton, feeling no better for having voiced her sentiments aloud, shifted her slim body slightly on the edge of the uncomfortable wooden chair that was situated to one side of the narrow, badly lit hallway, a thick stack of closely written papers lying forgotten in her lap as she waited for the summons that was so uncharacteristically late in coming this morning.

Raising one hand, she stifled a wide yawn, as she had been kept awake far into the night transcribing the Professor's latest additions to his epic book-in-progress on the history of upper-class English society; for besides acting as secretary, sounding board, and general dogsbody to him for as long as she could remember, Victoria also served as transcriptionist to the Professor, transforming his, at times, jumbled and confusing scribblings into legible final copies.

The Professor would not allow Victoria to recopy his notes into neat final copies during the daytime, and since her evenings were not known for their hours spent in any scintillating pursuit of pleasure, she could find no convincing reason to object to his directive that she fill them with more work.

As for the Professor, his lifelong struggle against insomnia made his evenings a prime time for visiting with the countless people he was always interviewing—all of them contenting themselves by prosing on long into the night over some obscure bit of family history of concern to, probably, none other than his subjects, another scholar, or himself.

Victoria had never been introduced to any of the Professor's nocturnal visitors, nor did she harbor any secret inclination to learn their identities, which the Professor guarded like some spoiled child hiding his treasured supply of tin soldiers from his mates. After all, if the Professor liked them, they would doubtless bore her to tears.

Hearing the ancient clock in the foyer groan, seem to collect itself, and then slowly chime ten times, she tentatively rose to her feet, torn between acknowledging that every minute that ticked by made it one minute less that she would be expected to sit in the gloomy library writing page after endless page of dictation until her fingers bent into painful cramps, and dreading the certain sharp scolding she would get for not rousing him when the Professor finally awakened on his own.

In the end, realizing that she wasn't exactly spending the interim in a mad indulgence of pleasure—seeing as how she had been sitting in the same spot like some stuffed owl ever since rising from the breakfast table—she made for the closed door and gave a short, barely audible knock.

There was no response. Victoria sighed and shook her head. ''He's probably curled up atop his desk again, afraid that the trip upstairs to his bed would rob him of his drowsiness, and taking his rest where he can,'' she decided, knocking again, a little louder this time. Then she pressed her ear against the wood, thinking that the Professor's stentorian snores should be audible even through the thickness of the door.

Five minutes passed in just this unproductive way, and Victoria chewed on her bottom lip, beginning to feel the first stirrings of apprehension. She looked about the hallway, wondering where Willie was and whether or not she should search out the housekeeper as a sort of reinforcement before daring to enter the library on her own.

But Willie was always entrenched in the kitchen at this

time of the morning, industriously scrubbing the very bottom out of some inoffensive pot, or shining an innocent piece of brass to within an inch of its life. She had her routine, Wilhelmina Flint did, and Victoria was loath to interrupt it. Besides, Willie had a habit of overreacting, and Victoria didn't feel up to dealing with the possibility of having to dispense hartshorn or burnt feathers at this particular moment.

Also, the Professor might be sick, or injured in a fall from the small ladder he used to reach the uppermost shelves of his bookcases. What a pother that would create. For if the Professor was hard to deal with when healthy, as an invalid he would be downright unbearable!

Victoria gave herself a mental kick, realizing she was only delaying the inevitable. She had hesitated too long as it was; it was time she stopped hemming and hawing like some vaporish miss and acted. So thinking, Victoria straightened her thin shoulders, turned the knob, and pushed on the door.

The room thus revealed was in complete disorder, with papers and books strewn everywhere the eye could see—which wasn't far, as the Professor's huge, footed globe was lying tipped over onto its side, blocking the heavy door from opening to more than a wide crack.

"Willie will doubtless suffer an apoplexy," she joked feebly, wondering if she herself was going to faint. No, she reminded herself grimly, only pretty girls are allowed to fall into a swoon at the first sign of trouble. Plain girls are expected to thrust out their chins and bear up nobly under the strain. "Just one more reason to curse my wretched fate," she grumbled under her breath, pushing her spectacles back up onto the bridge of her nose, taking a deep breath, and resigning herself to the inevitable.

Putting a shoulder to the door, she pushed the globe completely aside with some difficulty and entered the library, blinking furiously behind her rimless spectacles as her eyes struggled to become accustomed to the gloom. The heavy blue velvet draperies were tightly closed and all the candles had long since burned down to their sockets.

"Oh, Lord, I don't think I'm going to like this," she whispered, trying hard not to turn on her heels and flee the scene posthaste like the craven coward she told herself she was. Victoria could feel her heart starting to beat quickly, painfully against her rib cage, and she mentally berated herself for not having had the foresight to have acted sooner.

"Pro—, er, Professor?" she ventured nervously, hating the tremor she could hear creeping into her voice. She then advanced, oh so slowly, edging toward the cold fireplace to pick up the poker, then holding it ahead of her as she inched her way across the room, her gaze darting this way and that as she moved toward the front of the massive oak desk.

The Professor wasn't behind the desk; he didn't appear to be anywhere. Lowering the poker an inch or two, Victoria walked gingerly round to the rear of the desk, as she had decided that the intruder—for what else could possibly have caused such a mess except a housebreaker?—was long gone.

She looked up at the ceiling thoughtfully, for the Professor's chamber was directly above the library, and wondered if he was still abed, and as yet unaware of the ransacking of his sacred workplace. "Wouldn't that just be my wretched luck? I most definitely don't relish being the one landed with the duty of enlightening him with this marvelous little tidbit of information," Victoria admitted, grimacing as she cast her eyes around the room one more time.

"Oh," she groaned then, realizing at last that the stained, crumpled papers that littered the floor at her feet constituted at least three months of her painstaking labor, now ruined past redemption. "The only, the absolute *only* single thing in this entire world that could possibly be worse than having to transcribe all those boring notes is having to do them twice!"

She flung the heavy poker in the general direction of the

window embrasure in disgust, not caring in the slightest if her impetuous action caused more damage.

"Arrrgh!" The pain-filled moan emanated from the shallow window embrasure, and the startled Victoria involuntarily leaped nearly a foot off the floor in surprise before she could race to throw back the draperies, revealing the inelegantly sprawled figure of the Professor, his ample body lying half propped against the base of the window seat.

"Professor!" Victoria shrieked, dropping to her knees beside the man, who now seemed to have slipped into unconsciousness. For one horrifying moment she thought she had rendered him into this woeful condition with the poker, until a quick inspection showed her that it had come to rest on the tip of his left foot, which must have been sticking out from under the hem of the draperies all along, if only she could have located it amid the mess.

Running her hands inexpertly over the Professor's body, she didn't take long to discover that there appeared to be a shallow, bloody depression imprinted in the back of his skull. As she probed the wound gingerly with her fingertips, Victoria's stomach did a curious flip when she felt a small piece of bone move slightly beneath her fingers.

"The skull is broken," she said aloud, then swallowed down hard, commanding her protesting stomach to take a firm hold on her breakfast and keep it where it belonged.

"Ooohhh!" the Professor groaned mournfully, moving his head slightly and then opening one eye, which seemed to take an unconscionably long time in focusing on the woman kneeling in front of him. Reaching out one hand, he grabbed her wrist painfully hard before whispering, "Find him! Find him! Make him pay!"

"Professor! Are you all right?" Even as she asked the question, Victoria acknowledged its foolishness. Of course he wasn't all right. He was most probably dying, and all she could do was ask ridiculous questions. She may have long since ceased feeling any daughterly love for the man now lying in front of her, but she could still be outraged that anyone would try to kill him. "Who did this to you, Professor?" she asked, feeling him slipping away from her.

"Find him, I said," the Professor repeated, his words slurring badly. "He has to pay…always…must pay…promise me…can't let him…"

"He'll pay, Professor, I promise he'll pay. I won't let him get away with it," Victoria declared dutifully, wincing as the hand enclosing her wrist tightened like a vise, as if the Professor had put all his failing strength into this one last demand for obedience. "But you must tell me who he is. Professor? *Professor!*"

The hand relaxed its grip and slid to the floor. Professor Quennel Quinton was dead.

CHAPTER ONE

AS HE WAITED for the reading of the will to begin, the only sounds Patrick Sherbourne could hear in the small, dimly lit chamber were intermittent snifflings—emanating from a woman he took to be housekeeper to the deceased—and the labored creakings of his uncomfortable straight-backed wooden chair, the latter bringing to mind some of his least cherished schoolboy memories. He lifted his nose a fraction, as if testing the air for the scent of chalk and undercooked mutton, then looked disinterestedly about the room.

That must be the daughter, he thought, raising his quizzing glass for a closer inspection of the unprepossessing young woman who sat ramrod straight on the edge of a similar wooden chair situated at the extreme far side of the room, placing either him or her in isolation, depending upon how one chose to look at the thing.

No matter for wonder that Quennel kept her hidden all these years, he concluded after a moment, dropping his glass so that it hung halfway down his immaculate waistcoat, suspended from a thin black riband. The poor drab has to be five and twenty if she's a day, and about as colorful as a moulting crow perched on a fence.

She looks nervous, he decided, taking in the distressing way the young woman's pale, thin hands kept twisting agitatedly in her lap. Odd. Nervous she might be, but the drab doesn't look in the least bit grieved. Perhaps she's worried that her dearest papa didn't provide for her in his will.

That brought him back to the subject at hand, the reading

of Quennel Quinton's will. *Professor* Quinton, he amended mentally, recalling that the pompous, overweening man had always taken great pains to have himself addressed by that title, although what concern it could be to the fellow now that he was six feet underground, Patrick failed to comprehend.

The other thing that Sherbourne was unable to understand was the Quinton solicitor's demand for his presence in this tall, narrow house in Ablemarle Street, after one of the most woefully uninspiring funerals it had ever been his misfortune to view.

He had not met with Professor Quinton above three times in the man's lifetime—all of those meetings being at the Professor's instigation—and none of those occasions could have been called congenial. Indeed, if his memory served him true, the last interview had concluded on a somewhat heated note, with the irate Professor accusing Sherbourne of plagiarism once he found out that the Earl had entertained plans for compiling a history of his own and saw no need to contribute information to Quinton's effort.

Easing his upper body back slightly in the chair, he slipped one meticulously manicured hand inside a small pocket in his waistcoat and extracted his heavy gold watch, opening it just in time for it to chime out the hour of three in a clear, melodic song that drew him an instant look of censure from the moulting crow.

He returned her gaze along with a congenial smile, lifting his broad shoulders slightly while spreading his palms—as if to say he hadn't meant to interrupt the strained silence—but she merely lowered her curiously unnerving brown eyes before averting her head once more.

"Bloodless old maid," he muttered satisfyingly under his breath without real heat. "I should buy her a little canary in a gilt cage if I didn't believe she'd throttle it the first time it dared break into song."

"Prattling to yourself, my Lord Wickford? Bad sign, that. Mind if I sit my timid self down beside you? I feel this sudden, undeniable desire to have someone trustworthy about in order to guard my back. But perhaps I overreact. It may merely be something I ate that has put me so sadly out of coil."

Patrick, who also happened to be the Eleventh Earl of Wickford, looked up languidly to see the debonair Pierre Standish lowering his slim, elegant frame into the chair the man had moved to place just beside his own. "I didn't see you at the funeral, Pierre. It wasn't particularly jolly," Patrick whispered, leaning a bit closer to his companion. "By your presence, may I deduce that you are also mentioned in the late Professor's will?"

Standish carefully adjusted his lace shirt cuffs as he cast his gaze about the room with an air of bored indifference. "Funerals depress me, dearest," he answered at last in his deep, silk-smooth voice, causing every head in the room to turn immediately in his direction. "I would have sent my man, Duvall, here in my stead this afternoon, could I have but carried it off, but the Professor's solicitor expressly desired my presence. It crossed my mind—only fleetingly, you understand—to disappoint the gentleman anyway, but I restrained the impulse. Tiresome, you'll agree, but there it is."

He paused a moment, a pained expression crossing his handsome, tanned face before he spoke again in the same clear voice. "Tsk, tsk, Patrick. Can that poor, plain creature possibly be the so estimable daughter? Good gracious, how deflating! Whatever Quinton bequeathed to me I shall immediately deed over to the unfortunate lady. I should not sleep nights, else."

Sherbourne prudently lifted a hand to cover his smiling mouth before attempting a reply. "Although I am fully aware that you are cognizant of it, dare I remind you that voices rather tend to carry in quiet rooms? Behave yourself, Pierre, I beg you. The creature may have feelings.''

''Impossible, my darling man, utterly impossible,'' Standish replied quickly, although he did oblige his friend by lowering his voice ever so slightly. ''If it has feelings, it wouldn't be so heartless as to subject us to its so distressing sight, would it? Ah,'' he said more loudly as a middle-aged man of nondescript features entered the room and took up his position behind the Professor's scarred and battered desk. ''It would appear that the reading is about to commence. Shall we feign a polite interest in the proceedings, Patrick, or do you wish to abet my malicious self in creating a scene? I am not adverse, you know.''

''I'd rather not, Pierre—and *you* already have,'' Sherbourne answered, shaking his head in tolerant amusement. ''But I will admit to a recognition of the sort of uneasiness you are experiencing. At any moment I expect the proctor to come round, crudely demanding an inspection of our hands and nails as he searched for signs of poor hygiene. It is my conclusion that there lives in us both some radical, inbred objection to authority that compels us to automatically struggle against ever being relegated to the role of powerless standers-by.''

''How lovely that was, my dearest Patrick!'' Pierre exclaimed, reverently touching Sherbourne's arm. ''Perhaps even profound.''

The solicitor had begun to speak, to drone on insincerely for long, uncomfortable moments as to the sterling qualities of the deceased before clearing his throat and beginning the actual reading of the will, the first part of which dealt with nothing more than a series of high-flown, tongue-twisting legal phrases that could not possibly hold Sherbourne's interest.

''I wasn't aware you were acquainted with old Quinton,'' Patrick observed quietly to Standish, having realized at last that Pierre had never sufficiently answered his earlier query on the subject. As if they were exchanging confidences, he went on, "Indeed, friend, I am feeling particularly stupid in that I have failed to comprehend why either one of us should be found unhappily present here today. For myself, I can only say that the good Professor did not exactly clasp me close to his fatherly bosom whilst he was above ground."

"I knew the man but slightly, untold years ago in my grasstime," Standish replied, adding smoothly, "though I had foolishly not thought to inform you of that fact. I trust, dearest, that you will accept my apologies for this lapse."

"Why not just call me out, Pierre, and have done with it?" Sherbourne asked facetiously, slowly shaking his blond head, as he should have known he couldn't get past Standish so easily. "And please accept *my* apologies for my unthinking interrogation. I was striving only for a bit of mindless, time-passing conversation. I assure you it was never my intention to launch an inquisition."

"Are you quite set against starting one, then?" Standish asked glumly, appearing quite crestfallen. "A pity. I begin to believe I should have welcomed the diversion—if not the thumbscrews. Our prosy friend behind the desk is not exactly a scintillating orator, is he?"

Just then Patrick thought he caught a hint of something the solicitor was saying. "O-ho, friend, prepare yourself. Here we go. He's reading the gifts to the servants. We should be next, before the family bequests. What say you, Pierre? Do you suppose it would be crushingly bad *ton* if we were to spring ourselves from this mausoleum the moment we collect our booty?"

"*Shhh*, Patrick, I want to hear this. Oh, my dear man, did you hear that?"

"I'm afraid I missed it, Pierre," Patrick said, amused by the patently false concern on Standish's face.

"Quinton left his housekeeper of twenty-five years a miserly thirty pounds and a miniature of himself in a wooden frame!'' Standish pronounced the words in accents of outraged astonishment. "One can only hope the old dear robbed the bloody boor blind during his lifetime.''

The solicitor reddened painfully upon hearing this outburst from the rear of the room, then cleared his throat yet again before continuing with the next bequest, an even smaller portion for the kitchen maid.

"As the Irish say, my dear Patrick, Quinton was a generous man," Pierre ventured devilishly. "So generous that, if he had only an egg, he'd gladly give you the shell.''

This last remark was just too much—especially considering that the housekeeper, upon hearing it, gave out a great shout of laughter, totally disrupting the proceedings, while drawing Standish a chilling look from Miss Quinton. The angry solicitor removed his gaze from the document before him, prepared to impale the author of such blasphemy with a withering glare, but realized his error in time. A man did not point out the niceties of proper behavior to Pierre Standish—not if that man wished to die peacefully in his bed.

Flushing hotly to the top of his bald head, the solicitor quickly returned his attention to the will, reading importantly: "To Patrick Sherbourne, Eleventh Earl of Wickford, I hereby bestow all my considerable volumes of accumulated knowledge, as well as the research papers of a lifetime, with the sincere hope that he will, as it befits his moral responsibility as an honorable gentleman, continue my important work.''

"He never did!'' came the incredulous outburst from the housekeeper as she whirled about in her seat to look compassionately at Professor Quinton's only child. "Oh, Miss Victoria, I be that sorry!''

"Not half as sorry as I am,'' Patrick told Standish in an undertone. "I shall have to build another library at Wickford just to hold the stuff.''

"If I might continue?'' the solicitor asked as the housekeeper's exclamation had set the two other occupants of the room—a miserably out-of-place kitchen maid who was ten pounds richer than she had been that morning, and a man already mentioned in the will and identified as the Professor's tobacconist (and the recipient of all the Professor's extensive collection of pipes)—to fidgeting nervously in their chairs.

"It's all right, Willie, honestly," Victoria Quinton soothed softly, patting the housekeeper's bony hand. "I'm sure the Professor had his reasons."

Wilhelmina Flint sniffed hotly, then said waspishly, "He had reasons for everythin' he did—none of them holdin' a thimbleful of thought for anyone save hisself."

"Enough! What's done is done. Please continue, sir." Victoria said in a voice that fairly commanded the solicitor to get on with it.

"To Mr. Pierre Standish—who knows why—I bequeath in toto the private correspondence in my possession of one M. Anton Follet, to be found in a sealed wooden box presently in the possession of my trusted solicitor."

Upon hearing this last statement, Patrick stole a quick look at his friend, but could read no reaction on Pierre's carefully blank face.

"The remainder of my estate passes in its entirety to one Miss Victoria Louise Quinton, spinster. That's the last bequest," the solicitor told them, already removing his spectacles in preparation of quitting the premises. "Mr. Standish, I have the box in question, and the key, here on the desk. If you'd care to step up, I'll relinquish them as soon as you sign a receipt to that effect."

"My, my. Secret correspondence, Pierre?" Sherbourne suggested, looking at the other man intently. "Do you know this Follet fellow?"

"I know a great many people, Patrick," Standish answered evenly, already rising from his uncomfortable seat to bow slightly as the ladies quit the room, Miss Quinton in the lead, the uneven hem of her black gown sweeping the floor as she went. "Your recurrent curiosity, however, begs me ponder whether or not I should be performing a kindness by furnishing you with a comprehensive listing of my acquaintance, as a precaution against your spleen undergoing an injury, for example."

"Put m'foot in it again, didn't I, Pierre? And after I promised, too," Patrick remarked, grimacing comically at his faux pas. "I've no doubt you'll soon find me nattering with the dowagers at Almack's—lingering at the side of the room so as to catch up on all the latest *on-dits.* I implore you—can you think how to save me from that pitiful fate? Perhaps, in your kindness, even suggest a remedy?"

"A diverting interlude spent in the company of young Mademoiselle La Renoir might prove restorative," Standish offered softly, accurately identifying Wickford's latest dasher in keeping. "I hear the dear lady is inventive in the extreme—surely just the sort of diversion capable of ridding your mind of all its idle wonderings."

"While ridding my pocket of yet another layer of gold, for La Renoir goes through her ingenious paces best when inspired by the sparkle of diamonds." The Earl shook his head in the negative. "How jaded I have become, my friend, for I must admit that even Marie's seemingly endless repertoire of bedroom acrobatics have lost their ability to amuse me. I'd replace her, if not for the *ennui* of searching out a successor. My idle questions to you today are the most interest I have shown in anything for months. Perhaps I am past saving."

"Er, Mr. Standish," the solicitor prompted, pointedly holding his open watch in the palm of one hand.

Standish ignored the man as if he hadn't spoken. "Boredom can be the very death," he told Patrick sympathetically, idly stroking the thin, white, crescent-shaped scar that seemed to caress rather than mar the uppermost tip of his left cheekbone. "I was bored once, my dearest, so you may believe that I know whereof I speak. Ended by wounding my man in an ill-advised duel, as a matter of fact, and nearly had to fly the country. That woke me up to the seriousness of my problem, I must say! Once free of the benighted bolt hole I had been forced to run for until the stupid man recovered—for a more cowhanded man with a sword you have yet to see—I vowed to show a burning interest in all that had been so nearly lost to me."

"Such as?" Patrick prompted.

"Such as, my darling Patrick, an extreme curiosity about the human condition, in all its frailties. Oh yes—I also acquired an even more intense concern for my own preservation."

"I'd really rather not carve up some poor innocent, just to start my blood to pulsing with the thrill of life, if you don't mind, Pierre," Wickford pointed out wryly. "Although I am sure that is not what you are suggesting."

"What I am suggesting, darling, is that you look about yourself for some enterprise or pursuit that can serve to hold your interest for more than a sennight. In my case, the observation of my fellow creatures has proven to be endlessly engrossing. For you, well, perhaps Professor Quinton's papers will inspire you to complete his work."

"Or prod me into slitting my throat," the Earl muttered, shaking his head. "I do see your point, Pierre. I thank you, and I promise to give your suggestions my deepest consideration."

Extracting a perfumed handkerchief from inside his sleeve, Pierre waved it languidly before touching it lightly to the corners of his mouth, saying, "It was nothing, my darling man. But I'm afraid I really must leave you now, before our poor solicitor person suffers a spasm, dithering back and forth over the fear of offending me and his desire to return to his own hearth and slippers—although I fail to comprehend why anyone should fear me, as I am the most peaceful man in all England.''

"And I'm next in line for the throne," Sherbourne responded playfully, to be rewarded by one of Standish's rare genuine smiles.

"*Et tu,* darling?" he commented without rancor. "Ah well, I imagine this common misconception of my character is just a cross I must bear. Pray keep me informed of your progress, my dearest Patrick, for I shall fret endlessly until I know you are restored to your usual good frame.''

CHAPTER TWO

PATRICK REMAINED in his chair, idly watching Standish sign the receipt with a flourish and then depart, a small oblong wooden box tucked neatly under his arm. Perhaps he was desperate for diversion, but Patrick would have given a tidy sum to know the contents of that box. Pierre was a good friend, but not very forthcoming, and it was slowly dawning on Patrick just how little of a personal nature he really knew about Pierre Standish, even after serving with him in the Peninsula.

He looked around the book-lined room, wondering if M. Anton Follet was mentioned in any of the volumes, or in any of the papers holding Professor Quinton's extensive, although incomplete, history of the British upper class. His own research was devoid of any such reference, he knew, but then he had not gone much beyond a compilation of his and a half dozen other loosely related family histories before the whole idea had begun to pall and he had shelved the project (as he had so many others that he had begun in the years since his return to London from the war).

Rising stiffly from his chair—for he had spent the previous evening with Marie La Renoir and his muscles were still sending up protests—he realized that he and Miss Quinton, who had at some time reentered the library unnoticed by him to stand in the shallow window embrasure, were now the only occupants of the depressing room.

Steeling himself to pass a few moments in polite apology for having somehow usurped her claim on her father's life work (it would never occur to him that either he or Standish should apologize for their rudeness during the reading of the will for, in their minds, the crushing boredom of such an occasion had made them sinned against rather than sinning), he walked over to stand in front of her, a suitably solemn expression looking most out of place on his handsome, aristocratic face.

"Miss Quinton," he began carefully, "I can only tell you that your father's bequest came as a complete surprise to me. As I could not but help overhearing your housekeeper's refreshingly honest reaction at the time, I can only assume that you had a deep personal interest in his work."

Victoria Quinton turned around slowly to look at the Earl levelly, assessingly—dismissively. "Yes, you would have assumed that, wouldn't you?"

Patrick blinked once, looking at the young woman closely, unwilling to believe he had just been roundly insulted. She was standing stock-still in front of him, her hands clasped tightly together at her waist, the picture of dowdy dullness. He had to have been mistaken—the woman hadn't the wit to insult him. "I assure you," he then pressed on doggedly, "if there are any papers you particularly cherish—or any favorite books you would regret having pass out of your possession— you have only to mention them to me and I will not touch them."

"How condescending of you. In point of fact, sir, I want them all," Victoria Quinton replied shortly. "Indefinitely. Once I have discovered what I need to know, Lord Wickford, you are welcome to everything, down to the last bit of foolscap. Make a bonfire of it if you wish."

Not exactly the shy, retiring sort, considering her mousy exterior, Sherbourne thought, his curiosity reluctantly piqued. Possessing little that would appeal to the opposite sex, she had probably developed an animosity toward all men; no unmarried miss of his acquaintance would dream of speaking so to him. "Would it be crassly impolite of me to ask what it is you hope to discover?" he asked, staring at her intently.

Victoria turned smartly, her heavy black skirts rustling about her ankles, and headed for the hallway, clearly intending to usher her unwelcome visitor to the door. "It would be, although I am sure you feel that being an earl makes you exempt from any hint of rudeness. But I shall nevertheless satisfy your curiosity, considering your generosity in allowing me use of the Professor's collection. I shall even pretend that I did not overhear your complaints when you first heard of the bequest."

Patrick's dark eyes narrowed as he stared after this infuriating drab who dared to insult him. "How kind of you, Miss Quintin," he drawled softly as they stopped walking and faced each other. "I vow, madam, you fair bid to unman me."

Miss Quinton's left eyebrow rose a fraction. "Indeed," she pronounced flatly. "As I was about to say, sir: I have dedicated myself to the unmasking of the man who murdered the Professor. The answer lies in his papers, and I shall not rest until the perpetrator is exposed. And now, good day to you, sir."

She then moved to stand beside the open door that led down three shallow steps to the flagway lining the north side of Ablemarle Street. But her startling disclosure (and jarring candor) had halted Wickford—who could only view departing the house as his single most cherished goal in life—in his tracks, leaving him standing some distance from the exit.

"Find the murderer?" he repeated, not trying very hard to hide his smile. "How very enterprising of you, madam. Have you perhaps looked underneath your bed? I hear that many spinsters believe murderers lurk in such places."

Victoria's chin lifted at the insult. "I'm positive you are considered quite amusing by your friends in those ridiculous clubs on St. James's Street, but I can assure you that I am deadly serious.''

''But your father was killed by a burglar he must have discovered breaking into his library,'' Patrick pressed on, caught up in the argument against his will. ''Murder, yes, I agree, but it's not as if the man's identity could be found amid your father's research papers or personal library. I fear you will have to resign yourself to the sad fact that crimes like this often go unpunished. Law enforcement in London is sorry enough, but investigations of chance victims of violence like your father are virtually nonexistent.''

The front door closed with a decided crash as Victoria prepared to explain her reasons to the Earl—why, she did not stop to ask herself—so incensed was she by his condescending attitude. ''The Professor knew his murderer, probably opened the door to him, as a matter of fact. I have irrefutable evidence that proves my theory, but no one will listen to me. I have no recourse but to conduct my own investigation.''

''What is your evidence?'' Patrick asked, feeling a grudging respect for her dedication, if not her powers of deduction.

''That, Lord Wickford, is of no concern to you,'' she told him, pulling herself up to her full height. As she spoke she slipped a hand into the pocket of her gown, closing her fingers around the cold metal object that was her only lead toward discovering the identity of the murderer. ''Suffice it to say that I have in my possession a very incriminating clue that—while it does not allow me to point a finger at any one person—very definitely lends credence to the theory that *you,* sir, or one of a small group of other persons I shall be investigating with an eye toward motive, entered the Professor's library as a friend and then struck him down, leaving him to lie mortally injured. Before dying in my arms the Professor charged me with the duty of bringing his murderer to justice and, I say to you now in all sincerity, sir, that I shall do just that! All I ask of you is some time before you remove the collection. I will notify you when I no longer require it."

"Admirable sentiments, eloquently expressed, Miss Quinton," Patrick owned soberly, "although I feel I must at this point protest—just slightly, you understand—that you have numbered me among your suspects."

Bats in her belfry, Patrick then decided silently, becoming weary of the conversation. That's what happens to these dusty spinster types after a while. But aloud, he continued, "I'll respect your right to hold to your own counsel about your 'clue,' of course. But my dear Miss Quinton, you must know that I would be shirking my duty as a gentleman if I didn't offer you my services should you find yourself in need of them. That is, if you are willing to accept help from one of your suspects?"

"I shan't need your help," Victoria retorted confidently, deliberately ignoring the vague feeling of unease that had been growing ever since she first began this strange conversation. Longing to do Sherbourne an injury, she thought to herself: If I cannot throw actual brickbats at him, I can at least attack him verbally. "For now," she continued in a voice devoid of emotion, "it is enough that I have been able to interview my first suspect. I might add, sir, that I shall strive not to allow your boorish behavior today—and all I have read in the newspapers about your questionable pursuits—to prejudice me against you. At the moment, you are no more suspect than any of the other gentlemen who could have committed the crime.

"I apologize for baiting you so openly, Lord Wickford," she then conceded, her voice softening a bit, "but you are only the second suspect I have encountered today, you understand, the first having escaped before I could speak with him. I was merely testing your responses, feeling you out as it were," she added, not entirely truthfully, for in fact her opinion of him and his kind was not especially high.

Now Victoria had Sherbourne's complete attention. "Second suspect, you say? As I doubt that either the solicitor or that down-at-the-heels tradesman who scurried out of here with the Professor's collection of pipes is capable of murder, could you possibly be trying to tell me that Pierre Standish is also to be considered a suspect? My, my," he remarked, seeing the answer on her expressive face. "At least, Miss Quinton, you have put me in good company, although I imagine I should be feeling quite put out with you for even supposing I could have had anything to do with your father's death, except for the fact that I find it extremely difficult to take seriously anything you have said. Your last revealing statement implicating Mr. Standish has served to confirm my opinion of the worthlessness of your arguments."

Patrick smiled then, shaking his head in disbelief. "Therefore, I won't even dignify your assumption of my possible guilt with a question as to your reasons for it. I make no secret of my disagreement with your father when last we met, as I realize it is more than possible that you overheard us."

"I have not yet been able to ascertain a motive for you, or any of the suspects," Victoria was stung into saying. "To tell the truth, there may still be suspects I have not yet discovered. I am in no way prepared at this time to make any accusations."

"I shall sleep better knowing that, at least for now, you are only *assuming* to place guilt rather than running off to the authorities with a demand for my immediate arrest, I assure you," Patrick returned, bowing with an insulting lack of respect. "I shall also—need I even say it?—make it a point to enlighten Mr. Standish of his new status as a suspect in a murder, although telling him that he is not unique in his position, but has merely been lumped in with other would-be dastards, may not be a wise move on my part. Pierre does so hate running with the herd, you understand. But I'm sure you won't let Mr. Standish's righteous anger frighten you if he should happen to take umbrage at your accusation, for your motives are pure, aren't they, Miss Quinton? After all, you are only doing as any loving daughter might do, and you *are* a loving daughter, aren't you, Miss Quinton?''

Victoria's pale face became even more chalklike before a hot flush of color banded her features from neck to fore-head—the only portions of her anatomy Patrick could, or wished to, see—and she replied coldly, ''My feelings for and relationship with my late father are not at issue here, sir. The Professor was murdered, and I have undertaken the fulfill-ment of a dying man's last wish. It's the only honorable thing to do under the circumstances.''

Patrick looked about the drab hallway consideringly. ''You've led a rather quiet, almost sequestered life, Miss Quinton. Dare I suggest that you are contemplating using the Professor's death as an excuse to insert a bit of excitement into your previously humdrum existence? Although, looking at you, I can't imagine that you possess any real spunk, or you would have asserted yourself long since rather than live out your life in such dull drudgery, catering to the whims of an eccentric, totally unlikable man like the Professor. No, I must be mistaken. Obviously you believe yourself to be em-barked on a divine mission. Do you, perhaps, read Cervan-tes?''

''This is not some quixotic quest, sir, and I am not tilting at windmills. I have control of my mental faculties, and I am determined to succeed. I suggest we terminate this conver-sation now, so that I may get on with my investigation and you may repair to one of your ridiculous private clubs, where you can employ that inane grin you're wearing to good use as you regale your lowlife friends with what I am sure will be your highly amusing interpretation of my plans and mo-tives.''

Sherbourne's smile widened as he shook his head in dis-belief. ''I really must read the columns more often, if their gossip has indeed painted me as black as you believe me to be. At the very least, such a vice-ridden, pleasure-mad libertine as I should be enjoying himself much more than I think I am, don't you agree? Either that or—oh, please say it isn't so—you, Miss Quinton, have hidden away behind that dreary gown and atrocious coiffure a rather wildly romantic, highly inventive, and suggestible mind that is considerably more worldly than your prim façade, educated speech, and high-flown ideals indicate. Is that why you're so hostile, dear lady? Are you a bit *envious* of those lives you read about in the scandal sheets? Are you out to snare a murderer to fulfill the Professor's dying wish, or do you see this as a chance to deliver a slap in the face to a society that you equally covet and despise?''

''That's not true!'' Victoria exclaimed, aghast. ''How dare you insinuate that I have ulterior motives for my actions? You don't know me. You know less than nothing about me.'' The Earl's verbal darts were striking with amazing accuracy now, and all Victoria could think of was finding some way to make him leave before she could be tricked into saying something that confirmed his suspicions. ''Every word you utter convinces me more that you are the guilty party—attacking blindly in the hope you will somehow be able to dissuade me from my intentions. Let me tell you, sir, yours is an exercise in futility! I shall not be defeated by such an unwarranted personal attack!''

''As you say,'' Patrick answered, one finely arched eyebrow aloft. ''Well, good hunting, Miss Quinton. If you desire any assistance, or need rescuing when you find yourself in over your head, please do not hesitate to contact me.''

''I find it incumbent upon me to say that I cannot think of what possible use *you'd* suppose yourself to be,'' Victoria marveled nastily, ''considering your reputation for the aimless pursuit of pleasure, not to mention your renowned propensity for immature exploit.''

"Oh no, you misunderstand, Miss Quinton," the Earl informed her mildly. "I shan't come pelting into the fray on my white charger to *save* you, you understand, but I might be inclined to wander by and say 'I told you so' on my way to some nearby low gaming hell or depraved orgy." Moving once more toward the door, he added, "Now that we have exchanged the requisite pleasantries, I do believe I shall take my leave. Do please try not to weep as I pass out of your life forever, Miss Quinton. I'd wager a considerable sum that yours is not a face that would be enhanced by a maidenly show of tears."

"I never cry" was all Victoria answered, bent on correcting his misconception without seeming to take exception to his ungentlemanly remarks. The only outward sign that his insult had hit a tender spot was to be found in a slight widening of her curiously amber eyes, but it was enough to afford Patrick some small solace.

"I can believe that, Miss Quinton," he answered cheerfully, patting his hat down on his head at a jaunty angle as he prepared to leave before she said something that tried his overworked patience too high. "I imagine any emotion save your obvious contempt for your fellow man to be alien to one such as you. Indeed, it must gratify you in the extreme to be so superior to the rest of us poor mortals. When your father's papers pass into my possession—in other words, on the day when you finally are forced to admit defeat in your 'quixotic quest'—I shall be eager to inspect the Quinton family tree. It must be thick with truly outstanding specimens."

"You have not heard me boast of my ancestry, sir. It is you who carry a coat of arms on your coach door like a badge of honor, as if anything any of your ancestors has done can possibly reflect advantageously on you, who have done nothing to deserve the slightest honor at all."

Patrick's back stiffened as he swallowed down hard on an impulse to strangle the unnatural chit. He hadn't yet gotten through her iron-hard shell, no matter what he had thought earlier. He hadn't found a single chink in her armor of dislike and indifference that had refused to yield even an inch. She should be reduced to tears, not standing there toe-to-toe with him, trading insults.

"When first I saw you, Miss Quinton, I thought your father hid you away because of your lack of looks," he offered now, knowing he was behaving badly but somehow unable to help himself, for the woman seemed to bring out the worst in him. "I see now I was sadly mistaken. It was your serpent's tongue he strove so hard to conceal. Hasn't anyone ever told you it's not nice to go around antagonizing people with every other word that rolls off your agile tongue?"

Victoria took in the heightened color in Lord Wickford's thin cheeks and decided that she had tried him high enough for the moment. He had revealed nothing of himself save a reluctance to admit to anger and an ability to trade verbal insults without flinching, and he had appeared truly surprised to hear of her belief that her father had known his murderer.

Even so, she should have considered her tactics more closely before deciding to opt for a full, frontal assault. After all, hadn't Willie always told her that one caught more flies with honey than with vinegar? Victoria winced inwardly, wondering if the Earl was right—that she was, at three and twenty, taking on all the less-than-sterling traits of the waspish spinster.

Of course, she comforted herself, his surprise could have just as easily stemmed from his realization that she had somehow discovered some evidence that could incriminate him, she amended carefully, knowing it wouldn't be prudent to jump to any conclusions this early in the day.

She was just about to open her mouth and apologize for having behaved so shabbily when Sherbourne, who had just interrupted his latest move toward the front door as a sudden thought occurred to him, whirled to point a finger in her face and demand: "Pierre Standish, Miss Quinton. Humor me, if you please, and speculate for just a moment—what possible reason could *he* have had for putting a period to your father's existence?"

"Who is M. Anton Follet, Lord Wickford?" was Victoria's maddening reply.

Patrick inclined his head slightly, as if acknowledging a flush hit. "Ah, madam, such deep intrigue. I do so love cryptic questions, don't you?" His smile was all admiration as he ended silkily, "If this is a sample of your sleuthing, however, I suggest you repair to your knitting box without further delay."

"I don't knit."

Patrick's eyes closed in a weary show of despair. "This, I believe, is where I came in. *And*, madam, this is where I depart. Good day to you, Miss Quinton."

So saying, Sherbourne opened the front door and let it close softly behind his departing back.

It wasn't until his coach (the one with the gilt coat of arms on the doors) had delivered him to his own doorstep that Sherbourne realized he was more than just extremely angry. He was also confused, upset, and intensely curious about Pierre Standish, M. Anton Follet, Quennel Quinton, Miss Victoria Quinton's bizarre scheme, and the identity of the Professor's murderer.

It did not occur to him that the one thing he was not was bored.

CHAPTER THREE

"WHAT AN ODIOUS, odious man!" Victoria Quinton told the empty foyer once the Earl of Wickford had departed, having gained for himself—although it pained her, she had to acknowledge it—the last, telling thrust in their war of words. For at least one fleeting moment during their conversation she had felt the same impotent fury she had invariably experienced on the rare occasions when she had gone up against the Professor in a verbal battle before she had at last decided that she really didn't care enough about her father's view of life to try to convince him of her side on any subject.

Crossing the foyer to enter the small, shabby drawing room that—as the Professor had rarely visited it—she considered her own, Victoria walked over to stand directly in front of the wall mirror that hung above a small Sheraton side table, one of the few fine pieces of furniture that her mother had brought to the marriage.

The mirror hanging above it, on the other hand, was a later purchase of the Professor's, and it was exquisite only by way of its ornate ugliness. Peering through the virtual forest of carved wooden decoration that hemmed the mirror in from all sides, Victoria did her best to examine the features she saw reflected back at her.

"'Not a face that would be enhanced by a maidenly show of tears,'" she quoted, tilting her head this way and that as she leaned closer for a better view, as Victoria was markedly shortsighted without the spectacles she had chosen not to wear that afternoon.

"What Lord Wickford left unsaid was that if I had been so foolish as to ask him what would enhance my looks, he would have immediately suggested the prudent disposition of a large, concealing sack overtop my head." She smiled in spite of herself, causing a dimple Patrick Sherbourne had not been privileged to see to appear in one cheek, lending a bit of humanizing animation to her usually solemn face.

Putting a hand to her chin, she turned her head slowly from side to side once more, objectively noting both her positive and negative features. "The eyes aren't all that depressing, if I can only remember not to squint at anything beyond the range of ten feet." she mused aloud. "Although I do wish my brows were more winglike and less straight. I always look as if someone has his hand on the top of my head, pushing down."

Squinting a bit as she moved almost nose to nose with her reflection, she continued her inventory. "Nose,"she began, wrinkling up that particular feature experimentally a time or two. "Well," she concluded after a moment, "I do have one, not that it does much more than sit there, keeping my ridiculously long eyes from meeting in the middle, while my skin certainly is pale enough to pass inspection, although I do believe I should have considerably more color than this. In this old black gown I look less like one of the mourners and more like the corpse."

She stepped back a pace and deliberately pasted a bright smile on her face, exposing a full set of white, even teeth surrounded by a rather wide, full-lipped mouth that did not turn either up or down at the corners. Her neck—a rather long, swanlike bit of construction—did not seem to be sufficiently strong to hold up her head, and her small, nearly fleshless jaw, though strongly square boned, perched atop it at almost a perfect right angle, with no hint of a double chin.

Reaching a hand behind her, she pulled out the three pins holding up her long, dark brown hair, so that it fell straight as a poker from her center part to halfway down her back. "Ugh," she complained to the mirror, ruefully acknowledging that, although her hair was a good length, it was rather thin, and of a definitely unprepossessing color. "How could anyone with so much hair look so bald?" she asked herself, trying in vain to push at it so that it wouldn't just lay there, clinging to her head like a sticking plaster.

Then, holding her hands out in front of her, she inspected her long, slim, ink-stained fingers and blunt-cut nails before quickly hiding them again in the folds of her skirt. The Professor had told her repeatedly that her hands and feet were a disgrace, betraying physical frailty because of their slender, aristocratic construction.

"How I longed all through my childhood for a knock to come at the door and for someone to rush in to tell me that I wasn't really Victoria Quinton but a princess who had been stolen away by gypsies and sold to the Professor for a handful of silver coins," she reminisced, smiling a bit at the memory. Having no real recollection of the mother who had died while her only child was still quite young, Victoria had resorted to fantasy to explain away her unease at being unable to love the strange man who was her father. "Oh well," she acknowledged now with a wide grimace, "if my aristocratically slender bones didn't gain me a royal palace, at least they saved me from being hired out as a dray horse in order to bring a few more pennies into the house."

That brought her to the point she had been dreading, an inventory of her figure. "What there is of it," she said aloud, giving an involuntary gurgle of laughter. Victoria might have inherited her above-average height from the Professor, but she had been blessed—or blighted, according to the Professor, who would have liked it if she could have been physically suited for more of the housekeeping duties—with her mother's small-boned frame and inclination to thinness.

"Skinny as a rake, and considerably less shapely," she

amended, as her reflection told her clearly that the only things holding up her gown were her shoulders.

Victoria closed her eyes for a moment, sighed deeply, then lifted her chin and began twisting up her hair, fastening the anchoring pins with a total disregard for the pain her quick movements caused. "Point: Victoria Quinton, spinster, is an antidote," she declared, staring herself straight in the eyes. "Point: Mr. Pierre Standish insulted me openly and then all but cut me dead. Point: The Earl of Wickford did not hesitate in revealing to me his distaste for women of my sort." She stopped to take a breath, then ended, "Point: I don't care a snap about the first three points.

"Mr. Standish is a soulless devil, everyone knows that, and the Earl—well, he is the most excessively disagreeable, odious man I have ever met, not that I have even spoken to above two or three of that unimpressive gender in my entire life. I don't care a button what they think, and I am well shed of the pair of them!" She nodded her head decisively and her reflection nodded back to her.

She felt fairly good about herself and her deductions for a moment or two, until her mind, momentarily blunted by this rare display of self-interest, stabbed at her consciousness, rudely reminding her that she *did* need them. If she were ever to solve the puzzle of just who murdered the Professor, she needed them both very much.

Even worse, she acknowledged with a grimace, she needed to do something—something drastic—about making herself over into a young woman who could go about in public without either spooking the carriage horses or sending toddlers into shrieking fits of hysterics.

The two men who had been in the house in Ablemarle Street were not her only suspects—although they did for the moment stand at the head of the list of society gentlemen she had thus far compiled—and she must somehow inveigle introductions to certain others of the *ton* if her plan to ferret out the murderer was to have even the slimmest chance of succeeding.

Victoria pressed her fingertips to her temples, for she could feel a headache coming on, and looked about the room, searching for her spectacles. She still felt slightly uneasy about her decision not to wear the plain, rimless monstrosities, unwilling to recognize maidenly vanity even to herself, and decided to blame the insufferable Earl of Wickford, and not her foolishness, for the dull thump-thumping now going on just behind her eyes.

How she longed for her cozy bed and a few moments' rest, for she had been sleeping badly ever since the Professor's death three days earlier, but she discarded the idea immediately. "The Professor would have kittens if I dared to lie down in the middle of the afternoon," she scolded herself sternly. Although she had never been afraid of the man, she had found it easier to keep her thoughts to herself and display an outward show of obedience, thus saving herself many a lecture.

But then, just as she was about to head for her workbasket that stood in the corner and the mending that awaited her there, she brought herself up short, and a small smile lit her features. "And who's going to run tattling to him, Miss Quinton, if you do take to your bed—Saint Peter? You are your own mistress now, my dear," she reminded herself, a bit of a lilt coloring her voice. "You have longed for this day, dreamed about it for years, and now—through no fault of your own—it is here. You are free, Victoria Quinton, free to do whatever you will!"

Pivoting smartly on the heels of her sensible black kid half boots, she exited the small drawing room in a near skip, heading for the staircase.

It was perhaps only a small act of rebellion after so many years of doing only what she was told, but it was to set a precedent for the future.

CHAPTER FOUR

PATRICK HALTED on the threshold of the club's sedately decorated main salon and looked about for Pierre Standish, finally locating his quarry sitting alone and looking very much at his ease near one of the large floor-to-ceiling windows that overlooked the busy street below.

Sherbourne did not take himself immediately to that side of the room. Instead he spent several minutes wandering about in a seemingly aimless fashion, passing the time of day with some of his friends, although declining to sit and take refreshment with any of them.

He even took the time to place a wager with Lord Alvanley on the outcome of a mill that was to be held in the countryside later that week, before eventually arriving at his planned destination and sliding into a facing wing chair, a jaunty greeting on his smiling lips.

"Tsk, tsk. That took you precisely three minutes longer than it should have, my darling Patrick, although, in general, it was rather well done," Standish drawled amicably before returning his large gold watch to his pocket and looking up at Sherbourne for the first time.

"I beg your pardon, Pierre?" Patrick questioned, keeping a carefully blank look on his face as he adjusted his coattails before crossing his legs at the knee, allowing one elegantly fashioned Hessian to dangle.

"Yes, I believe you should," Standish answered smoothly as he motioned to a servant who was hovering nearby to fetch another glass for his lordship. "I recall that I have urged you to find an interest, my darling, but I fear your future does not lie in cloak-and-dagger machinations.''

Patrick shook his head in admiration, admitting defeat. ''How did you know I was looking for you particularly? I thought I was being quite smooth, actually.''

Pierre took up the glass the servant had brought and poured some rich-looking red liquid into it from a decanter before handing the glass to Wickford. ''I could, I suppose, say I have visited a wizened old gypsy in Europe who—because of some heroic service I rendered her—has given me the gift of foretelling events, causing you to look at me in awe, but honesty prevents me. Actually, dearest, I was at home when you called this morning but—how shall I say this without being indiscreet?—I was considerably engaged at the time.''

Taking a small sip of his wine, Patrick leaned back in his chair and quipped mischievously, ''My deepest apologies. I can only pray that I didn't interrupt at a critical moment? Some *indiscretions* have so little understanding of the link between concentration and performance.''

Pierre's dark eyes twinkled slightly in his otherwise emotionless face. ''I have amazing powers of concentration, thankfully. Besides, Patrick, you know I have always made it a point never to disappoint a lady.''

Patrick acknowledged his understanding with a slight nod of his head, knowing better than to dwell on the subject. Besides, he had not sought out Standish merely to spend a few pleasant minutes enjoying the verbal sparring that helped pass the time between noon and an evening's entertainment. ''Speaking of ladies, Pierre—''

''Not I, my dear, at least not literally,'' Standish said, a smile still lurking in his eyes.

Patrick chose to ignore this last statement, knowing that Pierre could keep a conversation jogging along in this lighthearted vein forever, without once saying anything to the point. He had met with his friend for a reason, and it was time the two of them got down to serious business. "There's something I think you should know, Pierre. Miss Quinton believes her father knew his murderer," he announced baldly, watching his friend closely for any reaction.

Pierre did not so much as blink. "How utterly amazing. I am, of course, astonished," he said in a tone that totally belied his statement.

"As usual, my friend, you react by not reacting. Perhaps a bit more information is required." Leaning forward a bit so that he could speak without fear of being overheard, he went on confidingly, "Does the fact that this same Miss Victoria Quinton considers you and me to be her prime suspects pique your interest in the slightest?"

"Are we, by God?" Standish responded, raising his dark brows a fraction. "I begin to believe you have awakened a slight curiosity on my part—perhaps even the faint glimmerings of interest. Perhaps you will oblige me by beginning with how you have come upon this charming little tidbit of information."

Patrick leaned back in the chair once again, satisfied at last with his friend's response. "The lady in question told me herself the day of the funeral, not that she wanted to, you understand."

"It's that pretty face, Patrick," Pierre interrupted, an earnest expression on his dark face. "I've noticed before the devastating way you have with the ladies. I imagine you've heard quite a few things over the years. Have you ever thought of writing your memoirs?"

"It was not my pretty face that did it, but her own satisfaction with her deductions that had her flinging her outlandish theory at my feet like a gauntlet," Sherbourne corrected testily. "Lord, man, at first she attacked me like a hound on a blood scent, trying, I believe, to frighten me into confessing."

"Quite the little Trojan, hmmm?"

"Quite the little idiot," Patrick amended. "She's taken it into her head to solve the mystery of the Professor's murder, you see, and believes the answer might lie somewhere in the papers I've inherited."

"And your thoughts on the subject?" Standish prodded, reaching for his wineglass.

Patrick smiled slightly, shaking his head. "I think the lady in question is a bit queer in her attic. Quinton was killed by a burglar; everybody knows that."

"Do they?" The question held no inflection, hinted of no hidden curiosity. It was just as if Standish, like Miss Quinton, had thrown out a suggestion, and now was waiting to see if his friend was going to pick it up.

Patrick slowly twirled the glass in his hand by its slender stem, watching the small bit of wine swirl around the bottom in a tight whirlpool as he considered Pierre's question. At last he raised his head a fraction, staring intently into the other man's eyes.

"Yes, darling?" Standish purred.

"Victoria Quinton may have the disposition of a cursed warthog—and a face to match—but she's sharp as needles, Pierre. Much as it pains me to admit it, I can't simply dismiss her assertions as daughterly grief. It's—it's as if she considers what she's doing as some sort of *duty*. Do you know, Pierre, I don't think she loved Quinton—or even *liked* him."

"Quennel Quinton was many things as I recall, but I know *I* did not find him to be especially lovable. Perhaps I have underestimated our little drab. She must have some intelligence," Pierre put in thoughtfully.

Patrick nodded in agreement. "A dedicated bluestocking, I'd say, which is why I cannot comfort myself by believing her theory to be some romantic bag of moonshine she's embraced merely in order to lend some sparkle to her humdrum existence. She's just not that sort of female."

Pierre directed a long, dispassionate stare at the man facing him before speaking again, all trace of mockery now gone from his voice. "You seem to have given our dowdy Miss Quinton and her assertions quite a bit of thought, Patrick. Perhaps you have even begun to question the reasons behind the Professor's demise yourself. Tell me, my dear, is this to be an intellectual exercise only, or do you plan to do something about it?"

Patrick lapsed into silence once more, absently raising his wineglass to take a drink before realizing it was empty, and then holding it out as Pierre refilled it from the decanter. Lifting the glass to his lips, he then downed its contents in one long gulp before rising to his feet. "She's a damned obstinate woman, Pierre, and she's deadly serious about this foolishness she's taken into her head. Somebody has to watch out for her, or she'll land in a scrape for sure."

Pierre put down his glass and applauded softly. "Congratulations, my darling man. You have come to exactly the correct decision. But do be careful, Sir Galahad—lest the lady decides to view her benefactor in a romantic light. You may save her from carelessly falling into the hands of a desperate murderer, only to have her end up casting herself into the Thames for love of you."

"Don't worry about that, Pierre," Patrick assured him. "Victoria Quinton hates the sight of me. She thinks I'm a terrible, shameless person. Useless too, I believe she said."

"I wait with bated breath, my dear one, to hear your opinion of her opinion."

Patrick slipped a snow-white lace handkerchief from his cuff and daintily dabbed at the corners of his mouth in imitation of one of his friend's little affectations before answering: "I was flattered, of course, my dear Pierre. What else could I be?"

CHAPTER FIVE

"YOU'RE LOOKING kinda peakedlike, Miss Victoria," Wilhelmina Flint remarked a week after the Professor's funeral as she lifted yet another stack of papers from the desk in the library in order to run her feather duster over its shiny surface. "Why don't I run myself on down to the kitchens and brew you up some of my black currant tea onc't I'm all finished puttin' this mess to rights?"

"Finish it, Willie?" Victoria questioned lightly, leaning back in the Professor's big leather chair to look up at the hovering housekeeper. "The only way this room could possibly get any cleaner would be if you were to dump all the furniture into the garden and whitewash the walls. Didn't you just dust in here this morning?"

Willie raised her chin and sniffed dismissively, although she wasn't really offended by her young mistress's words, considering that she had raised Miss Victoria since the girl was just out of soggy drawers and had therefore long ago become accustomed to her genial attempts to belittle her own love of cleanliness and order.

"Go away with you now, Missy," she said, going on with her work, which for the moment meant she was concentrating on chasing down yet another daring bit of lint that had somehow escaped her eagle eyes earlier.

While Wilhelmina tidied and fussed and generally stirred up more dust than her switching feathers could capture, Victoria sat at her ease, idly observing the hubbub as she gratefully abandoned her increasingly disquieting research for a few moments. Willie was a treasure, even with her seeming obsession with cleanliness, and Victoria knew it, just as she knew that the woman must never learn so much as the slightest hint of damning information coming to light about her longtime employer.

Although the housekeeper—who had left the countryside to be with her mistress in London when the Professor took the local squire's only daughter to wife—had never tried to replace Victoria's dead mother in her heart, Wilhelmina's brisk efficiency had always been liberally laced with affection for the plain, awkward child who received nothing but the most cursory notice from her busy professor father. If Victoria confided in her now, Wilhelmina would put a halt to the murder investigation immediately!

Victoria had grown to love the tall, rawboned redhead, and as she grew older she had secretly coveted Willie's buxomy, wide-hipped, narrow-waisted, hourglass figure, believing the housekeeper's ample curves and brilliant coloring to represent the epitome of feminine beauty.

Even now, with the once vibrant red hair showing traces of grey, Victoria could still see much of the full-blown beauty that had once been Wilhelmina's, and wondered yet again why she had never married. Surely there must have been plenty of opportunities. "Willie," she ventured now, "tell me truly—there must have been someone you wished to wed, maybe some farmer back in Sussex before you moved here? I mean, you didn't stay with us all these years just because of me, did you?"

The housekeeper stopped in the midst of rubbing a brass bookend with a corner of her starched white apron and peered intently at the serious young woman. "Because of you, Miss Victoria?" she questioned in a tone that hinted at the utter ridiculousness of such a question, then laughed out loud. "Lord love you, Missy, I should most certainly think not! It's crazy in love I was with the dear, sweet Professor, of course. That's why I stayed. It's as plain as the nose on your face!''

Now it was Victoria's turn to laugh, for if there were ever two people born to do murder to each other they were Wilhelmina Flint and Professor Quennel Quinton. Clearly Willie was doing her best not to load her young mistress down with yet another heavy dose of guilt, to be piled atop all the other guilt she was feeling over being unable to muster up any genuine grief over her father's death.

''I may have led a sheltered life, Willie, but I'm not a complete greenhead,'' Victoria reminded the housekeeper, sobering again. ''You and the Professor were many things to each other, but none of them were even remotely connected to anything of a romantic nature.''

''You're forgettin', Missy. The Professor left me that fine miniature of hisself. Wouldn't you be wonderin' why he should do such a thing?''

Victoria sat front once more, placing her elbows on the desk. ''That's another thing that puzzles me, Willie. There's something about that miniature that bothers me. I don't ever remember seeing it before, for one thing, but it's my inability to reconcile the miniature with the man I knew that is most difficult. I imagine it is hard to conjure up a real sense of recognition when faced with an image of one's parent at an age closer to one's own.''

Willie backed hurriedly away from the desk, turning her body slightly away from Victoria's as she extracted a cloth from one of her apron pockets, and then proceeded to make a great business out of dusting one of the uncomfortable wooden chairs that comprised the only seating for visitors in the room. ''Doesn't quite look like the old geezer, does it? It'd be the smile that's throwin' you off, I wager, Missy, seein' as how he did precious little of it in his lifetime.''

Victoria allowed a small, appreciative grin to show on her face before prudently hiding it with her hand. Willie had always been fairly outspoken about her lack of love for the Professor during his lifetime, but now that the man was gone she seemed to be pulling out all the stops. If she only knew… But no, Victoria didn't dare tell her.

"I won't scold you, Willie, even though I must remind you that you are being disrespectful of the dead. You have every right to be upset over the pittance he left you after all your years of service," Victoria went on, urging further confidences. "Even Mr. Pierre Standish—although he was extremely rude to voice his opinion aloud—said that thirty pounds was a most sorry sum."

"It was thirty pounds more than I was expectin', Missy," Wilhelmina replied, flicking her cloth briskly over the seat of the chair before sitting herself down with a thump and looking her mistress straight in the eyes. Victoria suppressed the sudden urge to flee, knowing that somehow the tables had been turned and Wilhelmina was about to ask some very probing questions of her own.

"What I wants to know now, Miss Victoria, is this—how much did the cheeseparin' old skinflint set by for you? I've been watchin' you and wonderin' what it is that's put you so badly off your feed. You've been sittin' in here day in, day out for over a week now, shufflin' those papers back and forth from one pile to another. It's bad news, isn't it?"

Victoria hesitated a moment, wondering if it was exactly fair to pour out at least a part of her troubles to Willie, who could do nothing more than commiserate with her—other than to throw a few colorful curses the Professor's way, of course—but she did feel a great need to talk to somebody.

"Well," she began slowly, a note of bitter self-mockery in her tone, "as you must know, Willie, there existed between the Professor and myself a certain, er, want of openness while he was alive."

"He treated you like an unpaid servant, lovin' and trustin' none but hisself and his useless scribblins'," Wilhelmina cut in candidly. "Let's call a spade a spade, Missy. There's naught but ourselves here to listen, you know."

Victoria lifted her head, throwing her long, slim neck and clearly defined, fragile, square jaw into prominence. "You're right, Willie, as usual," she said with some asperity. Then, losing a bit of her bravado, she began to ramble, hoping to change the subject. "It's time to call a spade a spade, whatever that silly saying means, for whatever else would one call it—a flowerpot? Willie, did you ever stop to consider just how silly some of our time-honored sayings are? Like 'right as a trivet.' Whatever could that mean? Could it just as easily be 'left as a trivet'? Or 'wrong as a trivet'? After all—"

"Are we soon goin' to be servin' tea in the parlor to the sheriff's officers?" Willie interrupted brusquely, not about to be sidetracked now that she had nearly gotten her mistress to the sticking point.

"You mean like Lord Barrymore did years ago, Willie?" Victoria asked, obviously still more than eager to digress from the distasteful subject of her current financial embarrassment. "I read somewhere in the Professor's notes that Lord Barrymore was dunned so much that the sheriff's officers seemed as much at home in his house as did his own servants."

Wilhelmina nodded impatiently. "Yes, yes. His lordship had them dress up as servants when he was throwin' a party. I know all about it, Missy. Us that serve know everythin'. Now stop tryin' to twist out of it and tell me—are we rolled up?"

It was no use, Victoria decided, opening her mouth to speak. "The Professor held the purse strings entirely, of course," she began slowly, "and I doubt even you could find anything unusual about that."

"Not out of the way, Missy, just stupid," Wilhelmina answered baldly. "As if there was yet a man born who knew the real cost of things—yellin' for fresh peas in the dead of winter like I was goin' to take m'self off out into the back garden and find 'em hangin' on the trees.''

"But although he kept the household on quite a strict budget," Victoria pressed on, wishing to get over this rough ground as smoothly as she could, "*he* always seemed to have funds enough to purchase his expensive books and his favorite tobaccos and, of course, his finely aged brandy. Oh dear, that sounded rather condemning, didn't it?"

"He knew how to live, that he did. I'll say that much for him," Wilhelmina put in thoughtfully. "I can't say I liked his choice of tailors, with the dull as ditchwater browns that he fancied for everything, but the quality was always there, wasn't it?"

Victoria nodded her head up and down firmly, as if Willie's confirmation of her assessment of the Professor's finances had reinforced her own feelings. "Naturally I assumed that the Professor had some private form of income—monies invested in the Exchange, or some income from an inheritance. You know what I mean."

Wilhelmina sat forward at attention. "But?"

"But his solicitor tells me he has no record of any such matters, and I have searched and searched this room without unearthing a single clue as to where the money came from. Even this house is rented."

Wilhelmina's expressive brows came together as she frowned, considering what she had just heard. "Are you tryin' to tell me that the old bas—, um, that the Professor left you without a penny to scratch with? I can't believe it! It doesn't make a whit of sense, Missy."

"Oh, there's some money in the house," Victoria explained hastily. "I found nearly one hundred and fifty pounds locked in a small tin box in the bottom drawer of his desk. There's more than enough to honor the Professor's bequests to you and Betty, and the rent for this quarter's already been paid. If nothing else, at least I didn't find any unpaid trades-men's bills.''

"So there's naught but a hundred pounds standin' betwixt you and the street?" Wilhelmina pursued intently, shaking her head in mingled anger and disgust. "You keep my thirty pounds. I've got more than enough put away that I don't need to be takin' the bread out of a child's mouth. Lucky thing for old Quennel that he's dead, let me tell you, for I'd like to strangle him with my own bare hands, and then go off to the hangman singin'!''

Victoria looked around the library at all the books the Professor had purchased over the years. "If only he hadn't chosen to leave the collection elsewhere," she said, sighing. "I'm sure I could have realized a considerable sum on its sale."

"The Earl didn't seem like he was over the moon to have been landed with the dusty stuff," Wilhelmina pointed out helpfully. "I'd be willin' to wager he could be talked into givin' it all back to you if you was to ask him."

Victoria fairly leaped from her chair to cross the room and look out the window at the small garden, hiding her flushed cheeks from the housekeeper's all-seeing eyes. "That man is utterly abominable!" she shot back with some heat. "I wouldn't ask the Earl of Wickford for a stale crust of bread if I were starving in a gutter!"

"Which you might very well be, Missy, if you don't rid your foolish head of this notion you've taken into it about finding the Professor's murderer," Wilhelmina supplied archly. "Better you spend the next few months sniffin' around for a husband to take care of you, I say."

"A husband! I have not the least expectation of such a thing!" Victoria, pulling a face, cried indignantly. "Oh, maybe once or twice—long ago—I had the usual dreams about falling in love with some handsome gentleman and living happily every after. But I'm three and twenty, Willie, and well past the usual age for marriage, even if I were so coldhearted a person as to seek matrimony simply as a way to save myself from having to make my own way in the world like any honest woman. Besides,'' she added, spreading her arms as if to invite Wilhelmina's inspection of her unprepossessing appearance, ''who do you propose as a suitable match for someone like me—the rat catcher?''

The housekeeper jumped to her feet, a quick flush deepening the color in her naturally rosy cheeks. ''Now see here, Missy, there's nothin' the matter with you that a bit of good food and some fresh air wouldn't put to rights! You're the spittin' picture of your blessed mother—Lord rest her soul and forgive her for being so weak as to allow herself to be married off to Quennel Quinton like she did—and she was a truly beautiful lady.''

Victoria's dark amber eyes softened as she shook her head slowly in the negative. ''Ah, Willie, you're a wonderful friend to me, truly you are. But then you didn't get to hear Lord Wickford's blighting assessment of my charms—or should I say my lack of them.''

''Knowing you, Miss Victoria, you probably laid him out in lavender with that sharp tongue of yours before his lordship even had the time to look at you.'' At Victoria's involuntary wince, Wilhelmina pressed her point home. ''Men are not so knowin' as they think they are, you understand. First you must present them with a pretty package—only then will they take the time to tug on the ribbons, like, and look a little deeper. Once he got to know you as I do, Lord Wickford would be like warm butter in your hands.''

Victoria walked back over to the desk and sat down wearily. ''I don't know, Willie. That description sounds rather messy to me. Besides, I don't like Lord Wickford. He's as shallow and vain...and...and arrogant as the rest of his sort. I have no desire to gain his approbation. I'd as lief retire to the country and raise dogs, really I would. But first I want to—that is, I *must* keep my promise to the Professor.''

"That again!" Wilhelmina exploded. "You owe that man nothin'—less than nothin' now that you know he left you without a feather to fly with. You have two months, or about that, before you must give up this house. Better to spend the time in thinkin' of yourself—not that selfish old man. Dyin' he was, and all he could think of was havin' you go harin' off to find out who did him in. You'd think that a body who knew he was about to meet his Maker would have a few thoughts about the poor innocent child he was about to leave behind. It's a bleedin' pity, that's what it is.''

Victoria pressed the knuckles of her closed fist to her mouth, fighting against the pain Wilhelmina's passionate words caused to clutch at her chest. The Professor had never once acted in an affectionate way toward his only offspring, so it would have been totally out of character for him to have had a kind word or two for her as he lay dying, but Victoria was human enough to have wished for more from her father.

In time Victoria, using the vivacious Wilhelmina as a yardstick against which to judge herself, had decided that she was the homely, helplessly ugly specimen the Professor said she was, and had therefore made no demur when he chose to have her dressed in nothing more colorful than mud brown and kept her closeted inside summer and winter, much to the detriment of her pale complexion.

If anything, Patrick Sherbourne's scathing description of her appearance—added to that of Pierre Standish—had put the final seal on her opinion of herself as being a truly undesirable female. She had a good brain—not even the Professor could quibble with that—but that brain told her that Wilhelmina's suggestion that she hang out her hopes for a husband was nothing more than an impossible dream.

No, Victoria told herself, reaching out blindly to pick up the first page of one of the stacks of paper lying in front of her, there existed unrealistic goals and attainable goals. Marriage was an unrealistic dream. Victoria was resigned to spending her life as one of the invisible people, destined to observe the world from the sidelines, in the role of governess, or perhaps as a spinster schoolteacher.

But before she resigned herself to the deadly dull existence that she felt to be her destiny, Victoria would take one slight detour into the world of excitement and intrigue, just as Patrick Sherbourne had so accurately surmised. She would play Bow Street Runner and ferret out the man who had murdered the Professor. She owed it to him, she comforted herself, having given him her solemn promise she would do it. But that wasn't really why she was looking forward to her investigation.

Opening the middle drawer of the desk, she slipped a hand inside to draw out the small enameled snuffbox Wilhelmina had found on the floor of the library the morning the Professor was discovered lying there injured. Holding the thing up to the light, she turned it slowly this way and that, admiring the detailed workmanship that had gone into the finely etched initials carved into its lid.

"P.S.," she read aloud, her eyes narrowing into slits as she contemplated just what those initials could mean. "Patrick Sherbourne. Pierre Standish. Somehow I hope it was one of them rather than any of the others I have discovered so far, for I do believe I would thoroughly enjoy handing over evidence condemning either of those gentlemen."

Wilhelmina shook her head in mingled dismay and disgust. "It's a sorry day, it was, that I showed you that snuffbox. I would have turned it over to that bumblin' constable if I had but known you'd take it into your head to think the thing belonged to the murderer."

"It has to, Willie," Victoria reminded the housekeeper. "Just think about it a moment. You clean this house almost hourly, bless you, so that snuffbox never could have escaped your broom unless it was dropped that same night by the murderer. I'm sure the Professor knew his killer; he just died before he could tell me who it was. After all, whoever it was had all night to ransack the library and find the box with the Professor's money in it. No burglar would have left empty-handed—only a man who had no need of funds would have done so.

"There's absolutely no doubt in my mind," Victoria said confidently, placing the snuffbox back into the drawer. "This is a very important clue, and it will lead me to the murderer, of that I am convinced. My only problems presently are money and time. I fear I may not have enough of either to do what must be done."

Wilhelmina had been still long enough. Reaching down to retrieve her cleaning rag, she began dusting the bookshelves even as she continued her arguments as to the impossibility of Victoria ever succeeding in her plan. "You'd have to go about in Society to rub up against folks like Lord Wickford and Mr. Standish, Missy. That takes money—money you don't have. It also takes knowin' the right people. You don't know anybody but me, and—lordy—I haven't been invited to sit down to tea with the Queen in ages."

Victoria allowed herself to be amused by Wilhelmina's small joke, but the housekeeper's bald truths could not be laughed away. "You're right, Willie. It's a difficult task I have set myself. Isn't it a shame I have no fairy godmother to come wave her wand over me and turn me into a rich, beautiful princess? It certainly would make things considerably easier, wouldn't it?"

FIVE HOURS LATER, Victoria closed the old journal with a snap and pushed it away from her before propping her elbows on the desk and lowering her chin into her hands. After her first, early successes in compiling a list of likely suspects she had somehow thought it would be only a matter of time before all the remaining pieces of the puzzle fell into place and she could identify the murderer.

But as the list of suspects grew, so too did the questions concerning exactly what the Professor had been up to, locked away in this library year after year. After all, aside from a few widely spaced magazine articles, his work had never been published—so what exactly was the source of his income? If he had no investments, no allowance from some inheritance she had never heard of, then she was at a loss to explain how they had lived in the relative comfort they had enjoyed all these years.

Victoria had also learned that the Professor had no arrangement with any publisher in the city concerning the publication of his "definitive history," which, as his transcriptionist, she knew to be years away from completion, so there was no point in pursuing that avenue in the hopes he had been receiving funds in anticipation of future profits.

"Still didn't find anything to the point, did you, Miss Victoria?" Wilhelmina observed as she reentered the library after finishing her own luncheon in the kitchen, shaking her head as if to say, I knew you wouldn't. "You should be out lookin' for a husband, and not sittin' in here diggin' into these dusty old books."

"Oh Willie, this is impossible!" Victoria complained, tucking a stray lock of hair behind her ear. "If I thought the Professor's manuscript was dull, let me tell you, his personal journals make them sound like racy novels in comparison."

"Like that Mrs. Radcliffe's *An Italian Romance,* what I found tucked in a hatbox, sittin' alongside your best bonnet?" Wilhelmina asked as she flicked her feather duster over a row of books sitting on the corner of the Professor's desk. "Mayhap I shoulda snuck in here of an evenin' and read some of his stuff m'self."

Retrieving the journal and placing it on the top of a small stack of similar books before slipping them all into a large side drawer, Victoria replied regretfully, "Alas, it was only a figure of speech, Willie. The Professor's writings, both public and private, were all as dry as dust. His journals ramble on for page after page about the most everyday things—as if the price of tallow candles in 1799 should be preserved for posterity."

"At least you won't have to go worryin' yourself that his lordship, the Earl of Wickford, will be readin' all about the Professor's wild and wicked past," the housekeeper offered, abandoning her dusting in order to run a finger along one of the windowsills, just to check up on the housemaid's efficiency.

"Wicked past? Willie, you know as well as I that the Professor's life was as ordinary as plain pudding. Why else do you think I have been reduced to reading Mrs Radcliffe?" Then, remembering just what Wilhelmina had said about discovering her latest hiding place for her lending library books, she went on: "About that hatbox, Willie—"

"I was just tidyin' things up a bit, Missy," the housekeeper put in hastily. "You know how lazy that Betty is. Why, if I'm not on her all the time, I swear she'd do nothin' more than wave kisses at the dirt as she breezed by. Did I tell you how I found her last week? There she was, plain as day, washin' down the front steps with—"

"That hatbox was at the very back of my wardrobe, secreted behind a dozen other boxes," Victoria persisted, knowing that Willie's love of cleanliness and order, and not nosiness, lay at the heart of the matter, but not adverse to seeing the housekeeper squirm a bit in her attempt to explain her motives. "There are times, Willie, that your dogged pursuit of demon dirt fairly boggles the mind."

Wilhelmina lifted her chin and assumed an injured air. "Well, you don't have to hit me over the head to make me know that you're pokin' fun at me, Miss Victoria. And me that's raised you since before you could so much as walk upright. Your darlin' mother gave me this position, and I have to say myself that I've served very well, but if you are wishful of makin' changes in the staff now that the old man got his notice to quit, why, I guess I can go to m'sister in Surrey.''

Victoria stood up and came around the desk to slip an arm around the older woman's shoulders. ''You'd leave me, Willie?'' she asked mournfully, resting her head against the side of Wilhelmina's ample bosom. ''You know I was only teasing, don't you?''

''Here now,'' Wilhelmina scolded, disengaging her mistress's arm before she succumbed to the urge to cradle Victoria in a motherly embrace as she had done years ago. ''That'll be enough of that, Missy. Besides,'' she continued after she had snatched up her feather duster and launched an attack on another row of books, ''now that the Professor isn't here to naysay anything, you can keep your books anywhere you want to, right?''

Victoria leaned back against the front of the desk, a slowly widening smile lighting her features as she contemplated the bookshelves as they would look when lined with row after row of her books—volumes that would reflect her deep love of art, music, and fine literature. ''I'll keep Mrs. Radcliffe on a top shelf, though, Willie, just so as not to injure some visitor's sensibilities,'' she decided, beginning to enjoy the thought of at last being her own mistress. But the smile faded as she remembered that hers was to be a short-lived independence.

''At least we won't be pinching pennies quite yet, Willie. I found another hundred pounds, stuck between the pages of one of the Professor's daily journals I was reading this afternoon,'' she told Wilhelmina now, for the time had more than passed to keep secrets from the housekeeper.

''Did you now?'' Wilhelmina observed, peering around the room as she contemplated the fortune that could be concealed between the covers of Quennel Quinton's extensive collection. "Do you suppose the money belongs to Lord Wickford now?"

Crossing her arms militantly across her chest, Victoria responded loftily, "The will said he was to get the collection. It mentioned nothing about anything hidden in the collection. Besides, he'd do nothing more lofty with the funds than to spend them on some painted dancer from Covent Garden or some such thing. No! I shall use the money to investigate the murder. I'm sure that's what the Professor would have wished me to do."

"Quennel Quinton never wished for anyone to do anything with money," declared a deep voice, "except give it to him so he could squirrel it away—and you know it, Willie Flint!"

"By the holy Peter!" Wilhelmina Flint screeched, throwing up her hands in dismay.

Victoria turned fearfully toward the doorway at the familiar tone of the man's voice, only to see the Professor standing just at the edge of the rug.

"Good afternoon, ladies. The door was open, so I let myself in," he said, just before Victoria Quinton, who had always thought herself above such missish displays, slid gracefully to the floor in a swoon.

CHAPTER SIX

VICTORIA RETURNED to consciousness slowly, her first thought concerning the fact that she was somehow lying down on the drawing room settee in the middle of the day with her shoes on. Her second thought was—naturally—that Willie would tear a wide strip off her if she could see her acting with such callous disregard toward the furniture.

Then vague memories of what had transpired in those last moments before her swoon sent her blood to pounding through her veins, and she opened her eyes a fraction, calling tentatively, "Professor?"

"Not likely" came the amused answer, and she turned her head warily on the pillow to peer at the elegantly clad man standing in the middle of the room.

"You!" she bit out, swinging her legs to the floor so that she could come to a sitting position, a move that sent the room spinning slightly before her eyes for a moment. "*Ohhh, my poor head!* What are you doing here, sirrah? How dare you remain alone in a room with an unconscious female? Have you no decency at all?"

Patrick Sherbourne, unruffled by this outburst, walked leisurely toward a small armless chair near the settee and sat down before deigning to answer. "You are correct, Miss Quinton, to point out my lapse in observing the proprieties."

"I should certainly hope so!" she said primly, arranging her skirts over her knees.

"However," he went on, undaunted, "in my own defense I must say that I have in the past had occasion to be alone in other rooms with other horizontal females, so you may see why I did not realize my error sooner.'' He paused a moment—for effect, Victoria was certain—then added, ''Of course, none of them were *unconscious* at the time, you understand. After all, I do have my reputation to maintain, don't I?''

Victoria's hands clenched into fists as she fought to take hold of her temper before it got the better of her, causing her to disgrace herself by picking up the statuette on the table in front of her and ramming it firmly into Lord Wickford's left ear. ''I withdraw my observation on the proprieties, sir. Clearly I am wasting my breath pointing out any impropriety to one such as you. But I would like to ask you a question, if I may?''

''You may,'' Patrick agreed, ''although I cannot promise to have the answer at my disposal. I've just arrived, you see. The front door opened at my knock—it was slightly ajar— and after debating a bit I decided it would be best if I entered and ascertained for myself whether or not there was anything amiss. After all, the burglar may have come back for a second go-round, mightn't he?''

''And I was just lying in here—alone?'' Self-consciously, Victoria raised a hand to assure herself that her black mourning gown was still securely buttoned up to her throat. ''Weren't you worried that I had been murdered?''

Patrick carefully removed a small speck of lint from his pantaloons and held it up to the light. ''That distressing thought had occurred to me, but of course I dismissed it at once,'' he answered languidly. ''You see, drawing on what I'd gleaned from our initial meeting, I deduced that there isn't a single soul in all the British Isles with enough moral courage to try to harm so much as a single hair on your head.''

''Indeed,'' Victoria said tartly.

''Yes, indeed. It would take a braver man than I to attempt to overpower you, Miss Quinton. Why, your tongue alone

could slice a man to ribbons before he could muster a coun-
terattack. Then there's your appearance…''

Victoria sat up very straight and glared at him from between narrowed eyelids. ''And what, pray tell me, is so very
intimidating about my appearance?''

Patrick ran his gaze over her figure, from her untidy topknot to the heavy black shoes sticking out from beneath the
hem of her woefully out-of-fashion gown, and shuddered delicately. ''Please don't force me, Miss Quinton. After all, I
am a gentleman.''

''Miss Victoria! You're awake!'' Wilhelmina burst into
the room like a whirlwind, a small glass vial held high in
one hand and a damp cloth clutched in the other. ''I was that
worried when you fainted, not that I blame you, for I don't.
I made Quentin wait in the library after he carried you in
here, so you wouldn't wake just to see his ugly puss and go
off again. Here, dearie, take a sniff of this,'' she ended, dropping to her knees beside the settee and taking the stopper out
of the vial.

''Oh, take it away, Willie!'' Victoria begged, pushing the
bottle back from her nose as the stinging fumes brought tears
to her eyes. But Wilhelmina's mention of someone named
Quentin brought her up short, and she grabbed the housekeeper's other wrist to hold her there. ''I thought I saw the
Professor come into the library, didn't I, Willie?''

Victoria's grip was painfully tight on Wilhelmina's wrist,
and the housekeeper hastily bobbed her head up and down
in the affirmative, hoping her answer would result in her freedom before her hand turned blue. ''Yes, yes, Miss Victoria,
you thought you saw the Professor,'' she agreed, tugging
hard until at last her wrist was free. ''Lord, you've got quite
a grip for such a scrawny thing, child.''

''Strong men quail before her, that's what I've heard,''
Sherbourne put in silkily as he helped the housekeeper to her

feet, and Victoria grumbled something unintelligible under her breath.

"Here, now," said a voice from the door. "Take your hands off my beloved, or prepare to defend yourself!"

"Beloved!" Wilhelmina scoffed, tossing her head so that her heavy mane of greying red hair shifted slightly in its pins. "That's a round tale, Quentin, if ever I heard one."

Both Patrick and Victoria were struck speechless by the sight of the man who was now standing in front of Wilhelmina, an ingratiating smile lighting his face.

At first sight there was no reason for either of them to believe they were seeing anyone but Quennel Quinton, but a few moments of careful observation banished that disquieting thought from both their heads.

Quennel Quinton had been a rather tall, portly man of about five and fifty years, with blue eyes and a blond fringe of hair ringing his otherwise bald head. The man Wilhelmina had addressed as Quentin was his exact double physically, except perhaps for the fact that his blue eyes seemed to sparkle with mischief, his rounded cheeks were as rosy as two ripe apples, and his mouth was arranged in an unabashed grin—something Quennel Quinton's mouth had never seemed able or willing to produce.

And there any attempt at making a comparison between the two men came to an abrupt end. Where Quennel had been sober, almost funereal in his dress, Quentin was clad in loud, flamboyantly styled emerald-green satin, with half a dozen gold chains spanning his considerable stomach. Three glittering rings pinched the pudgy fingers of both of his hands and a diamond as large as a pigeon egg nested in his cravat.

No, this certainly couldn't be Professor Quennel Quinton come back from the grave—not unless being tucked up temporarily underground had served to addle his senses beyond measure.

Quentin stood very still, seeming to enjoy the fuss his presence was making, as Patrick, quizzing glass stuck to his eye, walked in a slow circle around the man, inspecting him like a tout assessing a possible Derby entry, while Victoria, still sitting perched on the edge of the settee, openly goggled at him, her mouth slack.

"You're a relative, of course," Patrick said at last, allowing his quizzing glass to drop. "I don't believe we saw you at the funeral."

"Yes," Wilhelmina cut in, obviously not in the mood to kill the fatted calf for this supposed returned prodigal. "So seein' as how you're too late to either steal the pennies off his eyes or the brass nails from his coffin, why did you bother to come, Quentin? There's no money for you, you know. Not a single bent brass farthin'."

Quentin turned to Patrick, a sad smile on his face. "Ain't exactly tumblin' over herself to welcome me back, is she?" he asked blithely. "Ah well, it's not like I was expectin' her to fall on my neck weepin' with joy, you know. Give her time, your lordship, that's what I say. I know she still loves me."

"Love you? Love you!" Wilhelmina shot back heatedly. "You left me to rot while you went off chasin' rainbows. Snuffed my love like a candle, that's what you did. So if you think you can just come trippin' in here after all this time and call me your love, *Mr.* Quinton, let me tell you—"

Quentin winked at Sherbourne. "See? I told you. She's crazy in love with me."

"Oh, fie on you, Quentin Quinton!" Wilhelmina cried, flapping her great white apron a time or two in a shooing motion before raising it to cover her flaming cheeks as she ran from the room like a hysterical young girl.

All this time Victoria had been sitting there, her eyes going back and forth from Quentin to Wilhelmina to Patrick, like a helpless spectator trying her best to keep watch on a flying shuttlecock during a game of battledore, unable to summon up so much as a single question that had anything to do with the conversation then taking place. But now, with the housekeeper gone (taking with her the disquieting thought that the woman had a torrid romance hidden in her past), Victoria at last found her voice.

"Who—who are you?" she asked hollowly.

Sherbourne patted her on the shoulder in a maddeningly brotherly way. "Not a very original question, my dear Miss Quinton, and certainly not up to your usual standards, but I do believe you are heading in the right direction."

Turning her head slowly so that she could look directly into Wickford's eyes, she pronounced two words slowly and distinctly: "Go…*away.*"

"Here, now, young'un, is that any way to talk to his lordship?" Quentin scolded, looking from one to the other of the young people in consternation, finally directing his bright blue eyes at Sherbourne. "You are a lordship, ain't you, young fella? You look like a lordship."

"Patrick Sherbourne, Earl of Wickford, at your service," Patrick admitted, bowing in Quinton's direction. "My compliments, sir, and those of my tailor, who has repeatedly told me that clothes do make the man."

Quentin smiled again, clearly delighted to be in the presence of an earl, and held out his beefy, beringed hand. "Quentin Quinton, if you don't already know it. It's a pleasure to meet you, my lord."

Victoria stood up, exasperated beyond belief at the polite exchange taking place between the hated Wickford and this strange man who must surely be related to her, heaven only knew how. "Isn't this all just too pleasant for words," she bit out sarcastically. "Shall I ring for the tea tray now, or do you wish for me to withdraw so that the two of you can have a pleasant coze in my drawing room?"

"Feisty little thing, ain't she?" Quentin asked Patrick before lowering his considerable bulk into a nearby chair, whose springs protested loudly under the strain. "Reminds me of her mother, bless her dear departed soul, although she doesn't seem to have poor Elizabeth's looks. Pity. I had hoped—"

The sound of a heavy object hitting the far wall with some force brought Quentin up short, and both he and Patrick turned to look at Victoria, who was still on her feet, and looking more than a little incensed. "Will you please tell me who you are? I feel as if I've been somehow transported to Bedlam. Look what you made me do!"

Shebourne obligingly looked in the direction she was pointing and saw the heavy book that now lay against the base of the wall, its spine badly splintered. "Elizabeth, then, was also a bit overvolatile?" he asked Quentin placidly, ignoring the fact that Victoria was standing not two feet away from him, her hands clenched into tight fists.

"Not exactly overvolatile, your lordship," Quentin corrected, "but game as a pebble, dear Elizabeth was. Never did understand how she ended up with Quennel, but her father arranged the marriage, and there was nothing the poor child could do to gainsay it."

"*Ohhh!*"

"You screeched?" Sherbourne asked Victoria, who had just dropped heavily back down onto the settee, her amber eyes flashing fire. "Really, Miss Quinton. I know you are not in the custom of receiving visitors, but even the most elementary show of good manners seems to be beyond you. You are to entertain guests, not quiz them or—most definitely—subject them to the sight of ugly temper tantrums. Perhaps you should withdraw, just until you can gain control of yourself."

Quentin chuckled his appreciation of Sherbourne's wit, but his face sobered as he looked at the girl, who appeared to be on the verge of hysterics—or murder. "Victoria, my dear child," he said, frowning, "please forgive me for shocking you and then ignoring you. But I must say, I was a bit surprised that you refused to call me Uncle. I know your father and I didn't exactly get on over the years, but—"

"Uncle?" Victoria interrupted, slowly shaking her head. "I believe I must have misunderstood you, sir. The Professor had no brothers."

Quentin's troubled expression cleared as at last he understood Victoria's confusion and the reason he had not been informed of his brother's death. "No brothers, is it, niece? Well, tell me now, how do you like this? The departed Quennel was not only my brother, but my *twin* brother. I'm the older by five minutes," he added, turning to Sherbourne.

"And may I say you also were the recipient of all the looks and personality," Patrick replied, clearly amused. "I don't mean to pry, Mr. Quinton, but perhaps you will be good enough to answer one question. Where have you been keeping yourself, if Miss Quinton here has never heard of your existence?"

Quentin reached up to scratch at the bit of blond fuzz that sat above his left ear. "Well now, your lordship, that's a long story, and I'm feeling a mite parched. Victoria, do you think you could scratch up something in the way of some liquid refreshment for your poor black-sheep uncle?"

Victoria was still feeling disoriented, still struggling to take in what she had just heard. "I—I imagine I could have Willie make some tea," she offered weakly, never thinking to offer any of the Professor's private stock of brandy as she herself had never known the taste of strong spirits.

"Tea! That'd be the day. I should have known Quennel wouldn't have any good wine in the house. Cheap as a clipped farthing, that was my dear brother," Quentin retorted, winking at Patrick as he reached a hand inside his jacket and pulled out a flat silver flask. "Just fetch us a couple of glasses, niece. Right, your lordship?"

Patrick couldn't remember the last time he had been so

diverted. Whether it was the flask or Victoria's ridiculously shocked expression at the sight of it that set him off, even he couldn't have said, but suddenly he found himself lying back against the chair cushions, laughing out loud.

CHAPTER SEVEN

"AND THAT'S ABOUT IT, your lordship. Quentin married Elizabeth and the two of them traveled straight here to London, with my darling Willie coming along after leaving a message for me warning me never to darken her door again unless I was willing to give up my reckless ways."

Victoria and Patrick had been listening with great interest for nearly an hour as Quentin told them about his checkered youth in Sussex. The only sons of an impoverished, widowed cleric, Quennel and Quentin Quinton had been raised in a drafty, run-down rectory, dependent on Elizabeth's father, the local squire, for their daily bread.

Quennel had been a model son, if a bit dour for someone of his tender years, while Quentin had seemed to be the spawn of the devil, forever landing in scrapes from which his beleaguered father would have to extricate him. The only constant about Quentin was his devotion to Wilhelmina Flint, daughter of the local innkeeper, who was the most beautiful girl in the village, save Elizabeth, the squire's daughter.

"We were close as inkle-weavers once, Willie and me, if you take my meanin', your lordship." Quentin had told Patrick, giving the Earl a broad wink that caused a bit of pink to steal into Victoria's pale cheeks. "But I was a frisky colt, always on the go and wanting to see a bit of the world before I was ready to work in harness. So when Quennel and Elizabeth married, Willie went with them to London, leaving while I was gone from the village doing—well, it doesn't matter what I was doing, does it? After all, my niece is present, isn't she?''

Quentin was not very forthcoming on the courtship of Quennel and Elizabeth, merely saying, ''There's no accounting for tastes, is there?'' even if he himself did think it was ''a rum business all around.'' But the squire had a disky heart and probably wanted his only child settled before he was taken off, and heaven only knew Quennel wanted her. ''Quennel always took a shine to what he knew he shouldn't have,'' Quentin had told Victoria, who had not responded, but only sat on the settee in shocked silence.

''Well,'' Quentin had gone on jovially, as he had taken recourse to his flask more than a few times during his little talk and was feeling quite relaxed and at his ease, ''when I came home from one of my jaunts, m'father met me at the door with the news of Quennel's marriage and Willie's departure and wouldn't even so much as let me across his threshold. Told me I'd end in the workhouse, or worse, what with my feckless, adventuring ways, and sent me about my business without so much as a civil goodbye. Let me tell you, I went away a crushed man—forsaken by all I loved— and it took me more than a half dozen years before I even tried hunting down Willie and m'brother here in the city.''

''And by that time Elizabeth was dead and Willie refused to leave the young Victoria?'' Patrick had ventured, gaining himself a vigorous nod from Quentin, who was just then wiping a tear from his eye with a large white handkerchief.

Feeling a bit overset, Quentin had ended his story only a few moments later, and the trio had sat in silence for some minutes, each thinking his own thoughts.

Suddenly Victoria came out of the near trance she had been in since Quentin had begun speaking. ''Of course! That miniature the Professor left Willie in his will. It wasn't of him—it was of you!''

''Sent it to her from India along with a proposal of marriage and enough blunt for a one-way fare to join me," Quentin confirmed, looking confused. "Shipped it all off right after I made my first fortune. Why did Quennel have it?"

Patrick got to his feet and walked slowly across the room to look out the window that faced Ablemarle Street. "You know," he said reflectively to no one in particular, "I do believe it begins to look like Professor Quennel Quinton was not a particularly nice man. Mr. Quinton," he went on slowly, turning to face the other man, "I think it might be safe to suppose that your beloved Mrs. Flint never received your proposal—or the money for her fare to India."

"No! That's utterly preposterous, even for the Professor! I will not have you, a veritable stranger, speak so about him," Victoria objected quickly, hopping to her feet to glare accusingly at the Earl. "How dare you! You're an abominable, arrogant, and thoroughly odious man to suggest such a thing."

"On the contrary, Miss Quinton," Patrick corrected silkily, smiling at her in such a maddeningly sympathetic way that she longed to box his ears. "Being abominable, arrogant, and—what was that last brick you tossed at me?—oh yes, and odious, I am in the perfect position to recognize one of my own. Your father, you poor lamb, seems to have been a rotter of the first water. Keeping a man away from his true love, tsk, tsk. I do believe I might weep."

"You have no proof—"

Quentin raised a hand to place it soothingly on Victoria's forearm, gently pushing her back onto the settee. "Tell me, my dear," he asked quietly, "did you enjoy the books I sent you from Rome? And the lace and perfume I had shipped from France? Perhaps the ivory-sticked fan from Spain was your favorite? No? There were more gifts over the years, many more, but I can see from the look on your face that you never saw them. Wickford," he called softly, "do you think you could hunt up another glass? I do believe my niece here could use a swallow or two from my flask."

CHAPTER EIGHT

VICTORIA DIDN'T KNOW if she was on her head or on her heels. One moment she had been a penniless orphan, soon to be cast into the street with nowhere to go, no one to turn to, and the next she had been somehow transformed into the fortunate niece of one Quentin Quinton (late of the East India Company), a truly extraordinary man who wore pigeon-egg-sized diamonds in his cravat and prattled about presenting Victoria to Society as a well-dowered (if slightly long in the tooth) debutante.

Now, lying in her bed at the end of a most trying day, she thought back to the conversation that had taken place in the drawing room just before the Earl of Wickford had at last taken his leave of the premises.

"I believe the two of you should be alone to discuss these family matters," he had said once he had procured a glass for Victoria, filled it to the brim, and placed it into her trembling hand. "Although it has been heartwarming in the extreme to witness this joyous meeting, I begin to feel somewhat *de trop*. Quinton, it was a pleasure to meet you—a true pleasure—and I can only hope that you will bid me welcome if I chance to find myself in Ablemarle Street in the future."

Sherbourne, Victoria remembered now with a grimace, had then bowed to the both of them and taken his leave, lingering only long enough to toss a verbal bomb into the room by saying, "I suggest you have your intrepid niece tell you about her plans to collar the Professor's murderer, dear sir. It makes, I vow, for very interesting listening."

Victoria sat up in bed and reached behind herself for her pillow, which she punched a time or two with her fist before laying both it and herself down once more. "Oh, what a thoroughly insufferable man!" she said feelingly. "It wasn't enough for him to have been privy to the fact that the Professor kept me ignorant of my uncle's very existence. It wasn't sufficient revenge for him to have the satisfaction of learning that the Professor was not only an uncaring father but a mean one into the bargain. Oh no. He had to make it a point to disclose my plans to Uncle Quentin, as if to show the depths of my seemingly endless capacity for foolishness in trying to avenge a man not worth avenging."

Then a small, satisfied smile lit Victoria's woebegone countenance, as she remembered her uncle's reaction once she had shown him the snuffbox and repeated for him the Professor's last words. She could actually see the light of mischief creep into his bright blue eyes as Uncle Quentin's love of adventure quickly overrode the little bit of good sense the passing of the years had granted him.

"You'd have to go about in Society if you wanted to catch the murderer," Quentin had pointed out, still holding the snuffbox in one pudgy hand and lifting it to the light, the better to see the workmanship of the script engraving on its lid. "The Season's already started but, given enough money—which, as I figure it, is where I come in—I see no reason why we can't have you rigged out in fine style in time for you to hobnob with the lords and ladies at most of the festivities. Right, Willie?"

Victoria's smile faded as she remembered the battle that had taken place once Willie had entered the room to immediately put forth objections to Quentin's outlandish suggestion. "The girl's in mourning, you overstuffed dolt!" she had protested hotly, earning for herself naught but an amused chuckle and an "As if anyone gives a fig for dead professors these days," before Quentin demanded paper and pen be brought to him posthaste so that he could start making a list of every last item that was necessary for a "prime come-out, slap up to the echo or I'm a Dutchman!"

Her temples pounding, Victoria had taken refuge in the glass that her uncle had already refilled twice, drinking deeply until she chanced to look up and realized that Willie had somehow grown an extra head. Carefully setting her glass down on a side table, she had closed her eyes and counted to ten, opening them to find that, while the housekeeper's anatomy had returned to normal, her own stomach was beginning to feel decidedly unbalanced.

When Quentin had stopped for breath—he had been chattering nineteen to the dozen about ball gowns and modistes and jewelers, knowing that Wilhelmina would be hard-pressed to withhold her approval of anything that would serve to improve her dear Victoria's position in the world—Victoria had said thickly (for her tongue seemed to have grown two sizes in her mouth), "I doubt I'll take in Society."

And that, Victoria remembered now as she buried her face in her pillow, was when her dearest Wilhelmina and her newly discovered uncle had turned on her as one, united in their resolution to not only present Victoria to Society, but to make her its queen.

"Fresh air and vegetables," Wilhelmina had pronounced importantly, crossing her arms across her ample bosom as she looked to Quentin for confirmation.

"And red meat," Quentin had added, nodding his head in the affirmative. "And plenty of cow's milk. I'll have a cow brought to the door every morning. You can do that, you know, if you have the blunt."

"We'll have to do somethin' with that hair," the housekeeper had gone on, her eyes narrowing as she assessed her mistress. "There's just too much of it. Quentin, do you think you could—"

"Done!" he had promised warmly. "Then the child needs

rigging out from head to toe. Burn everything she owns, Willie my dear, and—''

''Stop it!'' Victoria remembered she had then screeched hysterically, clapping her hands to her ears as she had run from the room to hide in her chamber, where she still lay, desperately trying to discover some small bit of sanity still remaining in a world suddenly run mad.

''How I loathe and detest that odious Patrick Sherbourne!'' she said fervently into the darkness surrounding her bed. ''This is all his fault. Willie and Uncle Quentin will push me…and prod me…and dress me up like—like a plum pudding—and then push me into Society, just so people like Wickford can giggle up their sleeves at someone like me, the veriest nobody, trying to peacock about like I belong there. How on earth will I ever bear it?''

Her outburst over, Victoria took several deep breaths and closed her eyes, intent on taking refuge, at least for a little while, in sleep. But her eyes opened wide as yet another horrible thought invaded her weary brain. Sitting up straight in her bed once more, she wailed, ''My spectacles! What does it matter how I shall *bear* Society? Since I absolutely refuse to wear my horrid spectacles in public, what is more to the point is—how will I ever *see* it!''

CHAPTER NINE

"HAVE ANOTHER ONE of those muffins, Missy, and be sure to put a dollop or two of that nice honey Quentin brought home on top. And drink up all your milk," Wilhelmina prodded as she slipped a warmed plate holding two rashers of thick bacon in front of her mistress. "Your Uncle Quentin's payin' a pretty penny for it, you know."

Waiting only until she had chewed her piece of buttered toast sufficiently in order to swallow it without choking, Victoria complained, as she had at every meal for the past two weeks. "Couldn't you at least be a little more subtle, Willie? I feel like I'm being fattened up for Christmas dinner."

The housekeeper only sniffed dismissively, while covertly edging the muffin dish closer to Victoria's elbow. "Don't be silly, Missy."

"Silly, is it?" Victoria exclaimed. "I've already gained so much weight that none of my gowns feel comfortable, and still you and Uncle Quentin persist in force feeding me hourly from dawn till midnight. Confess, Willie, Uncle's out in the back garden right now, sharpening his axe. Do you plan to serve me up with an apple in my mouth? Heaven knows I've already been stuffed."

"Here now, Puddin', is that any way to talk to my poor, darling Willie?" Quentin Quinton admonished fondly as he entered the room, stopping only to ruffle the short cap of dark brown curls that were all that remained of Victoria's long tresses before snatching up a warm muffin and lowering his ample form into a chair.

"Dear Uncle," Victoria admonished after giving out a long-suffering sigh, "if you would please desist in addressing me by that ridiculous appellation, I should be most sincerely grateful."

Quentin wrinkled up his snub nose and turned to Wilhelmina for assistance. "Apple...what? What did she say, dearest? I love the little girl more than I can say—after all, she's m'only living relative—but I'll be dashed if I can understand her worth a groat when she starts in to spouting those jaw-breaking words."

Wilhelmina paused in the act of clearing away the empty egg platter long enough to notice that Quentin had poured honey all over his muffin and was now in danger of dribbling some of the sweet confection onto his cravat. Snatching up a large white linen serviette, she began tucking it firmly around his neck as she informed him sharply, "Miss Victoria says to stop calling her Puddin', just like I keep tellin' you to leave off callin' me dearest. I'm not your dearest, and I haven't been for more than twenty years. Here now, lift that mess of chins you call a neck and let me stuff this down under your collar."

Quentin leaned forward in his chair to give Victoria a broad wink. "She's crazy with love for me, Puddin'; always has been." Then, looking up at Wilhelmina, whose cheeks had turned bright pink as she realized what she had just done—being so familiar with the master of the house, even if he had been her childhood sweetheart—he smiled and said, "That's real Dresden lace on m'cuffs too, my dearest. Perhaps you'd like to have a go at tucking them up too?"

Prudently putting a hand to her mouth to hide her smile, Victoria shook her head, still able to marvel at the easy way Quentin had of disconcerting the usually unflappable Wilhelmina. In the two weeks since Quentin Quinton had moved his considerable baggage into the Professor's old bedroom, the one-time sweethearts had kept up a running battle—most of the skirmishes ending with the housekeeper fleeing the room in confusion.

Wilhelmina may have called Quentin a randy old goat when he snuck up behind her to deliver a quick pinch to her ample bottom, but Victoria could not help noticing that the woman had been taking even more than her usual care with her appearance of late, arranging her beautiful hair in a most becoming style—her white aprons starched and pressed to within an inch of their lives—while her accelerated house-cleaning had more than once reduced the kitchen maid to tears.

Then there was the matter of their meals, expanded in quality and quantity since his arrival, but also predominantly comprised of Quentin's favorite foods, personally prepared by the housekeeper herself. The large bowls of succulent sweetmeats—Quentin's particular favorites—that now sat on tables in nearly every room also gave mute proof to Wilhelmina's true feelings about the man who had deserted her all those years ago.

If these changes had been all that had occurred since she first discovered she had chanced to acquire a wealthy uncle, Victoria would have been a happy woman; watching Wilhelmina's courting had proved to be most amusing. But, as she already knew to her great despair, this was not the only change to have taken place in the tall, narrow house on Ablemarle Street.

Victoria had spent the last fortnight being stuck with pins jabbed at her by a small army of seamstresses, attacked by a scissors-wielding Frenchman with a heavy scent of garlic on his breath, marched up and down the narrow drawing room by a red-faced, puffing Italian dance-master who stood a full foot shorter than she, and drilled in the proper way to curtsy to a countess by a wizened old crone who had the best breeding, the smallest pension, and the least teeth of anyone Victoria had ever encountered.

Victoria crawled into bed every evening, exhausted, to dream of milliners and modistes and glovers, all pursuing her down dark alleyways, trying their best to catch her and measure every inch of her, from her nearly denuded head to her ludicrously painted toes, only to wake in the morning in time to face another day packed with unending struggles to maintain some control over her own body.

Now, looking down at the carefully sculpted nails on the tips of fingers that had been dipped into cucumber juice and massaged with crushed strawberries and cream until the ink stains had faded and the calluses had disappeared, Victoria wished yet again that she had had the good sense to deny even so much as ever *thinking* about discovering the identity of the Professor's murderer.

There were, she admitted to herself, certain things about her new situation that appealed to her, such as her twice daily airings in the small park nearby and the soft, silky feel of her new undergarments. But no matter how much of his vast fortune Uncle Quentin was willing to pour into the eager, waiting hands of London's merchants—and it appeared that his bounty, as well as his purse, was extremely generous— Victoria knew that mere window dressing was not enough to have her accepted with open arms by the *ton*.

Her background was unexceptionable enough, with no smell of the shop clinging to her, and once word of the ridiculously extravagant dowry Quentin had settled on her got round, Victoria was sure she would find at least a few invitations thrown her way; but she was likewise convinced that none of these invitations would put her within a hundred miles of any social gathering frequented by such exalted personages as the Earl of Wickford or Mr. Pierre Standish, her two most likely suspects.

Victoria bit down sharply on another thick piece of bacon as the thought of Patrick Sherbourne engendered in her a swift desire to indulge in some sort of physical exertion, and since Wilhelmina had threatened dire consequences if her young mistress were even to entertain the thought of lifting a finger to help with any domestic chores, chewing seemed to be the most exercise she was allowed.

How that infuriating man would chortle with glee if he could see Miss Victoria Quinton now—sitting politely at table, her elbows pressed primly at her sides, quietly partaking of her breakfast while her wayward uncle and optimistic housekeeper planned the social coup of the Season—Victoria thought helplessly, unable any longer to fight the urge to allow her shoulders to droop.

"Sit up straight!" Wilhelmina barked, sergeantlike, picking up immediately on Victoria's lapse. "Being tall is nothin' to be ashamed of, you know."

"Don't you know that even you can't fashion a silk purse out of a sow's ear?" Victoria responded somewhat lamely, pushing her shoulders back against the hard chair, for she had just graduated from the uncomfortable backboard the day before and could only hope the housekeeper wouldn't see fit to strap it back on her for her sins. "Besides, Willie, everyone knows Incomparables are always small, blonde, and dainty." And pretty, she added to herself.

"That, Puddin', was last year," Quentin told her bracingly. "This year there's to be something new for the gentlemen to wax poetic over, a tall, dark-haired beauty who's going to set this town on its ear!"

Victoria looked across the breakfast table at her uncle—sitting back in his chair, his thumbs hooked on the pockets of his pink satin waistcoat—sighed, and slowly shook her head. "I appreciate all that you're attempting to accomplish, Uncle Quentin, truly I do, and I'm overcome by your condescension. But it's plain as a pikestaff that I am not cut out for the social whirl. Why, I don't even have a female chaperone! Why don't we just stop now, before you waste any more money on such a wild scheme."

Quentin Quinton had the sort of round, cherubic face that could, when he applied himself, assume a sorrowful expression capable of wresting tears from a stone. Taking a deep, shuddering breath, he conjured up just such an expression now, seemingly suppressing a sob as he lamented, "That's it, then? You'd give up the quest just like that, at the first piddling roadblock? I had thought you had more of your mother in you, Puddin', really I did."

Victoria felt as if she had just kicked a kitten. Looking from her crestfallen uncle to the long-suffering expression now evident on Wilhelmina's face, she knew she was defeated. She had spent the past two weeks fighting every change, balking at every new gown or dancing lesson, but the time had passed for turning craven. She was committed to carrying out what had been—before Quentin arrived on the scene—only a wild, improbable flight of fancy. "Oh, all right!" she conceded grimly. "You may both take those tragedy queen looks off your faces. I have uttered my last objection."

"Then we may feel free to get on with it?" Quentin murmured artfully, not about to relinquish his woeful expression until he was sure he had gained a total victory.

"You are free to indulge yourselves to the top of your bents, both of you," Victoria declared fatalistically. "But I warn you—I am not so blind that I don't know that you have more than one reason for launching me into Society. Just don't go reserving St. Paul's for the wedding, if you please. Remember, it's a murderer we're after, and not a husband."

"A husband?" Wilhelmina repeated blankly, her eyes opened wide in innocence. "Quentin, did you hear that? Wherever did the girl get that silly idea? As if we'd ever let such a wild thought enter our heads."

"Not us, dearest, eh?" Quentin concurred, placidly reaching for a piece of bacon. "We know Puddin' would give us short shrift if ever we tried to play Cupid or some such thing.

Besides, I thought we agreed; it's m'poor brother's death we're out to avenge, heaven rest his soul." Raising his eyes to heaven, he then moved his lips as if in silent prayer.

Unable to watch this farce with a straight face any longer, Victoria picked up a muffin and lightly tossed it in her uncle's direction. Laughing, she scolded, "You two really bear off the palm, do you know that?"

Deftly catching the muffin, Quentin nodded to acknowledge this faint praise. "Pass the honey pot, Puddin', since it looks like you've taken over the serving this morning. Willie, my love, why don't you sit down and rest yourself a bit after fixing us this fine repast? There's enough here to feed a regiment. Repast," he repeated then, holding his knife up in front of him to admire its carved hilt. "I learned that word from a gentleman I met in Bombay. Secretary to a duke, he was, until he ran off with the Duke's money box. Lovely man. I learned a lot from him."

Wilhelmina looked nervously around the room, as if she expected the Professor to burst in at any moment to order her back to the kitchens before throwing Quentin out on his ear. "I really shouldn't—"

"Oh, don't talk fustian, Willie," Victoria pleaded, hopping up to pull out a chair for the housekeeper. "You're family."

Raising a hand to pat at the large knot of hair that lay at the base of her neck, Wilhelmina colored prettily, then sat down, a coquettish smile lighting her features. "Oh, isn't this grand!" she said, then giggled.

"Uncle," Victoria said, suddenly feeling inspired, "couldn't we get Willie a new wardrobe, and some lessons too? Then she could be my chaperone. I'd certainly feel less alone if I had Willie by my side when I went about town."

Quentin looked over at Wilhelmina, who had jumped to her feet the moment she had heard Victoria's suggestion, her usually pink complexion now suddenly chalk-white, and could not suppress a shout of laughter. "My Willie out in

Society? Lord, Puddin', why do you think she wouldn't leave with me all those years ago?"

"But—" Victoria protested, worrying that Wilhelmina might be insulted by his words.

"No," he pushed on, unheeding, "my Willie has no love of adventure in her heart, and the thought of sitting in some titled lady's parlor with a turban stuck on her head would be enough to send her scurrying right back to the country to hide her head in a haystack."

"He's right, Missy," the housekeeper agreed, hanging her head. "I never was the one for gaddin' about."

"Besides, I've already found a chaperone for you, and a right proper young woman at that," Quinton announced, gaining Victoria's undivided attention. "She'll be here within the week, if I read her letter right. She answered my advertisement in the newspapers, you know. Pretty handwriting. Puddin', do you really spell Saturday with two *T*'s?"

"Only one *T*, Uncle," Victoria informed him straight-faced. "But it's a common mistake."

"I thought so," Quentin said, looking a bit relieved. "She forgot the *E* too."

Victoria opened her mouth, thought better of what she was about to say, and asked for another piece of bacon.

Wilhelmina, still unsure whether to be relieved by Quentin's attempt at rescue or indignant over his low opinion of her courage, mustered enough spirit to sniff disparagingly at his description of the woman he had hired. "Chaperone, you say. That girl didn't sound to be more than eight and twenty herself, even if she is a widow. More like a companion, I'd say, and even then the tongues are sure to wag when the two of them go about together of an evening."

A young woman? More of a companion than a chaperone? Victoria felt her heart skip a beat as she thought of how lovely it would be to be able to converse with someone nearer her own age. She had never had a real friend—someone who might be able to answer some of the questions that had been plaguing her ever since she first set sight on Patrick Sherbourne and felt some strange stirrings deep inside her that she would rather die than mention to Wilhelmina. ''What's her name, Uncle, this companion you have secured for me?''

''Emma,'' Quentin told her, then added almost under his breath, ''Emma Hamilton.''

CHAPTER TEN

"I KNOW IT IS a *vastly* unfortunate name," the incredibly small, blonde-haired beauty apologized in her soft voice a week later as she sat in the Quinton drawing room, "but as I loved Harry dearly, it couldn't be helped. I do hope it won't cause you any undue embarrassment."

Victoria, who had been sitting across from her newly arrived companion—feeling taller and darker and homelier by the minute—could only shake her head and continue to stare at the fragile doll who was looking at her out of the widest, clearest blue eyes she had ever seen.

"Mama, bless her soul, for she has been gone these past seven years, used to say that I should have called myself Emma Connington-Hamilton, just to avoid confusion, you know, but I didn't think I could possibly do that without insulting Harry most dreadfully, don't you? I mean, after all, it wasn't as if *I* had ever danced on a tabletop for some wicked lords or draped shawls around myself and struck Attitudes for anyone who wished to see, was it?"

At last Victoria found her tongue. "Of course I don't mind about your name, Mrs. Hamilton. Only a poor-spirited person could be so cruel as to cast aspersions on you, or Lady Hamilton for that matter, as I for one believe we should thank her for making poor, brave Lord Nelson so happy in his last years. If your name offends anyone, it will only be because England should be ashamed to remember how shabbily it has treated Lady Hamilton, especially since Lord Nelson expressly asked the government to take care of her for him."

Emma smiled sweetly, showing off her perfect white teeth. "Oh, you are just as knowledgeable as Mr. Quinton said you were in his advertisement. Such a dear man, your uncle. How unusual for a female to know so much about matters of state. I must say I am impressed, Miss Quinton."

Victoria, who secretly wished she knew as much about dancing on tabletops and posing in Attitudes while dressed in draperies as she did about the less romantic features of the lives of Lady Emma Hamilton and Lord Horatio Nelson, could only sigh and say, "Please call me Victoria, Mrs. Hamilton. After all, we are going to be much in company with one another for the next few months, aren't we?"

"Oh dear, should I? I mean, you are my employer, after all, even if it is that wonderful Mr. Quinton who actually engaged my services as chaperone. Such a dear man, Mr. Quinton. Oh—I said that already, didn't I? Harry, rest his soul, always told me I should try more diligently to remember what I have said—or was it that I should be more diligent in saying only things worthy of being remembered? Ah, well," she concluded, folding her tiny hands daintily in her lap, "I don't believe it matters much now, does it? And please, Victoria, you must call me Emma. Only if you wish to, of course," she ended in a breathless rush.

"I would like that, um, above all things!" Victoria told the woman, lamely trying to sound more like a debutante. Victoria couldn't be certain, but she believed she was beginning to feel a headache behind her eyes. Was it possible that all Society females prattled on like Emma Hamilton? And if they did, how could someone like Patrick Sherbourne possibly help but seek his entertainment elsewhere, with women who, because of either their background or their profession, could at least be counted on to know whether or not the sky was blue—and then be able to say so with some measure of conviction!

"When do you plan your first foray into Society, Victoria?'' Emma asked then, belatedly remembering that she was in Ablemarle Street as an employee and not an invited guest. ''Have you a list of invitations you wish me to go through, to help you decide which entertainments would be best suited to an innocent young lady? That's what I did for Mrs. Witherspoon last year when I acted as companion for her dear Henrietta's come-out. Such a sweet girl, Henrietta. If only she could have done something about those dreadful teeth. I wonder who's chaperoning her this year.''

Wilhelmina came into the drawing room then, intent on ushering the new chaperone upstairs and helping her unpack her belongings (just to see if the beautiful but vacant-faced young woman had any clothing more suitable to her new post than the shabby blue traveling costume that had been inexpertly darned in at least three places), saving Victoria from having to admit that she had not as yet a single card of invitation to her credit, even though Uncle Quentin had sent announcements of her debut to the newspapers over a week earlier.

Once the two women had exited the room, Victoria stood up and reluctantly walked over to the mirror, the same one she had made use of after her first insulting interview with Patrick Sherbourne. Tilting her head to one side, she carefully assessed her new, shorter hairstyle, still trying to decide if she looked like a fashionable ingenue or a slightly long-haired peach.

Thrusting out her bottom lip, she then transferred her scrutiny to the modest strip of naked flesh showing above the scooped neckline of her green-sprigged muslin morning gown, comparing her still somewhat prominent, though straight, collarbones with the cushiony expanse of skin that had peeked out above Emma Hamilton's neckline.

''I may no longer resemble a plucked chicken—thanks to Willie's hourly meals—but I still look like I have more bones than any one female should. And entirely too much neck,'' she added, running a hand up her throat and over her finely chiseled jaw and then back down to her chest.

"Excuse me, ma'am, but the housemaid who answered the door led me to believe I would find Miss Quinton in this room. Would it be possible for you to—*Good God!* Miss Quinton, is that really you?"

Victoria's hand froze where it was, which was why she could feel the unsettling reaction Patrick Sherbourne's deep voice immediately effected on her heartbeat. Whirling stiffly to face him, she stifled the mad impulse to cross her spread palms over her exposed neckline and forced her hands to fold themselves together lightly at her waist, hoping against hope that she presented a picture of calm assurance.

"It *is* you," the Earl said again, as if confirming his own assumption. Holding out his right hand, he advanced toward her, smiling widely. "Miss Quinton, I have to own it. Please perceive me standing before you, openmouthed with astonishment."

Immediately Victoria's back was up, for she was certain this smiling man was enjoying himself quite royally, pretending that she had overnight turned from a moulting crow into an exotic, brilliantly plumed bird.

"Oh, do be quiet," she admonished, furious at feeling herself blushing as he continued to hold his hand out to her. "If I look a complete quiz, it is all your fault—telling Uncle Quentin about my plan to ferret out the Professor's murderer. Now, if you have done amusing yourself at my expense, I suggest you take yourself off on your usual immoral pursuits, as I have more than enough on my plate without having to stand here listening to your ludicrous outpourings of astonishment."

Dropping his ignored hand to his side, Patrick merely smiled all the more as he unabashedly quipped, "Oh dear, how distressing. Now you've gone and done it, Miss Quinton. Just as I was about to search out your uncle and kiss

him on both cheeks for having brought about a near mirac-
ulous transformation, you had to go and open your mouth.''
He shook his head in mock sorrow. ''Ruined the whole effect
in the twinkling of an eye. Pity, that.''

Victoria, who had not as yet had time to build up any real
confidence in her new, showier appearance, perversely took
comfort in Patrick's remarks. Peering across the room at him
carefully—and thanking her lucky stars that her spectacles
were tucked away safely in her pocket—she asked huskily,
''You—you actually *like* the way I look? You don't think I
look—*silly?*''

Sherbourne, whose palate had become more than a little
jaded—as he had limited his indulgences to only the most
sophisticated sort of female for more years than he cared to
count—found himself oddly touched by Victoria's artless
questions and decided to put himself out a bit for her.

Sticking his quizzing glass to his eye, he began a leisurely
stroll all the way around the young woman, touching her
lightly on the shoulder so that she remained facing front as
she tried to turn with him (his impersonal touch nearly turning Victoria's knees to water, had he only known).

What he saw pleased him more than he could have believed possible. He most especially liked the short cap of dark
brown curls that seemed somehow to soften, yet highlight
her finely boned cheeks and chin. Her curiously amber eyes
appeared to have grown in size beneath their straight, dark
brows, he realized, and how he had ever missed noticing her
wide, perfectly sculpted mouth he could not understand.

His circuit around her completed, he stood back several
paces and ran his eyes impersonally along her figure, taking
special note of her gracefully elongated throat and extraordinary posture. She was unfashionably thin, although not un-
healthily so, and the line of her bosom was far from imposing, but for the most part he believed he could safely say that
hers was a figure that would elicit quite a bit of envy among

many of the overly cushioned debutantes now in circulation—not that he would ever dare to voice that particular opinion to Victoria. After all, he valued his life!

Finally, just as Victoria thought she would not be able to stand still another moment, the Earl allowed his glass to drop and cleared his throat in order to pronounce his conclusions. "I make you my compliments, Miss Quinton. I would not go so far as to say that you have been transformed into an unbelievably ravishing creature, for you have not, but I do believe you have taken great strides since last I saw you in this room."

I will not be missish, I will not be missish, Victoria repeated over and over in her head, trying very hard not to cry out her disappointment at this faint praise. Instead, swallowing down hard on her feelings, she forced a laugh, trying to show the Earl that his opinion meant less than nothing to her.

Then, when he seemed about to expand on his conclusions, she broke in crushingly, "Thank you, sir, for that candidly expressed opinion. However, I do believe that you have overstepped the bounds of propriety in speaking so to a young woman not yet out. Therefore, I believe I find it incumbent upon myself to depress your attempts at familiarity and ask you to please leave."

Patrick raised his hands and applauded softly before declaring with maddening calm, "Well done, Miss Quinton. You have put me well and truly in my place. I commend you. Now, why don't you stop trying not to pout and be a good little girl and run to get your cloak. I, out of the goodness of my heart, have taken it upon myself to give you an airing in the park this afternoon."

Victoria looked at Sherbourne as if he had suddenly sprouted an extra head, disbelief written all over her expressive face. "Why would you want to do that?" she asked, suddenly suspicious of his motives.

"Ah, Miss Quinton, I am crushed, truly crushed," he answered sadly, shaking his handsome blond head. "Having seen your uncle's insertion in the *Morning Post* more than a week ago, I have been in danger of spraining my neck searching for you at every social gathering, but to no avail."

"You have?" Victoria breathed incredulously, her heart skipping a beat or two as she fleetingly entertained the idea that he might have been looking for her because he felt the same strange attraction that she did every time she thought of him.

"You are amazed, I know. So was I. At any rate, at long last my dullard brain realized that you had precious few acquaintances in town, a circumstance that would seem to make gaining any worthwhile invitations plaguey difficult. Remembering your uncle with kindness, I said to myself, 'Patrick, what would a gentleman do in such a situation?' I, of course, then replied, 'A gentleman would offer his services to the lady without delay'—especially when you consider that I am not without some reputation in this city."

Victoria sniffed derisively, giving up any lingering notion that he saw her in any sort of romantic light. "It is precisely that reputation which keeps me from accepting your charitable offer, sir, as I harbor no secret desire to become notorious. I may not get out into Society, but I too read the newspapers. Your name, like that of Mr. Standish, always seems to feature quite prominently in some of the columns."

"Notorious? Why, Miss Quinton, I do believe I am insulted," Patrick replied lightheartedly. "After all, I am considered quite the rage, you know."

Walking across the room to sit herself down on the settee before her quaking limbs failed her completely, Victoria retorted acidly, "*Rage,* you say, Lord Wickford? Yes, that word does seem to describe the reaction your presence evokes. Besides," she ended pettishly, "I do not believe I should like being indebted to you in any way."

Patrick didn't seem capable of taking the hint and going

away, for he merely acknowledged her insult with a nod before sitting down in the same chair he had occupied on his earlier visit, seemingly settling in for a lengthy chat. "I am boorish, of course, to remind you, Miss Quinton, but you are already indebted to me."

"How?" Victoria questioned dubiously. "Surely you cannot think I owe you some sort of recompense for having set my uncle onto this mad scheme to inveigle me into Society in order to unmask the Professor's killer?"

Sherbourne pulled out his pocket watch and checked on the time, shaking his head and muttering something about keeping his horses standing too long in the breeze before answering. "You seem to have conveniently forgotten that it is I who have so graciously allowed you to retain the Professor's collection in order to aid your amateur sleuthing, Miss Quinton. But never mind," he added, waving his hand dismissively, "for it was not nice in me to remind you, was it?"

Several thoughts went flashing through Victoria's mind in the next few moments. For one thing, she hadn't had so much as a free moment in the past weeks in which to continue her perusal of the Professor's collection—which had thus far unearthed over five hundred pounds hidden randomly among its pages, and little information of any merit.

Secondly, she spared a moment to deliver a mental kick to herself for being so lax as to forget that, in some perverted way, she did owe Lord Wickford a favor in exchange for his courtesy.

And finally, although she did not linger very long on the thought, she realized that the last, the absolutely last thing she wanted was to wave goodbye to any chance of ever seeing this same Lord Wickford again.

"Yes, Miss Quinton?" Patrick prodded wickedly, as Victoria's mouth had opened and closed several times without the young woman uttering a single sound. "Go right ahead, my dear lady. I have been keeping count, you know, and it is your turn to insult me.''

"Why would you want to set yourself up as my knight-errant?'' she asked baldly, surprising herself as much as him with her question.

It was a good question, though, Patrick admitted to himself. Just why was he going out of his way to help this peculiar young woman? Was he becoming altruistic in his declining years? Perhaps he would soon feel himself compelled to do "good works," just as his father had done once he had enjoyed seventy years of libertine, rakehell ways, hoping against hope that turning over a new leaf would perhaps gain him his entry into heaven.

Finally, unable to come up with any answer that lent him the least satisfaction, he quipped, "One drive through the park does not constitute an act of gallantry worthy of such a title, madam. A tastefully beribboned medal for bravery perhaps, considering the fact that I shall be opening myself to listening to your less than flattering remarks about me for the length of time it will take me to introduce you to a few of the more influential hostesses, but that is all. Now, Miss Quinton, are you going to come with me or not? If my new team is left standing much longer, my groom will scold me unmercifully all the way home.''

"What's this? A ride in the park? Sounds like a jolly fine idea to me, Puddin'. What are you waiting for? Go tell Willie to fetch your bonnet, and then you can be on your way—right after me and his lordship here have a little sip of something while we wait.''

"Yes, Uncle Quinton," Victoria breathed fatalistically, looking up to see her uncle already heading for the decanter that now stood on the table in front of the settee. At least the final decision had been taken out of her hands—allowing her to feel she had won a small victory. "But don't talk too long, as his lordship's horses are standing in the breeze," she added, silently praying that Quentin couldn't do too much damage with his bragging tongue before she could seek out her bonnet and return to the room.

"Nonsense, Miss Quinton," Sherbourne contradicted pleasantly, already rising to his feet. "I'll just step outside and instruct my groom to walk them a bit. After all, it's been quite some time since I've had a chance to speak with your uncle. I'm sure he has much to tell me about what you've been up to since last I saw you."

"I know," Victoria conceded gloomily, heading for the door as she muttered under her breath, "and that is precisely what I'm afraid of."

CHAPTER ELEVEN

THE PARK WAS A RIOT of lush greenery and colorful spring blooms, the whole scene washed clean by an early morning shower so that it smelled delicately of fragrant flowers and warm sunshine.

It presented such a delightful picture that it could only be deemed a pity that Victoria's visual appreciation of this beauty was limited to a range of slightly less than twenty-five feet in any direction.

Beyond that point, everything appeared to her as a sort of vague greenish mist below and even vaguer bluish mist above, although she wasn't about to admit that to the man sitting up beside her in the dashing vehicle she was convinced had been expressly designed by some perverse devil who knew about her unreasoning fear of high places.

So it was that—chary of confiding in anyone, and most especially the Earl, who she was sure would roast her unmercifully if he discovered her shortsightedness—she had spent the past ten minutes politely looking in any direction Patrick Sherbourne indicated, striving earnestly to comment intelligently on each one as he graciously pointed out the most interesting of the many buildings, monuments, and personages of merit they had passed along the way.

"Oh, do look over this way, Miss Quinton," Patrick was saying now, after they had been in the park only a few moments. "Why, I do believe it's Lord Storm exercising that extraordinary bit of blood and bone near the fringe of the park. Yes, yes, that's who it is all right, and there's the Duke of Avonall and his marvelously outspoken grandmother, the Dowager Duchess, over to our left, driving in that magnificent dark blue landaulet.''

Victoria obligingly turned in the direction he was indicating, truly wishing she could see these intriguing sights, and squinted hopefully into the distance, eventually singling out a largish blue blob that she believed to contain the famous Duke and the Dowager Duchess. ''I thought I had read somewhere that the Duke was taller,'' she commented, leaning forward a bit in the hope her eyes would focus better that way.

''He's sitting down, Miss Quinton,'' Patrick put in unnecessarily, trying hard not to smile as Victoria stared intently at the equipage he had pointed out—the one containing the immense person of Mrs. Imogene Throgmorton and her constant companion, her beloved sheepdog, Hercules.

The chit can't see more than an inch beyond the tip of her nose, he thought in amusement, though he was sure she would rather die than admit it. For all her protestations to the contrary and all her efforts to impress me with her disdain for the foibles of Society, she is just as vain as the rest of her species. Like asking my opinion of her new appearance earlier—a question that must have cost her pride dearly—it just goes to show that all women, plain or beautiful, have the same desire to be accepted, even admired, by the opposite sex.

Stealing a look out of the corners of his eyes, he inspected Victoria's profile—or at least as much of it as he could see, thanks to the sloping brim of her attractive bonnet—and decided that her face was really quite provocative. Piquant—that was the word he had been searching for ever since he had stumbled upon her intently inspecting herself in the drawing room mirror. Piquant, and rather endearing in a strange, unsettling sort of way.

Watch yourself, Sherbourne, he warned himself silently,

realizing that he was beginning to actually like this bright blue spinster with the poker-straight posture and the soft, unfocused amber eyes.

Puddin', her uncle had called her, an endearment that conjured up feelings of warmth and comfort and sweet deliciousness—hardly an apt description of the atrociously clad young woman who had only recently spared no effort in accusing him of being a possible murderer! Surely a change of hairdo and a new gown couldn't make that much of a difference in the girl.

"Does the Prince Regent often take the air in this park?" Victoria asked now, having tired of pretending an interest in the occupants of the blue vehicle which had passed nearly out of sight anyway—or at least she thought so.

"Not really," Patrick answered silkily, promptly giving in to the imp of mischief that had invaded him the moment he realized his thoughts had been taking him in a direction that did not suit his vision of himself as a carefree man about town. "But if by some chance his vehicle should happen by while we are here, I'll be sure to point him out to you. Even you couldn't miss 'His Royal Immenseness'."

Victoria's eyes snapped brilliantly as she whirled to face him, demanding, "And what is that last remark supposed to mean, sir?"

"It means, Miss Quinton," he responded jovially, "that you are as blind as the proverbial bat. Please, madam, end my suspense. Do you wear spectacles, or have you merely accustomed yourself to bumping into things? No, wait, I believe I have it—you have memorized the positioning of the furniture in your house, down to the last plant stand and footstool. Of course, it's that superior mind of yours. No wonder I didn't suspect anything earlier. My, what an enterprising young woman you are, to be sure."

"If you are quite done?" Victoria inquired repressively before bracing herself to do battle and exploding indignantly,

"I knew you were no gentleman! My eyesight is none of your concern, and certainly not open to discussion."

Patrick looked at Victoria as she sat stiffly beside him, clearly incensed at his audacity in pointing out what seemed to her to be a serious flaw, felt an involuntary twinge of pity for having amused himself at her expense, and then firmly quashed it with his next words. "Here now, Miss Quinton, don't climb up onto your high ropes on me, for after all, it was not I who mistook a dog for a duke."

Victoria turned once more on the seat to confront her tormentor. "I did *what?* Ohhh, you knew all along that I can't see clearly at any distance and you—you deliberately encouraged me to make a complete fool of myself." Twin flags of color flew brightly into Victoria's cheeks as she unwittingly showed the Earl more animation in that moment than she had at any time since they had first met.

"Yes," he admitted blithely (for he was, in truth, rather pleased with himself), his laughing eyes sparkling like black diamonds. "I did, didn't I? I really am quite a dreadful person, just as you thought."

Suddenly, unbidden, Victoria began to see the humor in the situation. Her chin wobbling a bit as she fought to withhold her amusement, she could only ask weakly, "Was—was it really a *dog?*"

"A rather large, shaggy sheepdog, actually," Patrick informed her, desperately striving to keep a rein on his dignity. "His, er, his name is *Her—Hercules!*" he added in a rush, just before his sense of the ridiculous got the better of him and he laughed aloud.

Victoria pressed one gloved hand to her mouth, trying with all her might to maintain some semblance of sanity in the midst of this totally insane conversation, but her efforts were without success. "His honor, the Duke of Hercules!" she could only gurgle incredulously, giving up the effort and dissolving into giggles—possibly the first spontaneous display of amusement she had shown since her nursery days.

When at last their shared laughter had trickled away, they looked at each other and smiled warily, aware of having established a sort of wary truce between them at long last. As if to test this new, fledgling friendship, Patrick, his expression sobering somewhat, leaned forward confidentially and said, "You know, being shortsighted is not something to be ashamed of, Miss Quinton. Everyone has something about themselves that they would rather not advertise to the world, but physical limitations or oddities really have very little to do with the worth of a person in the long run."

"It's very kind in you to say so, sir," Victoria began, finding the subject of her shortsightedness uncomfortable, "but then how many debutantes have you seen going down the dance in spectacles?"

"You have missed the point entirely, as usual," he said sadly, shaking his head. "Why, look at Lord Byron, for example. For Lord's sake, the man has a clubfoot—if you will forgive my ungentlemanly reference to a portion of the human anatomy. But does that stop him from being the toast of London? No, madam, it does not, and a clubfoot is far more evident than a pair of spectacles!"

Lifting her chin slightly as she turned front once more, Victoria said tightly, "You think I'm being foolish, don't you? Foolish, and horribly vain."

"If the slipper fits—"

"But I can't help it! Don't you understand? I know I'm no beauty, even you said so. I shall be nervous enough just attending the theatre, or some rout party. I simply cannot conceive going into Society with an unsightly pair of spectacles stuck to my nose!"

Sherbourne nodded, seeming to accept her words as he pulled his vehicle out of the line of carriages and drew the horses to a stop. "All right," he conceded equably enough, "if you insist. In that case, however, I must tell you that, because of my admiration for your extreme courage in trying to ferret out the Professor's murderer, I feel it only fitting to volunteer my services whenever you go into company. After all, it wouldn't do to have this Society you seem to hold in such awe observe you trying to engage in an uplifting discussion with some potted plant, now would it?"

The park suddenly seemed to be cloaked in a vivid red haze as Victoria lost her temper in that complete, heedless way only those who are usually even-tempered can do. Her coldly glittering amber eyes narrowed dangerously as she moved her face closer to Sherbourne's, and she spoke her next words through clenched teeth: "You're enjoying this, aren't you, every horrid, humiliating moment of it?"

"No, I—"

"Don't try to deny it!" she riposted swiftly, shutting him off. "This is just some sort of twisted game your type indulges in, playing with people as if they are puppets, making them dance on strings for your edification."

"Miss Quinton, please," Sherbourne interrupted, "you are in danger of becoming overwrought. I—"

But Victoria was beyond heeding. Angrily waving his words away, she continued in a fierce undertone, "Well, let me tell you, Lord High and Mighty Earl of Wickford, I shall have none of it! It was bad enough that you thought to amuse yourself at my expense, taking me out for a ride in the park just to poke fun at me, proving yet again what I already know—that I have been spinning daydreams in believing I should ever be able to enter Society in any but the most elementary way. But when you—"

"I did not," Patrick objected when Victoria stopped momentarily for breath. "Well, maybe I did—a bit—but I really didn't mean any harm, honestly. Please, Miss Quinton, if you would but let me get a word in edgewise—"

"No, I won't," Victoria answered belligerently. "You

don't deserve it. As I said, I can live with what you have tried to do to me. After all, my hopes were not all that high in the first place. But I will *not* have you raising Uncle Quentin's hopes by volunteering to present me to Society. That dear man has a heart of gold, which is the only reason I have allowed him to dress me up like some Christmas pudding and try to launch me as if I really were somebody worthy of presentation. To raise his expectations the way you have by showing up in Ablemarle Street this afternoon and treating him like some bosom beau, just to dash them all at the end—why, I think it is the most deceitful, odious thing anyone has ever done!''

"Hav-ing a spot of trou-ble are you, Wick-ford?'' a smoothly drawling masculine voice asked, stopping Patrick from indulging in what was his fondest desire at that moment—kissing the infuriating Miss Victoria Quinton square on her pouting full lips until she was too limp with passion to utter another word.

Shaking his head at the sound of the man's voice, both to bring himself back to reality and to rid his mind of the unsettling knowledge that he had been sitting in his high perch phaeton in the middle of the park, seriously considering making an utter fool of himself over an ungrateful, insulting—and not even very pretty—young woman who loathed the very air he breathed, he turned to greet George Brummell with almost unbelievable geniality. "Beau, my good friend! I didn't know you were back in town. It's so good to see you again. How is His Royal Highness? Is he with you?''

"Hard-ly, Patrick,'' Brummell replied in his usual languid way. "His Royal High-ness is still rus-ti-cating with *Mistress* Fitzherbert, I believe,'' he added, employing his usual derogatory way of referring to the Regent's long-standing companion, which was rumored to be one of the reasons the Beau had at last fallen out of favor with the royal personage. "But, my dear man, you are being sad-ly remiss. Must I beg?''

Sherbourne frowned a moment, still somewhat caught up in his feelings about the woman sitting so very still beside him, and unable to quickly understand that the Beau was asking for an introduction. "Oh, pardon me, George, I implore you. Please allow me to introduce my companion. Miss Victoria Quinton, may I present Mr. George Brummell?"

Beau, who had been standing in the path beside the halted vehicle, raised his hat and politely inclined his head. "Charmed, I am sure," he said smoothly, then mused, "Quin-ton, Quin-ton. Patrick I do believe you have been hiding this de-lightful crea-ture from me, for I do not re-call the name."

Victoria, who had now had ample time to regret her recent unladylike outburst, if not the sentiments she had expressed, could think of nothing but returning to Ablemarle Street as soon as possible and forgetting about the entire afternoon. She would then somehow convince her uncle that she was not suited for Society and, if necessary, invent some exotic illness that would keep her from ever leaving her room until the Season was over.

The man now standing before her, the famous Beau Brummell—and a person she should be trying to impress above all others—now seemed to be nothing more than an impediment to her plans. Therefore, never stopping to think about what she was saying, she merely returned his nod and told him flatly, "There is no reason to apologize for not recognizing my name, Mr. Brummell, as I am nobody at all, and entirely beneath your notice."

Patrick could only watch in amazement as Brummell's finely arched left eyebrow climbed ridiculously high on his forehead, signaling his astonishment. Now she's gone and done it, the Earl thought, wincing. Nothing like insulting the most influential man in all of England to set your toes straight on the path to social ruin, even if the fellow is slightly out of favor at the moment. Rushing into speech before the Beau could deliver one of his blighting snubs, he said hopefully, "Miss Quinton is so endearingly modest, isn't she, George?"

"Mod-est?" the Beau repeated coldly, seemingly surprised. "I think not, Patrick. I should instead call it immensely re-freshing. Of course Miss Quinton is no-body. Af-ter all, my dear boy, she heard me say I did not know her. *No*-body is *any*-body until *I* know them. However, my dear, candid lady, I do believe I shall make it my par-tic-u-lar proj-ect to in-tro-duce you. Will that suit, Patrick?"

Sherbourne smiled knowingly, realizing that Brummell had somehow decided to champion Miss Quinton in some sort of revenge against the Regent. After all, if George could take the unexceptional Victoria Quinton and turn her into the Success of the Season, it would be a sharp slap in the face for his former benefactor, who had openly prophesied that Brummell would soon realize his folly and come crawling back to him to apologize for his recent irreverent behavior.

"If you wish it, George," Patrick conceded cheerfully, "you could make my sainted great-grandmother into the rage, and the dear woman's been underground these twenty years."

"Pre-cisely, my dear boy, pre-cisely," the Beau confirmed shortly, already bored with the subject and longing to be on his way. "But I must toddle off now, as I am weary un-to death, having spent last eve-ning on the road. The scoundrel-ly landlord had the au-dac-i-ty to put me in a room with a *damp* stran-ger. I vow I did not sleep a wink all night."

As Patrick and Victoria watched the exquisitely dressed man walk away, nodding and bowing to everyone he passed, regally accepting their patronage as his right, Sherbourne muttered under his breath: "That was quite a coup, Miss Quinton. Beau can be quite an ugly customer, you know. If he takes it into his head to destroy somebody, they may as well sell up all their belongings and head for the Colonies, for nothing will save them."

Victoria was still watching the Beau's progress, impressed in spite of herself, and just a little bit encouraged about her chances of moving about in Society without making a complete fool of herself. Forgetting for a moment that she was not really speaking to him, she said to Sherbourne, "Mr. Brummell seemed to like me well enough, I believe. Perhaps he was amused by what I said to him. What do you think?"

Patrick once again found himself laughing out loud, causing the slight smile Victoria had been wearing to slowly slide from her face. "You mean that witty repartee you dazzled the Beau with, Miss Quinton? That 'I am nobody' drivel? Dear lady, please," he entreated earnestly as he set his team in motion, "I beg you. Whatever else you may attempt in this Season, please, *please,* do not entertain any notion of setting yourself up as a *wit!*"

CHAPTER TWELVE

DROPPING HEAVILY into a leather wing chair at White's, Patrick gratefully accepted a glass of wine from his friend Pierre Standish and drank its contents down in one long gulp. "I squired Miss Quinton around the park this afternoon," he then said by way of explanation when he saw the politely curious look on his friend's face at his action.

"How very enterprising of you, my dearest," Pierre responded levelly, absently stroking the scar on his left cheekbone. "Was your team unusually fractious, then? You seem quite fatigued."

"On the contrary, it was Miss Quinton who was being refractory, my friend, as is her custom," Sherbourne clarified, pouring himself another glassful. "I believed myself to be performing an altruistic act, and she all but boxed my ears for my pains. I tell you, Pierre, I don't think the woman is fully furnished in her upper rooms."

Pierre lifted his chin and lightly stroked his neck above his exquisitely crafted cravat, looking at Patrick from beneath his lowered eyelids. "One can only marvel at the fact that you persist in your attentions to the lady. Her looks have improved from unbearable to vaguely tolerable since the uncle's advent onto the scene—my valet, Duvall, frequents the park she walks in, you know—but really, darling, have you honestly convinced yourself that the monstrous dowry he bestowed on the chit will keep you warm at night—or do you plan a marriage of convenience only?"

Patrick's head came up like a shot. "Marriage?" he protested, aghast. "Whoever is speaking of marriage? Good God, man, how long have you been sitting here, if you have drunk enough to even consider such a thing? Besides," he added, narrowing his eyes slightly, "how does it happen that you know so much about Miss Quinton and her uncle? As far as I know, her outing with me this afternoon constituted her first public appearance. And this business about a dowry—really, Pierre, there are times when I actually believe you begin to frighten me."

Lowering his hand to press it lightly against his waistcoat, Standish dropped his chin slightly and winked at his friend. "Ah, my love, you are not so craven. You know that I have always made it a point to keep myself informed of the activities of those in my orbit. But I am not omnipotent, alas. Tell me, does the lady in question persist in her intention to unmask her departed papa's murderer, or has she merely been swept up in the social whirl at the insistence of dearest Quentin?"

"You know Quentin Quinton?"

Making a steeple of his slim, straight fingers, Pierre then tapped them lightly against his lips as he directed a long, dispassionate stare at his companion. "It is tactless in me to point this out, I know, but you should not answer a question with another question, my dear Patrick. In addition to bordering on the fringes of being rude, you will find that—at least where I am concerned—it is also quite an unfruitful exercise."

There were times when Sherbourne, usually a most peaceful fellow, longed for nothing more than to square off with Pierre Standish and bang away at him until they both were bloody and spent. This, he realized as he felt his left hand clenching into a fist at his side, was one of those times.

But now, as always, he brought himself up short, remembering that this cold, seemingly deliberately arrogant, heartless man was still the same fiercely loyal Pierre Standish who had stood staunchly at his back all through those incredibly dangerous days on the Peninsula Campaign.

He was also the same caring, compassionate friend who had nursed Sherbourne back to health when his horse was shot out from under him and he had lain unconscious for three days in some vile mountain hut; the same Pierre Standish who had drunk, and wenched, and caroused with him during the rare moments the enemy had been put to rout long enough for them to indulge themselves in some sanity-restoring frolic.

Patrick knew something had happened to change Pierre into the cold, calculating man who now sat across from him; something that had occurred at Standish's country estate upon their return to England, and even their close friendship had not been strong enough to encourage Pierre to confide in him.

Patrick shifted uncomfortably in his chair, longing to lean across the table and say, "Talk to me, Pierre. Tell me why you have taken on this ruthless exterior. Do you really delight in making all around you uneasy? Who did this to you? What can I do to help?"

But he didn't, of course, knowing the fragile relationship Pierre still allowed to exist between them would disappear at that instant, leaving him with no hope of ever helping his friend.

"Silence is also considered, I believe, to be rude, my dear sir," Pierre pointed out at last, as Patrick had gotten himself lost in a brown study. "Perhaps my question was too convoluted? Allow me to simplify and rephrase it: Does Miss Quinton persist in her quest?"

Patrick took a deep breath, then nodded twice in the affirmative. "She does," he answered grimly. "The inspiration behind launching her socially comes, I believe, mostly from the uncle, although Miss Quinton seems to be swimming from one deep gravy boat to another, considering that she has just this afternoon succeeded in catching Beau's eye. He means to make her a Success. I tell you, Pierre, I don't know where this whole business will end.''

''George has taken our little fledgling under his wing? Heavens, how very droll. The girl must be *aux anges*. Tell me, Patrick—does Beau realize the chit will be using *him* in order to further her investigation? My goodness, think of it, darling. Beau Brummell in the role of cat's-paw. But wait! Perhaps he too is a suspect? The mind begins to boggle.''

Patrick allowed a small smile to lighten his solemn expression, as it appeared he had just achieved the impossible. *He* was about to tell Pierre something! So gratifying was the feeling that he decided to drag out the moment, pausing to call a servant over to order dinner laid for two in the dining room before pouring another glass of wine for his friend.

''I told you I took Miss Quinton out for a ride this afternoon, Pierre,'' he began, edging his way into the story slowly. ''What I did not tell you is that I had a small, private conversation with Quentin Quinton while the lady went to fetch her bonnet and cloak. He is a delightful man, and most forthcoming.''

Reaching forward to pick up his wineglass, Pierre saluted his friend before taking a sip of the dark red liquid. ''Enjoy yourself, darling, you deserve it,'' he drawled amicably, leaning back once more.

Patrick felt a slight flush invade his cheeks. ''I didn't realize I was being so transparent, Pierre. Forgive me. At any rate, the uncle was a veritable fountain of information, believing me to be the best of good fellows since I championed him upon his arrival in Ablemarle Street, I imagine.''

''Don't forget that pretty face of yours, my dearest boy,'' Standish slid in gracefully. ''As I have told you before, it absolutely invites confidences.''

''From everyone but you,'' Patrick, grimacing slightly, said softly before getting back to the subject at hand. ''Quinton has entered into the investigation wholeheartedly since last I saw him. It seems that there is a most damning piece of evidence that Miss Quinton has unearthed, a snuffbox discovered lying near the body that fateful morning.''

"Ah, not only one clue to the murderer, but two," Standish observed quietly, his finger once more going to the crescent-shaped scar. "It would appear that the man was not only violent, but untidy as well. Continue, my dear, as I am breathless to learn more."

"There were initials engraved into the lid of the snuffbox," Patrick confided in an undertone, lest someone overhear. "The letters *P* and *S,* to be precise, which leaves our dear Beau out of the running but lands both you and me at the topmost spot on Miss Quinton's list of suspects."

"Not you, dear boy," Pierre corrected lightly. "At least, not anymore, as it would seem that you have become quite the fair-haired boy in Quentin's mind's eye. A word to the wise, my darling: I do believe I was more right than I thought when I said I scented some matchmaking in the air. Best check with the lady's modiste first thing tomorrow morning—just to see if the bride clothes have been ordered."

The room around them was becoming dim as the sunlight faded from the windows, and Patrick was forced into furious silence as a servant stopped nearby to light a brace of candles. While at first he was more than ready to jump into speech, roundly decrying Pierre's allusion to Quinton's possibly having plans for him concerning the infuriating Victoria Quinton, the Earl soon realized that he had nearly fallen for one of Pierre's oldest and best developed ploys—directing the conversation away from himself by introducing another topic that concerned him not at all.

So it was then that—when the servant, who seemed particularly inept with the tinderbox that day, finally moved away—Patrick looked levelly at his friend and said pointedly, "Then it would seem, my friend, that you now stand alone at the head of Miss Quinton's notorious list. Unless you have some other likely suspect in mind to keep you company, now that I am found to be without sin?''

"Ah, but I do, my darling man, I most assuredly do,'' Pierre answered placidly, rising to move off toward the dining room. "Two, as a matter of fact.''

"Two?" Sherbourne repeated, coming to his feet to follow Standish out of the room. "I believe I can come up with one. But can you really be thinking of our friend Mr. Spalding? No, no, my friend, not Philip. The man is a complete popinjay. He hardly has the backbone required to bash in someone's head—nor the stomach, I might add. Besides, what possible motive could he have? I doubt Philip was even acquainted with the Professor.''

"You'd rather believe I did the old boy in, then? I call that rather poor sporting of you, darling,'' Pierre pointed out as they sat themselves down in the dining room.

Patrick held up his hands as if to negate his last statements. "All right, all right, you've made your point. Philip Spalding is now officially a suspect. But who is the second man? I've searched my brain, but I'm afraid I've come up blank on any others with the same initials.''

With a look of disdain on his dark face, Pierre waved away the servant offering the soup course before lifting his knife to slice into the succulent fish that a second hovering servant had placed swiftly before him. Only after sampling the delicacy did he obligingly enlighten his dinner companion. "One Sir Perkin Seldon comes most easily to mind, I think.''

"*Sir Perky?*" Sherbourne exploded mirthfully. "I'd as lief believe *I* had done it in my sleep and failed to remember it when I awoke. Now really, Pierre—''

"Both gentlemen,'' Pierre answered evenly, although Patrick thought he could see a slight light of mischief lurking in the corners of the man's eyes.

"So now we have two more suspects, in addition to yourself, as so far the redoubtable Mr. Quinton hasn't absolved you by the simpleminded expedient of enlisting *you* in the marriage stakes. Now what? Do you plan to sit back and watch the circus that is sure to begin once Miss Quinton enters Society, or are you going to step entirely out of character and take an active role in this investigation?''

"You know me, darling. I much prefer to observe from a safe distance. Not,'' he added languidly, ''that I shouldn't enjoy pulling some of the strings from behind the curtain.''

"Leaving me to take center stage, I presume,'' Patrick pointed out good-naturedly, resigning himself to his fate. "All right, my friend, if needs must. I shall play your little game for you, as I feel I owe you that much.''

"On the contrary, my dear friend,'' Standish said in a curiously soft voice. "It is what *I* owe you.''

If Patrick disliked Pierre's cold unemotionality since his return to London over six years ago, he now found himself even more uncomfortable with this rare display of affection. "Please don't, Pierre. After all, he wasn't such a very large Frenchman,'' Patrick said lightly, thinking of the soldier he had shot just as the man was about to sink his saber into Standish's back. "Now, let us get back to the matter at hand, as I find I am beginning to look forward to Miss Quinton's come-out. General Standish, your loyal subordinate awaits his first order.''

"Major Standish will do, Corporal,'' Pierre corrected smoothly, acknowledging Sherbourne's compliment with a slight inclination of his head. "As to our plans for our suspects and the lady, why I do believe that I think it to be our duty to introduce Miss Quinton to both of them as soon as possible. Call it your Christian duty, if you will.''

"How do you propose we—I shall correct myself before you do—I mean, how do you propose that *I* arrange such a meeting?''

"Why Patrick, my darling boy,'' Standish scolded, shaking his head, "you don't mean to tell me that I have to think of everything, do you? Isn't it enough that I, your commanding officer, have given you an assignment? Do I have to hold your hand as well while you carry it out?''

CHAPTER THIRTEEN

VICTORIA STOOD ALONE in her darkened chamber, watching from behind the sheer underdraperies as the lamplighter moved slowly down the street, leaving the yellow glow of the lamp near Number Sixty-three behind him, then vanishing into the darkness.

Twin flames of light reflected on the smooth lenses of her spectacles as she stared into the heart of the soft glow as if it were some sort of divine fire wherein she could find the answers she sought.

For there *were* questions; so many questions.

Who had killed the Professor—and why?

Even more to the point, why was she, the man's unloved daughter, going to such lengths to unmask his murderer?

"Because you promised a dying man you would do just that, that's why," she reminded herself aloud, wincing at the sound of self-mockery she heard in her voice. She sighed deeply, then reluctantly admitted the truth. "Because you wanted some small bit of excitement before you resigned yourself to spending the rest of your days steeped in the same dreary dullness that has so far marked your existence, *that's* why."

Closing her eyes , she turned away from the window. "That may be how this whole crazy scheme began," she jibed scornfully, "but even that is not the whole truth, and you know it. Admit it, Victoria, you are allowing yourself to be carried along in this mad rush into Society so that you can be close to Patrick Sherbourne. You want to watch him as he goes gracefully down the dance, perhaps snatch a moment in conversation with him so that you can drink in his beauty, breathe the same air as he, delight in his smiles, and pray for the accidental brush of his arm against yours. In short, you, my dear, have read one too many Minerva Press novels, if you actually believe such a man would ever think to fix his interest with someone such as you!''

Clapping her hands to her burning cheeks, Victoria raced over to the bed and cast herself down on it, shaken to the core now that she had finally voiced her feelings aloud. What had begun as an investigation based on cold logic and Dame Reason had—within one bewitching twinkling of Sherbourne's dark eyes that fateful day the Professor's will was read—turned into a hopelessly convoluted melodrama, complete with a stars-in-her-eyes heroine mooning in her chamber over the prerequisite unattainable male.

"And I don't even *like* the man," she muttered wretchedly into her pillow. "He treats me like a particularly unlovely, backward child—when he isn't baiting me unmercifully, that is. Why, the only reason he comes around at all is for his own twisted amusement, as if I am some freak at the fair that he delights in tormenting, just to see me perform. I should hate him, actually," she vowed with some heat, pushing out her full bottom lip in a satisfied pout.

Then, turning over onto her back so that she could stare up at the shadows dancing on the ceiling above her flickering bedside lamp, Victoria slipped off her spectacles and began chewing on one earpiece, as she had done in her childhood. She could feel a soft curl of pleasure growing deep inside her as she remembered how cherished she had felt when Patrick had taken hold of her elbow in order to help her up into his phaeton just a few hours earlier.

Of course, he had not been quite so solicitous upon their return to Ablemarle Street, but she had decided to overlook this lapse, preferring to think that he had been put slightly out of coil by Mr. Brummell's kind attentions to her while they were in the park.

As for her impulsive outburst of temper—an unfortunate circumstance which her hindsight had thankfully colored in a more lenient hue—it had not been referred to again by either of them, leading Victoria to believe she had been forgiven.

"He couldn't have just been being polite in saying that my new appearance was pleasing either, for heaven knows he can be most brutally frank when it comes to compiling lists of my shortcomings," she mused, gnawing thoughtfully on one of the earpieces of her spectacles.

"And, although he was perfectly beastly in teasing me about my shortsightedness, he did offer to assist me in public so that I don't make a complete fool of myself by tumbling into a ditch or something. That is not the action of a completely selfish man. No," she decided, a slow smile teasing her lips, "the Earl has a good heart, I am sure of it—not like that Pierre Standish, who has no feelings at all."

Rising from the bed in order to search out her nightgown— the one the efficient Willie must have returned to the cupboard after Victoria had laid it on the bed not an hour earlier—unbuttoning her gown as she went, her smile faded as she remembered the mysterious locked box the solicitor had handed Mr. Standish.

"The Earl may no longer be a suspect," she declared with conviction as her simple dimity gown whispered softly past her slim hips to gather in a soft yellow pool around her feet, "but Mr. Pierre Standish certainly fits all the requirements. If only he and Patrick were not such obvious good friends. Proving Mr. Standish to be a murderer could make things very awkward for Patrick, but if I give up my search I will likewise relinquish my only reason for being in Society at all. And *that* I refuse to do!"

This little bit of introspection brought Victoria back to

thoughts of her discovery earlier in the evening of a secret compartment in the Professor's desk, although how it had remained a secret throughout Wilhelmina's twice-annual waxing and polishing, she was at a loss to understand. The contents of this compartment—a small ledger written in some sort of numbered code—had served to confirm Victoria's growing feeling of there being "something rotten in Denmark," although she had not as yet had time for a full study of the book.

"Tomorrow I shall closet myself in the library and devote my full attentions to breaking the Professor's code," she decided, walking toward her bed. "I always thought there was a darker side to the man, and now I have to discover if this darker side could be the real reason behind his murder. Indeed, I am almost beginning to feel empathy for whoever did him in. What an unnatural child I am! But," she ended on a sigh, "if the Professor was truly evil, it would go a long way in making me feel less an ungrateful daughter.

"I wonder," she added, hesitating a moment at the side of the bed. "Does Uncle Quentin have similar suspicions? And the Earl—perhaps he knows more than he is telling me, and that is why he has been so eager to lend me his assistance. This whole affair is becoming more and more curious."

She dragged back the worn cotton bedspread and slid gratefully between the covers, wriggling about slightly until she found her usual comfortable spot in the middle of the ancient mattress. "What a complete change from my former dull life. There are so many questions now, so many problems," she complained, stifling a yawn. "I should be feeling quite put upon, actually."

She slipped her hands behind her head, stretched out her legs until the covers came free from the bottom of the bed, and wiggled her bare toes. A wide grin split her face as she realized that she was not feeling the least depressed. "Actually, I can't remember the last time I was this happy!"

CHAPTER FOURTEEN

EMMA HAMILTON WAS FITTING into her new niche in the Quinton household with the ease of someone who has through necessity made a career out of making herself as amiable and comfortable as possible.

She complimented Wilhelmina on the woman's extraordinarily efficient housekeeping (while secretly wondering if she would ever again feel it safe to leave her knitting on a chair for a moment without it being whisked away into its basket while her back was turned).

She did her best to remain neutral during the constant mealtime wars (during which Wilhelmina and Quentin constantly bombarded Victoria with pleas to clear her plate, and the young lady counterattacked by way of fiercely lowered eyebrows, deadly verbal salvos, and, just once, a well-aimed dish of stewed plums).

She pasted a polite, if slightly bemused, smile on her face whenever Quentin decided to regale her with yet another implausible tale of his adventures in India, Africa, and Southern Europe (and did not whimper even once when he minutely described his interminable seasickness on the stormy voyage back to England).

But, for the most part, what Emma Hamilton really excelled at was The Nod.

She nodded her agreement to Wilhelmina's heavy, nearly indigestible menus, designed with Victoria's still-slim frame in mind.

She nodded her enthusiasm as Quentin proudly prosed on

at length that all his darling Puddin' needed was a wee bit of patina added to her polish before she surprised everyone and took the town by storm.

So dependent on others for her survival was Emma that she even bit her tongue and nodded her approval when Quentin showed her his latest surprise for Victoria—a heavy, three-inch-high diamond-encrusted pin fashioned in the shape of a *Q*, which was meant to be his present to her when she received her voucher for Almack's.

What Emma thought privately about all these things, no one knew, for no one ever bothered to ask her.

For amid the whirlwind of activity that was the Quinton household, Emma had become the single calm port in a sea ravaged by storms—nodding and knitting as Quentin entertained thoughts of renting out the entire Pulteney Hotel for a ball; patting her hankie delicately to her nose and nodding as Wilhelmina told her that Quentin Quinton was simply the shiftiest thing in nature, while reeking with the scent he had slipped into her apron pocket that morning; murmuring soft nothings and nodding as Victoria patiently explained that Society meant nothing to her, that discovering the Professor's murderer was the only reason she was allowing herself to be a party to the whole insane business going on around her.

Perhaps that was why Emma immediately became the center of everyone's attention two days after Victoria's ride in the park when she finally opened her sweet, rosebud-pink mouth and declared loudly: "*No!* Absolutely not! I cannot, I will not, allow it!"

"But why, Emma?" Victoria asked solicitously, going over to the settee to sit down beside her companion and take the woman's hand in hers. "After all, it is not as if Uncle Quentin cannot afford it. Besides, I think you've hurt his feelings. Just look at him standing over there, his poor chins dragging on the carpet—how can you be so cruel?"

Emma obediently looked over at Quinton, who did appear

to be almost comically crestfallen, and her bottom lip began to tremble. "Oh, you are all so kind, so well-intentioned—but you have no real conception of what is done and what is *just not done!*"

"Oh laws," Wilhelmina muttered under her breath, searching in one of her apron pockets for a large white handkerchief, which she held out to the whimpering woman. "Anybody would think we just told her we was goin' to sell her to a chimney sweep."

Shaking her head in silent warning, Victoria waved the housekeeper away. "You must come with me, Emma," she began bracingly. "After all, how can I attend a theatre engagement if my companion refuses to accompany me?"

Emma disengaged her hands from Victoria's and fluttered them agitatedly in her lap. "It—it's not that, Victoria, you dear, sweet girl. Of course I must accompany you to the theatre. But, good gracious, I cannot allow your uncle to purchase me a gown for the evening. I am a chaperone, not a young girl on the catch for a husband." She shook her head vehemently, setting her blonde ringlets to bouncing. "It—it just isn't *done*," she wailed again, unable to come up with anything more to the point that she could say on the subject.

"Heyday! Is that all that's got her blubbering and whining?" Quentin cut in, utterly blind to the effect his frank words might have on someone with Emma's tender sensibilities. "Good Lord, gel, I've got more of the ready than a body could spend in five lifetimes. Who's to say me nay if I want to shower a little of it on a fine, pretty miss like you? It's not like I had designs on you, or the like, seeing as how you know it's Wilhelmina holds m'heart. How did the girl get a maggoty idea like that into her head?"

"*Ohhh…*" Emma turned to Victoria in desperation, her china-blue eyes awash with tears.

"Uncle," Victoria warned quietly, wishing the well-meaning man would take the hint and withdraw before his plain speech could throw Emma into strong hysterics.

"Now don't you go pokering up on me, Puddin'," he responded, unrepentant. "Lord Wickford sent this here invitation for you and your companion to attend the theatre tomorrow night with him and one of his fancy friends. All I say is, why shouldn't little Emma here cast out a couple of lures while you're about it? You know—get herself some new duds like the ones I got you and, who knows, maybe she'll land herself a fine fish."

"Uncle!"

"Mr. Quinton!"

"Quentin!"

Quentin looked from one to another of the three women, sensing reactions of amused indignation, extreme embarrassment, and—from the love of his life—an immediate threat to his physical person, and threw up his hands as if to say, "I give up, do what you will," then quit the room, muttering under his breath about the injustice of it all. "Try to do something nice for a body, and what do you get?" the women could hear him asking as he strode away.

"You get a piece of my mind just as soon as I catch up with you, that's what you get!" Wilhelmina called after him, shaking her fist at his retreating back. "And close the door after you, Mr. Rich Man Quinton," she ordered. "Didn't you learn anythin' in that India of yours?"

A few minutes later, after Wilhelmina had also withdrawn, taking with her the sal volatile she had employed to good effect on the wilting Emma, Victoria embarked upon a lengthy rational discourse, which ended with her at last convincing her companion that accepting a few paltry gowns and other fripperies from Quentin did not constitute a rapid descent into the role of "fallen woman."

"It is so kind of you all to even think of me," Emma gushed gratefully, still dabbing Wilhelmina's enormous hankie to the corners of her eyes. "My jointure is rather small, you know, which is why I have been forced to, ah, I mean, so I find it helpful to lend my small consequence to less socially prominent young ladies like, er, that is—"

"I know just what you mean, dear lady," Victoria interrupted kindly, "and I can only say that Uncle Quentin couldn't have chosen better when he decided to ask you to join our rather strange little band. And I most assuredly am cognizant of the fact that I am certainly not going to be an easy debutante to launch. Why, any other chaperone would have thrown up her hands within an hour of arriving in Ablemarle Street, not that I could blame her."

Anyone who had the coach fare home to Hampstead Heath, Emma corrected silently, but she did not give voice to her thoughts. "Oh no, Victoria," she protested swiftly, careful to concentrate her remarks on her charge's last statement. "You must not say so! You are rather thin, and…and *tall,* and your coloring is not what is currently in fashion, but you are really a very striking girl."

"*Striking,* is it, Emma?" Victoria quipped, pulling a wry face. "You couldn't stretch that little fib wide enough to say *beautiful,* could you?"

"But you are not beautiful," Emma responded impulsively. "Beautiful is commonplace. You are—*different.* Yes, that's it; you're different. Your marvelous carriage, that long, slim neck, those curious amber eyes. I—I think you—oh dear, this will sound so silly, I know—but I think you have a way of *growing* on a person, Victoria."

"Rather like moss?" Victoria offered dryly, smiling a bit in spite of herself.

Emma waved her hands excitedly and pointed to Victoria's face. "There! There, you see it? There's that dimple. It's so unexpected, my dear, and should be most intriguing to a gentleman. Oh no, you must not be so hard on yourself. Your Uncle Quentin may be wishing for too much when he thinks you will become the Sensation, but you will have your share of beaux, believe me.''

Victoria lowered her head so that Emma couldn't see the embarrassed blush that had crept into her cheeks. If Emma thought she was passable, perhaps she did stand just a slight chance with Patrick Sherbourne. It was a wild dream, but it was heady nonetheless.

Then, reluctantly bringing herself back to the matter at hand, she remarked honestly, ''Well then, dear Emma, if I can be a moderate success, you, whose size and coloring are indeed the mode, should certainly take advantage of the opportunity Uncle Quentin has offered. After all, you told me your husband has been, er, gone for over five years. I'm sure he wouldn't mind if you enjoyed yourself.''

Coloring pretty, the older woman lowered her long eyelashes and gushed, ''Dear Harry. Oh yes, Victoria, I do believe Harry would tell me I was being silly, refusing this chance for a little excitement.''

Bless you Harry, Victoria offered silently, raising her eyes heavenward. She had been sitting in the drawing room for the past half hour listening to Emma, and she longed to retire to her chamber and think about the Earl's invitation, which had arrived just an hour earlier, setting off this entire chain of events. ''Of course,'' she agreed aloud.

''Not that I should wish to make a habit of it, you understand,'' Emma persisted, still trying to convince herself she was doing the right thing. ''I wouldn't care to be thought of as a *dashing* matron. After all, I am your chaperone. But,'' she began slowly, before ending in a rush, ''it would be the greatest good fun to have a new gown.''

Sensing her victory, Victoria reached up her hands to remove her spectacles and slipped them into the pocket of her morning gown. ''Then it's settled! We shall prevail upon Uncle Quentin to allow us to go to Bond Street directly after luncheon, and we shall both acquire stunning new gowns for the theatre. You, my dear friend, may act as my guide, as I do believe I am sufficiently 'different' already without pushing the point by wearing my spectacles out in public, don't you?''

CHAPTER FIFTEEN

"MISS VICTORIA AND Mrs. Hamilton aren't at home, you know," Wilhelmina warned the Earl of Wickford as she held out her hands to relieve him of his curly brimmed beaver and driving gloves. "They're off to Bond Street for some fancy new duds to wear to the theatre with you tomorrow night. You're welcome to wait, but only the good Lord knows how long they'll be, what with Missy takin' such care over every blessed penny she spends of Quen—, er, Mr. Quinton's money."

"Yes, thank you, Mrs. Flint, but I'm here to see Mr. Quinton," Patrick told her, handing the housekeeper his cloak just as soon as she was done flicking at his best hat with a small wire brush she had pulled from one of her many apron pockets.

"Quen— Mr. Quinton's in the library," she said then, carefully folding the cloak before draping it neatly over her forearm. "Locks himself in there now just like Missy does. And I'm *Miss* Flint, your lordship. A spinster's a spinster, I say, and I don't need to take on any hoity-toity airs like some I could name."

Wilhelmina shook her head sadly as she led the way toward the back of the house—as if resigned to the fact that she was one of the few remaining sane souls in a world gone mad—and leaving Sherbourne to follow dutifully along in her wake, feeling as if he had just been transported back to the nursery and firmly put in his place by his nanny. "Yes, ma'am—*Miss* Flint," he declared firmly. "Anything you say, *Miss* Flint."

"Like I told Missy over and over," she said then, oblivious to his sarcasm and doggedly returning to her original theme, "the daft man spends money like a drunken sailor out on a binge anyway, so what's a few pennies more for somethin' pretty for herself?"

"Or a few pennies piddled away on a butler and some other servants?" Patrick interjected mildly, just to hear the feisty housekeeper's reaction.

Wilhelmina skidded to a halt and turned to take umbrage at such a ridiculous suggestion. "A butler? Whatever for? Whyever should we be wantin' one of them useless, stiff-as-starch bodies around here?"

Patrick shrugged his shoulders, considering his answer. "Why, for one thing, a butler could answer the door for you."

"My legs look broke to you?" Wilhelmina scoffed, taking a large cloth from her apron pocket and (as long as they were just standing in the hallway and not really doing anything anyway), giving a nearby table a quick wipe.

The Earl frowned slightly, then pursued hopefully: "A butler could take charge of helping arriving guests with their outer garments—managing the disposition of their cloaks and hats and the like."

"Like I just did?" Wilhelmina asked incredulously, looking at him piercingly as she slipped the cloth back into her apron pocket.

"Exactly, Miss Flint!"

"After this butler you're talkin' about takes these cloaks," she pursued interestedly, "what does he do with them? Don't tell me any of those high and mighty blokes I've seen struttin' down the street with their noses higher than a lamppost hang them up either, 'cause I won't believe you."

Patrick smiled, beginning to realize how neatly he had

been cornered by the woman. "No, Miss Flint, the high and mighty butler does *not* usually deign to hang up the coats. He merely turns them over to a footman."

"And *he* hangs them up?" Wilhelmina pushed, smiling a bit herself.

"Uh…sometimes," he admitted, stroking his smooth chin. "It varies, depending on the size of the staff. Let's see, he could turn them over to an underfootman, who in turn could deliver them to a housemaid, who would then—"

"Who would then hand them back to the underfootman, to hand to the footman, to hand to the butler, because the bloomin' visitors would be ready to leave by then and *calling for their duds!*" Wilhelmina ended triumphantly, causing the two of them to go off into peals of laughter.

"What's going on out here, Willie my love?" Quentin asked from the doorway to the library. "You've got no need to go flirting with the Earl now that I'm home."

"Miss Flint wasn't trifling with my affections, Quentin," Patrick assured the man, "although I must say I am tempted. We were only indulging ourselves in a little game, and your dear lady has just neatly trumped my ace."

Quentin nodded, as if Wilhelmina's victory didn't surprise him in the slightest. "Always gets the last word, my Willie. She's going to make me a real brimstone of a wife, not that I'm complaining, you understand."

"Oh, fie on you, Quentin Quinton!" the housekeeper scolded, hiding her flaming cheeks in her hands. "I never said yes to you."

"You never said no, either, if I recollect correctly," Quentin reminded her, winking broadly in Patrick's direction. "Like that grand good time we two had down at the spinney when you—"

"Don't you go throwin' my past in my teeth, Quentin Quinton!" Wilhelmina shrieked, cutting off her beloved's flow of fond reminiscence.

"Now, now," Patrick interjected, hoping to calm the waters he had inadvertently stirred.

Wilhelmina wheeled around to face the Earl. "The man thinks a wife is part kitchen stove, part bed warmer. Would *you* marry a man like that?"

Patrick's lean cheeks puffed out a bit as he started to answer, then deflated again in an audible rush of released air as he stopped to consider just how he might best attack that particular question.

"Did you ever hear such a damned obstinate woman? It's a wonder to you that I still want to wed her, isn't it?" Quentin demanded, taking Sherbourne by the shoulder and turning him about rather sharply so that Quinton could look the younger man in the eyes.

Stepping hastily back two paces, Patrick spread his arms wide as if to distance himself from the two irate people and said genially, "Don't you go putting me in the middle of it, if you please. I hereby cast myself firmly in the role of innocent bystander! Somehow you have mistaken me for some wise Solomon, which I most assuredly am not. However, the answer, as far as I can see, lies quite simply in whether or not you two love each other now as you say you did all those years ago."

"*Well of course we do!*" the two answered in belligerent unison, immediately casting the hapless Earl in the role of instigator.

Patrick grinned at the pair of them. "Well, *I* believe you! You don't have to bite my head off!"

"Oh, laws!" Wilhelmina exclaimed, aghast, before clapping a hand to her mouth, having just then realized she had been arguing with a high-class nobleman as if he were "ordinary people." Then, before anyone could stop her, she scampered quickly away to the back of the narrow house to compose herself.

Patrick lowered his arms and took a step toward Quentin,

opening his mouth to apologize for upsetting Miss Flint, but Quentin forestalled him by reaching out to grab the Earl's right hand hard in his and pump it up and down vigorously.

"How can I ever thank you, son?" Quentin asked earnestly. "Willie's been avoiding me like some kind of plague ever since we found my letters to her tucked away in Quennel's desk. She didn't have to really believe that I sent for her until she saw them for herself, you understand. I think it gave her a bit of a shock to figure out that she's always been and always will be my one and only true love."

"I believe I can imagine how that knowledge could serve to unsettle a person," Patrick said dryly, trying without success to pry his hand from the other man's beefy grip.

Quentin chuckled shortly. "Knocked her for six, not to wrap it up in fine linen. Well, never mind that now, right? We'll be getting ourselves bracketed all nice and tight before the month's out, I'll wager, and we've got you to thank for it. This calls for a bottle of old Quennel's finest, damme if it doesn't!"

Leaving Sherbourne to stand by himself openmouthed in the hallway—massaging his sore right hand while he gathered his thoughts—Quentin fairly danced through the open library doorway and over to the full decanter and fine array of wineglasses set out on a silver tray on one corner of the desk.

"Here you go, my boy," Quentin said, offering the Earl a full glass as Patrick moved into the room. "Drink hearty!" he suggested before downing his own portion in one long gulp and then tossing the thin crystal goblet into the cold fireplace, where it shattered into a million needle-thin splinters. "A little trick I picked up somewhere on my travels," he informed his guest, who was observing him owlishly. "I think it has something to do with having good luck."

Patrick looked at the shards of broken crystal lying on the hearth and then back to the flamboyantly outfitted Quinton, who looked less like a man of the world and more like a delighted, oversized schoolboy than anyone he cared to think of at that moment. "Seems a capital idea to me, Quentin," he agreed, gifting the man with a slow, appreciative smile. "Here's to good luck!" he said, saluting the older man with his wineglass before draining its contents and sending it winging toward the fireplace, where it exploded in a satisfying crash.

The two men stood in companionable silence for a few moments, admiring their handiwork—Patrick privately thinking the exercise to be edifying in some strange way, although potentially quite wearing on the family crystal, and Quentin trying hard to keep a brave face once he realized there'd be the devil to pay if he couldn't clean up the mess without Wilhelmina getting wind of it—before Sherbourne cleared his throat and said in a businesslike voice: "Now tell me why you sent that note round to my town house, good sir. If I read it correctly, you believe Miss Quinton might be in some sort of danger."

Quentin immediately abandoned his role of jovial host and looked up at Sherbourne, mute appeal dulling his lively blue eyes. "It is Victoria—you're right enough about that, and about the danger too—if m'brother was half the bastard I'm beginning to think he was. It seems as if it wasn't enough for him to push poor Elizabeth's father into giving her to him in marriage, or working it so that Willie and me had our falling out. Oh yes, I suspected something havey-cavey about that business at the time, although it took Willie telling me about it last week to prove the whole of it. I tell you, son, the man was a real piece of work! Come round here behind the desk, and I'll show you what I mean."

The Earl followed silently as Quinton walked behind the large desk, pulled the top left drawer completely out, and reached a hand inside the resulting space. He heard the muted sound of a spring being released, then stepped back quickly as a section of what had appeared to be the solid base of the desk fell forward onto the floor.

"Very neat," Patrick commented, bending down to slip a hand inside the dark cavity and retrieve the slim ledger that lay inside. "Quennel's private account book, I presume?" he asked, rising to his feet and handing it to Quentin unopened.

Quinton nodded, saying, "I keep it there so as to make sure Victoria never gets her hands on it."

Patrick walked back around to the front of the desk, poured two full glasses of wine, handed one to Quinton, and then sat down in one of the uncomfortable straight-backed chairs. "What was the man dabbling in, then? Espionage?"

Taking a deep drink of his wine before answering, Quentin smiled as he quipped, "Selling secrets to Napoleon? No, it was nothing so dramatic as that. I can't be sure, but I'd say it was blackmail Quennel dealt in—with quite a bit of success, judging from the figures written down in this little book. After cutting his teeth so successfully on Elizabeth's father, I guess he decided to branch out a bit."

"Blackmail!" Sherbourne's head was immediately filled with a half-dozen divergent thoughts, ranging from his final meeting with the Professor to the small wooden box he had last seen tucked under Pierre Standish's arm. "Keep going, Quentin," he said softly. "I'd like to hear more. Although I believe I'd like you to start at the very beginning with Miss Quinton's grandfather, please."

Quinton sat down heavily in his brother's chair and spread his beringed hands on the surface of the desk, as if bracing himself for the task ahead. "That's a long story, my friend, and not really mine to tell," he said, sighing. "You'll keep it mum, won't you? Willie and I are the only ones left above ground who know the whole of it, and Elizabeth never gave permission for Willie to tell Victoria."

"You have my word, Quentin," Patrick vowed solemnly, looking the older man straight in the eye.

"Very well, then," Quentin returned, nodding. "Since there's no way to dress this up in fine linen, I might just as well come out and say it—Victoria *ain't* Quennel's daughter. Elizabeth fell head over ears in love with William Forester—son of the local doctor, you know, and a fine, tall figure of a fellow—but the poor lad died in a fall from a horse before they could be married."

"Now why do you suppose this little bit of information serves to so gladden my heart?" Sherbourne slid in quietly.

"I knew something about it because Quennel and I were studying our Latin grammars in the next room when the squire came to our father for advice, seeing as how Elizabeth had told her father she was breeding. Papa was the vicar, you'll recall. A few days later I got the itch to wander—Latin verbs always did that to me—and by the time I found my way home again the deed was done; Elizabeth and Quennel were married. You could have knocked me down with a feather—as Elizabeth never made much secret of her low opinion of m'brother. Now, you tell me—was it blackmail or not?"

Patrick chewed on the question for a moment, then answered, "It's all in how you look at it, I imagine. The squire may have felt Quennel was doing him a great favor. After all, the marriage certainly prevented a scandal, although it must have been dreadful for poor Elizabeth. First she lost her beloved William, and then she was forced into marriage with someone she particularly disliked."

"The squire died alone and quite penniless not six months after the marriage—and he had been comfortably plump in the pocket all his life," Quentin informed the Earl softly. "Quennel saved the squire all right, and then took the man's daughter and fortune for himself. Yes, I call it blackmail."

"Damme!" Patrick swore savagely, slamming his fist into his palm. "I wish Quennel were still alive so I could take my whip to him. Poor Elizabeth, she must have welcomed death.'' Then, looking carefully at Quentin, he asked, ''Why have you and Willie kept all this from Victoria? I can understand not telling her when she was still a girl, but don't you think it's time she knew? It's not as if you're preserving some fond memory of her father for her, you know. As a matter of fact, I think the knowledge would go a long way toward easing her mind about her less-than-daughterly feelings for the man.''

Quentin took another bracing drink from his glass. ''Willie was only following Elizabeth's instructions,'' he explained, looking into his glass as if for answers. ''I guess poor Elizabeth felt the child would have it bad enough once her mama was dead, without knowing that the man she was living with was no relation to her. Besides, knowing Victoria a bit now m'self, I'd say it wouldn't have taken much for her to confront Quennel with her knowledge and then strike out on her own, as if a young female with no money could make her way alone in this wicked city.''

''But she has you now, Quentin,'' Patrick put in gently. ''You may be no blood relation to her, but you are soon to wed Miss Flint, and it's clear Victoria considers the both of you as family. No, I can't agree with Elizabeth's logic anymore. You have to tell her.''

Quentin drained his glass in one swallow. ''I'll think on it, son,'' he promised quietly. ''I do love the lass, you know. She's a good girl; bright as a penny and has a kind heart. Besides, maybe then she'll give up this silly search for Quennel's murderer. As I said, I think she could be putting herself in real danger.''

Patrick poured the older man another liberal portion of wine. ''Tell me about it, Quentin. I think it's time I hear it all.''

Quinton started off slowly, telling Sherbourne how Victoria had thought the Professor had left her penniless until she had found the first small stack of currency tucked be-

tween the pages of one of his daily journals. This one discovery had been followed by others, the bills seemingly
placed randomly in various books throughout the library.

"She wasn't looking for money, you understand," he put
in to clarify the reason for the search. "She was looking for
names that fit the initials P.S."

"Ah, yes," Patrick said. "The notorious snuffbox you told
me about. Go on."

"Yes, well, while Victoria was looking for suspects, I
started smelling something fishy about this money that kept
turning up all over the place. I'm no Methodist, you understand, and I've seen a lot more of life than my dear, innocent
niece. I started coming downstairs after she was abed and
doing some snooping of my own. It wasn't long before this
whole business started to reek to high heaven."

"You found the Professor's hiding place and read his ledger," Sherbourne assumed correctly.

"You didn't look at it, so you don't know that there's
nothing there to read. It's just page after page of initials and
numbers, sort of like a code," Quentin told him, "but it
didn't take me long to figure it out. The initials stand for
names and the numbers are the amounts of money he had
gotten from each of his victims. Some of them must have
been paying Quennel for years. My brother may have told
everyone that he was writing a history of the English upper
classes, but what he was really doing was digging up any
dirt he could find on those poor unsuspecting souls and then
taking money *not* to write about them. He hid the money he
gouged out of each of them in places that mentioned their
names—a sort of filing system, I suppose. Lord, it pains me
to think we were related."

Sherbourne stood up and began a slow circuit of the room.
"It's beginning to become clear to me now," he said
thoughtfully. "My few meetings with Quennel were spent as
interviews, with him questioning me about my family history

for his manuscript. I was flattered, of course, but when I told him I had already done extensive work on a history myself and didn't see the need to continue our talks, he became quite agitated, telling me that none but a man as dedicated as he could ever possibly prepare the true, definitive history. So it was information for blackmail he was really after, was it?''

Patrick laughed at the thought. ''Let me tell you, friend, your brother would have caught cold there, as my family has always made it a point to be outrageous—and proud of it. We'd probably pay him to *print* what he learned! Oh, well. As for the Professor and myself, we parted in anger, to tell the truth, which is why I cannot understand his reasoning in leaving me his library and manuscripts.''

''Quennel was bloody vain, that's why,'' Quentin said shortly. ''He knew full well that Victoria would sell his books and abandon the project. By turning the stuff over to you, he wanted you to feel obligated to finish it for him so that he could live forever as a great historian. He was devilishly smart, you know. Papa wanted him to go into the church. Wouldn't that have been a rare treat!''

Sherbourne smiled his appreciation of the joke. ''But he was taking quite a chance, if you're right. How was he to know that I wouldn't merely publish his existing research— and heaven knows there are reams of it stacked on these shelves—with my own name on it?''

''He knew you are an honorable man, Patrick, that's how,'' Quinton informed him kindly. ''A successful criminal has to be an extremely good judge of people.''

''Does he now?'' Sherbourne countered dryly. ''Then Quennel certainly missed the mark if he thought Pierre Standish would just bow down to a demand for blackmail. Why, Pierre would kill him where he stood. *Oh my God, it couldn't be!*''

''You're right there, son, it couldn't be,'' Quentin hastened to tell the Earl, whose face now wore an eloquent expression of pain. "At least I couldn't find any mention of Mr. Standish—or yourself, of course—in the books and journals that held the money, although there's quite a few P.S.'s listed in the ledger. Whatever was in that box Quennel left to him— oh yes, Victoria told me about that—m'brother never made a penny-piece from it."

"Maybe he never had the chance," Patrick ventured against his will. "I don't like this, I don't like it at all. If there's a blackmailed murderer out there somewhere, Victoria's ridiculous investigation may force him into silencing her before he and his secret are uncovered. Quentin, give me the names of the other victims."

Searching among the small stacks of papers scattered over the desktop, Quentin unearthed a small sheet written in Victoria's delicate feminine handwriting and handed it to the Earl. "I have all those with the proper initials right here. Victoria has been going through the journals and writing down any names she could find that have the proper initials. We may have been poking at it from different ends, Puddin' and myself, but we came up with the same names. There's yours, right at the top of the list. You can see she's drawn a line through it. Guess you're off the hook as it were, right?"

Sherbourne studied the list in silence for a few moments. "Three of these gentlemen are dead, Quentin, poor fellows," he said presently. "Victoria has already crossed them off, as well as Peter Smithdon, who's off serving with Wellesley. That leaves Pierre, Philip Spalding, and Sir Perkin Seldon, the same two names Pierre—never mind. Well, let me tell you, Quentin, I don't like it. Burn it, there has to be someone else; somebody you've both overlooked."

"Why?"

"Why? Can you ask? Because neither Spalding nor Seldon are the sort to murder anybody, that's why!" Wickford gritted, angrily flinging Victoria's list onto the desk. "Spalding is a mincing fop who would swoon at the sight of blood, and Sir Perkin doesn't have the wit.''

Quentin lowered his gaze for a moment, considering the thing, then ventured weakly, ''Maybe one of them visited Quennel earlier that evening and after he left, a burglar crept in and conked the old bastard on the noggin? That would be a pretty turn of events, wouldn't it?''

Picking up the Professor's ledger of ill-gotten receipts and leafing through the many pages, noting dates that went back almost twenty years, Patrick replied bitterly, ''Whoever it was, the fellow deserves a medal. But you're right, Quentin. Victoria has to be stopped. This could get ugly before it's done.''

''Then you think it might be Standish? I know he's a particular friend of yours, but you have to admit, he's a bit of an odd, secret person.''

''Pierre does have some secret in his past, something that happened to him when he returned home after serving with me in the Peninsula, but although he hasn't felt inclined to confide in me, I can't believe it's so terrible that he'd murder to keep it hidden,'' Patrick said as if to himself, already heading for the hallway. ''I believe I'll go have another talk with him. He'll probably make an utter fool of me for my pains, but Victoria has to be protected at all costs. And tell her what you told me. She won't hate you for it, I promise you, and the information might just serve to make her abandon her silly scheme before she really and truly lands herself in the briars.''

Quentin sat back in his seat after the Earl's departure, a small, satisfied smile lighting his face just as Wilhelmina entered the room, a full dish of sweetmeats held in her hand as a peace offering. ''My, my. So the wind blows in that quarter, does it?'' he mused aloud, gaining himself a confused glance from the love of his life. ''It's just as I thought. Lord bless the boy. We'll have the Earl of Wickford legshackled to Victoria before he knows what hit him, Willie, and you have my word on it!''

"Of course we will," Wilhelmina answered flatly. "Was there ever any doubt? He may be an earl, but he's a good-hearted lad for all that."

Quentin rose from his chair and went around the desk to relieve the housekeeper of her sweet burden, tossing three of the sugary confections into his mouth for courage before pressing Wilhelmina into a nearby chair and saying seriously, "The boy wants us to tell Victoria about William Forester, my love. He says it's for the best."

"It's best to tell the child she was nearly born on the wrong side of the blanket?" Wilhelmina asked, cocking her head to one side. "Elizabeth always said we shouldn't take the chance, even though she was longin' to tell the child about her real father. I don't know, Quentin. But to say she's really a bas—, well, you know. Oh dear me, are you sure?"

"The Earl seems to think it's the lesser of two evils, I guess," he answered consideringly. "Hasn't kept him from tumbling into love with Puddin', has it? Besides, he says it will make Victoria happy. Come on, love, what do you say?"

Wilhelmina pulled the candy dish toward her and selected one of the confections for herself. "I'll think on it, Quentin," she promised, chewing thoughtfully. "I'll just have to think on it."

CHAPTER SIXTEEN

"HEYDAY, MY BOY, I thought it was you," Quentin called out heartily, rising from his comfortable seat in the Quinton drawing room to go into the hallway to greet Patrick and his companion, an exquisitely dressed young man who—rather like some ancient Greek whom Quentin remembered hearing about somewhere—had arrived bearing gifts. "I took care of that little business you suggested during our talk yesterday," he added under his breath as he put his arm through the Earl's and drew him into the room. "Puddin' was pleased no end to hear about her real, er, you know, just like you said, but she's standing fast on continuing the search. Can't figure women, can you?"

"I was afraid of that, my friend," Sherbourne whispered back. "Which makes me glad I planned this evening. You remember our plan, don't you? Good. Perceive our first suspect behind you now." More loudly, he said, "Good evening to you too, my friend," before reaching over to literally push his reluctant companion—who had been hovering in the hallway as if contemplating a last-minute escape—into the room ahead of him. "Please allow me to introduce you to—"

"You'd be Philip Spalding, wouldn't you?" Quentin interrupted, coming forward to grasp Spalding's hand in his fierce grip. "The good Earl sent round a note earlier telling us *you* were the one coming along tonight."

"Quentin," Patrick warned softly. For a conspirator, the Earl thought, friend Quinton was sadly lacking in subtlety.

"Huh?" Quinton asked before realizing he had nearly said

too much. "Well, never mind that. Come in, come right in, the both of you, and sit down. The ladies are still primping. Been in a rare dither all day, to say it plainly, with everything at sixes and sevens so that a man feels quite abandoned. What ho? Are those sweetmeats you've got tucked under your arm, friend?" he asked Philip, who was still staring at Quentin, a rather bemused expression on his handsome face.

"Yes, er, yes indeed, sir," Spalding admitted dazedly, finally finding his tongue. "They're for the ladies, you understand," he added swiftly, while taking a firm grip on the box as Quentin looked about to snatch it away.

"Oh, don't be impolite, Philip, old man," Patrick scolded mildly, already subsiding into what appeared to have become his favorite chair in the Quinton household. "Besides, I'll wager Mr. Quinton here would gladly trade you some of that lovely port I see standing over there on that side table, if only you were to let him have a small sampling of the delicious contents of that pretty little box. Wouldn't you, Quentin?" he asked, winking at the older man.

"I would at that, my boy," Quinton answered promptly, already moving toward the drinks table. "The gels will be a while yet, if Willie hasn't put an end to the fuss I heard going on up there as I passed by Victoria's door. Here you go, my boy," he said, handing a generously filled glass to Patrick. "As soft a port as you'll find, too, or at least it should be, considering what it put me back to get it."

"Indeed? Today's prices are intolerable, aren't they, what with the war and all," Philip said politely, accepting an equally full glass while trying mightily to hide the fact that he thought Mr. Quentin Quinton to be just the least bit common, for, after all, he was a guest in the man's house.

"That's quite a coat you've got on, fella," Quentin remarked jovially, still standing in front of Spalding, his body so close that the younger man involuntarily took a slight step backward. "How many men does it take to get you into it, anyway? I once heard of a fella who used two, one for each sleeve, if I remember it rightly.''

''I—why, I—'' Philip began falteringly, looking toward Patrick, who returned his look blandly.

''Sit down, man, sit down!'' Quentin then motioned, obviously not really interested in the answer to his question. Once Philip has hastened to obey—perching himself gingerly on one small corner of the settee—Quentin also sat, raising his glass to Philip and Patrick before downing its contents as if it were water and leaning forward to say, ''So you're Philip Spalding. As I said, I've heard about you,'' Lowering his voce slightly, he leaned forward and asked confidentially, ''Is it true, then? Don't worry that I won't keep it mum. We're all friends here. Tell me true. Do you really bathe in ass's milk?''

''*Patrick*—'' Philip sputtered, this time looking in his companion's direction with desperation evident in every perfectly sculpted feature on his handsome face.

Lifting his glass in a sort of salute, Patrick responded interestedly, ''Yes, Philip, pray do tell us. You simply cannot know how long I have agonized over the answer to that particular question. Ah, but here are the ladies,'' he said, rising languidly to his feet. ''It appears, Quentin, that we shall have to suspend this delicate discussion until another time.''

Quentin also rose, turning toward the open doorway in anticipation of seeing his niece and her young *dame de compagnie* fitted out in their new finery, and his expansive chest swelled proudly at the sight that met his eyes as Victoria and Emma walked into the room.

''Did you ever see two such beauties?'' he demanded rhetorically, already advancing toward Victoria, his pudgy hands outstretched in greeting. ''I tell you, my fine fellows, you'll have to watch yourselves if you don't want some other enterprising young bucks stealing a march on you. Surrounded by beaux, that's what they'll be, once this night is over.''

"Uncle Quentin, do control yourself," Victoria whispered fiercely, coloring hotly as she took his hands in hers and squeezed them in warning.

"Nonsense," Sherbourne admonished in his smooth voice, startling Victoria into giving a slight jump, for she had not noticed him coming to stand beside her, being fully occupied with trying to halt her uncle's embarrassing discourse. "Really, Miss Quinton, you must learn how to handle compliments with more grace. It isn't nice to contradict someone who is praising you."

Turning to look at the Earl for the first time—while maintaining her stern expression only through a commendable act of will, for the Earl of Wickford in evening dress was a sight to soften the strongest resolve—Victoria returned repressively, "I thank you for that information, sir, and please forgive my ignorance. You see, I have had such limited experience in dealing with flattery."

"Ah, that's more like it," Patrick exclaimed, inclining his head in her direction. "After all, what is left to a gentleman after a leading statement like that than to protest vehemently, and then go on to wax poetic over your shell-like ears, glorious hair, and alabaster skin, all of which pale beneath the sunshiny brightness of your smile?"

"I'm not smiling," Victoria pointed out unnecessarily, lifting her chin defiantly.

Sherbourne merely shrugged. "Forgive my lapse, my dear Miss Quinton, which I must tell you, I feel to be totally excusable, considering the fact that your ravishing appearance tonight has so set my treacherous heart to fluttering that I scarce know what to say."

Victoria looked at Patrick assessingly, her gaze scanning him from top to toe before going back to his face. She was in looks tonight; she knew that because her mirror did not lie, and her newfound sense of herself as a female emboldened her to respond evenly, "Better, Wickford, better. In fact, I am encouraged to believe that there's hope for you yet.''

Patrick stared back at her, nonplussed for just a moment, before throwing back his head and roaring with appreciation. The awkward miss was fast being replaced by a woman of the world, and he found himself looking forward to the remainder of the evening with every anticipation of being highly entertained.

Suddenly shocked by her display of forwardness, Victoria dropped her gaze to her satin-clad feet, secretly wondering if the new, snug-fitting slippers had somehow cut off the circulation to her head, thereby causing her to lose her customary common sense. But no, she countered mentally, that wasn't it. What had her so lighthearted, so utterly in alt, was the guilt-banishing news she had received the night before— the intelligence that the Professor was *not* her sire.

Indeed, after shedding a few heartfelt tears over the happiness denied her real parents, she had been floating through the hours, feeling almost reborn. She would have to take a firm hold on herself before she disgraced her beloved uncle by allowing her suddenly carefree heart to goad her into breaking into song!

Sensing her embarrassment, and not wishing to have her refining overlong on her rather forward comment, the Earl quickly sought out a diversion. Looking over toward Philip Spalding, who was still staring into Mrs. Hamilton's china-blue eyes with a look that could only be called adoring, Patrick leaned down to whisper to Victoria, ''Observe our friend Spalding, Miss Quinton.''

Victoria obliged, taking in the man's physical perfection only superficially for, to her, there was no handsomer man in England than the one now standing so close by her side. ''He seems much taken with Emma'' was all she said, finding vindication in the pressure she had been applying to Emma all day as her companion had tried every ploy in order to find a way not to wear the new finery Quentin had purchased for her for the evening. "One can only hope that he finds her company unexceptionable, for Emma has been most apprehensive about overstepping what she calls her place."

"Put your fears for Mrs. Hamilton to rest, Miss Quinton," Patrick offered bracingly. "If I am any judge, I do believe the gentleman to be utterly in thralldom. It's a sight to warm one's heart, although I do admit to a slight desire to go over there and close his mouth for him, as I do believe he is about to drool all over that pretty waistcoat he's wearing."

Victoria's head turned sharply in Emma's direction. She had forgotten about Philip Spalding, *suspect,* the moment Patrick had approached her, which was unforgivable, as the mission she had set herself for the evening—since learning the man was to be one of their party—involved discovering anything to the point that she could about the man. Frowning slightly as she took in the rapturous look on Emma's face, she said impetuously, "I hadn't planned on this."

Cocking one expressive eyebrow, Sherbourne quipped, "No! Don't tell me *you've* decided to hang out your cap for friend Philip? Dull sport, if you ask me."

"Can't you think of anything other than…than…" Words failed her and she left the sentence dangling as she spread her hands in disgust.

"Other than what, Miss Quinton?" Patrick pursued, not adverse to teasing her a little bit. "Romance? The sweet thrill of the chase? The anticipation of a small dalliance in some secluded garden? Or are my thoughts too ordinary, too tame? Perhaps you, who have enjoyed a lifetime of literary pursuit, are put more in mind of Casanova, or our friend Byron's scribblings—even some of the sentiments expressed by other, yet more worldly poets? Pray, enlighten me, as I wait with bated breath."

"Emma!" Victoria fairly exploded, rushing over to her companion (and away from Lord Wickford), for her newfound sophistication did not extend to listening to any more of Patrick's sallies. "As you have the advantage of me, do you think you could *formally* introduce me to Mr. Spalding?"

Emma, who had been drifting in a dream ever since first setting eyes on the glorious creature who, unbelievably, was returning her gaze with a look of near adoration, literally had to shake herself back to reality to effect the introductions, presenting Victoria as the charge she had been engaged to chaperone.

"Chaperone?" Philip chided solemnly, lifting Emma's hand to his lips. "What utter nonsense. Why, you can be but little removed from the schoolroom yourself."

"Oh, Mr. Spalding," Emma gushed, schoolgirllike, "surely you are funning me. I'm no such thing. Why, I'm already married…and…and a widow."

"No!" Philip protested vehemently, his rather high, thin voice (the sole blemish that marred his physical perfection, if one was willing to discount his rather shallow mental capacity) quavering with emotion. "I will not hear of it! That you, dearest lady, should have lived in this same world, trod the same earth, breathed the same sweet air, without my knowledge of your existence—why, it defies the imagination! My entire life until this moment is at once a sham, a joke, a hollow wasteland. Only tonight do I begin to live!"

"Oh, Mr. Spalding!" Emma breathed in ecstasy.

"Oh, Mr. Spalding!" Victoria scolded in shock.

"Oh, Mr. Spalding!" Quentin cheered in appreciation.

"Oh, good grief!" Patrick groaned in disgust, immediately earning for himself threatening black looks from the other three observers who, it seemed, agreed with everyone else's sentiments but his.

"You dare to doubt me?" Philip challenged rather shrilly, dropping Emma's hand and turning to confront his detractor. "I tell you, Patrick," he said in awful tones, "much as I responded with raillery when first presented with your plans for this evening, much as I sought excuses to rid myself of the necessity of lending myself to escorting two unknown females to the theatre, I could now go down on my knees to you in thanks.''

"No, you couldn't,'' Patrick pointed out cheerfully. "Your breeches are too tight.''

Drawing himself up to his full height, Philip Spalding reached a hand toward his left pocket, forgetting that he had left his gloves in the hallway, for he had every intention of slapping the Earl of Wickford firmly across his cheek. Dropping his hand back down to his side, he demanded haughtily, "Name your seconds, sir! For now you have gone too far!''

"Willie! Willie!'' Quentin bellowed in high good humor, running to the doorway to call the housekeeper before racing back to where Patrick and Philip stood, Sherbourne engagingly attractive in his amusement, Spalding magnficent in his fury. "Willie, you have to see this! They're going to fight a duel over Emma. What a rare treat! Come quick!''

Victoria grabbed onto her uncle's arm, as the agitated man seemed about to explode, and fairly shoved him behind her as she stepped between the two combatants—one now nearly doubled up with laughter, the other now standing quite rigid in his outraged dignity—and faced the Earl.

"Apologize, sir,'' she ordered, her stern expression not quite hiding her unspoken appreciation of the absolute silliness of the situation. "Poor Emma is nearly distracted with fear. Besides, Willie will be in here at any moment, probably waving a poker in her hand, daring anyone to be so foolish as to even *think* of spilling blood on her carpet.''

Wilhelmina did arrive, just as Victoria had predicted, although she arrived brandishing not a poker but a heavy black iron pot, and Patrick, who knew that Philip Spalding's only hope of besting him in a duel lay in the obscure chance that they exchanged calling cards at twenty paces, obligingly offered his apologies all round.

"I accept your apology," Philip said punctiliously, bowing with courtly grace before going over to tuck Emma's hand protectively through the crook of his elbow. "After all, I cannot forget that it is only because of you that I have been blessed with meeting this wonderful woman."

"Oh, Mr. Spalding," Emma gushed on a sigh.

"Oh, Mr. Spalding," Victoria trilled in warning.

"Oh, Mr. Spalding," Quentin breathed in anticipation.

"Oh no, you don't!" Patrick declared loudly, hastily draping Victoria's evening cloak about her shoulders and giving her a gentle nudge toward the doorway. "I don't believe I can allow this conversation to go any further. Spalding, old fellow, if you can stop ogling that poor lady long enough to help her with her cloak, I do believe we should be departing for the theatre. Quinton, your servant," he ended, already on his way out of the room, Victoria at his side, one hand to her mouth as she hid her involuntary grin of appreciation.

CHAPTER SEVENTEEN

"WHAT A WONDERFULLY comic expression on that actor's face, Miss Quinton," Patrick whispered into Victoria's ear. "But, of course, *The Critic* is one of Sheridan's best, you must agree, giving the actor much to work with. Ah, look now how he's waggling his eyebrows in ludicrous dismay, just so," he ended, aping the actor's facial acrobatics perfectly.

Victoria's eyebrows lowered menacingly as she turned her head slowly to stare daggers at her companion, who stopped waggling his eyebrows in order to grin at her irrepressibly. "Oh, do be quiet," she gritted tersely, hating the man for knowing that her vision of the characters on stage was limited to the coloring of their various costumes; she could barely see their faces, let alone their expressions.

"Then you aren't enjoying the play?" he pushed, feigning innocence.

"It's nice."

"Nice?" Sherbourne repeated. "You admit to this being your first visit to a theatre and after viewing the farce and a full act of Sheridan's play, the best you can do is to say it is nice? Why, my dear Miss Quinton, how you do run on."

Her full lips compressed into a tightly curved bow, Victoria said crushingly, "Lord Wickford...go...to... perdition."

"Isn't this a lovely evening?" Philip Spalding said blithely, leaning front a little to add his bit to the conversation. "I mean, we did have a bit of a pother earlier, that slight contretemps that I am sure we have all quite forgotten; but now, why I do believe we are all as merry as grigs. Aren't we, Em—, er, Mrs. Hamilton?''

"Right you are, Philip," Patrick agreed with a smile. Then, leaning closer to Victoria, he said confidingly, "Dead as a house, friend Philip is, for all his grand appearance.''

Lifting her program to cover the fact that she wanted nothing more than to go off into gales of laughter, Victoria turned her attention back to the stage, concentrating on remembering Wilhelmina's warning about squinting in public.

"Please, Miss Quinton," Patrick pursued in all seriousness, once Spalding had removed his face from between them and gone back to staring at Emma like a puppy at his first sign of a meaty bone, "I know you are dying to slip on your spectacles so that you might see what you're looking at. The lights are dim, and I promise not to stand up and whistle everyone's attention to this box."

"I am not quite such a zany, sir," she told him severely, refusing to turn her attention away from the stage. "I would have to be completely blind not to have noticed the stir Emma and I caused arriving in company with you and Mr. Spalding—and stone deaf not to hear the questions and speculations concerning our identities that went winging rapidly through the air while you and Mr. Spalding were disposing of our cloaks. It might interest you to know that we were first thought to be lightskirts, except for the fact that I am not quite pretty enough to fit that role.''

Patrick's eyes closed for a moment as he digested what she had said. So that was what had put her in such a strange mood, and after she had seemed so happy earlier. Damn! he silently swore, mentally kicking himself. He should have known that his appearance here with Victoria would cause a stir, especially with the handsome Spalding and the too-young, too-pretty Emma Hamilton acting as chaperone, but the anger her words provoked in him on Victoria's behalf seemed out of proportion to the insult, which was really no more than could have been expected from the gossip-mad *ton.*

"Would you like to retire?" he asked solicitously, already fairly certain of her answer. Miss Quinton, he had learned, was no simpering miss—it would be totally out of character for her to turn craven at the first hurdle.

Victoria turned to look at him, surprising him mightily by giving him a quick glimpse of her seldom-seen dimple as she smiled. "Actually, what I would like to do appalls even me, who has had years of solitude in which to develop a rather fertile imagination."

"You want to put out your tongue at the lot of them?" he asked, grinning a bit himself.

Looking at him askance, Victoria scolded, feeling carefree and happy once again. "And you call yourself a rakehell? For shame!"

"I never call myself a rakehell—I've never found the need," Sherbourne corrected scrupulously. "Now tell me, how would you revenge yourself on these unimportant people if you had the opportunity? I admit to being fascinated."

All at once Victoria was shaken with an almost overpowering urge to take the Earl's lean face between her hands and plant a smacking kiss squarely on his mouth, as all around her gentlemen cheered and ladies swooned.

"I, er, I…" she stammered, realizing she could not voice such outrageous thoughts aloud—most especially to Patrick! "I believe I should like to pour lemonade all over everyone sitting below us in the pit," she substituted swiftly, knowing it to be a paltry revenge indeed.

"I say," Philip Spalding ventured, leaning forward once again, "I hate to interrupt you, but the curtain has come down for intermission. Lemonade, anyone?"

Victoria bit down hard on her bottom lip and immediately took refuge once again behind her program.

"What a splendid good fellow you are, Philip," Patrick said in answer, trying hard not to look at Victoria. "Why don't you and Mrs. Hamilton run along ahead and secure us some before the crush becomes too thick, and we'll join you in a few minutes. Miss Quinton," he added, giving Victoria a quick wink, "you did say you desired lemonade, didn't you?"

"I did," Victoria, her gaze directed toward the empty stage, answered straight-faced, although her amber eyes were twinkling.

Patrick smiled knowingly. Covertly reaching out a hand and placing it warningly on her bare forearm, he said coolly, "Yes. Miss Quinton does indeed desire some lemonade, Spalding, just as you thought. Kindly procure her five dozen glasses, if you please."

"Five dozen gla— *What?*" Spalding gasped.

"You're too kind," Victoria gushed, turning toward Spalding and batting her eyelashes in imitation of an exotic-looking creature she had seen draped on some young buck's arm as they had entered the theatre.

Philip Spalding had a reputation for being kind, considerate, and always willing to put himself out for a lady, but this time he was having second thoughts. "I—I'll, um, I'll see what I can do. Sherbourne," he said in bewilderment before nodding in the Earl's direction and holding out a hand to Emma—who declined to leave her charge. Then he fairly fled from the box just before Patrick and Victoria, feeling very much in tune with each other, collapsed against each other in glee.

CHAPTER EIGHTEEN

THERE DID EXIST in London a few dedicated souls whose primary reason for being in attendance at the theatre that night was to view the goings-on taking place on the stage, but, for the majority, it was those periods of intermission that drew them, dressed in their silks and satins and glittering jewels.

For it was during those precious moments spent in the crowded hallways and foyers behind the boxes where those of the *ton* sat that people knew they would view the real drama of the evening. It was here that they all came, to see and be seen, to be brought up-to-date on the latest scandals, and to indulge in minor intrigues of their own.

During this, the first long intermission of the evening, an impeccably dressed Pierre Standish wended his way easily through the crush of people standing in the wide hallway behind the boxes to the place where Sir Perkin Seldon stood exchanging pleasantries with a minor member of Parliament, the chubby man's usual endearingly vacant grin demonstrating his willingness to agree with anything the ambitious man was saying as Sir Perkin unabashedly used his fingers to eat from the small plate of delicacies balanced in the other man's hand.

"Ah, Sir Perkin, here you are," Pierre drawled urbanely as he came up behind the verbose member of Parliament. "Stuck with yet another prosy bore, I see. You really must attempt to exhibit more discretion, my dear fellow. It is after all, only a small plate."

"How dare you! Just who do you think you are to—" the "prosy bore" objected hotly at once, only to cut short his tirade on a gasp as he turned his head and saw the man he believed he had been about to slice into ribbons with his eloquence; he ended by mumbling something incoherent into his highly starched cravat.

Raising one dark brow the merest fraction, Pierre intoned icily, "My dear fellow, excuse me, but I have no recollection of expressing any desire to have speech with you. Be a good sport, won't you, and toddle off now."

The man, his face now a most unbecoming shade of puce, obliged by immediately backing up three paces before turning on his heels and disappearing into the crowd, leaving Pierre to remark cordially to Sir Perkin, "I do believe I like that man, don't you? He's so very obedient; much like a spotted terrier I remember from my bucolic youth. Do you think he could be taught to fetch?"

Sir Perkin brought his bushy brown brows together and scratched at his shiny, balding pate before speaking. "He took his plate with him," he lamented briefly. "The ham was quite tasty, too." Then, his frown deepening, he asked, "Did—did you want to talk to me?"

"Now what idiot was it that said you were slow?" Standish returned with a slight smile, moving over to lean one strong shoulder against the stuccoed wall, his arms crossed in front of his chest to demonstrate that he was posing no threat to the small, chubby gentleman, but merely passing the time in idle conversation.

"But—but you never have before," Sir Perkin pointed out, a bit relaxed, but still quite obviously confused to have been singled out for such exalted—if not exactly sought after—attention. "Not that I mind, you understand," he pushed on quickly, as Standish tilted his head slightly to one side to stare at him inquisitively. "It ain't as if I go around in your circles, so to speak."

"Ah, my dear Sir Perkin—or perhaps you will allow me to call you Sir Perky, as do your intimates?" At the sight of Sir Perkin's eager expression and madly bobbing head, Pierre continued ambiguously, "Thank you, you sweet man. You are indeed as kind as your reputation would have me believe. I cannot imagine why I have waited so long to seek you out, can you?" Standish sighed audibly. "I must only blush as I admit that I do, alas, have an ulterior motive for approaching you at this time. Please forgive me, dear Sir Perky, for I mean to use you for a little project I have in mind."

Sir Perkin swallowed down hard, nearly choking on the bit of ham he had just removed from his pocket and popped into his mouth. "Forgive *you!*" he exclaimed, flattered as only the terribly naive or happily simpleminded can be.

Standish only blinked once and held his tongue, for it was clear his companion was not finished.

"Mr. Standish, I am your servant! I'll dine out for at least a month on just the story about how you routed old Simpson so famously a moment ago, and it's no wonder—with my pockets to let yet again—that I shall trade on it shamelessly," Sir Perkin added candidly, for it was common knowledge that the genial young man was in low water, and not above stuffing his pockets with tidbits from his hostesses' platters in order to feed his ravenous appetite.

Pierre smiled now in genuine amusement as Sir Perkin enlarged on his statement by giving his generous stomach a comforting rub at the thought of the delicious joints of fine beef and heaps of sweet pastries soon to be his. Obviously the intoxicating promise of unlimited food had banished any fear of Standish from Sir Perky's head.

CHAPTER NINETEEN

PHILIP SPALDING, being the dependable, trustworthy gentleman that he was, had already found his way to a refreshment booth, procured two glasses of lemonade—and two others containing a somewhat stronger liquid—and was returning to the box just as Patrick escorted Victoria and Mrs. Hamilton into the wide hallway.

"Isn't he just the most handsome, genteel gentleman you have ever seen?" Emma asked Victoria in a breathless voice, squeezing the younger woman's arm to hold her back as Sherbourne walked off in order to meet Philip halfway and relieve him of one of the glasses.

"The Earl?" Victoria asked, tongue in cheek, as she was still in a very good mood, her playful bantering with Patrick having eased any remaining apprehension about having decided that she could eliminate him as a suspect in the Professor's murder.

Emma's lips thinned a bit as she realized she was being teased. "As to the Earl, my dear, I was not so unattending that I did not notice the rather intimate exchange between the two of you when Mr. Spalding left the box. I would be shirking my duty as your chaperone if I did not point out that such familiar behavior is not acceptable. There, I've said it. Now let's enjoy ourselves, shall we?"

Victoria, unused to doing the unacceptable—and delighted to hear that she had—decided to take this gentle rebuke as a compliment to her easy adaptation to a new, more free life-style, and only quipped airily, "Am I to infer then that mooning over each other like two lovesick calves *is* acceptable, my dear, levelheaded chaperone?''

Emma's pretty face flushed becomingly, making her look like a young girl. ''Oh dear, is it that obvious? I vow I don't recall when I was ever thrown into such a pelter, even when I first met my dearest, departed Harry. Am I being a complete ninny, Victoria, do you think, or am I not being overly optimistic in believing that Mr. Spalding returns my regard?''

Now, here's a dilemma, Victoria thought, frowning. It's as plain as the diamond in Uncle Quentin's cravat that Mr. Spalding is quite enamored of Emma—and she of him—yet, because of his initials and some scant mention of him in the Professor's private papers, he has to remain a murder suspect. Oh, how she wished she could put a period to her investigation! But now, in addition to her own recently amended but still valid (at least in her mind) reason for going on with it, she had to be sure Emma wasn't in danger of falling in love with a murderer. The last, the absolute *last* thing Victoria wanted was to see her delightful widget of a chaperone hurt, and she knew she couldn't guarantee that such a thing wouldn't happen.

''I think Mr. Philip Spalding tumbled instantly and irrevocably into love with you from the first moment you stepped into the drawing room,'' Victoria said at last, seeing the nervous tears gathering in Emma's big blue eyes as she awaited an answer to her question.

''*Oh, Victoria—*''

''I also think that Mr. Philip Spalding cannot be entirely dismissed as a suspect in the Professor's murder, if you will forgive my reminding you that his initials match those engraved on the snuffbox I showed you,'' Victoria hastened to add as Emma looked about to swoon with delight. ''I'm sorry, my dear friend, but I do feel responsible for you, dragging you into my investigation this way.'' As she spoke, Victoria crossed her fingers tightly behind her back and

wished most earnestly that Philip Spalding was guilty of no
sin more serious than an excess of sensibility.

"*Oh!*" Emma breathed, startled out of her beatific dream.
"I forgot." She looked across the room at Spalding, whose
return had been delayed by the approach of two other gentlemen, before turning back to Victoria. Then, straightening
her back as if preparing to launch herself into battle, she
declared in utmost certainty, "I have never heard such a ridiculous piece of nonsense in my life! That sweet, wonderful
man—why, he wouldn't hurt a fly!"

Lifting one gloved hand to her chin, Victoria surveyed
Spalding as best she could as all four gentleman approached,
while Emma held her breath. "I think you may be right,"
Victoria said at last, stepping back a pace as it looked like
Emma was about to kiss her. "Mr. Spalding doesn't seem
capable of cold-blooded murder. Now, the man walking next
to him, well, I do believe you might not find yourself so
willing to champion *him.*"

Emma obligingly looked over at the tall, dark gentleman
Victoria had indicated. "That one? Oh my. *Oh my goodness!*
Isn't that Pierre Standish?" she asked in a quavering voice.
"They say he murdered his valet—or maybe it was his
groom. Oh dear, whyever would Mr. Spalding wish to pres-
ent Mr. Standish to us?"

"I rather doubt, dear Emma, that Mr. Spalding had anything to say about it, judging from the outraged expression
on his face," Victoria pointed out as her heartbeat began to
drum in her ears. What was Sherbourne about? she asked
herself, wondering when it was that she had lost control of
her own investigation. Drat her blabbermouth uncle, anyway,
and drat Patrick Sherbourne for putting his oar in where it
was neither wanted nor needed! Swallowing down hard on
her mingled anger and apprehension, she went on: "Mr.
Standish is a friend of the Earl's, you see, although I don't
believe I know the fourth gentleman."

Emma, who had deliberately fastened her gaze on the floor, looked up quickly before averting her gaze to the carpet once more. "Oh, that's only Sir Perky," she told Victoria dismissively. "I went down to supper with him once when I was first presented—before I met Harry, of course. The man gobbled up everything on my plate! But he's a sweet person, or at least he was then. Why would he be with Mr. Standish, do you suppose? It seems so—"

"Why, thank you, Mr. Spalding," Victoria said clearly, warning Emma into silence as she reached out a hand to remove a glass of lemonade from the tray the man had proffered with a slight bow. "Emma, do stop fretting about that uneven hem and look here—Mr. Spalding has thoughtfully brought us some refreshments. And some company?" she ended tentatively, tilting her head to one side as she looked directly into Standish's dark eyes and tried her best not to look frightened.

"Ah, the diplomatic Miss Quinton," Pierre said, bowing deeply from the waist, "we meet at last. I have been out of the city, you understand, and could not resist rushing to the theatre when I returned and found the Earl's message telling me he would be present here tonight. Such a dear man, such a good friend," he added scrupulously, turning to smile at Sherbourne, who was standing in thin-lipped silence. "Isn't that right, my dearest Patrick?"

"I have been trying to reach you since yesterday," the Earl replied shortly, a slight tic working in his cheek.

"Ah, yes," Pierre purred softly, neatly noting Patrick's agitation before turning back to Victoria and continuing suavely, "but I digress. When the dear Earl informed me that you were one of his party, why, I was quite naturally nearly overcome! Please, dear madam, allow me to at last apologize for my rudeness at not introducing myself after the reading of the Professor's will, but I had a pressing appointment and had to rush off."

"Really?" Victoria replied sweetly, only inclining her head slightly in acknowledgment of his bow. "I would have said your rush was more in the nature of a hasty retreat, if I am remembering the occasion correctly. I am so relieved to learn otherwise."

Patrick moved to stand beside Victoria as Pierre reached up to stroke the thin line of his scar with one manicured fingertip. "I believe the word you are searching for, Pierre my friend, is *touché*. Miss Quinton, would you please be so kind as to allow me to present to you and Mrs. Hamilton these two upstanding gentlemen—Mr. Pierre Standish and Sir Perkin Seldon?"

As Patrick identified the second man, Victoria's head turned sharply to look at Pierre, her eyes narrowed in speculation before widening at the look of smug satisfaction evident on his face. "Sir Perky" was really Sir Perkin Seldon— the fourth suspect? But how?… *Oh no! They both know! What did Uncle do—take an advertisement in* The Times? she thought wildly, her hands clenching at her sides momentarily as she silently cursed her prattlebox Uncle Quentin, who had admitted to her only last night that he had been keeping the Earl informed of all their discoveries about the Professor. Now Standish knew as well, and—dreadful beast that he was—the rotter was laughing at her! It is small comfort, she thought, that neither of the gentlemen knows about my true parentage, but it is absolutely the *only* thing that is keeping my feet from carrying me off somewhere private posthaste, where I might scream my vexation to the skies!

"Miss Quinton?" Patrick prodded, looking at her expectantly. "You have already acknowledged Mr. Standish—in a manner of speaking. Surely you don't wish to cut poor Sir Perkin, do you?"

Victoria opened her mouth to speak, then shut it again in order to collect her thoughts. This was what she had wanted—to be presented to Society and meet all four of the suspects she had gleaned from the Professor's papers—so why was she feeling so empty, so unbelievably disappointed?

She hadn't really believed that Patrick Sherbourne had taken a personal interest in her, had she? She couldn't have pinned her spinsterish hopes on his falling madly, passionately in love with her, could she? How could she—normally a most sensible person—have entertained, for even an instant, the ridiculous idea that the Earl had visions of romance in mind when he had issued his invitation to the theatre?

She should have realized that he was only funning with her, helping her as it were, in her "quixotic quest" (she flinched slightly as she recalled the term) to discover the Professor's murderer. And now, just to make matters worse, he had included his crony Pierre Standish in his scheme. Oh Victoria, she rued silently, only a silly spinster at her last prayers could have been so lamentably gullible!

Emma, sensing Victoria's tenseness, although not yet realizing that *all four* men standing in front of her bore the same possibly damning initials, stepped neatly into the breach as a proper chaperone should do, saying, "Sir Perkin, I vow it's been an age. I doubt you remember me at all. Of course, I was Emma Connington then."

Sir Perkin answered Emma absently, his rather small brown eyes intent on the person of Victoria Quinton. "Ain't she the daughter of that Professor fellow who slipped his wind some weeks ago?" he said, as if to himself. "No, couldn't be her. Not in mourning, is she?"

"Don't be vulgar, darling," Pierre breathed softly, "else I shall be forced to drop you."

But it was too late, for Victoria had come out of her brown study in time to hear Sir Perkin's words. "The Professor didn't wish for me to go into mourning, sir, and as an obedient, er, daughter, I have obliged. But tell me, how did you come to know the Professor? I don't believe I recall ever seeing you in Ablemarle Street."

Sir Perkin reached into his pockets with both hands, searching until he unearthed a crust of bread he had placed there earlier after dining at Lady Sefton's, and then popped the comforting morsel into his mouth. "I don't recall," he answered around the lump in his chubby cheek. "Ablemarle Street, you say? No, no, that wasn't it. I met him here and there, I imagine. I say, isn't that the warning bell? Best take our seats if we want to see the next act, right?" he said in a rush, already taking his leave.

"Do stay, dear Sir Perky," Standish commanded softly, halting the man in his tracks.

"Sir Perky's right, Standish," Philip Spalding put in scrupulously, looking about for a table on which to deposit the empty glasses he had thoughtfully gathered from his companions. "It wouldn't be proper to have the ladies miss a portion of their first theatre performance by standing about for a few minutes of idle chatter in the hallway."

"I stand corrected, of course," Pierre said bowing once again. "As usual, my dearest Philip, you are the epitome of polite behavior, while I remain the rudest beast in nature, attempting to steal a few more precious moments of Miss Quinton's delightful company. And yours as well, my dear Mrs. Hamilton. Ladies, your most obedient," he drawled softly before slipping a hand around Sir Perkin's elbow. "Come along, my informative friend, as I do believe you have served your purpose. I suggest we retire to White's, where I imagine they may be prevailed upon to serve us a late supper."

"Do you suppose they have ham?" Sir Perky queried anxiously as he allowed himself to be led off like an obedient puppy, its stubby tail wagging furiously in happy anticipation of a treat for performing as asked. "I'm particularly fond of ham, you know. Goodbye!" he remembered to call over his shoulder as he skipped along behind the long-legged Standish. "Been a pleasure and all that."

"Wasn't that odd?" Philip opined before dismissing the two gentlemen from his mind as he made to escort Emma back to her chair. "Has anyone ever remarked, my dear Mrs. Hamilton, on the absolute perfection of your earlobes?" Victoria could hear him saying as the two lovebirds drifted away.

"Miss Quinton?" Patrick then nudged, holding out his arm so that she might take it.

At last Victoria was free to speak her mind, and she immediately went on the attack. "You planned the whole ridiculous charade that occurred just now, didn't you?" she accused angrily, taking his arm with much more force than was proper. "You and that supercilious Pierre Standish. That's the only reason you offered to escort me here this evening, isn't it? Don't bother to protest your innocence to me, as I shan't believe a word of it," she rushed on as the Earl tried to slide in a word or two in his own defense. "Uncle Quentin told me that he had confided his fears for me in you, but then that poor, sweet, impressionable man couldn't have known that you'd then go haring off—rubbing your hands together in gleeful anticipation, no doubt—to spill the soup to Mr. Standish so that the two of you could concoct some silly schoolboy plot to unmask the murderer. And, please, I beg of you, *don't* go trying to fob me off with some farradiddle about doing it to *protect* me. You're enjoying yourself mightily," she fairly sneered, "and don't dare to deny it."

"One question at a time, if you please. As to your first question, I planned *half* of it," Patrick admitted, easing her tightly grasping fingers slightly away from the material of his jacket sleeve. "Once I knew exactly why Standish and I were suspects, I felt honor-bound to inform him of his position. It was my idea to bring Spalding along tonight, but Pierre has always been rather independent, and he must have decided to round up Sir Perky for you as well.

"By the by," he continued quietly, so that he could not

be overheard by the few persons still strolling about the hall-way, "even though I wasn't going to bring up the subject tonight, you must know that you have my deepest sympathy, my dear. Your life with Quennel Quinton must have been nearly intolerable. Indeed, Pierre was quite overcome when I had told him the whole of it—gave me his word then and there to help you in any way he could. Although you probably will refuse to understand it, you should be considering yourself quite honored. Pierre doesn't go out of his way for anyone very often."

"You know that he thinks he did it, don't you?" Victoria declared, still refusing to move.

"Perhaps you would clarify that a bit, please? Who do you mean by the second 'he'?"

"Mr. Standish thinks Sir Perkin Seldon is the murderer, of course," she spat back at him. "It's as plain as that scar on *his*—Standish's, I mean—face."

"Sir Perky a murderer? That harmless nodcock? Don't be ridiculous." So she had caught on to Pierre's cryptic remark about Sir Perky serving "his purpose," had she? Patrick's estimation of Victoria's intelligence, already high, increased by another giant leap.

Victoria sniffed her derision. "Ridiculous is precisely what I would be if I ever believed anything Pierre Standish had to say. The man is totally evil. Why, Emma told me just tonight that he has already murdered his valet."

"His groom," Sherbourne corrected. "That's old gossip. Besides, the man had the bad judgment to come at Pierre with a knife."

"With good reason, no doubt."

"So you've decided on Standish, then?" Patrick pursued thoughtfully, moving to face her in the now-empty hallway. "While I am greatly relieved to hear that you have abandoned your intention to see me swing from the gibbet, I find

I must protest. I know the man well, and Pierre Standish is no murderer.''

''And I'm no debutante,'' Victoria said coldly. ''As the farce is now over, I believe I should like you to take me home. After all, there is nothing left for you to do tonight.''

''Isn't there? You forget—I haven't yet answered your second question. If I recall correctly, it had something to do with my motive for escorting you here this evening. Perhaps this will serve as your answer,'' Patrick rasped in a low, determined voice before hauling her roughly into his arms.

Stepping out of Lady Wentworth's box in order to get away from her cloying perfume, George Brummell chanced to look to his left in time to see Patrick Sherbourne and Miss Victoria Quinton locked in a rather torrid embrace in the shadows.

Lifting his quizzing glass to his eye, Beau drawled thoughtfully, ''How ex-treme-ly in-ter-est-ing. Per-haps *I* shan't be needed af-ter all,'' before quietly stepping back the way he had come.

CHAPTER TWENTY

"IF I MIGHT SAY SO, Victoria my dear, you look a trifle cast down," Emma Hamilton commented, looking up from the small embroidery square she was working on as she bore her charge company in the sunlit Quinton library. "Perhaps the headache that intruded on last night's foray to the theatre has not fully abated. I could ask Miss Flint for some camphorated spirits of lavender, if you wish."

Victoria looked up from the Professor's vastly boring daily journal for the year 1810, which she had been studying for the past half hour (without really registering anything she had read), and removed her spectacles. Resting them on the desk, she reached up to massage her throbbing temples. "I'm really quite all right, Emma, thank you. It was so silly, you know, as I am rarely ever ill. I'm only sorry I had to cut short your evening. Mr. Spalding was most disappointed."

Emma's pretty face took on an adorably bemused expression. "He was sweet, wasn't he? I had half hoped that he'd pay a morning call today, but—"

"That would explain why you have deigned to wear one of the new gowns Uncle Quentin purchased," Victoria commented, smiling a bit in spite of her depressed mood. "That is a most becoming style."

Looking down at the flattering pink muslin gown that showed her petite figure to such advantage, Emma sighed soulfully, then said in a sad voice, "Yes, but as the hour grows late, I am realizing the foolishness of my hopes. Mr. Spalding is just the dearest, the sweetest gentleman I have ever met, but he must have realized that he is quite too important in Society to consider showing an interest in a Nobody like me.''

Victoria suddenly realized she was feeling even sorrier for her youthful chaperone than she was for herself. After all, at least she herself had not been foolish enough to consider that Patrick's impulsive actions at the theatre had really *meant* anything, had she? She shook her head emphatically and picked up her spectacles, once more anchoring the thin metal arms firmly around her ears. "True love does not regard such mundane things as social prominence as obstacles, Emma,'' she said kindly, knowing she sounded like one of the bird-witted characters in the marble-backed romances she loved so well. "If Mr. Spalding is genuinely attracted to you, he will find his way to Ablemarle Street—if not today, then very soon.''

Emma looked across at Victoria, who had already picked up the journal again and was now looking completely engrossed in what she found there. "You're so very level-headed, Victoria,'' she breathed in real admiration. "Another young woman would have let her head be turned upon finding herself the recipient of the attentions of anyone as handsome and rich and well placed as the Earl of Wickford—but you have not let it deter you so much as a jot from your original plan of unmasking your dear departed father's murderer.''

Victoria bit her bottom lip on the admission that nearly slipped out—an admission that could leave the gentle Emma no choice but to think her an unnatural "daughter.'' "Please, my dear friend,'' she pleaded at last, "don't try to make me into some sort of paragon, for I assure you, I am not.''

"Of course you are, Victoria,'' Emma protested hotly. "Why, look at you now! Only last night you had to leave the theatre early because you were ill; yet here you are, hard at work again the very next day. I feel so shallow and flighty, taxing you with my silly problems. How could I be such a thoughtless widget? Please forgive me!''

Slapping the journal down onto the desk with a bit more force than necessary, Victoria rose to her feet and came round to the front of the desk to face her friend. "Emma..." she began slowly, searching for the right words to confide in the other woman her *real* reason for deliberately trying to lose herself in work this morning, which was the *same* reason that she had pleaded a headache at the theatre the previous evening, and the *same* reason that she had spent the remainder of that endless night sleeplessly pacing her chamber.

"I bid you good morning, ladies."

Victoria wheeled sharply to see the Earl of Wickford stepping jauntily into the room, his curly brimmed beaver held in one hand, a highly polished wooden cane tucked under his other arm. He looked so handsome standing there in his impeccably tailored clothing that she suddenly found it difficult to breathe, let alone return his greeting.

"Miss Flint is busy in the foyer industriously attacking the bannister with some vile-smelling compound, so I volunteered to find my own way to the library. Mrs. Hamilton," he continued, turning to bow to Emma, "I discovered a certain lovesick young fellow lurking about outside on the doorstep as I approached, a rather lovely bouquet of flowers clenched in his paw."

"Oh!" Emma exclaimed, her hands going immediately to her perfectly arranged curls.

"Yes, indeed," Patrick drawled in amusement. "It was none other than our friend Mr. Philip Spalding. I put him in the drawing room for you, if that's all right? If you keep the door to the foyer open, I'm sure Miss Flint will be happy to act as chaperone."

Emma had risen halfway out of her chair, her embroidery square slipping to the floor unheeded, when she realized that she could not allow her charge to be alone with the Earl.

Looking from Sherbourne to Victoria and then back again, mute appeal in her eyes, she asked anxiously, "Whatever shall I do? This has never happened to me before, you understand, as I have never had a gentleman caller since poor Harry died."

"If you will allow me to suggest a solution, Mrs. Hamilton," Patrick said gently, "I do believe you might recall that the door to this room likewise opens onto the foyer. There's a lot to be said for small houses, is there not?"

"Yes!" Emma returned with unladylike enthusiasm, already heading for the doorway as Patrick slowly advanced across the carpeting, his gaze now firmly locked on Victoria's face. But before she could reach the hallway, Emma halted and turned to face her friend. "Victoria?" she breathed softly.

Standing very rigid and still, her gaze never leaving that of the man now standing a mere three feet away from her, Victoria answered tonelessly, "It's all right, Emma, run along," just as if her heart wasn't threatening to burst out of her breast.

"So?" PATRICK ASKED VICTORIA in a low, amused voice when the silence which descended after Emma left the room had stretched to nearly a full minute. "I'm waiting. Are you going to deliver that sharp slap to my face that you neglected to inflict last evening in favor of pleading a non-existent headache, or are you contemplating something entirely different? A friendly hello kiss would be nice, don't you think?"

Victoria opened her mouth and then shut it again with a snap before closing her eyes tightly and saying from between clenched teeth, "How can you be so provoking!"

Sherbourne grinned as he reached to gently remove Victoria's spectacles, causing her amber eyes to open wide in shock. "How can you be so adorably easy to provoke?" he countered, stepping past her to lay the spectacles on the desk-top before turning around and taking hold of her shoulders so that he could place a short, gentle kiss on her lips.

"Hello, Miss Victoria Quinton," he said huskily, loosening his grip and stepping slightly away from her.

Her amber eyes clouded momentarily, then sparkled angrily as she decided that the horrible man was amusing himself by trifling with her. "You are an out and out libertine!" she spat in some heat, beginning to pace swiftly up and down the length of the library, unable to stand still, yet remembering to keep her voice lowered so as not to have to deal with an infuriated housekeeper as well as an insufferable earl.

"That's me down to the ground all right," Patrick agreed amicably, resting lightly against the edge of the desk and watching interestedly as Victoria concentrated her pacing to a small area in front of him, the hem of her becoming light green sprigged muslin gown kicking out in front of her with each agitated step she took.

"Dead to all sense of shame, that's what you are," she went on passionately, waving her arms impotently. "You're not in the least penitent, are you? You're such an incorrigible flirt that you cannot even keep yourself in check when faced with such an unimpressive specimen as myself."

"Now I do believe I must object," Patrick countered suavely, pushing himself away from the desk to step in front of her, successfully putting an end to her tirade. "You may still be a bit scrawny, and maybe even a little fusty in your notions, but I wouldn't go so far as to say you're unimpressive.

"As a matter of fact," he went on doggedly when it looked as if Victoria was about to speak once more, "it would flatter you no end if I were to tell you that I am beginning to think of you as quite beautiful—in your own way—and extremely appealing. I even like the spectacles."

Victoria was going to faint, she was sure of it. Her body

was hot and cold at the same time, her limbs were trembling almost uncontrollably, and she seemed to have a cannonball lodged partway between her throat and her stomach. She opened her mouth to speak, to ask one of the several thousand questions she could think of, and croaked weakly, "You really like my spectacles?"

Patrick took another step forward, putting himself so close to her that she could feel his warm breath against her cheek as he leaned over slightly and said, "I positively adore them. I have dreams about them. I envy the fact that they are allowed such intimate contact with your petal-soft ears, your magnificent amber eyes, your perfect little nose."

"My nose is ordinary," she mumbled inanely, staring intently at his wondrously tied cravat. "It's just there to keep my eyes apart." Oh Lord, she thought silently, I sound like the village idiot! Why can't I say anything intelligent? Why can I hear my own heart beating? *Why,* she screamed silently as Sherbourne slowly lowered his head and began moving his mouth along one side of her elegantly long throat, *am I asking myself silly questions?* "Oh Patrick," she breathed, tilting her head ever so slightly so as to give him better access to the tender flesh underlining her jaw.

His lips blazed a white-hot trail along the fine line of her jaw and up over her chin, then began nibbling at the sensitive corners of her mouth until her own lips opened under the gentle assault and she gave herself up totally to his questing mouth, his strong arms, *and* his lean, hard body.

"Missy, I've finished with the bannister, and now I'll be wantin' to get in here and—*Oh Lord above, would you look at that! Quentin! Quentin Quinton, you come in here this minute and look at your niece!*" In an instant, Wilhelmina was gone, hotfooting off on the trail of Victoria's uncle.

At the sound of Wilhelmina Flint's shrill shrieks, Victoria had tried to jump away from Patrick's embrace, but he had held her fast against his broad chest, his strong arms still around her as if in protection. "Be still, my darling," he now admonished softly. "I do believe it would be best if I handle things from here on out."

"Dffft mffffnn mmmff!"

Patrick put a hand behind Victoria's neck and lifted her head slightly away from his chest. "What was that, my love? I'm afraid I wasn't attending. Tell me, does your uncle have any pistols in the house?"

"I *said*," Victoria gulped, trying to catch her breath, "don't do anything rash. I mean, after all, it's not like Willie is about to go screaming through the *ton* that you've compromised me or anything. Uncle Quentin is a man of the world; he'll understand. You had a momentary lapse, a, er, a sudden brainstorm, and shouldn't be held accountable for your actions. Besides, there's something about me you don't know. There's more than one scandal attached to me. You see, I'm not really the Professor's—"

"You couldn't have said all that," Patrick interrupted, smiling down at her before pushing her face back against his jacket front in order to shut off her impromptu confession, believing that, although there was a time and place for everything, this was neither. "As a matter of fact, you barely had time to *think* it. Now hush, pet, as methinks I hear the gentle footfalls of your uncle treading in this direction."

"Wickford?" Quentin Quinton rasped, still panting after his rapid descent of the stairs, Wilhelmina's prodding voice hurrying him as he went. "Willie's locked Emma and Mr. Spalding in the drawing room and told me to get myself into the library because you're mauling my Puddin'. She don't look mauled to me. The child looks damned comfortable, as a matter of fact. What's going on, my boy?"

"Felicitate me, Quentin," Patrick answered calmly, trying not to look like he was struggling to hold on to Victoria, who had begun squirming the moment her uncle had entered the room. "Your niece has just made me the happiest of men by graciously consenting to become my wife."

"She has!" Quentin shouted happily, her cherubic face splitting ear to ear in a wide grin.

"I have?" Victoria questioned wonderfully—and somewhat breathlessly, having at last freed herself.

"You have," Patrick pronounced calmly, sliding his arm around her waist and pulling her gently against his side.

"I didn't—"

"Yes, you did."

"I did? When?"

"Just now, you silly goose."

"Just now—*Ah,* you mean *just now!*"

"Precisely."

"Oh dear. But—"

All at once Quentin was upon them, lifting the bewildered Victoria into a crushing bear hug before setting her back down, grabbing onto the Earl's right hand and shaking it with considerable energy as he exclaimed happily, "I knew it was coming, you know. Oh yes, I did. Ask Willie, she'll tell you. Fell in love with her mind, didn't you? Bright blue she is, though she doesn't hit you over the head with it. Anybody can have a pretty face, right? My Puddin' here, well, she sort of grows on a body, slow-like."

"Like moss, as Emma hinted? Or perhaps you were thinking of a barnacle?" Victoria put in recklessly, beginning to believe that the Earl was serious—he actually meant to wed her.

Quentin grabbed Victoria's cheeks between his chubby, beringed hands and planted a kiss on her mouth. "See, what did I tell you! Sharp as a tack, that's my Puddin'!"

Sherbourne stood silently by until Quentin seemed to wind himself down, then suggested the man round up Wilhelmina and the unsuspecting couple she was holding prisoner in the drawing room so that they could all drink a toast to the upcoming nuptials, which he intended to have take place just as soon as possible without appearing unseemly.

Once Quinton had gone off to take charge of selecting just the proper vintage for a toast of this magnitude, Patrick turned to Victoria, a tender smile lighting his eyes. "You knew last night, of course, didn't you, my dearest love?"

Victoria gazed up at him unblinkingly.

"That was quite a convincing performance of outraged womanhood you put on earlier, but I understood that you didn't want to appear too anxious, knowing I had come here this morning with the express purpose of proposing to you. That's why I goaded you so shamelessly, to give you an opening."

"It was? You did?" Victoria blinked twice, trying to understand.

"Yes, of course I did. After all, you're an intelligent little minx, just like Quentin said. You had to know that I had to have been overcome with passion in order to be so rash as to kiss you in public, where all the world and his wife could see us. I nearly declared my intentions then and there, except for your nervous headache. But I'm glad I waited, although I will agree that this is not quite the romantic proposal I had envisioned, what with the entire household surrounding us."

A small crease appeared between Victoria's straight brows as she considered his words. He actually felt passion for her—she who only a few short weeks ago had felt her future lay in the bloodless profession of tending other people's offspring. "Wel-l-ll," she began slowly, considering what she should say. She may not be all that worldly-wise, but she instinctively knew that the last, the very last thing she should ever do would be to admit that she hadn't had the faintest suspicion of his intentions.

"Yes, pet?" he prodded, smiling down at her.

"Well, I don't wish to appear smug, Patrick, but I am, after all, a woman—"

"Not yet, my dearest darling," Patrick corrected mischievously, giving her rounded bottom a little squeeze. "That doesn't come until *after* the wedding."

"*Oh!*" Victoria exclaimed, blushing hotly just as Quentin and Wilhelmina came into the room loaded down with wineglasses and bottles of champagne, Emma and Philip in their wake, looking slightly bemused by it all.

"And never mind searching out my meaning in one of your books," he whispered in her ear before releasing her to accept Wilhelmina's effusive congratulations. "I do believe this is one question I'd prefer to answer myself!"

IT WASN'T UNTIL the impromptu betrothal party had wound down and the happy couple was left alone in the drawing room for the few minutes Emma felt were allowable under the circumstances that Victoria, her cheeks weary from smiling, took Patrick by the hand and led him to the settee. "I have something to tell you, my dearest. Something you should have been told before I allowed you to declare yourself," she began solemnly. "At first I was too overcome, and then I thought Uncle Quentin would take you to one side and inform you—but I can see that it is left to me, after all."

Patrick drew her hands into his and smiled soothingly, an endearingly loverlike expression of concern on his handsome face. "Sits it serious, my love?" he asked, already knowing what she was about to disclose. "Have you another fiancé hidden away somewhere whom I should know about?"

Victoria could feel the first stinging of the tears that were gathering behind her eyes as she shook her head and blurted out, "I have another *father* hidden away in my past, Patrick. The Professor married my mother knowing she was carrying another man's child!"

"*What?*" Sherbourne exclaimed, feigning surprise. "But how absolutely wonderful! It's comforting to know that this penchant for blackmailing isn't going to spring up some-where down the line in our children.''

"But—but, I'm a bastard," Victoria stammered. "At least, I think I am, technically. Doesn't that concern you in the slightest?"

"My second cousin Ferdy is rumored to be one of Prin-ney's covey of misbegotten offspring," the Earl countered, shrugging his shoulders as if to dismiss the subject. "I can't see where it makes a halfpenny of difference if your father was the son of a doc—*whoops!*''

"You knew!" Victoria exploded, pulling away her hands and bolting to her feet to stand looking down at the love of her life in accusation. "I should have known Uncle Quentin couldn't be trusted to keep silent. I vow that man's tongue is hinged at both ends!"

Patrick rose to stand beside her and slipped his arms around her stiff frame, pulling her against him as he soothed, "Quentin means well, my darling. Besides, what does it mat-ter—if we love each other?"

After sniffling inelegantly a time or two, Victoria raised her tear-drenched eyes to the Earl's face. "I do love you," she breathed softly, her bottom lip trembling just a bit.

"And I do love you," Patrick responded intensely, his arms tightening fractionally as he drew her more fully into his embrace. Then, easing the tense moment by employing one of his engaging grins, he added, "Convenient, isn't it, how that works out?"

CHAPTER TWENTY-ONE

THE NEXT WEEK PASSED in a dizzying daze of happiness for Victoria, who had finally come to accept the fact that Patrick Sherbourne, Earl of Wickford, was truly in love with her—no matter who she was—and wanted her to be his Countess. The beautiful ancestral betrothal ring of emeralds and diamonds encircling her finger proved it; the notice in the *Morning Post* proved it; the hustle and bustle of trying to gather her bride clothes in time for the wedding planned for the end of June proved it.

But most of all, Patrick himself proved it. He was endlessly loving, he was almost embarrassingly attentive, he was almost comical in his attempts to pull her behind closed doors in order to embrace her, and, best of all, he had agreed to help her solve the mystery of the Professor's death once and for all.

Although she couldn't quite agree with him and Quentin that she was in danger as long as the murderer might decide that he was still open to blackmail while the Professor's daughter was still alive, she allowed them to believe she did. After all, if Patrick knew her *real* reason for continuing the investigation (the one that had superseded every other reason she might have had previous to learning exactly what the contents of the Professor's ledger meant), he might just lock her in her bedchamber until the culprit was in gaol!

So in love was she that she had even agreed to allow Pierre Standish a small part in the investigation. It wasn't that she still thought him to be guilty that made her reluctant to have

Standish included in their plans, she had explained to Patrick; it was just that his friend made her nervous. He seemed to see everything, know everything—while the air of mystery that surrounded him resembled nothing more than a cold, impregnable fog.

By now Victoria, Patrick, and Quentin had been able to piece together the reasons behind each of the Professor's blackmail threats, using the information listed on the pages in his various journals where the packets of money had been discovered. At times damning, at other times downright silly, the reasons were many and varied, but all had seemed important enough to each victim to have him paying for their suppression in the Professor's "history."

After several informal meetings—peppered with Quentin Quinton's highly imaginative suggestions for ways to snare the murderer—it was Patrick who at last came up with the idea of placing both of the remaining suspects together in the same room and revealing the reasons they had been blackmailed in the first place—thus startling one of them into confessing.

It was to this end that Sherbourne had engineered the small, informal dinner party that was now taking place in the narrow house in Ablemarle Street, with Quentin Quinton cast in the role of host. Victoria and Patrick would have leading roles in the execution of their plan, and Patrick—with Victoria's reluctant agreement—had tracked Pierre down at one of his clubs, brought him up-to-date on just what was going forward, and then gained his promise of assistance in case things "got sticky."

Victoria stood near the doorway, dressed in a becoming ivory gown of finest watered silk; the soft brown ringlets that Wilhelmina had earlier combed so carefully over the curling stick framed her face while she watched the proceedings attentively. Slowly the room filled with guests—and murder suspects.

Patrick, looking even more handsome than usual in his severely tailored midnight-blue evening clothes, his dark blond hair showing an endearing tendency to fall forward onto his forehead, was standing beside Victoria, his hand reassuringly cupped around her elbow.

Sir Perkin Seldon, never tardy when free food was to be had, arrived a full quarter hour early, rushing through his expressions of delight at the engagement he had read about in the *Post* in order to divest the passing Wilhelmina of a heavy silver tray containing a multitude of fancy sandwiches which now, its contents badly depleted, resided on his generous lap as he reclined comfortably in Patrick's favorite chair.

Philip Spalding had been the second to arrive, bearing gifts for everyone as usual, and was already firmly ensconced on the drawing room settee beside a flustered Emma Hamilton, reading to her from an ode he had written, "To the Dimple in Her Rounded Chin."

The suspects now both in residence, they were awaiting only the arrival of their co-conspirator, Pierre Standish, who had told Patrick he would be happy to attend the party because "I have always been partial to the farce."

"Mr. Standish is late," Victoria whispered in Patrick's ear, waggling her fingers politely in Sir Perkin's direction as that man tried to get her attention. "You don't suppose he's changed his mind and decided not to—Oh, drat it anyway, what does that silly man want? Patrick, dear heart, please go see what's bothering Sir Perkin."

Looking over to where Sir Perkin sat gesturing very pointedly to the empty side of the silver tray, Patrick hazarded a guess at the problem. "I believe the slivered ham sandwiches Willie labored over were a tremendous hit with the man, though both the tongue and cucumber concoctions missed the mark. Excuse me a moment, my love, while I go search out your housekeeper before Sir Perky fades away to a mere shadow of himself.''

''Do that, darling,'' Pierre Standish drawled urbanely, causing Victoria to utter an audible gasp, as she had not realized that he had at last arrived. ''It will give me a moment to attempt to persuade Miss Quinton of the folly of her actions, agreeing to wed one such as you when everyone knows I am by far the better man.''

''That you are, Pierre, you sly dog.'' Sherbourne grinned, clasping Standish's hand in greeting. ''Why else do you think I snapped her up so quickly, before you could steal a march on me? I hope you're ready to play your part in our little melodrama?''

''Can you ask?'' he answered, raising one expressive eyebrow. ''I might even be inspired enough to create a small plot twist of my own, just to ensure that everyone has a lively evening.''

''How good of you to come, Mr. Standish,'' Victoria said, wishing yet again she could feel more at her ease in the man's presence. ''My uncle has gone off to seek out another bottle of sherry, but he should be back shortly. Ah, here he is now. Uncle Quentin,'' she called out quietly, stopping Quinton as he was just about to walk past them, a dusty bottle in one hand. ''Our final guest has arrived. Please come over here and allow me to introduce you.''

''My dear Mr. Quinton,'' Pierre said, bowing slightly in the older man's direction, ''it's good to see you again.''

''Good to see you too,'' Quentin responded, transferring the bottle to his left hand before wiping his right hand on his coat and extending it politely. ''Er, we've met?''

Pierre's dark face took on a hurt expression. ''How soon they forget,'' he bemoaned to Patrick, who was looking confused and a bit wary. ''Let me see if I can jog your memory, dear sir. Two months ago, at Ramsgate? A rather well-endowed barmaid named Rosie, I believe? I had docked my yacht there and retired to a nearby inn for a meal. Does it come back to you now, my dear fellow?''

Quinton's lively blue eyes widened in shock. Looking about himself swiftly for any sign of Wilhelmina, he leaned close to Pierre and whispered urgently, ''Keep your voice down, sir, I implore you. I had been at sea quite a long time, you understand, and needed a bit of comfort. Please, I'm soon to become a happily married man!''

''Your distress affects me deeply,'' Pierre replied, tongue in cheek. ''Surely my silence on the matter isn't an out of the way demand. But I would beg a boon, my dear fellow. Please, could you tell me why, since you have been in England for quite some time, you waited until after your brother's funeral to make your existence known to your niece?''

Victoria, who had been standing mute with shock ever since she realized that her Uncle Quentin and Pierre were acquainted, seconded this question, adding hopefully, ''But perhaps you hadn't yet come to London at the time the Professor was murdered?''

By this time Sir Perkin, whose hopes of securing more of the delicious ham had been raised, only to be shot down by Standish's arrival, had decided to take matters into his own hands, and approached the small group to tug on Patrick's sleeve. ''I say, Sherbourne,'' he said brashly, ''have you seen that buxomy redhead about lately? Surely you weren't planning on serving only one platter, were you? Though I could push on to Lady Beresford's. Her chef does a fine buffet.''

Patrick wasn't in the mood to worry about Sir Perkin's appetite. Pierre, drat the man, had been keeping information from him again, and now it appeared that the Professor's own brother could be a murder suspect. ''Run along over there and ask Mrs. Hamilton to help you,'' he said shortly, disengaging his arm from Seldon's grip. ''Just don't smile at her, else Spalding may call you out.''

Once the other man had toddled off, already calling plaintively to Emma, Patrick returned his attention to the matter at hand, saying, "Please, Quentin, we're all friends here. Answer Victoria's question."

Quentin took a deep breath, looking at each of them in turn, then said gloomily, "I was in London, all right. I came here directly from Ramsgate."

"Oh, Uncle!" Victoria sighed sadly. "Please, say no more! I don't want to hear any more, really I don't."

Suddenly the crestfallen man became indignant. "Well, I don't know why not, for pity's sake!" he exclaimed hotly. "All I did for nearly a month was kick my heels like some lovestruck lunatic while I waited for my new wardrobe to be finished. I had been in foreign parts for a long time, you know, and didn't want to present myself to Willie until I was fitted out fine as fivepence."

"Perfectly understandable," Pierre put in kindly, sneaking a quick look at Patrick.

"Then you didn't come to see the Professor? But I don't understand. Why didn't you attend the funeral?" Victoria asked, hating herself for needing to know.

"So much for my darling fiancée's declaration that she would be happier to remain in ignorance," Patrick put in, wrapping his arm around her waist. "Don't answer if you don't want to, Quentin. None of us here believes you conked your own brother over the head and then left him to die."

"It wasn't me, because I didn't think of it!" Quentin shot back tightly. "I was here, you know, that same night, only it was earlier in the evening I imagine, as the old bas—, er, m'brother was still very much alive. I'd come to see Willie, of course, but he told me she had moved back to the country to nurse her sick sister. Damn me for a fool, I believed him. By the time I had chased myself to Surrey and back again, Quennel had been carried to bed on six men's shoulders.

After that, I didn't see any reason to mention my first visit to anyone. I'm that sorry, you know, if I upset anybody.''

"Oh, Uncle," Victoria cried, embracing Quentin, "don't be sorry! *We're* sorry we questioned you. Besides, it's all Mr. Standish's fault for bringing it up in the first place, isn't that right, Patrick?"

The Earl pulled a wry face and looked at his friend, who was standing at his ease, surveying the touching scene unfolding in front of him. "Consider yourself reprimanded, please, dear Pierre, for I refuse to demand retribution. After all, I'm soon to be a married man, and must think of my poor wife and unborn children."

"I offer my apologies, of course, for departing from your prepared script for the evening, my friends," Pierre responded coolly. "I had already assured myself of friend Quinton's innocence, you know. I merely wished to introduce him as a suspect to prove to you all how misleading bits and pieces of seemingly damning evidence can be."

"And how some questions are best left unanswered? Such as an explanation of the contents of a certain wooden box now in your possession?" Victoria, who had grudgingly begun to admire this strange man, questioned incisively.

"Patrick you have unearthed a genuine jewel," Pierre said in a soft, drawling voice. "Guard her well."

CHAPTER TWENTY-TWO

AT THE CONCLUSION of the meal served in the narrow dining room, informal toasts were proposed all round to the happy couple before Wilhelmina (who had steadfastly refused to be one of the party) wheeled in the *pièce de résistance,* a five-tiered cake decorated with meringue swans and bits of greenery that elicited appreciative murmurs from everyone but Sir Perkin, who had immediately leaped to his feet to propose yet another toast—to the cook.

It was while the cake was being served that Patrick looked down the table at Victoria and gave her a barely perceptible nod. Promptly taking her cue, she turned to Philip Spalding, who was seated at her left, and said, "Patrick and I are leaving London within the week to visit his parents—they're spending the season in Bath, you know—to formally announce our engagement, but we wanted to have this small, intimate party here with my uncle in attendance." She then hesitated a moment before adding in a voice heavy with regret, "If only the Professor had been here to give me his blessing."

"Ah, yes," Spalding replied commiseratingly, "it is such a pity, isn't it?"

Victoria sighed deeply. "It seems it was only yesterday that I was sitting in the library, copying down his dictation. Patrick is going to complete the Professor's work, you know, so I believe we can look forward to having the history published in the next year or so."

"He isn't!" Philip exploded hoarsely, then quickly low-

ered his voice. "That is to say, he is? How wonderful. You must be very pleased, Miss Quinton."

Pierre Standish, seated on the opposite side of the table from Spalding, murmured smoothly, "Ah, Miss Quinton, well done. A flush hit, I'd say. May I?" he asked pleasantly, leaning forward slightly to look pointedly at the uncomfortably fidgeting Spalding.

"By all means, Mr. Standish," Victoria returned with utmost politeness. "After all, I believe I owe you at least that much."

"My dearest Philip," Pierre then began urbanely, addressing the patently confused man, "you seem to be upset about something. Perhaps the cake is too rich for your system—too laden with *cream* for your taste? A pity. I myself have quite a fondness for the stuff. As a matter of fact, I number among my happiest memories those times I would sneak off to the dairy when the servants were making cream. There was one dairymaid I remember in particular—"

Pierre's words were cut off as Spalding, suddenly comprehending, sprang to his feet, knocking over his chair in his haste as he accused dazedly, "You *know!* How do you know? He promised me no one would know. *He promised!*"

"Obviously there will be no need for the thumbscrews after all," Standish said to Victoria, his lips twitching in wry amusement. "I must admit I am surprised. I truly hadn't thought him to be our man. Perhaps a few more pointed questions are needed?"

"Philip!" Emma, tugging at his perfectly constructed coat sleeve, cried anxiously, unwittingly casting herself in the role of one of the man's tormentors. "Say it isn't so, *please!* Please say you didn't kill him!"

"Kill him?" Philip repeated hollowly, staring down at Emma, a confused look on his face. "Kill who?"

"Whom," Pierre slid in quietly, clearly enjoying himself.

"Why, the Professor, of course," Emma told him, tears

forming in her soft blue eyes as visions of her beloved—dirty, disheveled, and clad in tattered rags as he wallowed in his straw-lined cell—pushed her toward the edge of hysterics. "Was it you who killed the Professor?"

"*Arrrgh!*"

"Sir Perkin, are you all right?" Quentin asked, pounding the suddenly choking man sharply between the shoulder blades with one beefy fist.

Patrick and Pierre exchanged knowing looks, then turned to Victoria, who surprised them by looking a bit crestfallen rather than triumphant. "We wouldn't publish anything even remotely embarrassing, Mr. Spalding," she told Philip quietly. "Not that having a dairymaid for a great-grandmother is such a terrible thing."

"You know *too?*" Spalding asked, clearly agonized with shame. "The Professor promised me he'd burn his notes. I sold my matched bays to pay him what he—Oh, what difference does it make? Now that Standish knows too—and the rest of you—I imagine everyone will soon be snickering up their sleeves at me. I'll tell you what—I shall have to retire to the country, that's all there is for it, I guess."

"So dramatic, my dear Philip," Pierre drawled sarcastically. "Mrs. Hamilton," he went on, turning to look at Emma, who was crying silently into her handkerchief. "Has the knowledge you have gained in these past few minutes colored your opinion of dear Mr. Spalding here? Come, come. Don't be bashful; a man's future hangs in the balance."

Bright color suffused Emma's cheeks as she raised her face to peer up at Spalding. "I think he is still the grandest, most noble man that ever lived," she declared at last, before adding thoughtfully, "even if his great-grandmother *was* a Common Nobody."

"You do?" Philip squeaked incredulously. "Don't it even

bother you that I was so vain as to pay the Professor not to print that bit about my ancestry?''

"She thinks you hang out the sun, dear boy," Pierre snapped, beginning to lose patience with the ridiculous man. "Don't belabor the point. Now, why don't you escort Mrs. Hamilton to the drawing room—I'm sure you have quite a bit to discuss. Miss Quinton and the rest of us have pressing matters still to resolve.''

Offering his hand to Emma, who took it gingerly, Philip helped her to rise, then drew her arm lovingly through his and guided her slowly out of the room, his passionate gaze never leaving her beautiful face. "Was that your maternal or paternal great-grandmother, my dear Mr. Spalding?'' Emma was heard to ask pointedly as they walked along.

"Ah, true love," Pierre said emotionlessly once the couple had disappeared through the doors Wilhelmina needed no prompting to close in their wake. "I do not believe there is anything else in this entire mad world that I find so singularly dull and uninteresting.''

"And I believe you doth protest too much,'' Victoria replied bluntly, extremely curious about this enigmatic man who was her fiancé's dearest friend. "Someday I should like to hear the story of how you came to be the cynic you portray so convincingly.''

Pierre's dark face suddenly became an emotionless mask, his dark eyes unreadable. "I shall not soil your ears with that sad tale, my dearest Miss Quinton," he snapped coldly, then added more kindly, "Besides, I do believe Sir Perky is about to say something that will interest you. It seems I may have been right all along—though it is tactless in me to remind you, isn't it?''

Indeed, Sir Perkin was recovering from the fit of coughing that had been brought on by Emma's impulsive remarks, wiping at the stream of tears his choking had provoked with Quentin Quinton's immense handkerchief.

Rising to walk to the head of the table, Victoria gratefully sank into the chair Patrick had vacated for her and allowed her hands to be taken in Sir Perkin's compulsive grip.

"He tried to blackmail me too," he began almost incoherently, his lower lip trembling in his agitation.

"Yes, Sir Perky," Victoria assured him kindly, "I know; we all do now, having found certain incriminating papers in the Professor's library. You were not the only victim, I fear, as it appears the man blackmailed a great many people over the years. You just heard Mr. Spalding confess to having paid so that he could keep his own secret safe, didn't you? I can tell you in all honesty, Sir Perky, that Professor Quinton was a vile, soulless man."

"I can't really say I liked him above half myself," Sir Perky admitted, murmuring into his cravat.

"Have another piece of cake, Sir Perkin," Wilhelmina put in, placing a plate holding an immense slice of the dessert in front of the man, hoping he'd then release Victoria's hands. "After all," she said to Patrick as she stepped back to stand beside him, "Missy shouldn't be holdin' hands with a murderer, even if he is the sorriest-lookin' fella I've ever seen."

Wilhelmina's ploy worked, as food had always been a panacea to Sir Perkin, and he quickly shoveled two large bites into his mouth before talking around the resultant bulges in his cheeks. "The Professor called me to this house to talk about my family history—or so he said. I was flattered to have the Seldons included in his book, of course, and he did serve me the loveliest snack. Duck, I think it was; yes, it was duck. It was only after we had been talking for some time that I realized exactly what he was saying." Wiping some cake crumbs from his lips with his serviette, he looked up at Sherbourne and declared earnestly, "I couldn't believe it of him, I tell you. I just couldn't believe *any* of it!"

"Ah, the treachery of one's friends," Patrick commiserated, tongue-in-cheek."

Sir Perkin held one finger up in the air, signaling that he had something more to say just as soon as he had disposed of the forkful of cake he was at the moment aiming toward his mouth. "He wasn't my friend," he then corrected punctiliously.

"Very well, if you wish to split hairs at a time like this," Patrick said amiably. "Ah, the treachery of one's acquaintances! Is that better? But to continue: The Professor told you about the circumstances of your birth, didn't he?" Patrick was in a bit of a hurry to get this part of the questioning over, as he could see the tension was beginning to affect Victoria's nerves.

The man nodded his balding head up and down emphatically, licking a bit of meringue from his lips with the tip of his tongue. "It's not that I minded all that much being a bastard," he said in explanation, looking at Victoria for understanding. "It's just that—well—you see, Mama never told me!"

"How remiss of her," Pierre remarked silkily from his seat farther down the table. "Perhaps it slipped her mind."

"Yes!" Sir Perkin exclaimed, jumping on that excuse. "How good of you to see it that way, Mr. Standish. That's precisely what I thought myself, you know, but the Professor had all sorts of papers—church records and the like—that proved I was born before my parents were wed. I was shocked, I tell you," he then told Victoria earnestly, "truly shocked. I mean, everyone says I'm the living spit of my father." His emotional outburst over for the moment, he shoved another forkful of cake between his lips.

"But your father *is* your father," Victoria began hastily, then stopped, looking to Patrick in confusion, for she knew she shouldn't be speaking so freely about such things.

"What Miss Quinton is trying so delicately to say, Sir Perky," Patrick then explained, "is that you *are* your father's son. They were just a trifle tardy with the wedding ceremony, that's all, as christenings don't usually precede the marriage vows. But it was all in the papers the Professor had. Didn't you read them?''

''I—I didn't know.'' Sir Perkin looked at each of them in turn, swallowed hard, and then asked Wilhelmina if she could please pour him a bit of wine, as his throat was suddenly dry.

''Here you go, Sir Perkin,'' the housekeeper said bracingly, stepping forward smartly to refill his glass to the rim. ''Now don't you go gettin' all upset. Nobody's blamin' you. It was an accident, wasn't it?'' she urged, motherlike.

For a moment Victoria feared that Sir Perkin, now looking at the housekeeper like a lost puppy who had just been offered a meaty soup bone, was going to fling himself against Wilhelmina's starched apron and burst into tears, but then he took a deep breath and squared his shoulders, ready to own up to what he had done.

'It was me,'' he said dully at last, shrugging his shoulders. ''I did it. I killed him.''

''That's rich, upon my soul it is. Don't plague one with a bag of humbug, does he?'' Quentin remarked happily. ''No tippytoeing around the thing, that's for sure. Comes right to the point—bang—'It was me, I killed him.' You have to admire that in a man.''

''Uncle Quentin, please,'' Victoria hissed as Patrick covered his laugh with a discreet cough.

''I never really saw the papers,'' Sir Perkin then informed them, seeming suddenly eager to make a clean breast of everything. ''The Professor was just sort of waving them in front of my face, telling me that I was to pay him some ridiculous sum out of my quarterly allowance or else he'd publish the fact that I was a bas—, well, you know that part already. I tried to tell him that I didn't have a feather to fly with—everyone knows that—but he just kept waving those papers back and forth…back and forth…until I swear I couldn't see anything but those papers.''

''Poor little fella,'' Wilhelmina intoned sadly, wiping at her watery eyes with one corner of her apron.

''I guess I must have gone slightly out of my head,'' Sir Perkin then continued in a dull monotone, ''for suddenly there was this rather *red* haze in front of my eyes. I lunged for the papers—he held them up and away from me. I grabbed at his arm. We tussled back and forth a bit…with him just laughing and telling me I had to pay…then I somehow lost my grip on him. The Professor fell…hitting his head on the windowsill. It made an awful sound. Then he just sort of slid to the floor…and the papers scattered everywhere. He just lay there, propped against the window, his eyes looking at me but not really seeing anything, if you know what I mean.

''I didn't know what to *do!*'' he explained passionately, shaking his head. ''I hadn't meant to *hurt* him! He didn't look dead—what with his eyes open and all—and all I could think of was getting myself out of there before he started up and called for help. I closed the drapes over him, I think, and then gathered up my hat and gloves and got out of there as fast as I could.''

''Yes,'' Victoria concurred, reaching into her pocket and extracting the snuffbox to show to him, ''but you neglected to gather up more than the papers that concerned you before you left. You also forgot to take this with you. It has your initials on it; that's how we found you. Here,'' she said kindly, giving him back his property.

''Funny that he missed the snuffbox,'' Wilhelmina said to no one in particular, ''seein' as how he remembered to take up the duck. Weren't any bones in the library when I cleaned it, as I recollect.''

''You're going to call for the robin redbreasts now?'' Sir

Perkin asked Victoria, his chubby face chalky white. "It was an accident, but I still killed him."

"Now here's a dilemma," Pierre mocked, lightly stroking his scarred cheekbone. "I wonder, my dear Miss Quinton, is it a rule of English law that we hang the victim?"

"Don't be facetious, Mr. Standish!" Victoria said hotly, taking one of Sir Perkin's trembling hands in her own. "Although, to be perfectly truthful, I am embarrassed to admit that at first flush I was occupied only with the thrill of the search, and didn't really concern myself as to what I would *do* with the guilty party once I had found him. Indeed, you, Patrick, saw through my motives almost at once," she admitted honestly as her fiancé put a comforting hand on her shoulder.

"But I'm sure I never intended to turn the murderer over to Bow Street—at least not since I discovered what an out and out bounder the Professor really was, which didn't take very long once I was free to search the library at my leisure. Later, once I had uncovered the whole of the Professor's treachery—thanks to help from my Uncle Quentin and Patrick—I knew that it was imperative I continue my search. Oh, not because I was afraid the man might decide he needed to kill me as well to keep his secret safe—as you thought, Patrick, although I allowed you to think that I agreed with your theory."

"Then why, my dearest?" Patrick asked, confused.

Victoria looked up at her beloved, then across the table at the sorry-looking soul who sat quietly awaiting his fate. Squeezing Sir Perkin's fingers reassuringly, she explained, "Why, so that I could apologize to him and assure him that his secret was safe with me, of course."

"What!" Patrick exploded, his comforting hand suddenly digging into the tender flesh of her shoulder. "Do you actually mean to sit there and glibly tell me that the only reason you helped us arrange this whole scheme was so that we

could unmask Sir Perkin—in order that you might be able to *apologize to him?* That it has nearly always been your intention to apologize to the Professor's murderer—even before you allowed Quentin and me to help you? I don't believe it! You romantic idiot! Didn't you realize somewhere in your silly, romantic head that the murderer could have killed *you* as well when you gifted him with your polite apology—just in case you might someday have had second thoughts in the matter?''

"Mr. Standish could have killed me," Victoria corrected, quite calmly explaining her logic, "not that I would have considered going on with my plan if I discovered that *he* was the murderer. I'm not *that* much of a zany. Sir Perkin is much more understanding.''

"I don't believe any of this," Patrick grumbled, subsiding heavily into a chair beside his softly chuckling friend.

"I make no doubt, darling Patrick, that you'll be graying within the year," Pierre drawled, reaching for his wineglass. "Marriage has that effect on your gender, I'm told.''

Victoria refused to apologize for doing what she felt in her heart to be right. "I don't understand what all the fuss is about," she argued indignantly. "Even though investigating the murder seemed to be a golden opportunity for me to enjoy myself a little bit before hiring myself out as a governess or some such thing, from the very beginning I had a feeling that something was very, very wrong. As he lay dying, the Professor had kept impressing upon me the fact that I had to make his murderer 'pay.' At first I thought he meant the murderer should pay for his crime, but it soon became apparent to me that he had another sort of payment in mind entirely. Contrary to what I allowed you to believe, Patrick, I had discovered the Professor's private ledger and examined it long before you urged Uncle Quentin to show it to me. I had already known about the Professor's blackmailing activities for some time.''

Patrick tried to say something, only to be cut off by the love of his life as she continued matter-of-factly, "It was then that I stopped searching for the murderer out of some ridiculous loyalty to the Professor and pushed on for quite another reason entirely—to ease the poor murderer's conscience for having acted, under great distress I was sure, to remove a threat to his security. After all, I *too* had been living on the money the Professor was extorting from all those poor souls, although I didn't know it."

Sherbourne, his voice sounding strangely strained, muttered something that could have been "windmills," before slapping his forehead with his palm and exploding vehemently, "Of all the imbecilic, asinine, *quixotic*—"

Standish, who had risen languidly to his feet shut off the tirade with a warning shake of his head. "Let it go, dear boy," Pierre advised sagely. "Understanding the workings of a woman's mind is a lifelong study. You shan't be able to fathom such intricacies in one short evening. Now, if I might suggest you return your attentions to poor Sir Perky here, who is still looking a bit stunned by your fiancée's gracious forgiveness? Perhaps another slice of that delicious cake?"

Sir Perkin, who was feeling quite mellow, actually, now that he knew he wasn't about to be carted off to the guardhouse, rubbed his rounded stomach reflectively, saying, "Oh no, no, no! I couldn't eat another bite."

"I've got some cherry tarts in the kitchen left from luncheon," Wilhelmina suggested, having developed a real fondness for the chubby little man.

"You do?" Sir Perkin exclaimed, already rising to his feet. "You know, when I was just a lad in Wiltshire our cook would let me sit in her kitchen and watch her while she baked cherry tarts. I was always happy in the kitchens, what with all those wonderful smells and those lovely bowls to lick. I say, do you suppose...?"

Wilhelmina slipped an arm around Sir Perkin's shoulders and gave him a slight push toward the baize-covered door that led to the servants' portion of the house. "Done and done! You come with me and Quentin, Sir Perky," she said bracingly, "and you can watch me whilst I roll out a whole fresh batch. Right, Quentin?"

"Right you are, love," Quentin agreed, going ahead of them to open the door that led down a narrow hallway to the kitchen. "I could do with one of your cherry tarts m'self."

"And as the stage grows dim, the players drift away into the shadows, their stories told, their happiness assured." So saying, Pierre Standish made to move toward the hallway, adding, "I bid you good evening, my friends. It has been utterly delightful, I assure you—better than anything I have seen at Covent Garden in many a season—but a wise man knows when he has become dreadfully in the way. Isn't that correct, my dearest Patrick?"

Sherbourne, now standing before Victoria, his hands resting lightly on her shoulders as he gazed adoringly into her eyes, didn't bother to reply, knowing that Pierre had already slipped silently out of the room.

"I like him, you know," Victoria said of Standish as she reached her arms up and around Patrick's neck. "I know he's dangerous and secretive and all those other things, but I really do like him."

"I should box your ears," Patrick replied quietly, trying to look stern and failing badly in the effort. "You do know that, don't you? Why didn't you tell me what you planned to do when Sir Perkin confessed?"

"Do you know something, my dearest, most darling Patrick? You ask too many questions," Victoria replied sweetly, moving her lips to within a heartbeat of his—and effectively putting an end to their conversation.

EPILOGUE

"PERHAPS WE CAN TELL HIM we're keeping it for our oldest son to present to his wife," Victoria, trying to be helpful, suggested, holding the ornate diamond-encrusted brooch in front of her and looking at it assessingly.

"A brooch in the shape of a *Q* as a betrothal gift?" her husband quipped in amused disbelief. "At least it would be a true test of her devotion. After all, if the poor girl didn't really love our offspring, she'd run screaming posthaste for her papa to send a retraction to the newspapers, wouldn't she?"

Victoria giggled happily at the joke and then leaned back against Patrick's broad chest. "It is atrocious, isn't it? Dear Uncle Quentin, he means well."

"Wilhelmina was ecstatic about the necklace he gave her as a wedding token," the Earl said, his voice deliberately bland. "But then, of course, Willie does have a magnificent bosom, just the sort for showing such a heavy piece off to good advantage."

"Wretch!" Victoria shot back, poking him in the ribs with her elbow. Then, sobering slightly, she went on, "They're only gone a week and I miss them already. While neither may be related to me by blood, they're the only family—besides you, dearest, and the children we shall share—that I could ever want. Do you miss them too?"

Patrick leaned down to plant a soft kiss on the top of her head. "Yes, love, I do—and we are not the only ones. I hear Sir Perky has all but gone into mourning, now that his supply of tarts has been cut off. But they'll be happier in Surrey, love. Wilhelmina had no craving for London, even if Quentin's money could buy them a limited place in Society. And we'll visit them often, I promise. Just be glad Emma and Philip have at last set the date. I was beginning to think we had taken on a full-time boarder.''

"Emma or Philip?'' Victoria teased, looking out over the softly rolling hills of Sherbourne's country estate. "He certainly did make a pest of himself, didn't he, nearly drowning poor Emma with that constant shower of gifts he brought round to our town house almost daily. Honestly, to think he could actually believe dear, sweet Emma would consider him beneath her touch after finding out about his great-grandmother. I thought she'd have to compromise the silly man in order for him to believe she really did wish to become Mrs. Spalding.''

Shifting his weight slightly on the blanket they had spread out beneath one of the apple trees on the fringe of the orchard, Patrick reached his arms more fully around his wife and gave her slim waist a gentle squeeze. "Truth to tell, pet, I do think she was slightly taken aback for a while, before she considered all of her options. She made her point rather well at the end, I think, asking Spalding if he truly believed she wished to spend the rest of her life carrying around the name Emma Hamilton. All in all, I'd say the two of them were made for each other.''

"You would?'' Victoria asked, twisting her head around to look up at him.

"Not really,'' he answered in all honesty, "but it was either that or having the two of them underfoot indefinitely.''

"Oh you—'' she exclaimed in feigned exasperation, rolling over to pin him against the blanket. "Sometimes you are as maddeningly sarcastic as your friend Pierre Standish!''

"I kiss better than Pierre Standish, *darling*,'' Patrick declared, grinning up at her.

"You do?"

"Of course I do. Come here, minx, and I'll prove it."

"But however shall I know if you are telling the truth, having never kissed Pierre Standish?" Victoria asked, lifting a hand to remove her spectacles and lay them beside her on the blanket. "Perhaps you should write to Mr. Standish in London and apply to him for assistance in proving your point?"

"Pierre's not in London, pet," her husband informed her, slipping a hand behind her neck and slowly pulling her down to him. "He's been called to his father's estate in the country. It's strange, but I don't think he's been to visit his father since we first returned from the Peninsula to find his mother had died during his absence."

"I didn't know his father was still living. As a matter of fact, it never occurred to me that one such as Pierre ever *had* a father—yet alone a mother."

"Spawn of the devil, you mean," Patrick said, nuzzling her throat where it rose above the collar of her gown. "And to think that the poor fellow likes you."

Victoria pulled away slightly to protest. "I like him *too*. I just don't *understand* him, that's all. There are too many questions about him—too many questions and very few answers. Do you think we will ever learn just what is contained in that infernal wooden box? Or why he has changed so much since his return from the war?"

"Maybe we wouldn't like the answers," Patrick suggested thoughtfully, a small frown creasing the skin between his eyebrows. "Besides," he said, brightening, "I have already found all *my* answers—in you. Come here, my dearest wife, and tell me again: Who is your dearest, dearest love?"

"You are, of course." Victoria sighed on a smile, before settling her lips on his and surrendering to his embrace.

A long, lovely time later Patrick whispered into her ear, "Any more questions, my darling Victoria?"

His delighted wife only smiled.

THE ANONYMOUS
MISS ADDAMS

PROLOGUE

"AND I SAY she has to die! Damn it, can't you see? Haven't you been forever telling me that she has to go? It's the only way out, for both of us!"

"Not necessarily. You could always marry her," a female voice suggested. "You'd make a wonderfully handsome groom. And, please, my dearest, don't swear."

"Marry her? *Marry her!* Are you daft? Have you been sipping before noon again? How many times must I tell you? I'd druther shackle m'self to an ox—it would be easier to haul a dumb animal to the altar. Besides, the chit don't like me, not even above half."

"Can't hold that against the girl. You never were so popular as I'd like."

"That's nothing to the point! We're talking about her now. The only answer is to do away with her."

"All right, be bloodthirsty if you must. Boys will be boys. That leaves only the question—who and how do we handle disposing of the wretched girl?"

"That's two questions. I don't know *how* to do it, but I do know *who*. I've thought this out most carefully. We both do the deed. That way neither of us is apt to cry rope on the other."

There was a short silence while his co-conspirator weighed his latest suggestion. "You really believe that I'd be so mean-spirited as to lay information against my own—oh, all right. Don't pout, it makes nasty lines around your mouth. We both do it. Now—*how* do we do it?"

"An accident. It should look like an accident. The best murders are always made to look like accidents."

"That does leave out poison, firearms and a rope, doesn't it? Pity. I do so favor poison. It's so neat and reliable. A fall, perhaps? From the top of the tower? No, on second thought, that would be too messy. Think of the time we'd have cleaning the cobblestones. I suppose we must find another way."

"A riding accident, perhaps."

"That's brilliant! You were always so creative. A riding accident is perfect! She's always out and about somewhere on that terrible brute she rides. I'm more than surprised she hasn't snapped her neck a dozen times already, more's the pity that she hasn't. All right, a riding accident it is. Now, when do we do the deed?"

"She reaches her majority the tenth of October. The ninth ought to do it."

"That's cutting it a slice too fine, even for such a brilliant mind as yours. Something could go amiss and we wouldn't have time for a second chance. I would rather do it the first of the month. That way we won't have to waste any of her lovely money on birthday presents."

"Yes, why should we throw good money away on—I say! What was that?"

"Where?"

"Over there, behind the shrubbery. I saw something move. Blast it all, someone's been listening! Look! She's running away. Let me pass. I've got to catch her before she ruins everything!"

"Be careful of your breeches!" his companion cried after him. "This is only the second time you've worn them."

CHAPTER ONE

IT WAS A ROOM into which sunlight drifted, light-footedly skimming across the elegant furnishings, its brightness filtered by the gossamer-thin ivory silk curtains that floated at the tall windows.

The ceiling was also ivory, its stuccoed perimeter artfully molded into wreaths of flowers caught up by ram's heads, with dainty arabesques and marching lines of husks terminating in ribbon knots, while the walls had been painted by Cipriani himself and boasted tastefully romping nymphs, liquid-eyed goddesses, and a few doting *amorini*.

The furniture boasted the straight, clean lines of the brothers Adams—Robert and James—the dark, gilded mahogany vying with painted Wedgwood colors and the elegant blue and white satin striping of the upholstery.

To the awestruck observer, the entire room was a soul-soothing showplace, an exemplary example of the degree of refined elegance possible in an extraordinarily beautiful English country estate.

To Pierre Claghorn Standish, just then pacing the length of the Aubusson carpet, it was home.

"Oh, do sit down, Pierre," a man's voice requested wearily. "It's most fatiguing watching you prowl about the place like some petulant caged panther. I say panther because they are black, you know. Must you always wear that funereal color? It's really depressing. You remind me of an ink blot, marring the pristine perfection of my lovely blue and white copybook. It's jarring; upon my soul, it is. Look at me, for instance. This new green coat of mine is subdued, yet it whispers of life, of hope, of the glorious promise of spring. You look like the dead of winter—a very long, depressingly hard winter.''

Pierre ceased pacing to look at his father, who was sitting at his ease, his elbows propped on the arms of his chair, his long fingers spread wide apart and steepled as he gazed up at his son. ''Ah,'' André Standish said, his handsome face lighting as he smiled. ''I do believe I have succeeded in gaining your attention. How wonderful. I shall have to find some small way in which to reward myself. Perhaps a new pony for my stables? But to get back to the point. You have been here for three days, my son, visiting your poor, widowed father in his loneliness—a full two days longer than any of your infrequent visits to me in the past five years, seven months, and six days. I think we can safely assume the formalities have been dutifully observed. Do you not believe it is time for you to get to the point?''

Pierre looked at his father and saw himself as he would appear in thirty years. The man had once been as dark as he, although now his hair was nearly all silver, but his black eyes still flashed brightly in his lean, deeply tanned face. His body was still firmly muscled, thanks to an active, sporting life, and he had not given one inch to his advancing years. Pierre smiled, for he could do a lot worse than follow in his father's footsteps.

''What makes you think there is anything to discuss?'' Pierre asked, lowering himself into the chair facing his father. ''Perhaps you are entering into your dot-age and are only imagining things. Have you entertained that possibility, Father?''

André regarded him levelly. ''I would rather instead reflect on the grave injustice I have done you by not beating you more often during your youth,'' he answered cheerfully. ''You may be the scourge of London society, Pierre, if the papers and my correspondence are to be believed, but you are naught but a babe in arms when it comes to trying to fence with me, your sire and one time mentor. Now, if you have been unable to discover a way onto the subject, may I suggest that you begin by telling me all about the funeral of that dastardly fellow, Quennel Quinton? After all, he's been below ground feeding the worms for more than three months."

Only by the slight lifting of one finely sculpted eyebrow did Pierre Standish acknowledge that his father had surprised him by landing a flush hit. "Very good, Father," he complimented smoothly. "My congratulations to your network of spies. Perhaps you'd like to elaborate and tell me what I'm about to say next?"

André sighed and allowed his fingers to intertwine, lightly laying his chin on his clasped hands. "Must I, Pierre? It's all so mundane. Oh, very well. We could start with the box, I suppose."

Now Pierre couldn't contain his surprise. His eyes widened, and he leaned forward in his chair, gripping the armrests. "You *know?*" he questioned dumbly, as nothing more profound came to his lips.

André rose to go over to the drinks cabinet—an elegant piece containing several delicately carved shelves and holding a generous supply of assorted spirits—and took his time debating over just which crystal decanter held exactly the proper drink for the moment. "Yes," he said consideringly, finally selecting a deep burgundy and pouring generous amounts into two glasses, "I rather think this will do." Returning to his chair, he held out one glass to his son. "Here you go, Pierre. Red with meat—and confession. Rather apt, don't you think? And close your mouth, if you please. It's decidedly off-putting."

Pierre took the glass, automatically raising it to his lips, then shook his head as he watched André gracefully lower his body once more into the chair. "Much as I know you abhor hearing someone tell you what you already know, Father, I must say this out loud so that I can believe it. You knew Quennel Quinton was blackmailing Anton Follet? You knew the box left to me in Quinton's will was full of love letters Follet had written to—had written to—"

"My wife," André finished neatly. "Dearest Eleanore, your mother, to mimic you and likewise point out the obvious. Yes, of course I knew. Quinton first tried to blackmail me with those silly letters, but I convinced him of the futility of that particular course and suggested he apply to Follet instead. Follet's wife holds the purse strings, you understand. I imagine the poor fellow was put through hoops these past half-dozen years, sniffing about everywhere for the money to keep Quinton quiet. Why, the economies he must have been forced to endure! I do seem to remember hearing something about the man having to sell up most of his hunting stock at Tatt's. But then, one must pay the piper if one is going to commit things to paper. You'll remember, Pierre, that I always warned you against just that sort of foolishness."

It was taking some time for his father's words to sink in to Pierre's brain, and even then he missed the significance of the words "silly letters." "Quinton approached me within two months of arriving here after being invalided home from Spain, to learn that Mother had died. He waved the letters in front of me as he smiled—quite gleefully, I recall—and told me of Mother's romantic indiscretion, then said I would have to pay for his silence."

"Wasn't very smart, this man Quinton, was he? I'm astounded that he stayed above ground as long as he did."

Pierre laughed, a short, dissatisfied chuckle. "No, he was not very smart. I entertained the notion of ridding the world of the man, but rejected the idea as needlessly exertive. As you said, Father, I am your student, as well as adverse to being blackmailed. In the end, I, too, suggested he apply to

Follet for funds, with the stipulation that he leave me the letters in his will so that I might continue the blackmail myself. After all, Mother was dead. I needed to take my revenge somewhere.'' Pierre allowed his gaze to shift toward the carpet. "I didn't go through with my intention, I must admit, but it seemed a reasonably workable idea at the time. I was rather overset.''

"Oh, Pierre, let's not dress the matter up in fine linen. You were devastated! Otherwise, you would have repeatedly beaten Quinton about the head until he gave the damning letters over to you. You felt betrayed, by your mother and then by me, whom you felt must have been a dismal failure as a husband if my wife had been forced to seek love elsewhere. You stormed off to London in a childish snit and have returned here only sporadically ever since, duty calls to your aging father. Isn't that right, Pierre?''

Suddenly Pierre was angry. Very angry. He jumped up from his chair and stalked over to the window, to look out over the perfectly manicured gardens. "What did you expect me to do? Confront you? I had left here to fight on the Continent believing that you and Mother were the perfect couple. It certainly was the impression you gave. Then, shortly after I returned home, injured and weary, I learned that my sainted mother had not only died, but left behind her a legacy of shame and disgrace. I couldn't in good conscience intrude on your grief by telling you about it, yet at the same time I was angry with you for forcing her to indulge herself with someone like Follet. I had to get away before I exploded.''

It was quiet in the room for a few minutes, during which time the Standish butler entered and looked to his master for instructions concerning the serving of the evening meal, only to be waved closer so that he could hear a short, whispered instruction.

André Standish allowed his son time to compose himself, then walked over to place a hand on Pierre's shoulder. "Have you read Follet's searing love missives, my son, now that they are at last in your possession?'' he asked, his voice light. ''Or have you thought to tell me about them at last and then burn them, unread, like some brainless ninny out of a very bad pennypress novel?''

''No, I hadn't thought of burning them,'' Pierre answered, slowly gaining control of himself. He felt off balance, a feeling to which he was unaccustomed, and he disliked the sensation immensely. In London he was respected, even feared. Here, he was once again his father's son, standing in awe of the master. ''Nor have I read them. I couldn't bring myself that low. To be truthful, I don't know what I plan to do with them. That's why I'm here—prowling about your drawing room like a panther. What I don't know is what you hope to gain by dragging this old scandal out for an airing.''

''Here you are, sir.''

André turned to take the wooden box from the butler. ''Thank you, Hartley. You are obedience itself. You may retire now. See that we are not disturbed.''

''Very good, sir. Thank you, sir,'' the butler agreed, backing from the room, closing the double doors behind him as he went.

Pierre turned his head to see the offending box, then once more directed his gaze toward the gardens. ''Taken to burgling my rooms, have you, Father? I am discovering new, disturbing things about you with each passing moment. I don't want to hear those letters read, if that's what you have in mind. How could you read them and still retain any feeling for Mother?''

''Quite easily, I imagine,'' André replied, opening the box and picking up at random one of the dozen or so letters. ''I loved Eleanore very much, Pierre, and miss her more with each passing day. Oh, my, there seems to be the smell of old perfume about these letters. Follet was always the fop, as I remember. No wonder that servant I turned off for attempting to steal some of your dear mother's possessions took them posthaste to Quinton. Let's see, I think I can make out this dreadful chicken scrawl. Oh, the spelling! It's ludicrous! I'm afraid I must deny your request and read this one aloud. Prepare yourself, my son.''

André made a short business of clearing his throat and then began to read. '''My dearest dimpled darling, light of my deepest heart.''' He closed his eyes for a moment. ''Oh, that is dreadful, isn't it? I can barely read on but, for your sake, Pierre, I shall persevere. 'I sat awake till the wee morning hours just before dawn, my celestial love, thinking of you and our hasty, beatific meeting in the enchanted gardens last night. How I long to tell you all that is in my love-besieged heart, all the wonder and glory that I feel for you, but there seems no way we can escape for long your dastardly husband, André.' Oh, that is good,'' André stopped to comment. ''He used my name—just in case it had slipped your mother's mind, I suppose. No wonder Eleanore kept the letters; they're better than a night at Covent Garden.''

''That is sufficient, thank you. You may stop there,'' Pierre cut in, disgusted with his father's levity. ''Isn't it enough that she had an affair with the man? Must you read his reminiscences of it?''

''An affair?'' André repeated, his voice suddenly very cold, very hard. ''You insolent pup! How dare you! Haven't you heard a word I've read? The man was—is—an ass. A total ass! If his harridan of a wife hadn't hauled him off to Ireland, you would have discovered that for yourself. Do you really mean to stand there and tell me you still believe someone as wonderful, as intelligent as your mother would have given the idiot who wrote this drivel so much as the time of day? Why do you think I didn't kill Quinton when he first approached me? I laughed him out of the house!''

Pierre slowly turned away from the window to look piercingly at his father. "Are you telling me Follet's love was all one-sided?"

André smiled. "Ah, and to think for a moment there I was beginning to believe you were slow. Yes, Pierre, Follet's all-consuming passion for your mother was very much one-sided. To be perfectly frank, as I remember it, Eleanore considered him to be a toad. A particularly slimy toad." He tipped his head to one side, as if reliving some private memory. "I readily recall one evening—Follet was skipping about our first-floor balcony at the London town house reciting some terrible love poem he had written to her pert nose, or some such nonsense, and causing no end of racket—until your mother cut him off by dousing him with a pitcher of cold water."

Pierre smiled wanly, then returned to the drinks table to refill his glass. "All this time, wasted." He turned to his father. "If you knew what I was thinking all these years—and how you knew I shall not be so silly as to ask, considering that you know everything—why didn't you tell me? All these long years I've been warring with myself, trying to banish my love for my mother, trying to understand how human beings can be so fickle, so devious. And you knew—you knew!"

André put his arm around his son. "I must confess, I have known the whole truth for less than two years. It took me that long to figure out the reason for your defection, as I had taught you to hide your tracks very successfully. I had thought to tell you the truth then, but deep inside I was just the least bit put out that you could believe Quinton's obvious lies, and I made up my mind to wait until you came to your senses. And, never fear, you never stopped loving your mother. I see the flowers you order placed on her grave every week, and I've watched you when you visit the cemetery.

"But I've also watched you grow and mature these past years, even more than you did during your years with me, or your time spent on the Peninsula. You have become a devoted student of human nature, my son, taking all that I've taught you and honing it to a fine edge. Of course, you have become a shade too arrogant, and even, dare I say it, a bit cold—but I think we can safely assume that your arrogance has now suffered a healing setback.''

"This has all been in the way of a *lesson?*" Pierre asked, incredulous. "I can't believe it."

"Oh, dear," André remarked, looking at his son. "You're angry, aren't you? Good. You're very gifted, Pierre, gifted with money, breeding, intelligence and a very pretty face. I taught you all I could about being a gentleman. The war has taught you about the perfidies and cruelties of mankind. Now, Quennel Quinton has taught you never to accept anything at face value, even if it is personally painful for you to delve into a subject. He has also taught you a measure of humility, hasn't he, showing you that, for all your grand intelligence, you can still be duped. All round, I'd say the thing was a particularly satisfactory exercise."

"I exist only to please you, Father," Pierre drawled sarcastically.

"Of course you do," André acknowledged in complete seriousness. "Never forget it. The only obstacle to becoming a complete gentleman left before you now is for you to accomplish some good, unselfish work—some compassionate assistance to one of the helpless wretches of mankind. You have made a good start by helping your friend Sherbourne secure the affections of Quinton's supposed daughter, Victoria, but as you were trying to rid yourself of the title of murder suspect at the time, I cannot feel that your actions were completely altruistic. Yes, I would like to see you perform some good deed, with not a single thought of personal reward. Do you think you can handle that on your own, or shall I devise some scheme to set you on your way?"

Pierre stared at his father unblinkingly. "There are times

when I actually believe I could hate you, Father,'' he said, unable to hide a wry smile.

''Yes, of course,'' André replied silkily. ''Truthfully, I believe I should be disappointed in you if you were to fall on my neck, thanking me. Shall we go in to dinner?''

CHAPTER TWO

PIERRE LINGERED in the country with André for another two days, the two men rebuilding their former good relationship on a sounder, more solid base before the younger Standish reluctantly took his leave, his father's admonition—to find himself a humanizing good deed as soon as may be for the sake of his immortal soul—following after him as his coachman sprung the horses.

"A good deed," Pierre repeated, settling himself against the midnight-blue velvet squabs of the traveling coach that was the envy of London. "What do you think of that, Duvall, my friend?"

The manservant gave a Gallic shrug, shaking his head. *"Il vous rit au nez."*

"Father doesn't laugh in my *nose,* Duvall; he laughs in my face, and no, I don't think so. Not this time," Pierre corrected, smiling at the French interpretation of the old saying. "This time I think he is deadly serious, more's the pity. My dearest, most loving father thinks I need to—"

"Tomber à plat ventre," Duvall intoned gravely, folding his scrawny arms across his thin chest.

"Not really. You French may fall flat on your stomachs, Duvall. We English much prefer to land on our faces, if indeed we must take the fall at all. And how will you ever develop a workable knowledge of English if you insist upon lapsing into French the moment we are alone? Consider yourself forbidden the language from this moment, if you please."

"Your father, he wishes for you to fall flat on your face," Duvall recited obediently, then sighed deeply, so that his employer should be aware that he had injured him most gravely.

"Bless you, Duvall. Now, to get back to the point. I have been acting the fool these past years, a fact I will acknowledge only to you, and only this one time. There's nothing else for it—I must seek out a good deed and perform it with humble dedication and no thought for my own interests. Do you suppose the opportunity for good deeds lies thick on the ground in Mayfair? No, I imagine not. Ah, well, one can only strive to do one's best."

"Humph!" was the manservant's only reply before he turned his head to one side and ordered himself to go to sleep in the hope that the soft, well-sprung swaying of the traveling coach would not then turn his delicate Gallic stomach topsy-turvy.

Standish marveled silently yet again at the endless effrontery of his employee. The man, unlike the remainder of Pierre's acquaintances, had no fear of him—and precious little awe. It was refreshing, this lack of deference, which was why Pierre treasured the spritely little Frenchman, who had been displaced to Piccadilly during Napoleon's rush to conquer all the known world. Reaching across to lay a light blanket over the man's shoulders, for it was September and the morning was cool, Pierre sat back once more, determined to enjoy the passing scenery.

It was shortly after regaining the main roadway, following a leisurely lunch at the busy Rose and Cross Inn—Pierre being particularly fond of country-cured ham—that it happened. One of the two burly outriders accompanying the coach called out to the driver to stop at once, for there was something moving in the small mountain of baggage strapped in the boot of the coach.

"How wonderfully intriguing. Do you suppose it is an animal of some sort?" Pierre asked the two outriders, the coachman, and a slightly green-looking Duvall a minute later as the small group assembled behind the halted coach. He lightly prodded the canvas wrapping with the tip of his cane, just at the spot the outrider had indicated. "I do pray it is not a fox, for I will confess that I am not a devotee of blood sports. Oh, dear. It moved again just then, didn't it? My curiosity knows no bounds, I must tell you."

"It's a blinkin' stowaway, that's wot it tis," decided the second outrider, just home from an extended absence at sea, a trip prompted not by his desire to explore the world, but rather at the expressed insistence of a press gang that had tapped him on the noggin with a heavy club and tossed him aboard a merchantman bound for India. "Let's yank 'im out an' keelhaul 'im!"

Pierre turned to look at the man, a large, beefy fellow whose hamlike hands were already closed into tight fists. "So violent, my friend? Why don't we just boil the poor soul in oil and have done with it?"

Raising his voice slightly, Pierre went on, "You there— in the boot—I suggest you join us out here on the road, if you please. You can't be too comfortable in there, knowing the amount of baggage I deem necessary for travel through the wilds of Sussex. When did you decide to join us? Perhaps when my baggage was undone to unearth my personal linens and utensils back at the so lovely Rose and Whatever Inn? Come out now, we shan't hurt you."

"Oi can't," a high, whiny voice complained from beneath the canvas. "Yer gots me trussed up like a blinkin' goose in 'ere!"

Pierre tipped his head to one side, inspecting the canvas-covered boot. "Our unexpected passenger has a point there, gentlemen. It really was too bad of you, wasn't it, even as I applaud your obvious high regard for the welfare of my personal possessions. Perhaps one of you will be so good as to lend some assistance to our beleaguered stowaway before he causes himself an injury?''

Less than a minute later the canvas had been drawn away to reveal a very small, very dirty face. ''Hello. What have we here?'' Pierre asked, peering into the semidarkness of the boot.

''Yer gots Jeremy 'Olloway, that wot yer gots!'' the young boy shot back defiantly, pushing out his lower lip to blow a long strand of greasy blond hair from his eyes. ''Now, stands back whilst Oi boosts m'self outta this blinkin' 'ellhole!''

''How lovely,'' Pierre drawled. ''Such elegant speech. And a good day to you too, Master Holloway. Obviously, my friends, we have discovered a runaway young peer, bent on a lark in the country. Gentlemen, let us make our bows to Master Holloway.''

''That's no gentry mort,'' the burly outrider corrected, narrowly eyeing the young boy as he climbed down from his hiding place and quickly clamping a heavy hand on Jeremy's thin shoulder as the lad looked ready to bolt for the concealment of the trees on the side of the road. ''This 'ere ain't nothin' but a bleedin' sweep!''

''Oi'm not!'' Jeremy shot back, sticking out his chin, as if his denial could erase the damning evidence of his torn, sooty shirt and the scraped, burned-covered arms and legs that stuck out awkwardly from beneath his equally ragged, too-small suit of clothes.

''Of course you're not a sweep,'' Pierre agreed silkily, suppressing the need to touch his scented lace handkerchief to his nostrils as he looked at Jeremy and saw a quick solution to his need to do a good deed. ''But if you *were* a sweep, and running away from an evil master who abused you most abominably, I should think I could find it in my heart to take you up with us for a space, until, say, we reach London? Listening to your speech, and detecting a rightful disdain for those so troublesome 'aitches', I believe you might feel at home in Piccadilly?''

Jeremy, who had begun eyeing Pierre assessingly, positively blossomed at the mention of Piccadilly. Quickly suppressing his excitement, he scuffed one bare big toe in the dirt and remarked coolly: "If Oi *wuz* a sweep—which Oi'm not, o'course—Oi might wants ter take yer up on that, guv'nor. The Piccadilly thing, yer knows.''

Duvall immediately burst into a rapid stream of emotional French, wringing his hands as he alternately cursed and pleaded with his master to reconsider this folly. Better they should all bed down with *une mouffette,* a skunk! Oh, woe, oh, woe! Poor master, to have a cracked bell in his head. Poor Duvall, to be so overset that he could not even think which saint to pray to!

Jeremy stood stoically by, grimy paws jammed down hard on even grimier hips, waiting for the barrage of French to run itself down, then said, "Aw, dub yer mummer, froggie. Oi ain't 'eared such a ruckus since ol' 'awkins burnt 'isself wit 'is own poker!''

Duvall stopped in mid-exclamation to glare down at the boy, his lips pursed, his eyes bulging. *"Mon Dieu!"* he declared. "This insect, this crawling bug, he has called me a frog. I will not stand for such an insult!"

"Stand still," Pierre corrected smoothly, at last succumbing to the need to filter his breathing air through the handkerchief. "Now, if the histrionics are behind us—and I most sincerely pray that they are—I suggest that Jeremy crawl back into the boot, sans the cover, and the rest of us also return to our proper places. I wish to make London before Father Christmas.''

Satisfied that he was doing his good deed just as his father had recommended—and rescuing Jeremy from an evil master certainly seemed to qualify—Pierre once more settled himself against the midnight-blue velvet squabs and began mentally preparing a missive to his father detailing his charitable wonderfulness. "And that will be the end of that," he said aloud, eyeing Duvall levelly and daring the manservant to contradict him.

The coach had gone no more than a mile when it stopped once more, the coachman hauling on the reins so furiously that Pierre found himself clutching the handstrap for fear of tumbling onto the narrow width of flooring between the seats.

"I am a reasonably good man, a loving son," he assured himself calmly as he reached to open the small door that would allow him to converse with the driver. "I have my faults, I suppose, but I have never been a purposely *mean* person. Why then, Duvall, do you suppose I feel this overwhelming desire to draw and quarter my coachman?"

"If there truly is a God, the dirty little person will have been flung to the road on his dripping nose," Duvall grumbled by way of an answer, adjusting his jacket after picking himself up from the floor of the coach where, as his reflexes were not so swift as his employer's, the driver's abrupt stop had landed him.

"Driver?" Pierre inquired urbanely, holding open the small door. "May I assume you have an explanation, or have you merely decided it is time you took yourself into the bushes to answer nature's call?"

"Sorry, sir," the coachman mumbled apologetically, leaning down to peer into the darkened interior of the coach. "But you see, sir, there's a lady in the road. At least, I think it's a lady."

Pierre's left brow lifted fractionally. "A lady," he repeated consideringly. "How prudent of you not to run her down. My compliments on both your driving and your charity, although I cannot but wonder at your difficulty in deciding the gender of our roadblock. Perhaps now you might take it upon yourself to ask this lady to move?"

"I can't, sir," the coachman responded, the slight quiver

in his voice reflecting both his lingering shock at avoiding a calamity and his fearful respect of his employer. "Like I told yer—she's in the road. It's a lady for sure, 'cause I can see her feet. I think mayhap she's dead, and can't move."

Pierre's lips twitched as he remarked quietly, "Her feet? An odd way to determine gender, Duvall, wouldn't you say?" His next communication to the coachman followed, both his words and his offhand tone announcing that he was decidedly unimpressed. "Dead, you say, coachman? That *would* be an impediment to movement, wouldn't it?"

Duvall quickly blessed himself, muttering something in French that may have been "Blessed Mary protect us, and why couldn't it have been the sweep?"

"A dead lady in the middle of the road," Pierre mused again out loud, already moving toward the coach door. "I imagine I should see this deceased lady for myself." With one foot in the road, he paused to order quietly: "Arm yourself, coachman, and instruct the outriders to scan the trees for horsemen. This may be a trap. There are still robbers along this roadway.

"Although I would have thought it would be easier to throw a dead tree into the road, rather than a dead lady," he added under his breath as he disengaged Duvall's convulsive grip on his coattail. "Please, my good friend," he admonished with a smile. "Consider the fabric, if not your long hours with the iron."

Pierre stepped completely onto the roadway, nodding almost imperceptibly to the two outriders while noting with mingled comfort and amusement that the coachman was now brandishing a very mean-looking blunderbuss at the ready. A quick look to the rear of the coach assured him that his Good Deed was still firmly anchored in the boot, as the streetwise Jeremy Holloway's dirt-streaked face was peeping around the edge of the coach, his eyes wide as saucers.

"Oi've got yer back, guv'nor," the boy whispered hoarsely. "Don't yer go worryin' 'bout dat."

"Such loyalty deserves a reward," Pierre whispered back at the boy. "If we get out of this with our skin intact, Master Holloway, I shall allow you to sit up top with the coachman." As the coachman gave out with an audible groan, Pierre began strolling toward the standing horses, his demeanor decidedly casual, as if he were merely taking the air in the park.

Once he had come up beside the off-leader, he could see the woman, who was, just as the coachman had reported, lying facedown in the roadway and looking, for all intents and purposes, extremely dead. She was dressed in a man's drab grey cloak, its hood having fallen forward to hide her face as well as whatever gown she wore beneath its voluminous expanse. Her stockinged, shoeless feet—small feet attached to rather shapely slim ankles, he noted automatically, for he was a man who appreciated female beauty—extended from beneath the hem of the cloak, but her hands were pinned beneath her, out of sight.

He walked to within two paces of her, then used the tip of his cane to lightly nudge her in the rib cage. There was no response, either from the woman or from the heavily wooded perimeters of the road. If the woman was only feigning injury and in league with highwaymen, her compatriots were taking their sweet time in making their presence known.

Gingerly lowering himself onto his haunches, and being most careful not to muddy the knees of his skin-tight fawn buckskin breeches, Pierre took hold of the woman in the area of her shoulder and gently turned her onto her back.

"Ohh." The sound was soft, barely more than a faint expulsion of air, but it had come from the woman. Obviously she had not yet expired, not that her life expectancy could be numbered in more than a few minutes or hours if she were to continue to lie in the middle of the roadway.

"She toes-cocked, guv'nor, or wot?"

Jeremy's voice, coming from somewhere behind Pierre's left shoulder, made him realize that he had been paying attention to the woman when he should have been listening for highwaymen. "She's not dead, if that's what that colorful expression is meant to imply," he supplied tonelessly, pushing the hood from the woman's face so that he could get a better look at her.

What he saw made him inhale involuntarily, his left brow raising a fraction in surprise. The woman was little more than a girl, and she was exceedingly beautiful, in an ethereal way. Masses of softly waving hair the color of midnight tangled across her ashen, dirt-smeared face, trailing strands that lovingly clung to the small, finely sculpted features that carried the unmistakable stamp of good bloodlines.

Quickly seeking out her limp arm to feel for her pulse, Pierre mentally noted the fragile slimness of her wrist and the slender perfection of her hand and fingers. Her *cold* hand and *frigid* fingers.

"Master Holloway, be a good boy and go tell Duvall to bring me a blanket," Pierre ordered without looking away from the young woman's face, wrapping her once more in the worn grey cloak. "And have him bring my flask as well. This poor child is chilled through to the bone."

Once Duvall had brought the blanket, Pierre draped it over the young woman and hefted her upper body onto his knees, intent on forcing her to drink some of the warming brandy. It was no use. The brandy ran into her mouth, only to dribble back onto her chin. Handing the flask back to his manservant—who immediately took a restorative dose of the fiery liquid for himself—Pierre lifted the young woman completely into his arms and returned to the coach.

"Yer takin' 'er with us?" the seafaring outrider questioned worriedly. "Wimmen is bad luck aboard, that's wot they are.

Always wuz, always will be. Better yer toss 'er back. She's a small one anyways.''

Pierre silenced the man with a look. ''Turn this equipage about at once, if you please. I have a sudden desire to return to Standish Court. And don't spare the horses,'' he ordered the driver as he swept into the coach, the young woman lolling bonelessly in his arms.

Beneath his breath he added, ''I do begin to believe my loving parent has put a fatherly curse on me. I am suddenly overrun with unlooked-for Good Deeds. But, being a loving son, and not a greedy man, I also believe that at least one of these humanizing projects rightfully belongs to him. Duvall,'' he called out, ''tell the coachman that Jeremy is to ride atop with him.''

CHAPTER THREE

"Coo, GUV'NOR, would yer jist look at dat! Dat gentry mort looks jist like yer—wit a coffin o' snow plopped on 'is 'ead!"

André Standish leveled a cool, assessing look at the untidy urchin perched on top of the traveling coach, then descended the few remaining steps to the gravel drive and addressed his son through the lowered coach window. "An acquaintance of yours, Pierre? He has an interesting way with description. Have you lost your way and must retrace your steps, or have you somehow learned that cook is preparing your favorite meal for tonight—a lovely brown ragôut of lamb with peas— and it is your stomach that brings you back to me?"

"My current favorite meal is rare roasted beef with horse-radish sauce," Pierre corrected, "although I know it is rude of me to point out this single lapse in your seemingly fault-less store of information about me. And no," he said, shifting the human weight in his arms in preparation for leaving the coach, "much as I love you, I have not lost my way. May I infringe upon your affection by prevailing upon you to open this door?"

André complied with a courtly bow, flinging open the door and personally letting down the steps. A moment later, Pierre was standing beside him in the drive, the young woman still lying limply in his arms.

The older Standish gently pushed back the hood of the grey cloak, revealing the young woman's face. "I detect the smell of brandy. I foolishly thought I had raised you better than this. Surely you haven't taken to drugging your females, Pierre?''

''Not lately, Father. My coachman nearly ran over her as she lay in the road.''

''Unconscious? A head injury?'' André asked, not wasting time in useless questions as to how the female had come to be in the road in the first place.

''Most definitely unconscious.''

''Have you learned her name?'' André asked as the two men hurriedly mounted the steps to the house, Jeremy Holloway at their heels until Duvall stuck out one foot and tripped him so that he landed facedown in the drive.

''I like to think of her as Miss Penance,'' Pierre replied immediately. ''Whether she is mine or yours remains to be seen. Duvall,'' he called over his shoulder, ''I saw that. For shame. I would not have believed it of you. Now wash it and feed it and put it to bed.''

Duvall, having no trouble in understanding who ''it'' was, tottered over to lean against the side of the traveling coach and buried his head in his hands.

''SHE'S STILL SLEEPING?'' André asked the question three hours later as Pierre entered the drawing room, having excused himself after dinner to check on their patient.

''Hartley assures me that she'll sleep through to the morning,'' he told his father. ''It may only be a butler's opinion, but as the doctor said much the same thing before he left, I believe we can safely assume it's true. She's got a lump the size of a pigeon's egg on the side of her head.''

''Poor Miss Penance,'' André commented, accepting the snifter of brandy his son offered him. ''She'll have a bruiser of a headache when she wakes, I fear. Now, do you think it's possible for you to tell me about the urchin? We somehow neglected to speak of him over dinner, perhaps hoping to preserve our appetites, for he was most unappealing when last I saw him. Duvall appears to dislike him, a lack of affection that seems to be mutual. I happened to pass by the bedroom as your man was giving the boy a bath, you see. The language spewing forth from the pair of them was enough to put me to the blush.''

Pierre took a sip of brandy. "Duvall likes everyone very little, save me, of course, for whom he would gladly die if asked. A man could become quite full of himself, knowing that. But to answer your question, young Master Jeremy Holloway is a runaway—having escaped the life of a chimney sweep, if my powers of deduction are correct. He chose my coach as his route to freedom when we stopped for luncheon.''

"An enterprising young lad,'' André remarked, watching the burnished liquid swirl and gleam as he rubbed the brandy snifter lightly back and forth between his palms. "Oh, by the by—young Master Holloway would like to have a hot poker inserted in an area of Duvall's anatomy that is not usually spoken of in more polite circles. Duvall, in his turn, would like the boy deposited in a dirty sack posthaste and drowned in the goldfish pond—as I am convinced my understanding of gutter French is still reasonably accurate. My goodness, I begin to feel like a spy reporting to his superior.''

"Duvall likes to think of himself as bloodthirsty,'' Pierre remarked calmly. "Even taking Duvall's sensibilities into account, however,'' he went on silkily, "I do believe I shall take Jeremy as my Good Deed, and leave the disposition of Miss Penance to you.''

André blinked once. "Indeed,'' he drawled, setting the snifter down very carefully. "And might I ask why I'm to be gifted with an unknown female with a lump the size of a pigeon's egg on her pate?''

"Of course.'' Pierre lifted his own snifter and tipped it slightly in André's direction. "I won't even remind you of how you maneuvered me so meanly once you learned about Quinton. Shall we drink to *poetic justice,* Father?''

THE MORNING ARRIVED very early, very abruptly and in full voice.

"How dare you! Get your hands off me! At once! Do you hear me?''

Obviously the injured young lady had come to her senses with a vengeance. Mere seconds after her screams had stopped, Pierre—who had been sleeping most peacefully in the adjoining chamber—skidded to a halt just inside the bedroom that had been assigned to Miss Penance, still tying the sash of his maroon banyan around his trim waist.

"I imagine you can be heard in Bond Street, brat,'' he commented, running his fingers through his sleep-mussed hair and ruefully looking down at his bare legs and feet. Raising his head, he addressed the butler, whom he espied backing toward the door to the hall, a china cup and saucer nervously chattering against the silver tray he was clutching with two hands, his face white with shock. "Ah, Hartley, dear fellow, what seems to be the matter?''

Hartley's lips moved, quivered actually, but no words came forth.

"What seems to be the problem?'' the woman asked. "What seems to be the problem! I awoke to see this *man* leaning over my bed! *That's* the problem! And why are you asking him? And who are you? You're not even dressed, for pity's sake. What has the world come to when a lady can't get some sleep without all the world creeping into her bedchamber, with only the good Lord knows what on their minds, that's what I want to know. Well, don't just stand there with your mouths at half cock. You both have some explaining to do!''

"Hartley, you may retire now,'' Pierre offered kindly as the elderly butler looked about to expire from mingled shock and indignation. "And please accept my congratulations. I didn't know you were still considered to be such a danger to the ladies."

Leaning his shoulder against the doorjamb, his arms folded against his chest, one bare leg crossed negligently over the other at the ankles, Pierre then allowed his gaze to take a slow, leisurely assessment of the young woman occupying the bed.

She was still as beautiful as his initial impression of her had indicated, with her small features lovingly framed by a heavy mass of coal-black hair, her pale skin made creamy where her slim throat rose above the fine white lawn of Eleanore Standish's nightgown. His first sight of her long-lashed, blue-violet eyes only reconfirmed his opinion. However, she might not be quite as young as he had first thought, for the light of intelligence burned brightly in her eyes. "Unless it's fever," he hedged aloud, knowing his wits weren't usually at their sharpest this early in the day. His early morning wits or the lack of them to one side for the moment, Miss Penance was still a most remarkably beautiful young woman.

"Well?" she asked, pushing her hands straight out in front of her, palms upward and gesturing toward him. "Have you somehow been turned to marble, sir? Perhaps I should remind you of your current situation? You're in a lady's bedchamber without invitation. I suggest you retire before I'm forced to do you an injury."

Pierre smiled. "Oh, Father's going to adore you," he said silkily. "What's your name, little Amazon? We can't go on calling you Miss Penance, although my spur of the moment christening now seems to border on the inspired. Please, madam, give me a name."

"My name?" she croaked, wincing.

"Your name," Pierre repeated. "As you're sleeping in my father's house, I don't believe it is an out-of-the-way demand."

Miss Penance slumped against the pillows, suddenly appearing to be even smaller than she had before, her chin on her chest. "So you don't know who I am, either," she said in a small voice, all her bravado deserting her. "I had hoped—"

She sniffed, a portion of her spunk reasserting itself. "I should have known I'd be looking for mare's nests, asking for some spark of intelligence from a man who has that much hair on his legs and is vain enough to consider showing it off to strangers."

"Eight to five you're a parson's eldest," Pierre was stung into replying. "And a Methodist parson to boot. Only the worse sort of strumpet or a holier-than-thou old maid would even dare utter the word 'leg' in front of a gentleman. Somehow, I can't quite picture you in the role of strumpet. You dislike men entirely too much. Which leaves us with only the other alternative. Now, are you really trying to tell me that you have no recollection of your own name?"

"Don't be ridiculous! Of course I know my own name! Everyone knows his own name," she shot back at him. "I just—" Her voice began to lose some of its confidence. "I just seem to have, um, momentarily *misplaced* the memory. It'll come to me any time now. I'm sure of it."

"How reassuring," Pierre soothed, slowly advancing into the room. "And, of course, once you succeed in locating this truant name, you'll doubtless inform me as to why you were lying unconscious in the middle of the roadway just north of here, obstructing traffic and upsetting my coachman no end. It's the merest bagatelle—no more than a trifling inconvenience—this temporary lapse."

The violet eyes shot blue-purple flame. "Oh, do be quiet, Mr.—"

"Standish," Pierre supplied immediately, lowering himself into a seated position on the bottom of the bed. "Pierre

Standish. See how easy that was. Now you try it. How utterly charmed I am to meet you, Miss—''

She nodded her head three times, as if the movement would jog her memory. ''Miss…Miss…oh, drat! I don't know! *I don't know!*''

''Quietly, my dear Miss Forgetful, quietly,'' Pierre scolded absently. ''We shall abandon this exercise momentarily, as it seems only to annoy you, and speak of other things. How is your head? You sustained a rather nasty bump on it, one way or another.''

She reached up to gingerly inspect the lump she had discovered earlier upon awakening. ''It's still there, if that's any answer,'' she told him. ''Your guess is as good as mine as to how I came to have it. And, even though I am sure it matters little to you, it hurts like the very devil.''

Pierre frowned at her use of the word ''devil.'' Tipping his head to one side, he commented, ''I believe we can dispense with the notion that you are a parson's daughter. Your language is too broad.''

''Then I am to be the worst sort of strumpet?'' she asked, narrowing her eyes belligerently. ''Thank you. Thank you very much.''

Pierre shook his head, ''No, not a strumpet, either. You're much too insulting. You'd have starved by now.''

''Perhaps I am a thief,'' she suggested, pulling the blankets more firmly under her chin. ''Perhaps you should be locking up your family silver at this very moment, for fear I shall lope off with it the instant I find my clothes. I may assume that I have some clothing somewhere? Not that I'm likely to recognize it any more than I recognize this nightgown I have on now.''

''There's no reason for you to recognize it. It was my mother's,'' Pierre told her. ''She died several years ago.''

''I'm surprised.''

"Surprised that my mother is deceased?" Pierre questioned, looking at her oddly.

"Surprised that she lived so long, with you for a son," she answered meanly, for even a fool could see that she was feeling very mean.

"*Touché,* madam. I believe that evens up our insults quite nicely." Pierre rose from the bed and turned from her before he spoke again. "I'll send a maid with some breakfast," he said just as he reached the doorway to his own bedchamber. "That is, if I recover from the wounds your tongue has inflicted. Later, when you are more rested, my father will doubtless wish to interview you. Pray don't repeat your latest attempt at nastiness to him, for he loved my mother very much."

"I'm sorry," she called after him. "Really, I'm sorry. I shouldn't have said that. It's just…it's just that I'm really very upset. I mean, I don't even know where I am, let alone who I am. Please—forgive me."

Pierre turned to look at the young woman now sitting up in the bed, her violet eyes drenched with tears. "Neither of us has been very nice, have we?" he said. "It happens that way with some people, I've heard. We have already decided not to like each other, no matter how little Dame Reason is involved in the decision. Let us agree to forgive each other, madam, and have done with it."

"Agreed!" she said smiling for the first time, the unexpected beauty of it making a direct hit on Pierre's senses, so that he blinked twice, said nothing, and left the room, suddenly uncomfortable at being dressed in nothing more than his banyan.

A HOT BATH HELPED to ease the soreness she had felt over every inch of her body from the moment she had first awakened in the beautiful, sunlit bedchamber.

The young maid who had introduced herself as Susan had

carefully washed her hair, massaging away some of her tension and banishing the headache that had been pounding against her temples.

The meal of poached eggs, country bacon, toast, and tea had erased the gnawing hunger that had made her believe her stomach must have been worrying that her throat had somehow been cut.

But nothing could ease the terrible, blood-chilling panic that shivered through her body each time she attempted to remember who she was, or where she lived, or how she had come to be lying unconscious in the middle of a roadway.

"I just don't remember!" she said out loud as she sat at the dressing table in the nightgown and robe Susan had brought her after her bath, glaring at her unfamiliar reflection, her chin in her hands. "I don't remember anything; nothing before waking up here this morning."

"There are many who would not curse such a lapse, but rather rejoice in it. Good afternoon, Miss Penance. I'm André Standish, your host. Forgive me, but I did knock."

"You—you look just like him," she was stung into saying as she stared into the mirror, where André's reflection smiled back at her. "If it weren't for the color of your hair, I'd swear—"

"Ah, you'd swear," André interrupted. "I see my son has not exaggerated. You are an enigma, aren't you, Miss Penance? You have the look and accent of a lady, but your conversation is sprinkled with words most well-brought-up young females have been taught to shun. Of course, there was a time, more years ago than I care to recall, when all the best ladies were shockingly frank in their speech, but that time has since passed, more's the pity. Perhaps you were raised solely by your father, or a doting uncle. That would explain it, wouldn't it?"

She sat quite still, listening to the sound of his voice more than his actual words. His tone was so gentle, so reassuring.

"No," she answered, suddenly sleepy, and wondering why she felt she could lean her head against his arm and doze, secure in the knowledge that he'd never hurt her. "No, I don't think so. Men seem to frighten me—except you, that is. I was very afraid of your son this morning. I don't think I've been around men very much."

"Pierre can be most formidable, even in his banyan. *Especially* in his banyan, I imagine." André laid a hand on her shoulder. "You're frightened, and with every right. Forgive me for trying to prod you into memory. There's no rush, you know. We shall take this thing one day at a time. Now, come lie down on the bed for a while. You must be exhausted. I've already sent for the doctor, but he is busy with someone who is really ill and not merely confused by a bump on the head. He sent along a note assuring me that you'll remember everything in time. He will be here tomorrow to answer any questions you might have."

She allowed herself to be helped into bed. Looking up at André, she said, "You're not at all like your son after all. You're very nice."

"Pierre's a beast, I'm ashamed to say. Quite uncivilized," André confessed with a smile and a slight shake of his silver head. "Were I you, I should stay as far removed from him as possible. Now, get some rest while I go downstairs and cudgel my brain into coming up with a female companion for you. It isn't correct for you to be the lone young woman in a masculine household."

She was very sleepy, but she didn't miss the meaning of his words. "Then—then you think I'm a young lady?"

"Was there ever any doubt?" André replied, winking at her as he closed the door behind him.

CHAPTER FOUR

THE YOUNG LADY Pierre had dubbed Miss Penance walked aimlessly along the twisting gravel paths of the substantial Standish Court ornamental gardens, idly swinging a yellow chip straw bonnet by its pink satin ribbons, her feet dragging only a little in the soft, too-large kid slippers that had once belonged to Eleanore Standish.

The gardens were glorious, a fairyland of flowers and evergreens and whimsical statuary, all bathed in the warmth of a sunny late summer's afternoon. It was a perfect place to spend a few quiet moments, which was the reason André Standish had suggested it to her earlier, after she had risen from her nap.

So far, neither her nap, the walk, nor the peacefulness of her surroundings had jogged her memory. She had been without it for only a few hours, but she measured its loss minute by minute, and the gravity and scope of that loss were gnawing at her, causing the still tender bump on her head to throb most painfully.

She could be anybody—or nobody. It would be awful to be a Nobody. No one would send out an alarm for a Nobody. A Nobody could disappear from the face of the earth without a trace and no one would care, no one would feel the loss. A Somebody would be missed, and an immediate search would be instituted. Besides, she didn't feel like a Nobody; she felt like a Somebody.

''That's no great help,'' she told herself out loud. ''Everybody wants to be a Somebody. Now, how do you suppose I know that?''

Her seemingly selective memory was what really upset and confused her. How could she know so much and still not know who she was? She knew the name of that flower climbing the trellis over there—it was a morning glory, a purple one.

She knew she was in Sussex, for Susan had told her. She knew Sussex was in England, and that Susan had not told her. She knew where Austria was, and could name at least three principal crops of France. She knew the Italian word for head was *capo,* but did not know how she knew it.

She was sure she had always particularly favored chicken as it had been presented to her for luncheon in her room, and could name the ingredients used in its preparation. She had counted to three thousand as she had sat in her bath, and probably could have continued to count for the remainder of the day without problem.

So why couldn't she remember her name?

She could be married, for pity's sake! That thought stopped her short, and she bit her lip in trepidation. She could have a husband somewhere. Children. Crying for her, missing her. No, she didn't feel married. Could a person feel married? How did being unmarried feel?

She could be a bad person. Why, she could be a thief, as she had suggested to Pierre Standish. Perhaps she had been discovered with her hand in some good wife's silver drawer, and had been running from the constable when she had fallen, hitting her head on a stone.

She could be a murderess! She could have murdered a man—her husband, perhaps?—and been fleeing the scene of that dastardly crime in the dead man's cloak when she had somehow come to grief in the middle of the roadway.

Pierre Standish had certainly been unflattering when he pointed out that her speech, although cultured in accent, contained a few expressions that were not normally considered to be ladylike. Ladies did not rob or murder.

The thought of Pierre Standish had her moving again, as if she could distance herself from thinking of the man. How dare he enter her bedchamber in such a state of indecent undress! And once he had realized what he had done, why hadn't he excused himself and retired, as any reasonable man would have done, rather than plunk himself down on the bottom of her bed so familiarly and immediately commence insulting her? He hadn't had an ounce of pity for her plight. As a matter of fact, he seemed to find the entire situation vaguely amusing. No wonder her language had not been the best.

No, she didn't know much, but she knew she didn't like Pierre Standish.

She did like André Standish, however. The older Standish was kindness itself, fatherly, and certainly sympathetic to her plight. After all, hadn't he told her not to worry, that his hospitality was hers until she rediscovered her identity, and even beyond, if that discovery proved to present new problems for her? Hadn't he assigned Susan as her personal maid, and even promised to provide a female chaperone as soon as may be? Hadn't he even gifted her with the use of his late wife's entire wardrobe?

The gown she was wearing now was six years out of fashion and marred by the helpful but vaguely inept alterations Susan had performed on the bodice, waist and hem as her new mistress napped, but it was still a most beautiful creation of sprigged muslin and cotton lace.

She smoothed the skirt of the gown with her hands, grateful once again for being able to wear it, and then purposely made her mind go blank, concentrating on nothing as she continued to walk, not knowing that her appearance was more than passably pleasing, it was beautiful.

Her hair, that unbelievably thick and lengthy mane of

softly waving ebony, was tucked into a huge topknot, with several errant curling tendrils clinging to her forehead, cheeks and nape.

Her face was flawless, except for a lingering paleness and a vaguely cloudy look to her unusual violet eyes. Her mouth, generous and wide, drooped imperceptibly at the corners as she stopped in front of a rose bush, picked a large red bloom, and began methodically stripping away its petals, tossing them over the bush.

She looked young, innocent, vulnerable, and just a little sad.

"'*Ey!* Gets yourself somewhere else, fer criminy's sake! Yer wants ter blow m'lay?''

She turned her head this way and that, trying to figure out where the voice was coming from.

"Oi says, take yerself off, yer ninny. Find yerself yer own 'idey-'ole.''

"Hidey-hole?" she repeated, leaning forward a little, as she was sure that voice had come from behind the rose bush. "Who or what are you hiding from?''

"The froggie, o'course. Who else do yer think? Now, take yerself off!''

She wasn't afraid, for the voice sounded very young and more than a little frightened. Her smooth brow furrowed in confusion at his words, though, and she asked, "Hiding from a frog, are you? Well, if that isn't above everything silly! I would imagine you'd be more likely to come upon a frog in the gardens, wouldn't you? If you don't wish to come face-to-face with one, don't you think it would be preferable to hide where frogs don't go?''

Jeremy Holloway was so overcome by this blatant idiocy that he forgot himself and stood up, just to get a good look at the woman who could spout anything so ridiculous. "Yer dicked in the nob, lady?'' he exclaimed in consternation, then quickly ducked again, whining, "Yer seen me now. Yer gonna cry beef on me?"

She leaned forward some more and was able to see a boy as he crouched on all fours, ready to scurry off to find a new hidey-hole. "If you mean, am I going to turn you in, no, I don't think I am. After all, who would I turn you in to in the first place?"

"Dat froggie, dat's who! And all because Oi gots a few active citizens. Oi asks yer—is dat fair? Show me a lily white wot's ain't gots some, dat's wot Oi says."

Her head was reeling. "Are you speaking English?" she questioned, careful not to move for fear the boy would run off before she could get a good look at him.

All was quiet for a few moments, but at last, his decision made, Jeremy poked his head above the rose bush, looked furtively right and left, and then abandoned his hiding place. "Yer the one m' gingerbread man found in the road yester-dee," he told her unnecessarily. "*Yer* cleaned up right well, Oi suppose. But not this cove. Not Jeremy 'Olloway. No-body's gonna dunk this cove in Adam's ale agin."

"Thank you, I think," she answered, beating down the urge to step back a pace or two, for, in truth, Jeremy didn't smell too fresh. The boy was filthy, his clothing ragged and three sizes too small. "You might too. I imagine Adam's ale is water? What's a lily white, Jeremy, and whose citizens are active? And a gingerbread man?"

With an expression on his thin face that suggested she must be the most ignorant person ever to walk the earth, Jeremy supplied impatiently, "A lily white's a sweep, o' course. Everyun knows dat. Oi'm really a 'prentice, or Oi wuz, till yesterdee. My mum sold me ter ol' 'Awkins fer 'alf a crown, which is more than m' brother went fer. Wot else? Oh, yer. A gingerbread man is a rich gentry cove, like Mr. Standish. 'Appy now? Yer asks more questions than a parson."

"Lily white because they're so very dirty? Oh, that's very good," she commented, smiling at Jeremy, her heart wrung by his offhanded reference to what must have been a terrible experience. "But what's an active citizen?"

Jeremy put his head down, scuffing one bare foot against the gravel path. "Lice," he mumbled, then raised his head to fairly shout: "An' 'e ain't stickin' Jeremy 'Olloway's 'air in no tar an' shavin' it! Oi'll skewer 'im first—an' so Oi told 'im, jist afore Oi kicked 'im an' loped off! 'E didn't foller me, 'cause 'e 'ates the ground Oi dirties an' wants me gone. 'E telled me so 'imself."

"*Mon Dieu!* There you are, you *vilain moineau,* you nasty sparrow! Please to grab his ear, mademoiselle, so that I might cage him! I have the water hot, and the scissors is at the ready!"

More rapidly than she could react, the scene exploded before her eyes. A thin, harried-looking Frenchman appeared in front of her, a stout rope in one hand, a large empty sack in the other, and Jeremy Holloway disappeared, faster than a gold piece vanishes into a beggar's pocket.

"You have let for him to escape me again!" the Frenchman accused, his watery eyes narrowed as he glared at her.

"You frightened him, the poor boy," she accused, feeling protective.

"Please not to put in your grain of salt, mademoiselle," he returned nastily, drawing himself up to his full height. "I have been run to the rags searching for the small monster. I have been made sore with trying."

She understood. In that moment she understood something else as well—Jeremy's words coming back to her—and the light of battle entered her eyes. "Oh, do be quiet, *froggie,*" she ordered, privately pleased with herself.

"*Froggie!*" The servant's head snapped back with the insult, as if he had been slapped.

They stood there, the pair of them frozen in their aggressive stances for several seconds, then Duvall opened his mouth to speak. Fortunately for his opponent, something else took his attention just as he was about to begin, for his response to her name-calling was sure to be terrible, if unintelligible to anyone not familiar with gutter French.

"I say, Duvall, must I do everything for you?" asked a weary voice from somewhere behind them, and both of them turned to see Pierre Standish coming down the pathway, Jeremy Holloway's left earlobe firmly inched between his thumb and forefinger. "I set you a simple chore, and now, more than four and twenty hours later, the evidence of your failure has barreled into me as I attempted to take the afternoon air. I cannot adequately express my disappointment, Duvall, truly I cannot. Ah, good afternoon, Miss Penance. You're looking well. My congratulations on your rapid recovery since this morning. One can only hope your disposition is now as sunny as your appearance."

She placed her fists on her hips. "You let go of that poor, innocent boy this instant, you monster!"

Pierre's social smile remained intact. "Oh dear, I deduce that I have once again raised myself up only to open myself to a fall. Obviously you are to be perpetually tiresome, Miss Penance. But it is of no matter if you are quite set on such a course, as *you* are not my problem. This urchin, however, *is* my concern. Be still, Master Holloway, if you please," he asked of the squirming Jeremy, "as it would pain me to box your ears. Duvall, are you going to allow me to be thwarted in my zeal to accomplish a good deed? If nothing else, please consider the fate of my immortal soul."

Duvall began to wring his hands, his entire posture one of pitiable subservience. "Ask of me to cut off my two hands, good sir, and I will gladly make them a gift to you. Have my tongue to be ripped out with the pincers and served up to the dogs for dinner—order hot spikes to be driven under my fingernails. Anything, dear sir! Anything but, but''—he gestured toward Jeremy—''but this!''

"Come, come, Duvall," Pierre scolded, advancing another step. "Don't be so bashful. How often have I begged you to consider yourself free to express your innermost thoughts? Tell me how you *really* feel. Help him, Miss Penance. Explain to my dear Duvall that he shouldn't keep such a tight rein on his emotions."

Miss Penance, as even she had begun to think of herself, narrowed her eyes as she ran her gaze assessingly up and down the elegantly clad Pierre Standish. "You look better dressed," she said at last, although the tone of her voice did not hint at any great improvement over his banyan and bare, hairy legs. "The only thing remaining to be done to make you passably bearable would be to put a gag in your mouth. You are, Mr. Standish, by and large, the most insufferable, arrogant, nasty creature it has ever been my misfortune to encounter! How dare you maul that poor child that way? How dare you insult this man, who is obviously your slave?"

Ignoring her insults, Pierre honed in on one thing she had said. "Of *all* the creatures you have met, Miss Penance? May I deduce from this that you have regained your memory? Shall I have Duvall order a celebratory feast?"

Quick tears sprang to her eyes. "How I loathe you, Mr. Standish," she gritted out from between clenched teeth. "No, I have not yet regained my memory, sir. But I *have* met your father, your beleaguered servant, and this poor underfed, persecuted boy—and each of them is twice the man you are. You—you idiotic, conceited *fop!*"

"God's beard! She makes of you a mockery, good sir! It is of the most deplorable!" Duvall exclaimed, taking three steps away from her in order to distance himself from her disparaging words.

Jeremy halted in his struggle to free himself from Pierre's painful grip, his mouth hanging wide as he gasped at Miss

Penance. "Dicked in the nob, dat's wot she is," he said at last. "Dat's thanks, ain't it, guv'nor—and atter all yer done fer 'er! Does yer wants me ter level 'er? She's jist m' size, so's it'd be a fair fight."

Pierre looked down on the recently liberated chimney sweep. "I'd rather you allowed Duvall to make you presentable, Master Holloway, if you are cudgeling your brain for a way to express your thanks to me. Duvall? You agree?"

"Ask of me to cut off my two hands, good sir, and I will gladly make them a gift to you. Have my tongue to be ripped out with the pincers and—" Duvall stopped himself, taking a deep breath and squaring his shoulders. "Yes, sir," he ended fatalistically. "Very good, sir."

"You both are so kind, you threaten to unman me," Pierre drawled, a smile lurking in his dark eyes as he looked over to see Miss Penance holding back her fury with an effort. "Please leave us now, before I embarrass myself by falling on your necks in gratitude for your loyalty."

Jeremy and Duvall reached the end of the path before Miss Penance said, her voice measured, "You…make…me…*ill!* I suppose you think *I'm* supposed to be feeling three kinds of a fool for berating you when you are so obviously deserving of my thanks for not allowing me to lie in the road when you discovered me? That is the point of this exercise, is it not? Well, please do not hold your breath waiting for my thanks, for you will only succeed in turning that insufferably arrogant face of yours a hideous purple!"

Pierre walked over to a nearby bench and motioned for her to sit down. "You're right, of course," he agreed, settling himself beside her. "I was the most horrid of selfish creatures to have spirited you away from your so comfortable resting place. How could I have been such a cad? How will you ever forgive me for my callous disregard for your privacy? Shall I order the horses put to immediately, so that I can return you there before bedtime?"

"Don't be any more foolish than you can help. That's not what I meant, and you know it!" she countered, longing to punch him squarely in his aristocratically perfect nose. "Obviously you have somehow rescued Jeremy as well, and probably done something for that poor, nervous Duvall so that he looks upon you as a near god. But if you have some twisted desire to surround yourself with fawning admirers, I'm afraid that in this case you have badly missed the mark. I may have been born, figuratively speaking, only this morning, but I do possess some basic common sense. You could not care less what happens to me. You're only using me in some twisted, obscure way that benefits you, and I have to tell you, I resent it. I resent it most thoroughly! The moment I have recovered my memory I will be more than pleased to wave you a fond farewell as I go out of your life forever!"

"Such a passionate—dare I also mention, lengthy?—speech. You see me prostrate before you, devastated by your eloquent, long-winded vehemence," Pierre drawled, stifling a yawn.

"*Oh!*" she exploded, jumping to her feet. "I can only hope I discover that I *am* a murderess, so I can kill you with a clear conscience!"

Watching as she ran back toward the house, leaving one too-large shoe behind on the gravel path in her haste, Pierre raised his hand to absently stroke the small crescent-shaped scar that seemed to caress his left cheekbone. "Such a darling girl," he mused aloud. "I believe I have been more than justly revenged on my loving father."

CHAPTER FIVE

"SHE'S *WHERE!* I don't believe it! I refuse to believe it!" cried a female voice. "Quickly, fetch me my hartshorn. I feel faint!"

"Rubbish. You never faint, for all your moaning. You're strong as an ox," replied her male companion.

"Oxen, always oxen! Have you no other animal to use as a comparison? To think that your last tutor told me you showed an active imagination. It's a good thing I turned him off when I caught him winking at the upstairs maid, or I'd show him an active imagination! And have some pity on your elders. My poor heart could give out at any moment."

"It would be a better job to stop worrying about your heart and begin worrying about your neck! About both our necks."

"Why? We haven't done anything, have we? They can't hang a person for merely *talking* about murder. Besides, it's only her word against ours. Oh, why did she have to end up there? Anywhere but Standish Court. André Standish! He's completely, utterly ruthless. My blood runs cold at the very thought of him. He's so smooth, so mysterious. He seems to know everything."

"It's not the father who worries me. It's the son. I heard all about Pierre Standish when I was in London for the Season. He's like the father, but meaner. Killed his groom, you know—just for saddling the wrong horse. I do wish, though, that my man had his way with a cravat."

"But it has been five days since you went chasing off after her, and nothing has happened. I have been worried to death, waiting for you to return, waiting for the constable to come carry me away to some terrible, smelly gaol. Now you come back here, telling me she's not twenty miles from this wretched hovel you've rented, and with André Standish of all people. How could you have hidden in the bushes, watching the son cart her away like that? What are we going to do when they confront us?''

"Why, we're going to deny everything, of course. It's her word against ours, after all, and besides, no one has been murdered—yet. Of course, there's always the possibility she'll die, for she was unconscious when Standish lifted her into his coach. God, to think that I had finally run her to ground, just to have her bolt away from me into the roadway as we heard a carriage approach. You cannot know how prodigiously I hated hiding in the hedgerow while Standish all but plucked her out of my hands. Yes, it would serve her right to die from the tumble she took. That would solve the problem quite nicely.''

"Then we'd be free of her forever! Oh, that's above everything wonderful. But what if she lives? No, you have to go back to Standish Court. You have to go back, and silence her once and for all.''

"With Pierre Standish there to guard her? And you said you loved me. But you're right. She has to die now, or everything is ruined.''

"Yes, yes, it does present a problem. But we have no choice. Besides, you don't have to leave straight away. It can wait until tomorrow. Sit down, my dear, you look weary. Other than the fact that you couldn't apprehend that dreadful girl, was it a nice trip? The countryside is so pleasing this time of year.''

JEREMY HOLLOWAY RAN halfway down the length of the shiny black and white tiled foyer in his stockinged feet, an oversized knitted cap pulled down over his ears, then skidded the rest of the way on the slippery floor, whistling through the gap between his front teeth as he held his arms wide to maintain his balance. He quickly held his hands out in front of him before he cannoned into the closed doors to the drawing room.

Grinning from ear to ear in enjoyment of this new amusement, he turned himself about, ready to attack the slippery floor from the other direction, only to feel his shoulders firmly grasped by a pair of strong hands. Looking up—looking a long way up—he saw his new master staring down at him, his left eyebrow arched inquisitively.

"Good morning, Master Holloway," Pierre said quietly. "May I be so bold as to assume you are prepared to explain what you're doing?"

"'Allo there, guv'nor!" Jeremy chirped brightly, his quick mind working feverishly for an explanation. "Givin' a bit o' polish ter the floor, Oi am. 'Artley, yer pantler, asked me ter, yer see, an' Oi'm jist obligin' 'im—doin' 'im a bit of a favor, like. 'E's been ever so kind ter me, yer understands."

"Ah, yes, dearest Hartley. Wasn't that kind of him—and kind of you. Kind and thoughtful—and utter rubbish. Tell me, Master Holloway. Was it enjoyable?"

Jeremy swallowed hard on the enormous lump in his throat and rolled his eyes as if attempting to discover the nearest exit. "Jist cuff me good an' gets it over, guv'nor," he said at last, as Pierre's hands still held him firmly in place. "Oi can takes it."

"He will do nothing of the sort!" Miss Penance exclaimed militantly from behind Pierre. "Mr. Standish, you will please release that poor child at once. Or have you rescued him from his terrible former life only to beat him yourself?"

Recognizing opportunity when it appeared, Jeremy immediately burst into noisy tears, wrenching himself free of Pierre and immediately burying his head against his latest savior's waist. "Oi didn't mean nothin' by it, 'onest, miss.

The floor wuz jist there—yer knows. So pretty, so shiny. Don't let 'im beat me, miss, pleez! Ol' man 'Awkins, 'e beat me all the time.''

"Don't you worry, Jeremy. I won't let him so much as lay a finger on you,'' Miss Penance assured him, her arms wrapped tightly around Jeremy's thin shoulders, her violet eyes glaring at the man she considered to be the bully of the piece. "You're terrible with children, you know,'' she told Pierre condescendingly.

Pierre, who was always appreciative of outstanding theatrical performances, showed his appreciation now, clapping most politely as he commended softly, "Bravo! Bravo! I tell you both, I am most deeply affected. I don't know whether to toss roses at your feet or go off into the woods and fall on my sword. What a cad I am, what a cold, unfeeling monster! I should be horsewhipped.''

"I agree. I might only pray that I can be the one to wield the whip, sirrah!''

"My word, really? Such a Trojan you are, Miss Penance. Is that blood I see in your eyes?''

Jeremy pulled his face free from Miss Penance's smothering embrace to see that the two adults had all but forgotten him as they stared at each other, his female protector with some heat, his male protector with barely suppressed amusement. Clearly his presence was no longer required, and he carefully disengaged his hands from Miss Penance's waist and ran for the safety of the servant's quarters, careful both to pick up his still new shoes and to refrain from sliding as he neared the door that led to the kitchens.

"Now here's a dilemma,'' Pierre said after a space, his gaze never leaving the shining violet glare that still bore into him. "It would appear, Miss Penance, that the object of our latest contretemps has succeeded in eluding both my cruel, animalistic wrath and your fierce, motherly protection. Do we continue to stand here, staring at each other until one of us crumbles under the strain, or do we agree to a cessation of hostilities—only until the next time, of course—so that I might continue toward the breakfast room without fear of feeling a shaft of cold steel plunge between my shoulder blades?''

Miss Penance, who had already begun to feel rather foolish—not that she for one moment would let that insufferable prig know it!—lowered her chin and stepped back three paces, motioning for Pierre to precede her toward the breakfast room. ''Hunger alone makes me accompany you, sir,'' she told him, then gasped as he took her arm so that they walked together down the hallway to breakfast.

The room was empty of other occupants when they arrived, Miss Penance quickly disengaging her arm from Pierre's grasp as she made for the side table that held an enormous array of hot and cold food. After piling eggs and kippers and toast indiscriminately on her plate, she retreated to the far end of the long dining table and sat down, as far away from Pierre Standish and the coffee pot as she could. After all, it was one thing to share a table with the man. It was asking entirely too much to believe she would pour for him as well.

Putting a forkful of eggs into her mouth—while trying not to notice either the absence of salt or the salt cellar that sat directly in front of Pierre halfway down the table—she lowered her gaze in the hope her long black lashes would disguise the fact that she was staring at him.

There was no denying it, more's the pity, he really was a very nicely set-up man. Thin but well muscled, and taller than she by at least a foot, he wore his clothes well, even if he seemed to wear nothing but whitest white and blackest black. Of course, the white of his cravat showed his tanned skin to advantage, while the black of his clothes almost exactly matched the dead-of-night shade of his hair—which didn't mean that she found him attractive, for she did not.

Of course she didn't.

She lowered her gaze to her plate, somewhat alarmed to see the kippers she had placed there, for she didn't think she was going to like them. They looked so *dead*. Pushing them to one side with her fork, she took a deep breath and lifted another forkful of eggs to her mouth.

"Salt?" Pierre asked just as she closed her mouth around the fork, his voice dripping innocent inquiry.

"No," she snapped, adding, "thank you," only because she knew it was polite to do so. Glaring at him once again— she seemed always to be glaring at him—she stabbed her fork into the food on her plate and took a whopping mouthful of kippers, her eyes immediately widening in shock. "Mmmfff!" she mumbled, knowing that, no matter how un-ladylike it would be, there was simply no way in the world she was going to swallow the nastiness now filling her mouth.

Pierre, his face determinedly blank, propped his elbow on the table and with chin in palm, inquired sweetly, "Coffee, Miss Penance?"

Her teeth firmly clenched, her lips nearly disappearing as she drew them into a thin line, Miss Penance could only glare at him and shake her head—vehemently. "Mmmfff!" she repeated, tears beginning to sting her eyes.

"I'll take that as a no," Pierre answered amicably. "Perhaps you'd care for a glass of milk? After all, kippers can be very, um, salty."

Her hands digging into the serviette in her lap, she used her tongue to shift the kippers to one side of her mouth, still refusing to chew.

"Not very talkative, are you, Miss Penance. Miss Penance," he repeated, sitting back at his ease. "We have to do something about that name, don't we? I mean, it was all right for a while, but you've been with us for three days now, and to tell the truth, it is beginning to weary me. Have you any suggestions for a replacement?''

The eggs in her stomach—the unsalted eggs in her suddenly unsettled stomach—were threatening to revolt, forcing her to bolt from the room or to dispose of the kippers posthaste, either solution bound to be remarked upon by the still solicitously smiling Pierre Standish.

''Miss Penance, much as I am enjoying this, enough is enough.'' Pierre rose, reaching for the water pitcher and an empty glass. ''Here. What's the matter? Kippers got your tongue?''

That did it! The serviette found its way to her lips and she rid herself of the kippers just as Pierre waved a glass of water in her face. She grabbed it, too grateful to refuse his help, and downed the cool liquid as fast as she could, not caring about anything except ridding herself of the taste of salted herring. ''Oh!'' she exclaimed, gasping, once the glass was empty. ''That was horrid!''

''It's an acquired taste,'' Pierre told her, sitting down once more. ''I believe it is safe to say that you, Miss Penance, have not acquired it.''

Using the handkerchief she had unearthed from her pocket to dab at her moist eyes, Miss Penance responded grudgingly, ''Apparently not. Thank you. I'll see that the serviette is laundered.''

Pierre ignored this last statement, choosing rather to go back to the subject of her name. ''I have been giving it some thought,'' he began, knowing she would have no choice but to follow where he was leading, ''and I have decided to call you Miss Addams—as in Adam and Eve, you understand—but with two D's, so as to not be too ordinary. Not being particularly partial to the name Eve, however, I shall leave the matter of your first name entirely to you.''

''Well, isn't that too bloody generous of you,'' the newly

250 THE ANONYMOUS MISS ADDAMS

christened Miss Addams began furiously. "I'd just as soon you—"

"Your language, Miss Addams, please! Consider my tender ears."

She ignored him, continuing, "I'd just as soon you left the entire matter to me, or to your father, as he has informed me that *he* is to be my guardian until such time as I remember exactly who I am."

"My father, yes. And how is that gentleman? I have not seen him above once since he scolded me for distressing you with the sight of my legs. He warned me that I might have compromised you, but I disabused him of that assumption, considering that you are quite the most uncompromising female I have ever encountered."

"Caroline!"

"I beg your pardon?"

"Caroline. You're not deaf. Dumb?—well, that is arguable, I believe. I wish to be called Caroline. Caroline Addams."

"Caroline." Pierre raised his left eyebrow, a mannerism that was becoming increasingly infuriating to Caroline Addams. "That may be an unfortunate choice. Heaven knows it hasn't done Caroline Lamb a world of good. Are you quite settled on it, then?"

She crossed her arms at her waist. "Completely and irrevocably," she declared.

"There is nothing complete and irrevocable in this life, Miss Addams, except our assurance of one day leaving it." Pierre looked down at his plate, realizing he had quite lost his appetite. He rose, carefully pushing in his chair. "Now, if you'll excuse me?"

"Never!" Caroline answered quickly, knowing she was behaving most childishly, but also knowing that she had been provoked. After all, he was the one who seemed to like her best when cast in the role of shrew. ''I shall be happy to see you go, but I shall never excuse you.''

He stopped, his hand still on the back of the chair, and looked consideringly down the table at her. ''You know, Miss Addams,'' he said, almost as if he was saying the words as he thought them, ''I am almost convinced that you are deliberately provoking me.''

Caroline's mouth opened wide as she raised her hands to her cheeks in feigned shock. ''No! Whatever would make you think that, Mr. Standish?''

He ignored her obvious dramatics. ''The question then is: why? Perhaps you are fighting some wild attraction for me? Oh dear, that must be it. It was the legs, wasn't it? Admit it, Miss Addams. I most particularly remember your fascination with my legs. You're mad with love for me.''

''I'm what?'' she exclaimed, feeling her cheeks beginning to flame. Now he had gone too far. ''You're depraved!''

''So I've been told,'' Pierre admitted, turning to go. ''But I've never before heard the accusation voiced in the way of a complaint. Ah, well, I think I shall go now, to beat my devoted valet heavily about the head and shoulders, in order to regain some of my trampled self-esteem. Good day, Miss Addams. I leave you to enjoy the rest of your delicious meal in peace.''

''And good riddance to him!'' Caroline concluded heatedly as Pierre closed the door behind him. So aggravated was she that she vented her anger by giving her serviette a wicked shake, intending to spread it across her knees once again, only to send the rejected bite of kippers skidding across the parquet floor.

A few moments later the sunny breakfast room was entirely empty of human occupation, with only two uneaten plates of rapidly congealing food left behind to show that the room had ever been occupied.

CHAPTER SIX

ANDRÉ LOOKED UP from the letter he was penning in the supposed privacy of his study to see his son enter the room, an unusually enigmatic smile on his darkly handsome face. "Have you succeeded in finding something to amuse you, my boy? You look almost pleased. Much as it reveals the weakness of my old age, I must tell you, it's unnerving to observe you so happy."

Pierre settled himself comfortably in an oversized burgundy leather wing chair, draping one long, elegant booted leg over the arm of the chair. "This is not happiness you see upon my face, Father. It is an outward sign of my depravity. I have this on good authority, you understand. Your son is hopelessly, but happily, depraved."

The older Standish signed his name to the bottom of the sheet with his usual flourish and carefully laid down his pen before remarking on his son's nonsense. "You've been teasing our little guest again, haven't you, Pierre? It really is too bad of you. What was it this time? Have you been showing her your legs again?"

"Nothing so daring. I merely told her I've decided on a surname for her. Addams—with two *D*'s of course, to raise her from the ordinary. She, in her turn, linked Addams with Caroline, a mundane but serviceable appellation, barely worthy of a young lady who might well be a missing heiress. Of course, she might just as easily be a fleeing housemaid, which would make her choice of name smack of a pushy young lady dangerously overreaching herself, but I was not so boorish as to point that out to her.''

"Of course," André answered, rolling his eyes. "You are, if nothing else, discreet."

"I'll ignore that outburst. We were rubbing along together fairly well, Miss Addams and I—except for the kippers, of course—when suddenly, inexplicably, she turned hostile. It wasn't a pretty sight, I can tell you. She is a most highly strung female.''

After sanding the letter and then shaking the excess into a small dish, André folded the single heavy ivory vellum sheet and applied a small wax seal. "I refuse to discuss kippers with you, Pierre, no matter how you dangle them before my curiosity. I've just completed a communication to my solicitor in London, requesting that he send us a suitable chaperone posthaste. Shall I amend it, asking him to send me a bodyguard as well, or are you done with trying to drive my anonymous ward out of her wits?''

Pierre lifted a hand to lightly stroke his scarred cheekbone. "Anonymous. The Anonymous Miss Addams. It does have a poetic ring about it, doesn't it? I must have been inspired. I should like the bodyguard, I suppose, although I believe your concern is misplaced. Miss Addams is in no danger from me, but rather the opposite. As a matter of fact, that is why I am here, pestering you in your private sanctum. I do believe I shall be reconvening my remove to London before my poor, abused confidence sustains some irreparable damage from your ward's pointed tongue.''

André tapped the folded letter lightly against his chin as he studied his son's negligent pose. "She's routed you then, my son? I grow to like our Miss Addams more with each passing moment.''

The left eyebrow that had so infuriated Caroline earlier now moved in a slight upward direction, rather like a silent punctuation of Pierre's thoughts. "Feeling rather full of yourself, aren't you, Father?'' Pierre drawled, turning to place both his feet on the floor. ''But you couldn't be more wrong. I have responsibilities, you know.''

''You do?'' André questioned with patent incredulity. ''I should deeply appreciate a partial listing of these 'responsibilities,' as I cannot imagine anything more pressing in your life than an appointment with your tailor.''

''Responsibilities,'' Pierre pursued, undaunted. ''I have a household in town that I have been sadly neglecting this past fortnight. I have important papers of some sort or other to sign, or at least I believe I do. It is difficult to keep track of such things. And, oh yes, I have promised Master Holloway that I would return him to his beloved Piccadilly. It's enough that Duvall has cut off all the poor boy's hair and scrubbed him until his nose shines brighter than the sun. I can't disappoint the little scamp now.''

André coughed, covering his mouth, and with it, his smile. ''You mean to make me believe you are going to toss young Master Holloway straight back into the den of inhuman thieves that first sold him into service? You may be many things, Pierre, but you cannot convince me that you, my only son and light of my life, are stupid.''

As Pierre had no intention of returning Jeremy to any woman who would sell him to a sweep for a half a crown, he lowered his eyes, avoiding his father's gaze. ''I only mean to have the boy pay a flying visit to the place, seeing his former home from the safety of my carriage. Only then will I be able to resign him to living in the country, surrounded by the lesser evils of clean, fresh air and ample food. The boy has a romantic vision of his former home and hearth that only a good dose of reality can hope to dispel. Then I shall install him at my estate in Surrey, out of harm's way. Now, having bared my soul to you, and only to you, for I wouldn't wish the world to think I have become soft, have I succeeded in reaffirming your fatherly faith in me?''

André crossed the room to look down at his son. "You are being kind, Pierre. Why?"

"Kind, Father? Please. I am never kind. I am merely, to quote you, lending a bit of 'compassionate assistance to one of the helpless wretches of mankind, without a single thought of personal reward.' Did I get that just right, Father? I should so hate to misquote your immortal words of wisdom."

"You're running away," André announced incontrovertibly, smiling down on his son. "Oh, this is gratifying in the extreme. I'd always hoped to live long enough to see such a day."

"You're dangerously twisted, Father," Pierre warned, rising to his feet. "If I am an unnatural son, you are a most irregular parent. Loving you as I do, I hesitate to point that out, but the need for self-preservation compels me. No, sir. I am not running away. I am leaving. There is a vast difference between the two."

André, his expression serious, only nodded. "I'll bid Miss Addams your farewells for you. I see no need to expose either of you to each other again, considering the adverse effect you seem to have on one another."

"How utterly kind of you," Pierre drawled sweetly. "And shall you hold tight to my hand until I reach the safety of my carriage? Really, Father, you are most hopelessly heavy-handed in this previously untried role of matchmaker. Oh, yes," he said as his father showed signs of protesting. "You are become most sadly lacking in Machiavellian skills, dearest Father, probably just one more damning effect of rapidly encroaching old age. Speaking as one who once stood in awe of your skills, I must tell you, it's a sad, extremely sad, spectacle to witness."

Unruffled by this masterful put-down, André only smiled and said, "Again you overreact, my son. My concern was solely for Miss Addams. I would never think to exhaust myself in order to comfort you."

Pierre bowed, silently acknowledging André's denial. "Your reassurances do comfort me nonetheless. Now, if you'll excuse me, I should like to track down Duvall and make him the happiest man on earth by ordering him to pack. He has never been enamored of the country, you understand, much preferring the hustle and bustle of city life."

André regarded the letter in his hand. "You have just given me an idea. Familiar as I am with your neck or nothing approach to travel, perhaps you will favor me by delivering this missive in person once you reach London, saving me considerable time in my quest for a suitable chaperone for Miss Addams?"

Bowing once more, Pierre answered, "As I live only to bring ease to your declining years, it would be my pleasure to play post boy. I should even be willing to take on the task of ferreting out this suitable chaperone myself, as I have some firm ideas on just what sort of female is needed."

"You do," André commented blandly. "I should like to hear a list of your specifications."

"She should be strong, both in back and in heart," Pierre began, ticking off his fingers one by one. "She should have at least a nodding acquaintance with stable speech, so as not to be shocked when Miss Addams's command of polite conversation deserts her. Also, along with the usual virtues of pristine morals, a watchful eye, and no annoying habits— such as picking her teeth with the tines of her fork or ferreting out your private stock of port and commandeering it for herself—she should be at least ten years your senior. I should not wish to exchange one possible compromise for another."

Now it was André's turn to bow. "You are too kind, my son. Have I neglected to mention that I have instructed cook to prepare rare roasted beef with horseradish sauce for dinner this evening?" With a slight self-deprecatory grimace and a wave of one elegant hand, he pushed the question aside. "Please forgive me—it was but a momentary lapse."

Pierre opened his mouth to, his father was sure, graciously accept his apologies—a terribly lowering prospect for one who still considered himself his son's superior when it came to subterfuge—when a shrill female screech interrupted.

"What the devil?" Pierre exclaimed, already moving toward the open French doors that led straight onto the garden, his father close on his heels.

Caroline Addams's small, muslin-clad body shot into the room. Stopping abruptly, her head still turned partway around, as if trying to catch sight of the demon that was pursuing her, she crashed directly into Pierre's chest. "Ooof!" she exclaimed as her breath left her body, and held tight to Pierre's arms to steady herself.

"Add one more requirement to that list I gave you, please, Father," Pierre said, unruffled. "This chaperone of yours must be extremely fit and fleet of foot if she hopes to keep your Miss Addams in tow. Either that, or might I suggest leading strings?"

Caroline, having recovered sufficient breath to speak, immediately went on the attack. "Unhand me, you idiot!" she demanded, pushing free of his too-familiar clutches, refusing to consider that she might be the cause of their current situation. "And don't just stand there with that stupid, smug smirk on your face! I could have been murdered!"

Pierre's "stupid, smug smirk" remained firmly in place. "Nonsense, my dear Miss Addams with two *D*'s. You were in no danger of being murdered. After all, think of it—*I* was nowhere about. Unless, perhaps, you have succeeded in making other enemies during your short sojourn under my father's protection?"

"Sarcasm! Always sarcasm. And bad sarcasm at that," Caroline retorted. "Do you never tire of hearing the sound of your own voice?" She ran over to where André was standing, silently watching and listening to this exchange of unpleasantness between his son and his ward. "Mr. Standish! You believe me, don't you?"

André put a comforting arm around her shoulders and drew her close in what he would have termed a fatherly embrace. "Of course I believe you, my dear," he informed her. "Only one question, if you please. What was it that you said?"

She pulled away from André, no longer frightened but extremely angry. "I was accosted in the gardens, of course," she told them both, looking from one to the other of the Standishes hoping she had shocked them.

"You ran afoul of one of the gardeners?" Pierre suggested, stifling a yawn. "They're very possessive of their greenery. You should really try to keep to the paths, and not trample on the posies."

"I did not!" she contradicted defiantly. "I was merely walking down one of the paths—near those delightful shrubberies you showed me yesterday, Mr. Standish," she elaborated, turning to André, whom she would much rather speak to and look at, Pierre's silently mocking eyes infuriating her to the point where she knew she would soon lose all control over her nerves. "Suddenly, out of nowhere, there was this—this *man!* He must have been as big as a house! He was looking at me in the most prodigiously speculative way, and he had a large sack in his hand. He took two steps toward me, and I screamed. You may have heard me."

"Prinny and his court heard you," Pierre slid in quietly, "and they're in Brighton, I believe, eating seventeen-course meals and doing whatever else it is they do. You probably disturbed a poacher clumsily plying his trade too close to the house. The poor man is most likely miles from here by now, still running as if all the hounds of hell were after him, and with his hands clapped to his ringing ears."

Caroline stared at André, trying to gauge his opinion. What she saw was not encouraging. Her arms flapping wildly, like a small, flightless bird, she began swooping about the study, her too large shoes flop-flopping as she went. "You don't believe me—either of you! What must I do to convince you—*die* for you?"

"So dramatic, my dear girl," Pierre remarked, looking at his father from beneath lowered lids. André nodded, only slightly, and his son nodded in return, the two reaching out to each other in silent communion. "But I must admit," Pierre began carefully, "you do begin to interest me. Tell me about this terrible man with the large sack. Was he more than ten feet tall? Did he drool, or just shoot sparks of blue fire from his one, horrible bulbous eye?"

Caroline stopped her furious fluttering and subsided heavily into the oversized wing chair Pierre had vacated a few minutes earlier. "Oh, shut up," she grumbled, allowing her chin to drop onto her chest. "Mr. Standish," she said crushingly, looking up through her long black lashes at André, "I hate to be the one to cause you pain, but I believe your dearest late wife must have somehow played you false. This idiotic ninny cannot possibly be your son, no matter how much he resembles you physically. You have been kindness itself to me, while he is the meanest, most obtuse, self-important, belittling—"

"—beast in nature," Pierre finished helpfully when Caroline seemed to lose her train of thought.

She sat up very straight, the toes of her too big shoes barely touching the floor. "See!" she exclaimed, pointing an accusing finger at Pierre. "Now, you've heard it out of his own mouth! Oh, please, sir, send him away so that I can tell you about the man in the garden."

André shooed Pierre away with a wave of his hand, but his son withdrew no further than the French doors, idly casting his gaze over the garden as he appeared to ignore the occupants of the room. Pouring a small glass of sherry for his ward, André proffered it to her and took possession of the facing wing chair, his elbows on the arms of the chair, his hands elegantly cupped beneath his chin.

"Ignore him, my dear," he told Caroline. "Heaven knows it is difficult, but I have every confidence you can manage it if you try. Now, tell me about this man you saw tippy-tocing about in my garden."

Caroline took a small, tentative sip of the sherry, then downed the rest in one gulp, shivering only slightly at its immediate impact on her system. "With pleasure, Mr. Standish," she said, sitting up very straight. "As I said, I was taking the air in the garden, near the decorative shrubbery, when I heard a noise in the bushes. I looked up just in time to see this man—not nearly so tall as yourself, sir, now that I am no longer in danger and can think more clearly, but still with two eyes and no sign of drool about his mouth—standing not three feet away from me, a large sack held open in both hands, just as if he was preparing to bring it down over my head. He wore a hat pulled down around his ears, so that I couldn't see his face too clearly, but he was very menacing, I'm convinced of that."

"You must have been terrified," André allowed, deftly removing the glass from her hand.

"I was. I said something to him—I don't remember just what—and screamed and ran straight to this room, and the man didn't follow. Now, are you going to do anything about it or not?" she ended, despising the slightly shrill sound of her last question, for she did not like letting either Standish know that she was still frightened. "I mean, if you think anything needs to be done," she added weakly.

"That was a very good explanation, my dear. Very clear, very concise and very unnerving," André pronounced, looking over to where Pierre was standing, his hands clasped behind his back, still staring into the garden. "What say you about all this, Pierre?"

He turned to face the occupants of the room. "I say, dear

Father, that unless we have a remarkably shortsighted poacher who mistook Miss Addams here for a pheasant, then we shall have to investigate this incident most thoroughly. After all, we cannot have a guest in our house disturbed in this way, can we?''

''We, Pierre?'' André repeated pointedly, raising his eyebrows. ''But I thought you were about to depart for the metropolis. Have you had a sudden change of heart, a rare stab of consideration?''

''Oh, dear,'' Pierre said, one hand to his heart. ''Do you think so? I should hope not. Perhaps I'm sickening for something.''

Caroline bounded from her chair, heading for the door to the hallway. ''You're sickening all right!'' she shot back over her shoulder before slamming the door behind her with a mighty bang.

''I think she's a trifle upset,'' Pierre remarked placidly, staring at the closed door. ''The child's disenchantment with me to one side, however, the fact that we have no clear idea as to who she is begs me to ponder the possibility that she might be correct—and that someone is trying to murder her.''

André, careful to conceal his smile from his son, ripped the letter to his solicitor neatly in two and tossed the halves into the cold hearth. ''Then you'll be staying to dinner, Pierre? Cook will be most pleased, although I image that, conversely, your devoted Duvall will be devastated.''

CHAPTER SEVEN

IT WAS EARLY in the morning, and the noise of uncooperative horses being put into harness in the courtyard in preparation for another long day on the road filtered through to the common room, where many of the inn's patrons were partaking of their breakfast.

Off in one shadow-darkened corner of the large, low-ceilinged room sat a conservatively dressed couple, by outward appearances and by their signatures on the inn register, mother and son, the two deep in some serious discussion in between taking hearty bites of an equally hearty fare.

"I still don't see why you couldn't have sprung for a private dining chamber," the young man was saying, his thin, sad face wearing a disheartened frown that seemed comfortably at home there. "It's bloody dangerous, sitting out in the open this way, exposing ourselves to anyone who might come through the door."

"I keep telling you not to swear in front of me. Just like your father, aren't you?" the woman retorted around a mouthful of eggs. "Always reaching into my pockets for your own comfort. They are not bottomless, you know. Besides, you worry too much."

"You weren't the one who had to run and scramble for miles and then hide in that thorny thicket yesterday until it was dark," the man grumbled, rubbing at an angry-looking scratch that ran down one side of his face. "She was screaming to wake the dead. I was sure someone was going to clap me on the shoulder at any moment, and haul me off for attempted kidnapping.''

''You don't even know if she saw you,'' the woman pointed out. ''A mouse could have run across her toes, setting her off.''

''You still think I'm lying, don't you? You think I never went to the Standish house at all, but only sat in the bushes somewhere all day, out of harm's way, before coming back to you with some moonshine story about nearly being caught. That's simply unloving of you, do you know that?''

''Then she just mustn't have seen you clearly, dearest,'' the woman conceded, seeing that the young man's bottom lip was trembling, as if he were close to tears. ''You were wearing a hat. And don't pout. Your face might freeze that way. Mother believes you. You said you were half hidden behind the ornamental shrubbery. Yes, she didn't see you clearly, that's the only logical explanation. You'll just have to try again. Pass me one of those delicious-looking biscuits, if you please. The food here is quite remarkably fine for such an out-of-the-way place, don't you think?''

The biscuits were passed, along with a small crock of fresh creamed butter that was the private pride of the innkeeper of the Scarlet Cow, who would have blushed to the top of his bald pate if he could have heard this great praise. ''Didn't see me? Damn it! What does it take to convince you? We've been over this a dozen times. Then why did she set to screeching like a greased pig in a trap and go haring off back to the house as fast as her two legs could carry her? Answer me that if you can, you daft woman!''

''Your language, please. Don't break my heart. But it *doesn't* make sense. If she had seen you, the two of us would be before the local constable at this very moment, trying to explain our way out of the hangman's noose. It wouldn't have taken that frightening André Standish a full day and night to ferret us out, seeing as how we're strangers, and staying at this inn not two miles distance from his front door. Why hasn't she cried rope on us? Knowing her, I'm sure she would delight in seeing our necks stretched.''

''More to the point—why did she look at me so blankly and then ask me who I am? Anyone would think the chit didn't recognize me. Either that, or she's more of a cool fish than we thought and is running some rig of her own, to get revenge on us, as it were. Kindly leave one of those biscuits for me, if you please.''

''A rig of her own? Don't be silly, she's only a girl, and hasn't the wit. No, it can't be that. Perhaps she was just shocked by your sudden presence, and forgot your name for a moment.''

''Forgot my name? You named me Ursley, Mother, remember? *Ursley!* A person doesn't forget a name like that. God knows I can't. I couldn't even be called by any other name than Ursley. Not Diccon, or Billy, or even Georgie. You cursed me when you gave me this name, and I shan't ever forget it.''

''It is a family name, and very distinguished, or at least it was until your dearest father so carelessly botched our last endeavor—bless his dear, departed soul and may I be forever grateful that the poison I chose did not cause him to suffer unduly.'' She buttered another biscuit. ''I dislike seeing this pettish streak in you, Ursley. Have you been getting quite enough sleep these past few days? And, if you'll remember, your classmates called you Stinker at school. Surely that qualifies as a pet name?''

Ursley ignored his mother's casual mention of her murder of his father by way of a gooey strawberry tart laced with arsenic, for he saw nothing wrong in it, as the man had become an embarrassment to all of them. The only thing that worried him was that he himself was in danger of going down to defeat himself in their current project. It was a thought that could destroy a man's appetite and make him overly anxious to succeed.

He took refuge from his thoughts in another attack. "If you had wished to help me compile a list of grievances against you, Mother, the name Stinker would come second on my list. First of course, is the problem of our little eavesdropper. And I still say she didn't recognize me. I think she must have hit her head as she fell onto the roadway that first time I was chasing her, and can't remember anything."

Ursley's mother thoroughly chewed the last biscuit and swallowed. "Yes, I have heard of strange things like that occurring after an injury to the head. I'll agree that you have a point that bears investigation—though, of course, whether this new development will help or further complicate matters remains to be seen. Let me think on it until it's time for luncheon. There must be some way we can be sure. Perhaps we shall not have to kill her after all. Having her insane and locked up snugly in some asylum would be equally as lovely as having her dead, and quite less the bother."

"And live in constant terror that someday she'll wake up screaming 'That horrible man, Ursley Merrydell, and his wicked mother are trying to murder me?' Oh, no, madam, I should think not!"

"No, no. *I* should think not, as well. But we're going to have to be very careful. If only we could find some way to get ourselves into the Standish household. You know, that is a male household. It would be a shame if the girl's reputation should suffer irreparable damage just because there is no good woman in the house to protect it, don't you think, Ursley? I am a very good chaperone, thanks to your father's unforgivable failure to leave us reasonably provided for, and have impeccable references. Go take a walk to settle your meal, dearest, while I think on this a bit longer, and we'll talk again over luncheon. I wonder…"

CAROLINE HAD LAIN awake in her bed for half the night, racking her brain for some elusive memory, some forgotten fact, some small, enlightening clue that might serve to help her rediscover her identity. When the morning came she had nothing to show for her pains except slightly puffy eyes and a lingering headache. A headache that was about to become much worse.

She approached the sunny breakfast room warily—hoping to avoid bumping into Pierre, who would most certainly destroy her appetite with his unnerving presence—and succeeded in dining in solitary splendor. It was just as she was touching the fine white linen serviette to her lips one final time that the sound of a carriage moving off down the drive came to her ears.

Idly curious, and hoping against hope that Pierre had once more changed his mind and was already on his way to London—and out of her life—she drifted into the drawing room to see that same infuriating man standing at the mantel, dressed in his usual impeccable black and white, frowning over a missive he held in one hand.

"Bad news?" she ventured softly, hoping against hope that he had just learned his horses had all lost at the races and his cook had run off with the upstairs maid, taking all his silver plate with them. "You look faintly downpin, although I have found, with your usually unreadable expressions, it is difficult to tell just what is going on inside that head of yours—if, indeed, anything does."

"Ah, Miss Addams. You're awake, and as full of compliments as ever." Pierre unhurriedly folded the letter he had been reading, pocketed it in his jacket, and turned to look at his father's ward. She was coming more into her looks with each passing day, a thought that did little to change his opinion of her. Pretty is as pretty does, someone had once said, and Miss Caroline Addams had been remarkably unpretty in her treatment of him. Not that he cared one way or the other what her opinion of him was, he reminded himself with a slight mental jolt.

Her midnight hair was once more a cascading tumble of curls, reminding him of the way she had looked that first morning when Hartley had startled her from her slumbers and he had burst into her chamber, hairy legs and all. How could something so angelically beautiful, so fragilely constructed, so infinitely appealing, be such an unremitting pain in the—

"You will be devastated to hear the news, I imagine," he said, bursting into speech before he could finish his last thought. "My dearest father has seen fit to desert us."

"What! He couldn't have! He wouldn't have!" Caroline looked to the window, as if she could see the carriage that had recently pulled away and somehow call it back, then over to Pierre, her quick mind registering the fact that he appeared mildly pleased at her nearly hysterical reaction to his news. She cleared her throat, folding her hands together at her waist. "I see," she said, striving to be calm. "A family emergency, no doubt? Perhaps he knew he could not stay under the same roof as you any longer without succumbing to the urge to strangle you?"

"Strangle me? My own father?" Pierre motioned to a nearby chair, politely inviting her to seat herself so that he could do the same.

"Yes," she said, spreading her skirts around her as she chose a chair as far away from him as possible. "Don't feign surprise. I imagine you inspire that sort of feeling in most of your acquaintances."

"Don't judge everyone else's reactions by your own, Miss Addams. I am quite well thought of by many people, unbelievable as that might seem to you."

"I'm not speaking of your paramours, Mr. Standish," Caroline countered smoothly, then gave a silent gasp at the lengths to which her impudent tongue could take her when she was in his company.

Pierre smiled. Her looks improved even more when she was flustered. "We could sit here all morning, listening to you tear strips off my consequence, but I believe we have other matters to discuss. My father, by way of this letter he left before sneaking out of the house like some mischievous youth embarking on a spree, has charged me with your welfare while he travels to London on some trumped-up excuse about how he needs to personally choose a suitable chaperone for you. He is as transparent in his motives, I'm afraid, as a pane of freshly scrubbed window glass."

"His motives?" Caroline asked, not liking the way Pierre was looking at her. He was entirely too familiar in his speech, and always had been, which was bad enough, but now he was looking at her in a way that made her wish she could throw her hand protectively across her breasts, hiding herself from his too observant eyes.

"Father would like it immensely if we were to tumble into love, Miss Addams," Pierre said baldly, not seeing any reason to dress the thing up in fine linen. As a rule, he disliked being obvious, but his father was forcing his hand.

"With each other?" she squeaked, knowing her eyes were as wide as saucers.

"No, Miss Addams," Pierre returned suavely. "I am to fall madly in love with the tweeny, that charming birdbrain servant who bursts into giggles each time I happen to pass her in the hallway, and you are to have your heart stolen away by my so-estimable man, Duvall. And here I have always prided myself on my lucidity. I thought I was being so clear. Please forgive me."

Caroline was on her feet in a flash, wishing she was a man so that she could call this smug, maddening man out and then run him through. That alternative not being open to her, she walked purposefully across the room and leaned down to go eye to eye with him. "Don't...be...facetious!" she said, punctuating each word with a sharp stab of her index finger against his pristine white shirtfront.

As she jabbed her finger the last time, Pierre lifted his right hand and neatly grabbed her wrist, pulling her down to within inches of his face. "Don't…be…stupid," he warned silkily, his black eyes flashing dangerously as his smile chilled her to the bone. He held her prisoner for another moment, an eternity during which she more than realized how vulnerable she was, before releasing her as he had captured her.

She quickly retreated to her own chair, subsiding into it before her knees, curiously wobbly, buckled completely. "I—I'm sorry," she said, shaking her head. "I don't know what's come over me. I'm not usually so forward."

Pierre did not miss the implication of this last statement. Perhaps he had somehow, accidentally, jiggled her memory. "You're not, Miss Addams? Tell me, please. How can you be so sure?"

A sudden vision of herself not more than a year younger than she was now, dressed in a rather low-cut white gown and laughing delightedly as she went down the dance with some scarlet-jacketed lieutenant flirting for all she was worth, flashed into her mind. "Oh, dear Lord," she breathed, all color leaving her face as she pressed her hands to her cheeks. "You were right about me. I *am* a strumpet!"

Pierre folded his hands beneath his chin, much as his father had done the day before while Caroline told them about the intruder in the garden. "I must tell you, Miss Addams, my mind begins to boggle with your every new revelation. First you regale us with tales of bogey-men in the greenery, and now you confess to being a fallen woman. Tell me, are you an accomplished strumpet, do you suppose, or only a recent practitioner of the oldest profession? You barely seem old enough to have been plying your trade for any great length of time."

Caroline closed her eyes, feeling slightly queasy, and the

picture in her mind reappeared. She could see the entire ball-room now, and even make out one or two faces other than her own. It was a lovely ballroom, if slightly rustic, the sort of room to be found in a smaller city, although how she knew that she couldn't remember, and the people looked to be highly respectable—even stuffy. A woman dressed all in pur-ple, and with a most uncomplimentary silver turban banding her head, was regarding her in a clearly condemning way, as if she heartily disapproved of her conduct.

She squeezed her eyes tightly shut, scrunching up her en-tire face—bringing a genuine smile to Pierre's face at the sight of her wrinkled-up nose—hoping for more, hoping to hear bits and pieces of conversation, for it would seem that she was talking to her dancing partner. The image visible inside her closed eyelids wavered slightly, distorting the dis-approving, turbaned lady's face most grotesquely, and then was gone, as quickly as it had come.

She opened her eyes. "I'm not a strumpet," she said softly and to no one in particular, relief clearly evident in her voice. "I'm only distressingly forward, if the ugly purple lady is to be believed."

"I can't know how you feel on the subject, but for myself, I've never put much credence in ugly purple ladies," Pierre supplied helpfully, rising leisurely to his feet. Crossing the room to the drinks cabinet, he poured Caroline a small glass of sherry and delivered it to her. "I shouldn't like for this imbibing of spirits to become a habit, Miss Addams, but I think you could do with a small restorative. May I take it you've had a flash of memory?"

Caroline shook her head, declining the drink, then nodded. "I saw myself at a country ball, flirting most prodigiously with some lieutenant as we went down the dance, shocking the purple lady with my forwardness," she told him, almost immediately regretting having shared the memory with him. "It was not really helpful, as I recognized nothing of the scene save my own grinning face. There wasn't even any music. If only I could call the scene back again, and try to move it past that moment in the dance.''

She felt Pierre's hand on her arm, and was startled by the gentleness his touch conveyed, a gentleness so in contrast with his usual condescending treatment of both her and her plight. ''Don't push, Miss Addams. There are ways and there are ways. Small, unexpected flashes of memory are only one of them. By one method or another your past will be revealed to you. In the meantime, as Cervantes said: 'Patience, and shuffle the cards.'''

'''There is a strange charm in the thoughts of a good legacy, or the hopes of an estate, which wondrously alleviates the sorrow that men would otherwise feel for the death of friends.' My goodness! Where did *that* come from?'' Caroline exclaimed, amazed at the words from Cervantes's *Don Quixote* that she had just quoted.

''My congratulations, Miss Addams,'' Pierre murmured, looking down on her. ''You become curiouser and curiouser. That you know Miguel de Cervantes's work is surprise enough. Your choice of quote, however, is considerably more than mildly intriguing.''

Caroline brightened. ''Yes. Yes, it is, isn't it? What do you suppose it means?''

Pierre lightly stroked the scar on his cheekbone with the smallest finger of his left hand. ''I believe it means that you have had a difficult morning and should indulge yourself in a small liedown in your chamber like a good child. Now, if you'll excuse me, I believe my father's defection leaves me with the sure-to-be fatiguing bother of having to discuss tonight's menu with cook.''

''That's it? That's all you have to say?'' Caroline hopped to her feet, longing to stomp her foot in disgust, refraining only because Pierre was sure to comment on this display of immaturity and at last succeed in maddening her past the point of all rational thought.

Pierre turned back to her, his expression politely inquiring, "You want more?" he asked solicitously before producing a bored grimace. "Of course, how boorish of me. I seem to have temporarily mislaid my manners." He bowed deeply, mockingly, from the waist. "Good morning to you, Miss Addams. As I will be lunching with father's steward, I pray that, after you have sufficiently recovered in the privacy of your chamber, you will enjoy the remainder of your day until we meet again at dinner."

Caroline watched, openmouthed and silently seething, until Pierre had sauntered from the drawing room, then headed straight to her chamber, exiting it not fifteen minutes later, clad in Eleanore Standish's altered riding habit, the too-large boots clomping heavily against the stairs she took at a rapid pace. She didn't know if she was a good horsewoman, or even if she had ever ridden in the first place, but she'd rather break her neck clearing a five-barred gate than bow to the autocratic Pierre Standish's high-handed direction of her life!

CHAPTER EIGHT

SHE WAS HALFWAY to the stables before realizing that the day was much too pretty to be spent thinking about either André Standish's defection or the maddening Pierre Standish and his obvious wish to make her life as uncomfortable as possible. She would be happy today, if only to make him miserable!

Her furious pace immediately slackening to a leisurely stroll, Eleanore Standish's intricately braided leather riding crop slapping softly against her skirts, Caroline took a deep breath of fresh country air into her lungs and looked about at the gloriously landscaped grounds that made up a small part of the vast Standish holdings. All at once her fingers began to tingle as she longed for her brushes, wishing to capture the scene with the watercolors from her paintbox.

"I paint!" she said out loud, halting in her tracks as the realization that she had discovered something else about herself penetrated her brain. "Ladies paint. Ladies, and the daughters of good houses. I dance, even if I do flirt. I dance, I paint, and I can quote Cervantes." Her smile was as brilliant as the late morning sun. "I *am* a Somebody!"

Her happiness was fleeting. "Of course, a governess must also know those things," she pointed out to herself as she continued toward the stables. "A governess, or a schoolmistress. No. I'm too young to be a schoolmistress. A governess is possible, even if the thought of being one is terribly lowering. But would a governess dance? No wonder the purple lady was frowning. I probably overstepped myself while supposedly chaperoning her daughters—two of them, and both as uninspiring as their mother, no doubt—and got myself turned off for my pains, without a reference. I've been wandering the world on my own ever since, with neither family nor friends to ease my plight, until I finally got myself into a scrape that ended with me lying facedown in the roadway, dressed in a man's cloak, and minus my shoes. How thoroughly depressing.''

'''Ey! Yer al-ays prate ter yerself? Sumthin' havey-cavey 'bout folks who jaw bang when nobody's there ter 'ear 'em.''

Caroline stopped walking and looked around until she discovered the source of the voice that had interrupted her imaginings. She found it sitting perched atop a granite pedestal that supported a lovely statue of a Grecian maiden pouring water into the small, stone-edged pool that surrounded the statue like a miniature moat.

''Jeremy Holloway!'' she exclaimed in relief, for it wouldn't have done for Pierre to have overheard her romantic imaginings or she would never, she was sure, hear the end of it. Waving to Jeremy gaily, she redirected her steps until she was in front of the pool. Sitting down on the low stone wall at the water's edge, she looked inquiringly at the young sweep. ''What are you doing here? Did you wade across? I thought you detested Adam's ale.''

He ignored her questions, seemingly more concerned with her welfare. ''They'll takes yer away an' fix yer up wit yer own straight-waistcoat iffen yer keeps it up, yer knows that, don't yer? Oi lifted the blunt from a gentry mort an' went ter see the loonies in Bedlam onct on a Sunday. There's all manner of dicked-in-the-nob folks locked up inside, all jist singin' and dancin' and talkin' ter themselves nineteen ter the dozen. Ain't a pretty sight, Oi tell yer. Yer'd best be careful.''

''Thank you, Jeremy, for the advice. I'll do my best not to let that happen to me.'' Caroline allowed her fingertips to dangle in the cool water, trying to catch the ever-widening ripples caused by the water pouring from the Grecian maiden's stone pitcher. "How are you now, Jeremy, now that your active citizens have been routed?" she asked, careful to keep her gaze diverted from the boy's all-but-bald head until he could replace the knitted cap he constantly wore.

"Oi wuz jist lookin' at m'self in the water," he mumbled, carefully pulling the cap down over the light golden fuzz that barely covered his head. "Oi'm goin' ter kill dat frog, yer know," he added matter-of-factly. "Oi bit 'im good, but Oi'm still goin' ter kill 'im. 'E deserves it, Oi'm thinkin'."

"I understand," Caroline returned sympathetically. "But it had to be done. There's no other way to rid yourself of the pesky little creatures, unfortunately. Your hair will soon grow back, twice as thick and long as before. But must you really kill him, Jeremy? Guv'nor will be grievously saddened, you know, for Duvall is the only person in the world, save you, who can tolerate him."

"Guv'nor likes the froggie?" Jeremy sounded dubious, understandably depressed by what he could only see as a serious flaw in his otherwise perfect savior. "Well, mebbe Oi'll only 'urt 'im bad."

Caroline suppressed a grin and nodded her agreement with this generous concession on the sweep's part. "That's very kind of you, Jeremy," she told him. "Now, would you like to accompany me to the stables? I have a wish to see if I can ride."

As Jeremy's face twisted into an expression of wary incomprehension, Caroline held out her hand, helping him to leap from the pedestal to the wall to the ground, then explained her predicament as they walked together.

"So you see," she ended as Jeremy lifted the latch that allowed them to push back a section of fence and enter the yard, "I have absolutely no memory of anything about myself, other than those few things I just told you."

She felt Jeremy's hand take hold of hers. "Oi'll 'elp yer," he told her, his protective urges coming to the fore. "It's a terrible thing, bein' away from all yer know. That's 'ow Oi wuz when 'Awkins took me."

Caroline felt the back of her throat stinging with emotion as she looked into the boy's open, childish face. "Thank you so much, Jeremy, for understanding. You have no idea what it means to me to—oh! Jeremy, just look at him! Isn't he a beauty?"

The horse being led into the stable yard was no more than three years old, a huge, sleek, black satin creature with a wide white blaze running the length of his handsome, intelligent face. His form was fluid, hinting of speed even as he was walked slowly in a wide circle, his muscles rippling along his strong flanks, his ears and tail nervously twitching at the sound of Caroline's voice.

Jeremy stopped short in his tracks, eyeing the huge horse warily. "A beauty, is it? 'E looks like a bleedin' devil ter these peepers."

"Nonsense." She approached the stallion fearlessly, taking the reins from the startled groom. Stroking the horse's velvety nose, Caroline murmured fulsome compliments to his handsomeness, then allowed him to nuzzle her open palm. "Sugar, Jeremy," she said, still using the same soothing tone. "Ask the groom for some sugar. This darling creature and I have got to get to know each other."

After doing her bidding, Jeremy approached the stallion gingerly and all but flung the sugar lump at Caroline before quickly scurrying away for, being a child of the city, he had long ago learned to keep his frail body a safe distance from deadly hooves. "The groom says 'is moniker is Obtuse, wotever that means. Be careful-like. 'E looks like a killer iffen Oi ever seen one."

"He doesn't mean it, sweetheart," Caroline assured the horse, feeding it the sugar. "You're just a great big baby, aren't you, Obtuse? Obtuse. You have to be Pierre's mount. No one else would think to saddle you with such an unsuitable name.''

As if to confirm her thought, the groom came up to her and told her that Mr. Pierre was most protective of his horseflesh, horseflesh that had been left in the groom's charge, and now that the young miss had petted the horse—and this next bit he would appreciate very much—perhaps she'd be willing to give him back into his hands.

''I have Mr. Pierre's generous permission to ride Obtuse,'' she lied with a quick coolness that surprised even her, looking directly into the groom's eyes as she uttered the blatant untruth. ''Please see that he is saddled for me immediately.''

There are many things a groom can do on his own with his master's horse. He can curry the horse, feed the horse, exercise the horse, and even get kicked in the rump by the horse if he isn't careful. All this and more can a groom do on his own. There are some things he cannot do. He cannot buy or sell the horse, beat the horse, or even get bucked off the horse, as he may not mount the horse without his master's permission.

But there is a higher rule, one that the groom knew stood head and shoulders above the rest. He cannot, under pain of instant dismissal, contradict a guest. Caroline, dragging this bit of knowledge from the depths of her memory, knew it as well, and her triumphant smile blighted the man with its brilliance.

Obtuse was fitted with a sidesaddle, and within five minutes Caroline was on his back, galloping out of the stable yard with the nervous, grumbling groom riding behind them on a mount that could not hold a candle to the stallion's speed.

''I can ride!'' Caroline shouted delightedly into the wind that was rushing by her as Obtuse headed for the open field. ''I can ride!''

HE RODE LIKE A MAN possessed, quietly cursing the groom who had come pelting back to the stables, having lost Caroline somewhere in the dense trees.

He cursed the soft ground that slowed his mount's progress and the mount itself for not being the more fleet-footed Obtuse.

He cursed his father for having saddled him with the responsibility of someone else's welfare and for that same man's premeditated defection.

But most of all he cursed Caroline Addams, the willful, headstrong idiot of a girl who had ridden off over the countryside without a thought to the danger she might well find there.

Pierre urged his mount into a full gallop, hoping against hope that he would find Caroline still in one piece. "So that I might have the pleasure of killing her myself," he declared through gritted teeth.

She was in danger, he just knew it. No stranger to peril, he had long ago recognized its smell, its chilling effect on his bones, its capacity to swoop down and destroy everything in its path. He had met danger face-to-face on the Peninsula, slept with it lying by his side, fought with it on more battlefields than he cared to recall, and watched its victims being sucked down into the greedy Spanish mud.

To look at him, Pierre appeared to be a gentleman giving his horse its head, for his impatience was rigidly controlled, a lesson learned long ago. It was an inward battle he was fighting now or, more clearly, two battles, one with his old enemy, danger, and another, even more terrifying, that raged between his heart and his head.

His head told him that Caroline Addams was the last, absolutely the very last person in the world who should matter to him. His heart, beating hurtfully in tune with his mount's galloping hooves, fought to tell him that Caroline Addams was the only person in the world who could ever really matter to him.

Suddenly, just as he pulled his horse to a skidding, plunging halt at the crest of a slight hill in order to scan the horizon, he spied Obtuse tied to a branch of a small tree, a grazing grey gelding tied beside him. His rapidly pounding heart stopped in mid-argument before beginning to beat rapidly again, now more in fear than in anger. Caroline was nowhere to be seen.

Dismounting, and checking to be sure that his pistol was still tucked into his waistband at his back, he proceeded slowly, his eyes scanning the open field and border of trees, his ears alert.

"Oh, Sir John, really?" he heard after a moment, his entire body swinging about at the sound of Caroline's voice, followed by the lilting song of her delighted laugh. "Admit it, sir, you're funning me. Nobody could be that contrary, not even Pierre Standish."

"It's true, I swear it," came a male voice, obviously belonging to the unseen Sir John. "He has always been an odd duck. You can never know what he is thinking."

"But to cut a man dead on Bond Street just because he didn't like the style of his jacket? And the man actually broke down and *cried?* It sounds so incredibly silly."

Pierre pushed back the branches of a wild flowering bush and stepped into the small clearing to see Caroline sitting at her ease on a fallen log, Sir John Oakvale lying at her feet, one hand propped against his cheek,

She looked beautiful sitting there, her entire blue velvet clad figure softly dappled by sun and shade, her expression one of delight, the disapproving frown she customarily donned while in his presence nowhere in evidence. Her smile, the same innocently devastating smile he had glimpsed that first morning of their acquaintance, was now directed at Sir John Oakvale.

Pierre sensed danger again, this time emanating from himself, whom he knew to be capable of falling on Sir John and beating the grinning nodcock into a bloody pulp. He carefully schooled his features into their usual faintly bored expression.

"Hardly silly, Miss Addams," Pierre drawled, masterfully containing himself and stepping completely into the clearing. "The man was utterly crushed, as well he should have been, for I am known to be a most demanding arbiter of the best fashions. He retired to his estates that same day, a broken man, so that I could not tell him that the whole thing was my fault. I had gotten a bit of smut in my eye, you understand, so that in actuality I had passed by him without seeing him. You did remember to tell her that, didn't you, Oakley?"

Sir John scrambled to his feet, hastily brushing dirt and leaves from his buckskins. "Standish!" he exclaimed, looking as guilty as a young lad caught with his hands in the honey pot. "We didn't hear you ride up. And it's Oak*vale*," he added pettishly, wishing he could refrain from correcting Pierre but unable to restrain himself.

"Of course it is, Oakmont. How could I be so forgetful? Do forgive me," Pierre said silkily, walking over to Caroline and extending his hand to her. "You have been very naughty, haven't you, Miss Addams. My groom is quite destroyed by your capriciousness. I left him in the stable yard, a shadow of his former self, as he is sure you are dead and I shall blame him. Or was it that he was sure Obtuse was dead, and I shall demand his life in forfeit? Yes, I'm convinced it was the latter. Only the loss of my dearest Obtuse could serve to put me in a rage."

"My loss would doubtless be cause for a celebration, isn't that correct, Mr. Standish?" Caroline asked, ignoring his hand and rising without aid.

"I shall leave that determination to your own judgment," Pierre offered magnanimously.

"Of course you will. I shall apologize to your groom, for

it is my fault he is upset. Your sensibilities and their condition are your own problem, thank goodness, and I care not whether they have or haven't suffered permanent damage. Sir John,'' she said, walking over to where that man stood, looking about to bolt for the safety of the trees, ''it was so very nice to meet you. Perhaps you shall agree to visit me at the Standish home, in order to help me pass these long, tedious days?''

Sir John blushed from his intricately tied cravat to the roots of his wavy blond hair, pleased that Caroline had found his company entertaining. Heaven only knew his father didn't, which was why he had been out riding in the first place, finding that being away from home for as many hours as possible during his duty visits to that same home was less taxing on his easily overset nerves.

Sir John, young, boyishly handsome, and a great pet of the London ladies, who found his company pleasant without being threatening, had come upon Caroline in the field separating his father's small holding from the larger Standish estate. The sight of her had gone a long way toward reconciling him to his enforced visit home, even if the thought that he would have to endure the sure to be uncomfortable presence of Pierre Standish whenever he called on Miss Addams was distasteful to him.

Bowing over Caroline's hand, Sir John said brightly, ''I should be honored to visit you, Miss Addams.''

Pierre, one foot perched on the fallen log, raised a hand to stifle a yawn. ''I had a premonition you would say just that, you dear man, and in just that way. How utterly deflating. I suppose you'll expect me to serve as host, in my father's absence. Oh, very well. Mapletree, please, consider my father's home your home, for the duration.''

''That's *Oak*tree!'' Caroline fumed, hands on hips, knowing Pierre was taking great pains to get Sir John's name wrong, an insult so blatant she was surprised he would sink to it, for his cuts were usually more subtle.

Sir John coughed slightly and cleared his throat. "Actually, Miss Addams, it's Oak*vale*," he corrected apologetically. "For myself, I don't mind but Father is rather starchy about people getting it right."

"As well he should be! It's a lovely name," Caroline responded, horrified by her mistake even as she caught Pierre's gaze and found the corners of her lips twitching as a silent message of shared humor flashed between them. Her expression hardened, for she was angry with herself at even this small intimacy with a man she loathed. "Mr. Standish, I've just had a thought."

"You have, Miss Addams? Might I convey my congratulations?" Pierre cut in, seemingly occupied with removing a spot of dust from his brilliantly shined boots. "I refuse further comment, as it would be beneath me."

"Really?" Caroline retorted, obviously not believing him for a moment. "I would have thought you beneath nothing. To continue, sir; if you are not ready to return to the estate, Sir John can bear me company home."

Pierre removed his foot from the log and took a firm grip on Caroline's upper arm. "Much as I detest denying Sir John this opportunity to ingratiate himself with me by performing this kindness, I feel that, as your host, I must cut short my own pleasure and escort you safely back to the stables. My dear fellow, excuse me, but you do understand—don't you, Oakvale?"

So pleased was Sir John that Pierre had deigned to use his correct name, he acquiesced immediately, causing Caroline's upper lip to curl in disdain as he bowed once more over her hand and departed before Pierre could ruin the moment with another of his crushing remarks.

"And now, madam," Pierre said softly as they watched Sir John ride away, his tone so mild that Caroline had no idea of what was to come, "if it isn't an out-of-the-way demand, and putting momentarily to one side your heartless disregard for my groom as well as your kidnapping of Obtuse, do you think you could possibly explain your reasons for deliberately putting yourself in danger?"

CHAPTER NINE

"DANGER? WHAT DANGER are you talking about, Mr. Standish?" Caroline questioned hotly, immediately going on the offensive. "Oh, just a moment. *Could* it be? Is it *possible?* Surely you cannot be referring to the 'shortsighted poacher' in the garden? That man, whose presence you did not even choose to investigate by exerting yourself to the point of making an actual search for him, in the unlikely chance I may have been correct and the fellow *was* trying to kidnap or murder me? That man, whose presence in your garden, on your property, was so innocent that your father, who has set himself up as my guardian, has taken himself off to parts unknown, leaving a worthless dandy like you as my only protector? Please, please, good sir, enlighten this poor, confused lady. Is that the *danger* to which you are referring so obliquely?"

"That's the way, Miss Addams. Be nasty," Pierre urged reassuringly. "It's good for the soul. Rage at me, and don't forget a single insult. We, both dissolute father and reprobate son, have done just as you say. We have treated you as if you were naught but an infant, pooh-poohing your fears and not giving your story of the man in the garden the credit you are convinced it deserves."

Caroline was not mollified, as she was certain he did not want her to be. He was smooth. He had only agreed that he and André had not believed her, not that they had been wrong. He was never serious, but constantly flippant, and most incisively cutting. Well, she would not rise to his bait and give him the satisfaction of seeing her lose her temper. If he thought he could push her, she would show him she was capable of pushing back.

"I am pleased to see you have finally decided to believe me," she answered sweetly, just as if she had taken his words to heart, carefully removing her arm from his grasp and heading for her mount. "If your presence at this moment is a belated show of concern, I shall accept your apology."

"I didn't offer one," Pierre pointed out, making a cup of his joined hands and giving her a mounting step to help her into the saddle. "But, then, you already know that, don't you? I merely listed a few Standish failings. Personally, I'm rather proud of them. And, you must admit, your own behavior begs another question. Would a prudent woman ride out alone if she was really convinced she was in danger?"

He had her there, not that she would give him the satisfaction of agreeing with him. She looked down at him from atop Obtuse, knowing she was going to regret her next question. "If you don't believe me about the man, then why did you say I was in danger in the first place? You make precious little sense, Mr. Standish."

"Call me Pierre, Caroline. I think we have outlived the need for such formalities. You're riding my horse, for one thing, a horse that has known none but me on his back, surely a sign that you feel you know me well enough to make free with my possessions. Also, we should remember that we have seen each other in a state of undress. Yes, I would say the time for formalities has passed."

"Answer the question, *Pierre*," Caroline gritted, wondering why she stood here listening to his nonsense, when it would be so easy, so very easy, to spur Obtuse into an instant gallop and leave the insufferable man in the dust. "You did think I was putting myself in danger by riding out alone because of the man I saw in the gardens. That's why you came after me. Admit it."

"I could, I suppose, say that you may have unconsciously put yourself in some peril from some unknown gentleman set on doing you harm. I could say it, but I won't, for I don't believe it."

Caroline could have burst into tears. She was right. He still didn't believe her! He was deliberately leading her on, making her think he was concerned for her safety—concerned for *her*. He didn't care two sticks for her! It was his horse he had come after, and now he was just getting some of his own back, leading her on with all this talk about danger, because he felt she deserved punishment. "I could detest you with very little effort," she said meanly, glaring down at him. "*Very* little effort."

Pierre placed a hand on his heart. "Please, Caroline, your vehemence threatens to crush me." Before she could answer, or even think of something vile enough to say that would do justice to the way she felt at this obvious untruth, his hand moved, delivering a sharp slap to Obtuse's flank, and she was fully occupied in controlling the stallion as it began to race back to the stables.

Several minutes later, as the groom helped her from the saddle, Pierre rode into the yard on his slower mount, tipping his hat to her. "How could you have done that?" she yelled to him. "I could have been killed!"

"As much as I dislike explaining myself, I shall answer you. If you weren't a superior horsewoman I would have found you in the field an hour past, your obstinate little neck broken in several places," Pierre answered as another groom raced to the horse's head so that his master's son could dismount. "I know your limits, Caroline, perhaps better than you do yourself. I suggest you reflect on that for the remainder of the afternoon."

"I detest you!" she said, flinging the words at his departing back, causing the groom, who was about to walk Obtuse in order to cool him, to shake his head in silent condemnation.

"He's arrogant, insufferable, and entirely too sure of himself. I really, *really* detest that man," Caroline consoled herself repeatedly as she stalked back to the house, rhythmically slapping the riding crop against her thigh. Perhaps if she repeated the words often enough she could make herself believe them.

"*C'EST BON POUR LES CHIENS;* it is good for the dogs, and nothing else. *Mon Dieu,* how could this have happened?" Duvall was inconsolable. His master's best jacket was ruined past all repair, covered with horsehair and splashed with flecks of sticky, drying foam that had come from the mouth of the horse he had stretched to its limits during the search for that ungrateful Miss Addams. The valet held the offending jacket at arm's length in front of him by the tips of two fingers, his expression eloquent with disgust.

"First she arrives like a hair in the soup. That was the first sin, but not the last. We cannot escape from this terrible place to London because of her. The dirty little person is still with us because of her. But now, but now—this is the sideways of enough! Now she has caused for the so-beautiful jacket to be destroyed. I warn you, master, you won't buy another like this for a mouthful of bread."

Pierre, who had been listening to this tirade, and much more, from his valet all during his bath and while he was dressing for dinner, took one last look at himself in the mirror over his dressing table and was tolerably pleased with what he saw reflected there. "Your concern for my finances warms my heart, Duvall, even as your ceaseless chatter fatigues me. Kindly dispose of the thing. The smell of horse goes badly with the scent I have chosen for this evening."

Duvall was past caring whether or not he was displeasing his employer. After all, hadn't he, for two long hours only that morning, brushed this very coat into an absolute *merveille* of perfection? If his master had felt the need to go chasing after the so stupid Englishwoman, the least he could have done was think of his poor valet's dedicated efforts and changed his jacket before leaving. Where was the man's gratitude, his consideration? Duvall took one last, sorrowful look at the jacket, then dropped it out the open window onto the ground below, planning to fetch it later, in the hope he could at least rescue the silver buttons.

"And it has all gone for nothingness anyway," Duvall mused aloud. "She did not even have the decency to be killed. A fine jacket, ruined, and all for the wild geese chase. *C'est incroyable!*"

"Your logic never ceases to amaze me, Duvall," Pierre said, turning to his valet. "If Miss Addams had been murdered, then the sacrifice of my jacket would have been acceptable? Do you dislike women so much?"

"*Appeler un chat un chat;* to call a cat a cat, I say," Duvall responded reasonably. "A woman you can get anywhere, but a perfect jacket is not so easy to find."

Pierre's smile disappeared. "For the most part, my rationalizing friend, I agree with you. However, I value this particular woman a bit more than that. Someone is trying to kill Miss Addams, or at least make off with her. She was lucky today, if it can be called lucky to have had Oakvale for company, but at least his unlooked-for presence served to keep her safe from whoever is after her."

Taking his cue from his master, Duvall pushed all remaining regrets concerning the demise of the jacket from his mind and concentrated on the matter at hand. "The man in the gardens is then real?"

Pierre chose a ring from the tray on top of the dressing table and slipped it on the smallest finger of his left hand. "Someone did a good job of trampling down the shrubbery out there," he told the valet as he held his hand in front of him, considering the appropriateness of his choice of gold-encircled onyx over the plain gold ring he usually wore with this particular ensemble. "Not that I would tell Miss Addams that, of course. I see no good reason to alarm her. Unless, of course, she persists in trying to slip her leash." He turned to the valet, holding out his hand for that man's opinion. "What do you think, Duvall? Too much?"

Duvall, pleased that his employer had applied to him for guidance, immediately exploded into a torrent of complimentary French, extolling the man's utter perfection. Monsieur's frame was exquisite, honoring the very fabric of which his ensemble had been constructed. The cravat, it was how you say, a triumph! The hair, so full, so thick with health, fit his head like a crown to a king. And the shoes! The shoes were—

"Fairly comfortable, thank you," Pierre broke in, moving toward the door. "Thank you, Duvall, for that rousing declaration. If you are correct, Miss Addams will swoon at the sight of me. That only leaves me with the question of whether I should welcome such an occurrence—or do my best to avoid it."

Duvall opened his mouth to give his opinion, but his master had shut the door behind him before he could voice it.

PIERRE STANDISH EXCELLED at polite yet interesting dinner table conversation, which was one of the many reasons he was welcomed everywhere in Mayfair, even if his hosts were never quite sure if their guest was laughing with them or at them.

He was also considered to be quite a success with the ladies, although he never seemed to exert himself to gain their good opinion. It was just that he was so very handsome, and so strangely mysterious, his dark good looks and incisive mind compelling all the young belles, and more than a few of their mothers, to try to discover the key to his locked heart. His massive fortune only added to the sweetness of the pie.

The masculine portion of society, whether they be titled lords, war heroes, or refined gentlemen of quality, were equally desirous of gaining Pierre's regard, but for the most part they were more than a little in awe of the man. He did not give of himself, did not engage in polite conversation or welcome confidences as much as he seemed to use some strange sixth sense to ferret out the motives and shortcomings of his fellow man.

While many prided themselves on being numbered among his acquaintance, and would have liked to know him better, only a few trusted friends were allowed into his inner circle. Partly this was due to Pierre's upbringing, and a father who had taught him that a man should consider himself blessed if he could number his real, true friends on the fingers of one hand. The unfortunate affair of Quennel Quinton's blackmail scheme had served to harden him, making him appear even more formidable than he was before serving in the Peninsula.

The women could not know that Pierre had been harboring an unfavorable opinion of the inconstancy of a female's affection, nor the men be aware that he had begun to look on all of mankind with a faintly jaundiced eye.

Caroline Addams, not knowing that she had been treated to a greater degree of friendliness by Pierre than almost every other female in England—thanks in part to André's admonition to find himself a redeeming charitable project—was also without knowledge of Pierre's reputation. She only knew that he was extremely handsome, curiously reticent and maddeningly intriguing.

Like many of her sex, she wished she could somehow peel away the world-weary façade Pierre wore and get to know something of the real man that lay beneath the polished exterior. She wanted to see him react, whether in anger or passion she did not know. He was so cool, so controlled, so very perfect. His perfection, she had found, was the most annoying thing about him, and she longed to see him ruffled, on edge, unsure of himself.

"Human," she said aloud, walking into the drawing room a few minutes before the dinner gong was due to be rung. "That's what I want to see. Some sort of human emotion—and I don't count that dratted eyebrow as a display of anything other than disdain. I want to see him with his feathers ruffled, off his stride. And I want to be the one who causes his dishevelment."

"You said something, miss?"

Caroline whirled around, nearly tripping on the overly long hem of Eleanore Standish's gown. "Oh, Hartley, you startled me! I didn't see you over there. No, er, no, I didn't say anything. Did you think I said something? Oh, dear, I must have been talking to myself. I do that sometimes, don't you? Jeremy says it's a bad sign, and I might end up part of the Sunday show in Bethlehem Hospital. That would be too bad, wouldn't it?" She laughed weakly as the old retainer regarded her owlishly. "Yes, ahem, excuse me. I seem to be babbling. Did you want something, Hartley?"

Hartley shook his head while still looking at her strangely, then bowed himself out of the room. "There!" Caroline groused, dropping heavily into a nearby chair. "That is a fine example of what I'm talking about! Hartley startled me, and I proceeded to make a cake of myself trying to explain what I was doing. Pierre, on the other hand, wouldn't have been overset in the least. He probably would have turned, oh so slowly on his heels, lifted that dratted eyebrow of his just so"—she tilted her chin upward and tried her best to imitate Pierre's haughty glance—"and said, 'Ah, Hartley, you are here. How fortunate. If it would not be too great an exertion on your part, might I trouble you for a glass of port?'"

"I make it a point never to drink port before a meal myself, Caroline, as it ruins the palate. But, as Hartley isn't here, might I play the part of loyal servant and fetch you a small glass of sherry?''

For the second time in as many minutes, Caroline found herself flying into nervous speech. ''Pierre! I didn't see you there. Well, of course I didn't see you there, for you weren't there, were you, or at least you weren't there a moment ago. You are here now though, aren't you? Oh, wasn't that the dinner gong? My, I'm starving. An afternoon on horseback will do that to one, won't it? Shall we go in? It wouldn't do to have the meal cool, would it?'' She hated herself for what she was doing, and longed to slap her hand over her mouth to stop the flow of words, but she couldn't.

Only Pierre's left eyebrow, the one he was raising in that oh-so-sophisticated way, could put a bridle on her runaway tongue. That, and his next words: ''Caroline, far be it from me to criticize, but you are babbling. Has Sir John's company this afternoon so titillated you that you are reduced to the simplest of chattering females? It would be such a pity, for I had thought you above such failings.''

Her eyes narrowed as she stood, intent on saying something so mean, so cutting, that he would flee the room in fear of her wrath. She glared at him while summoning something sufficiently nasty to say, her gaze raking him from his perfectly combed head to his brilliantly polished shoes. He looked, a part of her brain registered automatically, incredibly handsome in his ebony and white evening dress.

''Why must you always be so damnably perfect?'' she blurted without thinking of the consequences, suddenly feeling undersized and dowdy in her borrowed finery. ''Perfect speech, perfect clothes, perfect control—nobody should be so damnably perfect. Listen to me—I'm swearing like some fishwife! Oh! You make me so angry!''

Pierre didn't so much as blink, a lack of reaction that made Caroline mentally strike another black mark against him in the copybook she had begun keeping in her brain. "Well? Aren't you going to say something?"

She watched as Pierre walked toward her, holding out his arm so that she might take it and together they could proceed to the dinner table. "What would you like me to say, Caroline? You are obviously overwrought, and you are correct— it is entirely my fault. This perfection you speak of is my personal curse, but I did not mean to inflict it on you. Perhaps if I were to slurp during the soup course? Or would you rather I ate my peas with a knife? I should be willing to do anything to oblige you."

She stopped, tugging on his arm so that his progress was halted as well. Looking up at him consideringly, she gave in to impulse and raised a hand, deliberately mussing the front of his hair so that it hung over his forehead. "There," she said, standing back to admire her handiwork. "That's more like it. You look almost human, Pierre. Now I believe I can do justice to my dinner."

She took one step toward the dining room before Pierre's hand snaked out to grab her arm and pull her back. Without a word, he hauled her into his arms and kissed her, hard and long and quite thoroughly. When he released her, she was breathing heavily, her cheeks flushed a becoming pink and her lips softly swollen. "What—what did you do that for?" Caroline squeaked when at last she could speak.

Pierre studied his handiwork for a moment, gently running a fingertip across her slightly parted lips. "There," he said, smiling. "Now I *feel* human, and I, too, can enjoy my dinner."

CHAPTER TEN

IT WAS A LOVELY country village lined with small thatched cottages, a pond at its center, and boasting not two but three perfectly wonderful little shops whose window displays captured Caroline's interest. So far she had purchased a wide yellow satin ribbon for her hair, a snow-white linen handkerchief with a delicate pink and green embroidered hem, a pair of tan leather riding gloves, and an ample supply of sugary hard candies, which she and her maid, Susan, were already sharing.

She disliked the idea that she had been reduced to spending Pierre Standish's money, but she was totally without funds of her own. She had fought and conquered her misgivings, knowing that, while there were a myriad of things she could continue to either borrow from Eleanore Standish's wardrobe or do without, there were also certain things she desperately needed.

The most important thing, the primary reason she had come to the village, was to purchase shoes that fit her. She was tired of retracing her steps to retrieve Eleanore's too-big slippers that kept falling off her feet. Of course, this didn't explain the purchases already lying in the basket Susan was carrying, but Caroline wasn't going to think about them now. She was just going to enjoy herself. She deserved it. She had earned every last copper penny of the money, too—having to endure Pierre Standish's insulting embrace.

Even now, the morning after her disgrace, her cheeks burned with embarrassment and indignation. And something more, something that she would rather not think about. For Caroline knew that most of her discomfort derived from the fact that she had enjoyed his kiss and had not fought to free herself from his arms.

For that, Pierre Standish would most certainly pay! She might just purchase a pair of riding boots. A very expensive pair of riding boots. She smiled wickedly. She might even kick him with them!

"Oh, look, Susan," she exclaimed, pulling the maid to a stop in front of a shop window. "There are just heaps and heaps of lovely shoes in here. Come along. I can't wait to get out of these uncomfortable slippers."

"DID YOU SEE THAT? She walked straight past us, just as if we weren't even here. Now do you believe me? She's dicked in the nob, just like I said."

A curiously pleased smile on her face, Amity Merrydell looked on as her quarry and the quarry's maid disappeared into the small shop. "I never said I didn't believe you, Ursley. Why must you malign me so? I told you—I have a plan."

Ursley sniffed derisively and leaned against the thin railing beside the street. "Some plan. We've been walking up and down this village day in and day out, with you all the time muttering about this great plan you have. All I see is that we are the ones who should be in that shop, for my boots are nearly worn through."

"Have you no faith in me? I knew she'd show up in the village sooner or later. It was too risky, trying to let her get a look at us at Standish's house. Now, come with me!" Grabbing her son by the elbow so that she could pull him into the small lane that ran beside the shop, Amity delivered a sharp slap to his cheek, just to be certain she had gained his undivided attention, then whispered, "Now listen to me and do precisely as I say."

"*Ow!* That hurt, Mama," Ursley whined, rubbing his stinging face. "You always do that. Why do you *always* do that."

Amity ignored him, leaning forward so that mother and son were nose to nose. "We can't afford to bungle. Now, this is what you must do…"

CAROLINE WAS CONFUSED. There were so many pretty slippers and jean half boots, so many lovely colors and styles, that she couldn't make up her mind. Some she could have worn straight out of the shop, while some would take at least a week to be handcrafted to her measurements and then delivered. She would take the black slippers, of course, and perhaps the pink satin with the lovely grosgrain bows at the toe, but could she really decline a pair of white dancing slippers without regretting their absence?

"Oh, Susan," she said on a sigh, sitting back against the hard wooden chair to gaze down at her outstretched feet. "These are absolutely lovely. But I only have two feet, don't I? I really mustn't be greedy. Which do you prefer, the pink or the white?"

Susan, who had never owned more than two pair of shoes in her life—the ones on her feet and the ones she had just worn out—only shook her head. "It's perishin' difficult, miss, fer sure," she agreed, then spied the cobbler leaning over his counter to get a better look at Caroline's carelessly displayed shapely lower legs. "But, please, miss, lower yer skirts. Yer ankles are stickin' out for all the world and his wife to goggle at."

Caroline looked up to see the cobbler turning away, a sheepish expression on his face. "Sorry, Susan," she said, wondering yet again if she really was a lady of quality, for she seemed sadly prone to behaving like the worst sort of wayward creature. "I think I'll take these black ones and order the white ones. And the riding boots, of course. That goes without saying.''

The door to the shop opened and a man entered, a young man dressed in what, considering the way he strutted into the place, he must have believed to be the height of fashion. He was not overly tall—not much taller than Caroline herself—and rather underfed, even hungry-looking, with a nose that could only be called unfortunate. His hair, once he had tipped his curly brimmed beaver jauntily in her direction and tucked it beneath his arm, was revealed to be mousy brown in color, and woefully sparse for a man so young. If Pierre Standish were to stand beside him, or even Sir John Oakvale, the man would escape notice, even if his hair suddenly caught fire.

Caroline quickly took all this in, then just as swiftly dismissed the gentleman from her mind and turned her attention back to her toes, wiggling them in pleasure as she realized that the slippers were a perfect fit.

''Good morning to you, you lovely creature,'' Ursley Merrydell drawled, making an elegant leg in front of Caroline. ''I was just passing by this charming shop, out on the strut as it were, when I chanced to peep through the window and see you sitting here. As soon as I did my heart was smitten by your lovely face and form. Might I be so bold as to ask you to join me at the local inn for a repast—and possibly even greater pleasures?''

Caroline's jaw dropped a fraction as she stared up at the author of such an audacious speech. How dare he accost a gently reared female in this way? The man didn't look bosky. Or was it obvious that she *wasn't* what she hoped she was, and this strange man had instinctively recognized her as the sort of fast female who would welcome his less than innocent advances?

She was figuratively nailed to her chair by his words, and before she could think of a reply, Susan, who was standing behind Caroline, rushed into angry speech. ''Away with yer now, yer filthy beast. This here lady's under Mr. André Standish's protection.''

Ursley leered down at Caroline. ''Standish's turtledove, are you? Well, from what I hear, he's away from home right now. And while the cat's away—'' He didn't finish his sentence, only reached down to take hold of Caroline's upper arm and pulled her to her feet.

Caroline tried to shake him off, turning her head to yell to the cobbler, ''Do something, for pity's sake!'' just to have the cobbler retreat at once through the curtain at the back of his shop, leaving her alone with only Susan for protection. ''Oh, that's just fine!'' Caroline exploded, realizing that if she were going to be shed of this manhandling brute she would have to do it herself.

Her attacker now had both his hands on her, drawing her toward his descending mouth. ''You'll get no order from me!'' she yelled to the cowardly shopkeeper, twisting her head from side to side, trying to elude Ursley's lips. Why did she have to be so small? Even this skinny snake could hold her immobile with ease. Tears of frustration stung her eyes, which made her even angrier. ''Let go of me, or I'll bite your ugly nose!'' she warned impotently, for she could not move so much as an inch, his grip was so firm. Then, suddenly, her body went very still. Didn't she know this man? Hadn't they met somewhere before? No, it was impossible. If he knew her he would have immediately said something, would have called her by name.

Susan raced around the chair to begin whipping pieces of rock-hard candy straight at Ursley's head, screaming for him to ''leave go, afore I brains yer!'' while Caroline did her best to kick her attacker in the shins. It was unbelievable! She was being attacked right in the middle of the village, and in broad daylight.

The door to the shop slammed open and an older woman bounded through the door, her reticule already swinging above her head much the way David must have swung his slingshot as he prepared to slay Goliath. "Away with you, you nasty varlet!" she screamed at the top of her lungs, the reticule connecting with Ursley's head for at least a half-dozen bruising blows. "Is there no safety for poor unguarded females in this terrible place!" With her free hand drawn into a tight fist, she then began beating against Ursley's back, causing him to stagger slightly and ease his hold on Caroline.

"Hey, not so hard!" he protested, turning to look at this new threat.

"If I were a man, I'd horsewhip you!" the lady warned fiercely, brandishing her reticule yet again. "I'm weary unto death with watching you young jackanapes assault unprotected females. A dozen years or more I've chaperoned young ladies of good birth and breeding, keeping them safe from the likes of you. Run along, varlet, or I'll have the constable on you!"

Ursley, who was feeling battered, threw the woman a foul look and made a break for the door, only to slip on one of Susan's pieces of candy ammunition, sense his feet sliding out from beneath him, and go crashing to the floor. His curly brimmed beaver, his most recent and therefore most prized possession, broke his fall, giving its life to save its owner. "Oh, no, not my beaver!" he exclaimed, sounding perilously close to tears.

By this time Caroline had recovered and was the next one to attack, picking up a nearby wooden clog that had obviously been fashioned to fit a very large foot and promptly tapping Ursley sharply atop his sparsely haired head. "Assault defenseless women, will you? Sit still, so I can hit you again!"

Scrambling on all fours, Ursley reached the doorway and quickly hauled himself up by grabbing on to the still open door. "Fie on you!" he shouted dramatically, waving a fist in the air, his other hand clutching the worse-for-wear headgear. "I wouldn't have tried my evil wiles on you had I known you had a chaperone."

A moment later he was gone, running down the flagway toward the safety of the inn, cursing his mother's heavy-handedness with the reticule and wishing he had not allowed himself to be a part of this charade.

Caroline, seated once more in her chair, fanned herself with her new handkerchief. "Where is your chaperone, miss, so that I might put a flea in her ear for leaving her charge unguarded?" her rescuer asked, dabbing at her damp upper lip with the edge of her sleeve.

Caroline looked up at the tall, angular, rawboned woman who had so recently wielded her reticule like a regular Trojan, and smiled. "I have no chaperone, ma'am," she told her. "I am the ward of André Standish, but it is a male household. However, I should very much like to take you to meet Pierre Standish, who is in charge of me in his father's absence. I do believe he would like to deliver his thanks to you in person, for he is endlessly concerned for my well-being."

Ignoring this invitation, the woman frowned, bringing her heavy black brows crashing together over the bridge of her nose. "No chaperone? It's unthinkable!" She fell silent, biting her bottom lip as if considering something known only to her. "Excuse me, miss, but are you happy without a proper chaperone, without some other gently raised female to bear you company and instruct you in how to go along? I am between positions now, having had my last charge married off quite successfully. If you would wish to engage my services, at least until your guardian can find a suitable chaperone of his own choosing, I should be happy to show you my references."

It was Caroline's turn to frown. She hadn't really thought about it. Susan was her companion, of sorts, although she wasn't much of a conversationalist. Then again, Susan couldn't sit at the dinner table as a buffer between her and Pierre. She most certainly couldn't have saved her from Pierre's kiss last night in the drawing room.

A chaperone. Caroline smiled. What a splendid idea. A chaperone would go a long way toward putting a spoke in Pierre's wheels, wouldn't it? Rising, she held out her hands. "Excuse me for being so rude, but I do want to offer you my heartfelt thanks for saving me from that brute. My name is Caroline Addams, and you're—?"

"Caroline Addams? If you say—er, I'm Mrs. Merrydell, Mrs. Amity Merrydell," Amity offered quickly, taking Caroline's hand in her much larger one and shaking it heartily as a smile split her long, horsey face. "I know the way of it was unfortunate, Miss Addams, but I must say that it's a pleasure to meet you."

Caroline tipped her head to one side, gazing up at the tall, rather formidable-looking woman whose strong grip was in danger of crushing her fingers. Pierre would dislike the slightly overwhelming woman on sight. Wasn't that just terrible? Caroline smiled, feeling very pleased with herself. She would do nicely. Oh, yes, Mrs. Amity Merrydell would do very nicely indeed. "Oh, on the contrary, Mrs. Merrydell," she corrected sweetly, "I do believe that, in this case, the pleasure is entirely mine."

"I HATE MY MOTHER," Ursley Merrydell muttered morosely, staring drunkenly at his battered hat as he sat in a corner of the common room at the small inn. "She's mean, and she's nasty, and she likes hitting me. She's a hateful, hateful woman."

He picked up his mug of ale, his fourth in less than an hour, and drained its contents in one long gulp. "Nasty woman," he said again, gingerly touching his fingertips to the side of his head, tracing the edges of the small lump that had been raised by something heavy in his mother's reticule.

"Probably a rock she put in there, just for me. She's a nasty woman. Nasty, nasty, nasty."

She always had a plan, his mother did. Ursley had grown up listening to his mother's plans, the endless schemes she had concocted, designed to make them rich with only a minimum of effort. She and his father had once worked together, but that was all over now because his father had learned to love his gin too much and had bungled one too many of those neverending schemes.

"Poor Dada," Ursley said, his lower lip quivering as he considered his dead father, this time with sympathy for what must have been a wretched lifetime spent with Amity. "Why did I have to take after you? Why couldn't I have been big, like Mama? She hits so hard, Dada. I don't like it when she hits me. And after I was the one who figured out all about this losing her memory business in the first place. Mama wouldn't have had a plan at all if it weren't for me."

Ursley was seven and twenty, old enough by far to be on his own, if only he knew it, which he didn't. He had relied on his mother for all of his life, and it hadn't occurred to him to do things any other way. Most of the time she treated him very well, telling him how she loved him and buying him pretty things. It was only at moments like this, when she was hot on a plan, that she turned mean. And it was only at times like this, when Ursley was hurting, that a small, niggling thought having something to do with putting an ocean between himself and his battering mother appealed to him.

But there was all that lovely money to consider. He waved his hand halfheartedly at the barmaid, who plunked another heavy mug of ale in front of him, some of the dark, foamy liquid slopping over the top to splash on his hat. "Cow," he said, sneering as her generously rounded hips swished away from his table toward a group of men who had just come through the door. Ursley sneered not because he was angry but because he had earlier asked her to come up to his room after closing and she had laughed in his face.

Money. That's what he needed. The barmaid wouldn't laugh at him if he had gold to dangle in front of her greedy little face. Nobody would laugh then. And nobody would hit him, not ever again.

He lifted the mug and drank deeply. He'd go along with his mother's plan for now. He had seen her ride out of the village in the Standish carriage, and he acknowledged her plan certainly appeared to be working. If the rest went as well, they'd soon have more money than they'd ever dreamed of—lovely money, and a house all their own. Then his mother would take him to London for a Season, and he would marry a beautiful heiress who would bring them even more lovely money. It was a marvelous plan, a wonderful idea, and he still believed it, because it was a nice thing to believe.

But he wouldn't wait forever. If his abused head hadn't taught him anything else, it had taught him that he was all but through listening to Mama.

CHAPTER ELEVEN

PIERRE PACED the Aubusson carpet that covered the floor of his father's study, mentally ticking off the passing seconds on the mantel clock with each long, impatient stride and idly wondering if he was fast on his way to losing his senses.

Caroline had not been gone above two hours, surely not an unconscionable amount of time for a trip to the village and back, with space in there somewhere for whatever wildly expensive purchases she had decided upon as a perfect punishment for his unseemly advances last night before dinner. Besides, Susan was with her, as were his own coachman and a burly groom he had sent along for good measure. What could possibly happen to her?

Nothing could happen to her. He was overreacting, that was all, scratching around the barnyard like a hysterical old hen with but a single chick. He was taking this Good Deed thing beyond the bounds of common sense, and it was all his beloved father's fault. His beloved, *absent* father.

André's defection bothered Pierre, not because the man had gone to London, but because it had not occurred to Pierre that he would. He was slipping; he should have seen it coming. But Pierre, as his father had accused, had become over-weeningly arrogant, and had forgotten that André had taught him everything he knew.

Obviously the teacher had thought it was time to give the student another lesson: never assume. Pierre knew he had *assumed* his father would react in a certain way and had proceeded to base his own actions on that assumption. He should have known his father had always made it a point never to do the expected.

André was off somewhere, doing typical André things, which could mean anything from selecting just the sort of chaperone he would wish for Caroline, to discovering, in his own inimitable way, his ward's true identity.

"Both, probably," Pierre said aloud, shaking his head. "While reducing his son to the role of nursemaid." He stopped his interminable pacing for, besides making him look silly, the exercise was wearying, and he sank into a chair. This wasn't like him; it wasn't like him at all. He enjoyed being an observer, but a contributing observer, not just an impotent bystander relegated to a minor role.

He could have hired a man, a dozen men, to ensure Caroline's safety. That was elementary. Discovering who she was, who was intent on harming her, and why—those were important things.

"Obviously too important to entrust to a mere son," Pierre remarked to the empty room. "I do believe I am insulted. Now, what in blazes was that?"

He had heard the sound of something breakable hitting the tiled foyer floor, followed by a deep, masculine shout. Pierre only had time to turn his head toward the sound before the door crashed open, banging loudly against the wall, and Jeremy charged into the room, looking back over his shoulder as if the hounds of hell were after him.

"Yer'll not git yer maggoty mitts on me agin, yer beetle-browed bogey!" he shouted as he ran. "Oi'm not goin' no-wheres with the likes of yer!"

Pierre stood up in time to catch Jeremy by the shoulders, effectively halting him in his tracks. "I assume there's some reasonable explanation for this interruption, my young friend?" he asked, looking over Jeremy's head to the hallway. "There are, after all, more elegant ways of entering a room."

Jeremy looked up at Pierre, his eyes wide with fright even as a new determination squared his jaw. "'E's not gonna snaffle me, is 'e, guv'nor? Yer said yer wuz gonna take me ter Piccadilly. Yer can't lets 'im take me."

"I don't recall expressing any wish to be shed of you," Pierre responded, "although I must admit that the lapse amazes even me." He released Jeremy's shoulders, only to have the boy fall to the carpet and wrap his arms convulsively around Pierre's knees. "I think it only fair to warn you, brat, that I am known to dislike dramatic displays," he added, looking down at Jeremy's fuzzy yellow head.

"There yer be, yer dirty, snivelin' heathen!"

Pierre looked up to see that there was now a very large, very dirty man standing on his father's lovely Aubusson carpet. He pointed out as much to the man. "You're standing on my father's Aubusson carpet, my good fellow," he said, his voice smooth as finest velvet. "My gratitude would know no bounds if you would remove your boots from it at once."

The man halted in his tracks, looked about as if wondering how he had happened to enter the elegant room, then backed up until his boots were once more touching polished wood, two feet away from the carpet.

"I do so admire obedience," Pierre complimented, nodding in the man's direction. "I don't believe we've been introduced. Master Holloway—as you appear to have the advantage of knowing the name of our unexpected visitor—would you be so kind as to do the honors?"

Jeremy spoke from the presumed safety of his position, still at Pierre's feet. He was safe now, he was sure, as the "guv'nor" was all powerful and would let no harm come to him. "Dat's 'im, the sweep. Dat's ol' 'Awkins. 'E's come ter do yer da's chimleys an' spotted me. Slit 'is slimy gizzard, guv'nor! Chop up 'is liver an' lights an' feed 'em ter the crows!"

"So bloodthirsty, Master Holloway. I cannot fathom why

you and Duvall do not hit it off. You have so much in common." Pierre's left eyebrow lifted fractionally as he turned his attention back to the man. "So, you're Mr. Hawkins?" he remarked silkily. "This young lad has mentioned you more than once, as you've made a strong impression on him—most frequently with a fireplace poker, as I recall. I must say I'm surprised. My compliments to you. I hadn't thought a creature such as you could actually walk upright."

The sweep master's huge hands bunched into tight fists, and he took two steps forward, his boots once again on the carpet.

"Tut-tut!" Pierre admonished pleasantly. "The carpet, sir, if you'll recall."

Hawkins backed up, although if anyone had asked him why he had done so he would have been hard-pressed to explain. The gentry mort hadn't been born that could scare Jacky Hawkins. There was just something about this particular one that had made him consider a small retreat preferable to whatever unspoken alternative Pierre Standish might have in mind. His voice rose, to cover his sudden attack of cowardliness. "Dat there boy belongs ter me," he whined, pointing a grimy finger at Jeremy. "Oi paid fer him right an' tight. Oi don't want no trouble, guv'nor. Oi only wants wot's mine."

Pierre appeared to be unmoved by Hawkins's logic. "Master Holloway," he questioned softly, "much as I have recently developed a most prodigious aversion to assumption, may I assume that you do not wish to reenter Mr. Hawkins's employ?"

"Oi'd druther 'ave a bleedin' stick stuffed up m' nose!" Jeremy lifted his head to demonstrate, with the use of his index finger. "Jist like this!"

Pierre shuddered delicately. "There you have it, Mr. Hawkins, straight from the boy's, er, mouth. Now, if you'll excuse us, I believe this young man and I have wearied of this conversation. Please be so good as to close the door behind you as you leave the room and, I believe, this house. Your services are no longer required.''

Hawkins slammed his hamlike fists against his hips as his face turned a violent purple. "Oi ain't steppin' one foot nowheres till Oi 'ave that kiddy back right an' tight. 'E's mine, Oi says.''

"Yes, you did say, Mr. Hawkins," Pierre said consideringly. "How fatiguing it is to listen to it a second time, for it now becomes my sad chore to repeat myself by again requesting your immediate departure.''

Hawkins knew he could break Pierre Standish in half, just as if he were a dry stick. He was twice his size, wasn't he, and no stranger to fighting. So why was he standing there like a stuffed bear, doing nothing? Why, indeed? He took one step onto the carpet.

Pierre's left eyebrow rose the merest fraction.

"Oi'm out good blunt for that worthless brat!" Hawkins shouted, shaking his fist at Jeremy. But for all his bellowing, he didn't bring his second foot forward.

"Are you suggesting that I reimburse you, Mr. Hawkins?" Pierre smiled, and Hawkins shivered. "I'm afraid I shall have to disappoint you there, as I do not traffic in human souls, either in the buying or the selling of them.''

"Oi'll have the law on yer! Yer nuthin' but a thievin' lowdown bastard!''

"Oh, dear, really?" Pierre leaned down to touch Jeremy's shoulder. "Excuse me, Master Holloway, but I must implore you to remove your arms, as I believe your convulsive grip has served to put my feet to sleep. Ah, thank you, that's much better.'' He stepped away from the child without moving closer to Hawkins.

"Don't leave me, guv'nor!" Jeremy screeched, panic-stricken at this seeming desertion by the one man he had grown to trust. "Wot are yer gonna do now?"

Pierre turned back to the boy, smiling widely. "Do, Master Holloway? Why, I would have thought you'd know. I'm going to challenge our Mr. Hawkins to a duel, as any gentleman must do when his honesty and honour have been impugned. First I will slap him, with a glove or handkerchief of course, as I would not wish to soil my hand, and then I shall ask Mr. Hawkins to name his weapon of choice. I favor pistols, or even swords, but as I have not had the chance for more than a few rounds with Gentleman Jackson in these past months, fisticuffs would appeal to me as well. What say you, Mr. Hawkins?"

Pierre looked to where Hawkins had been standing a moment earlier, to see that the room was now empty of anyone save Jeremy and himself.

"How odd," he remarked, shaking his head. "It would appear, Master Holloway, that your Mr. Hawkins has undergone a change of heart. Pity. A duel would have filled an hour nicely."

Jeremy hopped to his feet, punching the air as he danced about the room in imitation of some bruiser he had once seen perform an impromptu demonstration of the manly science of fisticuffs on a street corner. "Yer woulda kilt 'im, guv'nor," he assured Pierre. "Yer woulda shoved yer fives right square in 'is ivories, so dat 'is daylights popped out. It'd 'ave been grand ter see ol' 'Awkins arsy varsey, 'is applecart spilled, guv'nor. Real grand! Wot a sight fer sore eyes it'd 'ave been!"

"Please remember that a gentleman is never vulgar in victory, Master Holloway, any more than he is ungracious in defeat," Pierre admonished, patting the boy on the head. "Now run off and see if you can be of some help in the kitchens. Or you might wish for me to ring for Duvall, so that you might have another bath?"

Jeremy ran from the room as fast as his legs would carry him, and Pierre settled once more into a chair, looking toward the mantel clock and wondering where the devil Caroline could be, the incident with Hawkins, which had been at best only a small diversion, already forgotten.

It never occurred to him, that, had Caroline seen his protection of Jeremy, her low opinion of him would have undergone a considerable change for the better.

THE NEARER THE carriage carried her to Standish Court the more apprehensive Caroline became about her impetuous decision to employ Mrs. Merrydell.

The woman was not at all what she would have had in mind for a chaperone, if indeed she had ever considered the requirements for such a person.

Her references, which the woman had produced from the single piece of luggage that the coachman had picked up from the local inn and insisted Caroline read as they rode along in the carriage, were impeccable; three letters, all signed by titled ladies whose penmanship was only slightly superior to their imaginative spelling.

It was the woman herself who bothered Caroline. She was loud, for one thing, and rather coarse, and had a disconcerting habit of nudging Caroline none too gently in the ribs to emphasize her stories of how she had contrived to successfully "pop off" many an eligible young miss in her time.

Knowing that her own language could at times stray embarrassingly close to the barracks, Caroline tried hard to overcome her objections to Mrs. Merrydell's speech, but there was a world of difference between a good swear-word when it fit the situation and talking openly about such things as "firm little titties" when the woman described the physical attributes of her last charge.

What had begun as a ploy to infuriate Pierre Standish had rapidly descended into a ticklish situation that was, among other things, fast giving Caroline the headache. Even Susan, who was for the most part a placid sort, was showing signs of wishing to stuff something in Mrs. Merrydell's mouth in order to shut her up.

As the carriage stopped in front of the main entrance to Standish Court, Caroline soothed herself with the thought that Pierre would have Mrs. Merrydell's measure in less than a heartbeat, and would immediately show her the door, if only to thwart his unloved Good Deed. He would instinctively know that she had engaged the woman only to inconvenience him and would refuse to allow her to remain as chaperone.

She smiled as the groom lowered the steps and held out his hand to help her down. Pierre would take care of everything. For once she was glad for his interference in her life.

Leading the way, Caroline swept across the foyer after learning Pierre's whereabouts from the footman, ignoring something he tried to tell her about a rare goings-on just having taken place, and knocked at André's study door. "Come along, Mrs. Merrydell, and meet your new employer," she urged as that woman hesitated a moment, assessing a large vase that stood in a corner of the foyer as if considering what price it would bring in the open market.

When no one called for her to enter, Caroline knocked a second time, then opened the door.

"Ah, Miss Addams," Pierre drawled, rising languidly from his chair. "Please forgive me for not begging you to enter, but I was enjoying the notion that there are still people in this world who ask permission to enter a room. You've concluded your visit to the village?"

Caroline stood in the doorway, not understanding what he was referring to and suddenly reluctant to enter. He seemed inordinately happy, and that disturbed her. "I have," she answered shortly.

"And now you've come to show me your purchases. How gratifying. Please, don't hover in the doorway. Come in, and let me see what you've got. There wouldn't be a surprise for me, would there?"

She tipped her head to one side, as if considering the question. "Wel-l-l, *actually*," she began, sliding her hands behind her back and crossing her fingers for luck, "there is one little surprise."

"Really? I am, of course, breathless to learn more," Pierre told her, advancing across the room. "Now what, I must ask myself, would Miss Addams consider to be a suitable gift for me?"

"Oooff!" Caroline felt a none-too-gentle poke in the back and staggered three full steps into the room.

"Enough of this shilly-shallying!" Mrs. Merrydell protested, pushing past Caroline to confront Pierre. "This here gel was being attacked in the village, no thanks to you, until I came to her rescue. No chaperone," she said, shaking her head. "It's shameful, that's what it is. But that's all over now, for Amity Merrydell is here. Are you the one who is in charge? You look mighty young to me. There isn't anything havey-cavey going on, is there? I'm a good woman, and I won't be a party to any shifty dealings."

Pierre, staring past Mrs. Merrydell to Caroline, blinked once, then waited for his Good Deed to speak.

"I—she—that is, I—hired her," Caroline gulped out, wondering if that bump on her head had proved to shake out her common sense as well as her memory. She must be the victim of a temporary mental aberration! How else could she explain Mrs. Merrydell?

Pierre nodded. "You hired her," he repeated, his voice calm. "I see."

And he did see. He saw everything. That was what was so maddening. He always saw everything, drat him anyway. Caroline longed to fly at him and shake him into reacting. "A strange man made advances toward me while I was being fitted for some shoes—lovely shoes, in white, and a black pair, and some riding boots as well, but that's nothing to the point now, is it?—and Mrs. Merrydell rescued me and, and

I hired her as my chaperone.'' He'd done it again—he had her babbling like the village idiot!

"How very enterprising of you,'' Pierre said coolly, but he was looking at Mrs. Merrydell as he said it. "Please excuse me—Mrs. Merrydell, I believe you said? You must think I am the rudest beast in nature. Won't you ladies be seated while I ring for some refreshments. You must both still be terribly overset. Only then will I prevail upon you for details of what must have been a truly terrifying ordeal.''

"That's it?'' Caroline asked incredulously, unable and unwilling to believe Pierre was taking her news so well. "That's all you have to say?''

He tugged on the bell rope, then turned to look at her inquiringly. "What else is there to say? I should have liked to have been there, to protect you, but we were fortunate enough to have found a protector in the so estimable Mrs. Merrydell, who immediately took you under her wing. You seem to have no end of protectors, Miss Addams, which is fortunate for you, as you seem to have an inordinate need for protection.

"Mrs. Merrydell?'' he said, looking toward the woman now seated comfortably in his father's chair. "Do you by chance play the harp? My father and I would so enjoy it if you could instruct Miss Addams in its use. Oh dear, I can see by your expression that you do not. A pity, but there it is. Doubtless you have many other skills. Ah, Hartley, there you are, prompt as usual. Would you be so kind as to procure some refreshments for the ladies? Ladies, just tell Hartley every little thing you require.''

Caroline stomped across the room to stand toe-to-toe with Pierre. "I don't *require* anything, you dolt,'' she hissed at him from behind clenched teeth. "Why are you doing this? You know full well Mrs. Merrydell is completely unacceptable. I only brought her to upset you. For God's sake—*get rid of her!*''

Pierre waved a hand at Mrs. Merrydell, who was busily ordering a meal fit for a smithy who had just completed twelve full hours at his forge, and drawled urbanely, "Why, Caroline, my dear, whatever do you mean? I think Mrs. Merrydell is an admirable choice for a chaperone. Sturdy, firmminded, and not about to take any nonsense. Just what I would have wished for you myself."

"I *despise* you," Caroline whispered harshly, knowing that he had bested her once again.

Pierre lifted her chin with one long finger and smiled down into her face. "No, darling girl, you don't. Why that pleases me I am not sure, but I am confident I will work it out in time. Now, be a good little charge and go have some tea. I just remembered that I have somehow promised Master Holloway a chess lesson this afternoon."

Caroline was staring at him, unable to move. "A—a chess lesson?" she asked, incredulous.

"Yes," he answered, letting go of her chin. "My kindness astonishes even me. Ladies, your most obedient," he said, bowing elegantly before leaving Caroline alone in the room with a grinning Mrs. Merrydell.

CHAPTER TWELVE

THE DOCTOR LEANED over Caroline as he examined the bump on her head. "Ah, good, very good. The swelling has gone down quite nicely, Miss Addams, as I'm sure you are already aware. Physically, I would say you have completely recovered, which is no great surprise for, as I told Mr. Standish after the first examination, you are young and healthy."

"Young, healthy and *anonymous,* Doctor Burgess," Caroline pointed out.

The doctor frowned his concern. "You've remembered nothing?"

Glad his examination was over, she patted her hair back in place, "Mere snatches, Doctor Burgess. Nothing that means anything."

"Snatches? You've remembered snatches? What sort of snatches?" Mrs. Merrydell, who had been sitting at her ease in a corner of the bedchamber, hastily hopped to her feet to approach her charge in what could only be termed a challenging manner. "Naughty, secretive girl. You only said you had lost your memory in an accident. You told me nothing of snatches!"

Caroline, who had wearied of Mrs. Merrydell's constant company within minutes of meeting her and who had—thanks to that perverse Pierre Standish—had to endure the crude woman from morning to night for three full days, ignored this latest outburst and directed her reply to the doctor. "I know that I can ride, paint and dance. Nothing more. Nothing even remotely personal."

"I see," said Doctor Burgess, frowning down on her from overtop his spectacles.

"Wonderful!" exclaimed Mrs. Merrydell, adding quickly, "That is to say, it's a start, my dear, a start. You shouldn't force yourself to remember—should she, Doctor? I mean, it might be injurious—to her spleen, or something."

Doctor Burgess who, if truth be told, had no real knowledge of Caroline's particular complaint outside of the meager bits he had gleaned from one of his medical books, hastily agreed with the woman. "That goes without saying, Mrs. Merrydell. We wouldn't wish to fall victim to a brain fever, would we?"

Caroline looked back and forth between the two faces hovering above her and shook her head. "No, I imagine *we* wouldn't. But what if I never remember who I am? I can't spend the remainder of my life not knowing my own name. I would surely go insane."

"Oh, but we can't count on—that is, we shouldn't even *think* of such a terrible thing! Most assuredly not!" Mrs. Merrydell protested, grabbing Caroline's two hands and squeezing them convulsively. "You will just have to take each day as it comes, my dear. Isn't that the ticket, Doctor?"

Doctor Burgess was beginning to tire of his role as acquiescent bystander and walked to the side table to retrieve his bag. He snapped it closed with some force. The Merrydell woman wasn't a doctor, after all. It was time he took charge of the situation. "I begin to think Miss Addams must have some terrible secret locked inside her memory, some awful event that has made it preferable for her to forget everything that has happened to her. This might be the time to call in the local constable. Perhaps he can shed some light on the situation."

"The constable!" Caroline and Mrs. Merrydell cried in unison.

Now the center of attention, Doctor Burgess nodded

thoughtfully. "The constable," he repeated solemnly. "If there has been any terrible accident in the neighborhood he would know of it, as well as whether or not a young lady of Miss Addams's description has gone missing. Yes, I think that is a sterling idea. I wonder why Mr. Standish hasn't thought of it himself."

"Ah, good doctor, but he has."

Three heads turned to see Pierre Standish standing in the doorway, his arms folded across his chest. "Pierre!" Caroline cried, hopping down from the bed to approach him. "You spoke with the constable about me?" She couldn't decide if she should be glad that he had exerted himself for her or angry that he had thought she was notorious enough to be known to the local constable.

Taking her elbow so that he could lead her to a nearby chair, Pierre answered, "Not I, actually, but my father. He ordered a thorough inquiry to be launched throughout the district, but to no avail. So sorry to disappoint you, Doctor, but that is neither here nor there, is it? How is our patient? Will she live?"

Doctor Burgess cleared his throat and puffed out his chest, clearly taking full credit for what he told Pierre was Miss Addams's astonishing recovery from a terrible blow to the head. "There is no reason for me to attend her again, unless you wish me to, of course. There is really nothing else I can do for her at this time."

Mrs. Merrydell was quick to agree, pointing out that she was in charge now and perfectly capable of supervising Miss Addams's welfare. "She's in no danger while *I'm* about!" she ended determinedly.

"Danger, Miss Merrydell?" Pierre repeated, his smooth voice tinged with surprise. "Whoever said Miss Addams was in any danger? Surely I haven't spoken of danger. We were speaking only of unfortunate accidents, I believe."

Taking refuge in righteous anger, Mrs. Merrydell placed

her hands on her hips and challenged hotly, "And just who was it who saved her from that cheeky dandy in the village, Mr. Standish? There is no end of danger to a well-bred young woman left to fend for herself. Heaven only knows what trouble she could have gotten herself into if *I* hadn't been there to save her."

Caroline shook her head slowly as she rose to cross to the bed, wearied to death by Mrs. Merrydell's constant repetition of her bravery in rescuing her at the shoemaker's. "I think I should like to lie down for a while, if you don't mind," she said in a voice all but dripping with maidenly fatigue, hoping everyone would take her hint and withdraw so that she might have a moment's peace. "We can regroup at luncheon to hear, while eating our stuffed capon, Mrs. Merrydell's hundredth reenactment of her daring rescue."

"Well! That's gratitude for you," Mrs. Merrydell said, sniffing. "Not that I'm not used to it, as a chaperone often feels she has taken a viper to her bosom," she added as she headed for the hallway. "Doctor Burgess, please allow me to show you the door."

Caroline stretched out on the satin coverlet, closing her weary eyes. Her headache, which had abated within hours of her awakening after the accident, had returned at almost the exact moment Mrs. Merrydell had entered her life, the constant dull ache behind her eyes showing every indication of becoming a permanent part of her. She would do anything—anything—to be shed of the woman.

"Another headache, Caroline?" Pierre questioned solicitously, startling her, for his voice came from directly beside the bed. "I wouldn't want to think you were going into a sad decline. Father would be so angry with me. Is there anything I can do?"

Without opening her eyes, she suggested dully, "You could have dear, sweet Mrs. Amity Merrydell bound and gagged and set on a freighter heading for the West Indies at dawn. That would go a long way toward alleviating my pain.''

''No,'' he answered, chuckling softly at her show of vehemence. ''As much as I regret it, I cannot do that. I still have need of the woman.''

Caroline's eyes popped open and she glared at him. ''Whatever for? Or have you not yet wearied of your latest revenge on me? I admit it, the woman was a mistake. I only brought her here to get some of my own back on you. I never thought you'd open your father's house to her.'' Her eyes narrowed as a sudden thought hit her. ''What do you know that I don't know?''

Pierre reached down to stroke a finger along Caroline's jaw. ''Almost everything, infant, almost everything. Have a nice nap and we'll take this up later, as I'm sure you will not be satisfied until you have asked me at least a dozen new questions, for which, I regret, I as yet have no answers.''

As CAROLINE SUSPECTED, luncheon with Pierre and Mrs. Merrydell did not shed any new light on either her identity or Pierre's reason for allowing Mrs. Merrydell to continue to run tame in his father's household. In fact, other than to ask some probing questions concerning her chaperone's last few employment situations, Pierre kept the conversation very light and very general. All in all, if it wasn't for cook's disarming way with capons, the meal would have been a total waste of Caroline's time.

Hoping that putting some fresh air and distance between herself and her resident dragon would serve to clear her head, Caroline changed into her riding habit immediately after luncheon and departed for the stables. The first person she met there was Jeremy, whom, she realized, she hadn't seen in several days.

''How are you going on, Jeremy?'' she asked conversationally while waiting for the groom to saddle Lady, the mare

Pierre had set aside for her personal use. Lady was a far cry from Obtuse, but she was spirited enough, and Caroline had already grown to love her gentle ways.

"Oi'm learnin' ter be a groom, missy," he told her proudly, standing tall. "Oi doesn't like it much bein' inside, so guv'nor 'as me workin' 'ere. Oi've all but decided not ter go back ta Piccadilly. Did yer 'ear 'ow guv'nor set ol' 'Awkins ter the rightabout? It waz a rare sight ter see, Oi tells yer, a rare sight!"

"Guv—er, Mr. Standish routed your former master?" she asked, sorting through Jeremy's heavily accented slang. "I knew a sweep was coming, of course, but I never thought it could have been *your* sweep. Oh, this is delicious. Tell me about it."

As she urged Lady into a canter that would not outdistance the groom Pierre had assigned to her, Caroline considered all that Jeremy had told her. Even leaving off some of the lad's sure to be broad exaggerations, Pierre had done a wonderful thing, a wonderfully unselfish thing, by defending the little sweep. "And it was totally out of character," she mused aloud. "I will never understand the man. Not that I wish to," she added hastily, the memory of Pierre's kiss once again entering her mind unbidden.

Pierre was a puzzle she was not ready to solve, for her own puzzle, the one of her true identity, must necessarily take first place of importance in her mind. All her energies must be—had to be—directed toward learning who she really was. The doctor's words returned to her, making her wonder if she could have been involved in some sort of carriage accident, hitting her head and then wandering off, only to faint in the roadway where Pierre had first seen her.

It seemed a logical explanation, but if there had been an accident surely André Standish's inquiries would have discovered the event. No, there had to be another reason for what had happened to her.

She continued to ride Lady across the open fields, the breeze lifting her dark curls and putting an attractive blush on her cheeks. She thought about the cloak she had been wearing, the man's cloak she had examined without a hint of recognition. Where had the cloak come from? Who had it belonged to? Why had she been wearing it, instead of some cloak of her own?

"And I was barefoot," she said aloud, Lady's pointed ears flicking alertly at the sound of her mistress's voice. "How far could I have gone on foot without shoes? Not any great distance, surely. After all, my feet were barely bruised."

Out of the corner of her eyes she saw a lone horseman approaching, and shivered in sudden panic, only to relax when she recognized the handsome, vacant face of Sir John Oakvale. She smiled as he waved gaily and "yoo-hooed" her, silently admonishing herself for becoming so skittish over the doctor's speculative prattling and Mrs. Merrydell's melodramatic ramblings about danger. She was in no danger; the idea was ridiculous! Of course, there had been that man in the gardens, she reminded herself fleetingly, but the incident had come to nothing. Determinedly widening her smile, she banished her dark thoughts.

"Good afternoon to you, Miss Addams," Sir John said, pulling his mount up beside Lady so that the horses could walk together. "I was hoping to pay a call on you before this, but m' father's been ill, you understand, so I've had to curtail my social activities for a time."

"Oh, dear. Nothing serious, I hope," Caroline returned politely.

Sir John shook his head. "No, just a small tea party with the aunts and, of course, the dance over at the squire's. I really didn't miss anything of importance."

Caroline barely suppressed a giggle. "I meant your *father*, Sir John."

"You did? Of course you did!" he exclaimed, hooting

with laughter. "How silly of me. Just a touch of the gout, though it makes him growl like a bear with a sore paw. How are you going along with Pierre Standish now that his father has flown the coop? Not that you haven't got yourself a real dragon of a chaperone."

Caroline's head snapped slightly back. "Gossip, Sir John?" she admonished regally. "I would have thought gentlemen to be above such things. Have I become a topic of conversation in the neighborhood?"

Sir John cast a wary glance behind him at the groom who was riding in their wake. "No, no! Of course not! Dear me, I wouldn't think of it. It's just that it's so dashed dull in the country, you understand. A nameless young lady is just the thing to set all the biddies to tittering behind their fans. Jealous, too, I imagine, seeing as how you've captured the elusive Pierre Standish for your very own."

Caroline bristled. "I have not *captured* anyone, and do not care to do so. It's the furthest thing from my mind. You will make that perfectly clear to the ladies, won't you, Sir John?"

Sir John nodded furiously, knowing he had gone too far. "Oh, look, there's that stand of trees we visited upon our first meeting. I think my mount can outrun your mare. Shall we race, Miss Adams?"

Angry that she had allowed herself to be flustered by Sir John's mention of Pierre, Caroline immediately took up the challenge and, before the groom could utter a word of censure, the two spurred their mounts into a gallop. Sir John's mount, a showy but heavy-rumped grey, was no match for Lady, and soon Caroline was two lengths ahead of him, turning her head to laugh back at his rapidly diminishing figure.

Without warning, the sidesaddle began to shift beneath her, and she had to turn her full attention to controlling Lady, who momentarily misplaced her gentle disposition at this startling development. Hauling on the reins with more force than delicacy, for her entire body was now shifting dangerously toward the ground, Caroline clenched her teeth and held on for all she was worth.

With a sickening lurch, the girth slipped completely sideways and Caroline, her foot still in the stirrups, was flung backwards onto the ground and dragged along the surface of the field, pulled by one caught leg.

Lady's hooves flashed dangerously close to her head as clumps of dirt and sharp stones bit into her back. There was no chance to wonder how the girth had loosened, or why. She felt no pain, for there wasn't time for such an indulgence; she only knew she had to free her foot before she was either trampled or dragged to her death.

How she did it she would never know, but she raised a hand to grab convulsively onto part of the saddle and levered herself upward until she could swing her booted foot free of the stirrup. Within a heartbeat she crashed back toward the ground, only to roll over and over in the dirt until her soft body was rudely introduced to an unfortunately placed boulder that put a sudden halt to her progress.

A moment later Sir John was by her side, holding her limp hand in his and moaning, "My God, Miss Addams, please, please don't be dead. If you're dead Standish will kill me!"

PIERRE PACED the sunlit drawing room, idly wondering if he should send word to the stables to have Obtuse saddled so that he could join Caroline on her ride. He could stand the exercise, he knew, for he felt like a caged lion trapped within doors on such a fine day, but still he didn't pull the bell rope and give the order.

It would be entirely too dangerous, being alone with Caroline, with none but the birds and the horses to act as chaperones. He was too attracted to her, and she was too attracted to him.

He smiled at this last thought. Yes, Caroline Addams was attracted to him, even if she would rather die than admit it.

This attraction was a comforting yet unsettling thought. Certainly he hadn't encouraged her; quite the opposite. But it was true nevertheless, and he was secretly pleased.

It was also an impossible situation. He was years older than she, for one thing, not that anyone put much stock in such things. More important was that no one knew just who Caroline really was. She was a lady, of that he was sure; a very young, very beautiful lady of quality. But was she titled? Was she married? Was she eligible or ineligible?

And what was she eligible for? he asked himself, still pacing the carpet for all he was worth. Surely his mind wasn't running toward thoughts of matrimony? The notion was ludicrous. He, Pierre Claghorn Standish, in the role of doting bridegroom? It was past imagining.

But there was the kiss to consider, that one brief interlude when he had held her in his arms. Her touch had brought with it a startling revelation. He was vulnerable to a woman's charms—to a certain woman's charms.

Perhaps she reminded him of his mother, dressed in his mother's gowns as she was. But no. He wasn't that uncomplicated, or that gullible. It was Caroline herself who intrigued him; the Caroline whose astonishingly beautiful eyes were the unknowing mirror of her soul; the Caroline who spat fire and passion and clear, insightful intelligence; the Caroline who championed a young chimney sweep and had no idea what to do with a mouthful of unwanted kippers.

Oh, he was definitely in serious trouble, Pierre decided, shaking his head in a fine imitation of self-pity. How André would crow if he could but see him now. There was nothing else for it—he would have to ferret out her true identity as soon as possible and then put half a country between them. Perhaps an ocean wouldn't be far enough.

"Master Pierre?" Hartley's voice came from a doorway, interrupting Pierre's disquieting train of thought. "There's a lady here to see you, sir. I told her I'd ask if you're receiving today.''

''A lady?'' Pierre mused almost to himself. ''This is unexpected. Does the plot perhaps begin to thicken?'' More loudly he bade Hartley to show the lady in at once, and a few moments later a handsome young woman dressed in fashionable traveling clothes sailed through the door. ''Victoria!'' he exclaimed in real delight, holding out both hands to his visitor. ''I don't believe it. Is Patrick with you? Surely he hasn't let you out of his sight already?''

Victoria Quinton Sherbourne, now Countess Wickford, was definitely in looks this day, her soft, rose-colored gown giving a decided bloom to her cheeks, the sparkle in her intelligent eyes and the enchanting dimple in her left cheek making it possible for the people she met to forget that she was not a classically beautiful woman. Her appearance was a far cry from the too-thin, drab, sad creature Pierre had first seen in Quennel Quinton's library the day that unlovely man's will had been read. It was remarkable how being loved, and in love, could bring such marvelous changes in a person.

After allowing Pierre to kiss her on the cheek—a display of affection he had never employed with her before—she stood back, used the index finger of her left hand to push her spectacles more firmly onto her nose, and said wonderingly, ''Good Lord, Pierre, your father was correct. You *have* mellowed. I never would have believed it. Patrick will be devastated to have missed it. I must meet the young lady at once and offer her my congratulations.''

CHAPTER THIRTEEN

"AND SO," VICTORIA concluded as she sat at her ease on one of the satin settees in the drawing room a few minutes later, gracefully pouring tea into a bone china cup, "no matter how great the inducement—and I must tell you that your father has quite a way with explanation, revealing just enough to pique an overwhelming interest and not a jot more—there was just no possible way for Patrick to abandon his project at such a crucial point and join me on this terribly unsubtle, curiosity-satisfying expedition."

"Expedition?" Pierre cut in, waving away her offer of tea and hot buttered scones in favor of a slightly stronger liquid refreshment. "Does dearest Patrick believe I am a mountain to be climbed? I assure you, I am the most uncomplicated of men, with nothing to hide."

"Perhaps expedition is too harsh a term for it. Let's just call it a friendly visit," Victoria corrected, obviously aware she had somehow struck a nerve and deciding to twist the knife a bit, in a friendly way, of course. "It goes without saying that Patrick sends his most profound regrets, as well as his equally profound professions of anguish at not being privileged to see you, his unflappable friend, at sixes and sevens."

She set down her teacup and leaned forward expectantly. "You are at sixes and sevens, aren't you, Pierre? I cannot tell you how depressing it would be to find that you are still your usual self, infuriatingly secretive and most maddeningly heart-whole."

''My father has painted you a melodramatic picture of his only son as a brokenhearted swain, perhaps even entertaining thoughts of suicide? I must remember to be kinder to him in future, as it is evident he is fast entering his dotage.''

''Oh? Then you deny being interested in the poor, nameless girl whom you brought to your father's house to recover from some accident?'' Victoria countered, peering intently at him overtop her spectacles. ''When Patrick questioned your father as to your motive, he told us you were already on the way to being well and truly smitten. I haven't heard my husband laugh so heartily since my uncle Quentin forwarded us a jeweled camel saddle he had acquired somewhere in his many travels, just in case Patrick should ever decide to keep his own dromedary. I cannot tell you how let down I am to know that you aren't head over ears in love with the girl. And Patrick? Why, it is your dearest friend who might become suicidal at this news! For shame, Pierre. The least you could do is tell me you've been turned down by the creature and are even now in the midst of a sad decline.''

Pierre shook his head slowly. ''Hanging is definitely too good for me,'' he drawled in his most deliberately maddening way. ''Perhaps if I gave myself up to be boiled in oil it might, in some small way, earn me a measure of forgiveness in your eyes. Please, dearest Victoria, tell me how I can make you happy. I should not sleep nights, else.''

Victoria threw back her head and laughed. ''Oh, Pierre, it really is good to be in your company again. Only you can deliver an insult in the form of an apology.''

He tipped his glass to her, smiling slightly. ''Just as it is good to have you here, my good friend, someone who appreciates my feeble attempt at wit without being so thin-skinned as to be insulted.''

''Oh, dear.'' Victoria grimaced comically, then sobered. ''Please don't tell me this Miss Caroline Addams—as your father tells me you call her—has no sense of humor. That really would be too bad of her, wouldn't it? But it is possible you are wrong, isn't it? I mean, I was once considered to be totally humorless, but that was only because there was so little to laugh about in my life. I believe I have made great strides, thanks to Patrick. Perhaps your Miss Addams has only misplaced her humor along with her memory? It is merely a thought, something to consider.''

Pierre lifted a hand to absently stroke the small scar on his cheekbone. "I shall take your thoughts and suppositions under advisement," he agreed amicably, setting down his glass before rising and holding out a hand to her. "Your chamber should be ready by now, Victoria, if you'd like to refresh yourself.''

She took his hand and also rose, to stand directly in front of him. "End of discussion, Pierre?" she asked, blighting him with her smile. "Very well, but only for now, and only because the trip has worn me to a frazzle, and I find I would very much like a liedown on my bed. I shall reconvene my inquisition over the dining table tonight, when your Miss Addams is present.''

"Was there ever any doubt of it?" Pierre countered, lifting her hand to his lips. "I have known you without funds, without future, without hope—but I have never known you without questions. It is good to see that you have brought the best of you into your new life, as I believe I would miss that inquisitive, incisive mind.''

Victoria impetuously stood on tiptoe to kiss him on the cheek, something she wouldn't have even considered doing a few months earlier. "And to think that I once didn't believe I could like you," she quipped cheekily just as a loud commotion in the foyer turned both their heads in the direction of the doorway.

"Master Pierre! Master Pierre!" Hartley shouted, racing into the room. "You must come quickly. There's been a terrible accident.''

"Accident?" Pierre asked curtly while Victoria noticed that the skin over his high cheekbones was suddenly drawn tight, his hold on her hand painfully snug. "What sort of accident?"

"A riding accident, Master Pierre," Hartley responded, gasping for air, for he was not a young man anymore and was clearly overset with his news. "With Miss Addams's horse! She's been badly hurt. The groom just rode in to tell us that she's lying in the fields and—"

Pierre was already out of the room and bounding across the lawns to the stables, not hearing anything more, and Hartley was left to finish telling his story to Lady Wickford, who quickly led the old man to a chair and poured him a bracing cup of tea.

"Sir John Oakvale is with her, but the groom says she won't wake up, and she's terribly pale," Hartley told her, his hands shaking so badly that the tea slopped onto the saucer. "I shouldn't be here, my lady, sitting with you. Oh, but it's wonderful of you to understand. My knees are shaking like dry bones in a sack. Why, if anything should happen to Miss Addams, Master Pierre might have all our heads!"

"He loves the young lady that much, then?" Victoria asked carefully, handing the butler a pristine white linen cloth with which to blot at the hot tea that had splashed onto his trousers.

Hartley bobbed his head emphatically. "He loves her dearly, my lady, and so all of us belowstairs say, except that Frenchie valet of Master Pierre's, Duvall, who doesn't love anything save his position."

"How very interesting," Victoria mused, turning to look out the window, as if she could see all the way to the field where Caroline lay unconscious, Pierre already racing to her side. "Then for everyone's sake, Hartley, I do hope she'll be all right."

SHE WAS FLOATING in a truly wonderful dream, mercifully cut off from the world and its less than rosy realities, being carried high above the earth in the most gentle, comforting, safe embrace imaginable. There was no fear, no pain, no reason for worry or doubt. There was just peace, and the heady feeling of being totally and completely cherished. Even loved.

She hadn't always felt this peaceful, she knew. First there had been the sickening sensation of falling, of losing her grip, followed by the painful buffeting of her body as her head and shoulders bounced about while her left leg was being pulled from its socket. Then terror had overwhelmed her, only to be superseded by the sure, unspoken, mind-destroying realization that she was about to die without ever having lived.

All this and more she had known in the space of a half-dozen heartbeats, then just as quickly forgotten at the moment she was lifted high against the chest of the strong angel who now held her to him, keeping her from harm, banishing all her fear, all her pain.

She moved her head slightly, wishing to press it against his chest, just to see if angels had heartbeats, too, and the pain came back, washing over her in wave after nauseating wave. She groaned aloud, unable to open her eyes but nevertheless sure she was no longer with the angel, but on a bed of nails instead, with a rock for her pillow.

"Caroline?" The voice she heard was low, masculine, and concerned. "Caroline, you're coming awake now, much as you would rather not, I'm sure. Open your eyes, Caroline. Please."

It was Pierre's voice she heard, although she was fully prepared to ignore it in the hope she might then be able to return to her lovely dream—that loving embrace. It was his last word that changed her mind, for that single, simple entreaty spoke volumes. He was worried about her. Poor man, she had caused him no end of trouble, hadn't she? She didn't want him to worry about her. She didn't want Pierre's concern, she wanted his—

"Pierre?" The voice was a whisper, a female whisper. "How is she? Before he left, Doctor Burgess was kind enough to tell me she should be fine, but that was hours ago. Shouldn't she be awake by now?"

It wasn't Mrs. Merrydell's voice. Caroline was sure of that. Mrs. Merrydell had an irritating, penetrating voice, like a pieman calling out his wares beneath her window. This voice was too sweet, too cultured to be that of her unfortunate choice of chaperone. Besides, the voice had called him Pierre, not Mr. Standish. No servant would do so, not even the encroaching Mrs. Merrydell.

Pierre must have turned slightly away from the bed to face the woman, for Caroline felt a slight tug on her hand, letting her know that he had been standing beside her, his hand wrapped snugly in hers. The realization that he had allowed this slight, unconscious intimacy had the effect of bringing stinging tears to her eyes.

"She stirred slightly just a moment ago, Victoria. Waking up will be painful for her, what with the blow to her head and the bruises on her back, which Burgess told me about, so I imagine she's fighting to stay unconscious."

Victoria. Who was Victoria? Caroline focused all her attention on the voices floating above her.

"You poor darling, you've been standing here all evening long, letting her hold your hand," Victoria said gently. "Please, at least let me get you a chair before you fall down. And you haven't eaten a thing."

Darling. She called him darling. Caroline didn't think she liked that.

"Thank you, but no. I'm fine. I can't ignore the fact that Caroline's had two bad blows to the head in such a short time. Stronger persons than she have been rendered permanently damaged. Why don't you retire now, my dear, you too have had quite a long day."

My dear. He called her my dear. Caroline liked that even less.

"I'm awake," she said abruptly, and not very civilly, knowing she just had to open her eyes and get a good look at "my dear" Victoria or else go mad. "I hope I'm not interrupting anything, but it's rather difficult to sleep when people insist on holding conversations within inches of my ear. Who are you?" she ended shortly, glaring up at Victoria.

Pierre stepped to one side, not letting loose his grip on Caroline's hand, and introduced Victoria to her.

"You're a countess?" Caroline heard herself asking stupidly. "I didn't know a countess could wear spectacles. At least not one so young and beautiful as you."

Victoria laughed and bent to kiss Caroline's cheek. "André told me you were outspoken, but I think I like you better this way than if you had been a simpering miss. I know I definitely like you better awake. You've had us all very worried, especially Pierre, who has stood by your side ever since carrying you home on his horse. How do you feel, Caroline? And, please, call me Victoria. My title is quite new and still makes me nervous."

Caroline's gaze shifted quickly to Pierre's face, not without pain. "You—you carried me?" she asked him, remembering again how safe she had felt, and marveling that she could ever have believed herself safe in his embrace. Safe was not a word she associated with this disturbing man. "Please allow me to thank you, Pierre," she said with dull politeness.

"So grudging, Caroline? One can only suppose you would rather I had left it to that brainless twit, Oatcake? He wanted to bring you home on a gate, doubtless finishing the job the fall began."

"His name is Oakvale, as you very well know," Caroline

shot back, wondering if he actually believed it would injure him in some way to accept her thanks and be done with it. "Poor Sir John. He must have been very frightened by it all. I know I was. Not everyone can be as coolly detached as you, you know."

"I'll just leave you two to sort this out," Victoria interrupted, her voice tinged with humor as Pierre and Caroline glared at each other. "I'll stop by to see you in the morning, my dear. We really do have *so* much to talk about."

Caroline quickly murmured her good-night to Victoria, still not knowing exactly who she was but content to wait till morning for an explanation. Right now all she could think of was her accident, an event that was more important to her at this moment than either Sir John's lack of good sense or Pierre's uncharacteristically gentle treatment of her injured body.

But any questions she might have had about her fall were to be delayed, for, as Victoria opened the door to the hallway, Mrs. Merrydell charged into the room with, Caroline thought randomly, much the same grace that might be employed by a trumpeting rogue elephant trampling down some unfortunate native village that stood in its path.

"And it's about time, too!" Mrs. Merrydell exploded, her long strides eating up the space between door and bed in less than a heartbeat. "Whoever heard of the chaperone being forced to cool her heels in a hallway while the randy son of the household sits alone in a darkened bedchamber with a poor, defenseless girl? I'm half surprised her skirts aren't over her head, and that's a fact!"

Pierre stopped the woman in her tracks by the numbing frost of his black, icy stare. "Don't be vulgar, Mrs. Merrydell, or I shall be forced to have you removed—from the premises as well as from this room."

Mrs. Merrydell blustered for a moment or two, muttering random snatches such as "Well, I never—" and, "If you think for one moment that—'' before ending quite humbly, ''Please forgive me, sir. I'm quite overwrought with fear for poor, dear Miss Caroline.''

''Of course you are,'' Pierre answered smoothly. ''It is just, you see, that we would rather you were overwrought from a distance. You do understand me—don't you, dear Mrs. Merrydell?''

The woman looked about herself distractedly. ''But—but—who will stay with her tonight? Surely, sir, you don't mean to—''

''Her maid will keep vigil,'' Pierre responded, earning himself a thankful squeeze of Caroline's hand on his. ''Your duties do not include nursing, madam. And now, if you don't mind, Miss Caroline and I have something to discuss—in private.''

Clearly Mrs. Merrydell was torn. One part of her wished for nothing more than to escape Pierre's piercing gaze with as much haste as possible, while another part of her dearly wished to remain, whether to protect her charge or to eavesdrop on some clandestine goings-on, Caroline couldn't be sure. In the end, personal protection won out, and Mrs. Merrydell retired, closing the door behind her so softly that it stayed open a crack.

Pierre saw the woman's lapse as well. He raised Caroline's hand to his lips, kissed it, and then released it to cross the room and firmly shut the door, turning the key in the lock. ''The woman is necessary for the moment, but extremely tiresome,'' he remarked as he returned to Caroline's bedside and once more took up her hand, an unconscious gesture that immediately set her heart to pounding in her chest. ''Are you up to talking about your accident just yet, Caroline, or shall I call your maid?''

''No, I want to talk,'' Caroline assured him hurriedly, struggling to sit up in bed. ''Oh, my back!'' she exclaimed as the slight exertion set off a small explosion of pain. "Did Lady step on me?"

"Doctor Burgess doesn't think so," Pierre told her, helping her to sit up by adjusting the pillows behind her head. "You were bruised by the rocks and stones you were dragged over until you were able to free your foot from the stirrup. According to Oakvale, you were a regular acrobat. I believe he has tumbled into love with you as a result, and would think it the best of good fun if you could run away together to join a traveling fair. He would, on consideration, make a tolerable juggler, wouldn't he?"

Caroline giggled, then caught herself up short as her chest ached. "That's not very nice, Pierre. Sir John thinks very highly of you."

Pierre let go of her hand to pull a chair over to the bed, but he did not sit down. "Don't defend him until you hear his latest bit of genius. It is Romeo Oatcake's considered opinion that, as one bump on the head served to remove your memory, this second bump has just as surely caused it to return. He was truly astonished that I had not thought of such a thing myself and conked you on your noggin a fortnight ago. When last I saw him he was preparing to call on you formally, only if your recovered memory means you have discovered that you are an heiress, of course. Not quite the sharpest knife in the cabinet, is he, poor fellow?"

"Of course," Caroline answered distractedly, ignoring his disparaging remarks about Sir John's brainpower, her mind busy with other thoughts. "Although I certainly wasn't actively seeking another bump on my head, and appreciate the fact that you abstained from giving me one, Sir John's idea does hold some merit. What one bump took away, another bump just might return. Except for one thing. I haven't remembered anything more. As far as I know, my name is

Caroline Addams and my life began the day you found me in the roadway.''

She looked over at Pierre, her clear blue-violet eyes narrowed thoughtfully. ''But *you* couldn't have known that until I told you. That would be impossible. Wouldn't it?''

CHAPTER FOURTEEN

"I DON'T KNOW, Caroline. Would it be possible? Perhaps I am fey. My maternal grandmother was originally from a small village in County Cork, and you know what has been said about the Irish."

"Don't try to fob me off with any of your nonsense, Pierre," Caroline warned, pouting. "There is just no way you could know whether I had regained my memory or not without me telling you. Unless,"—she stopped for a moment, her features assembling themselves in a thoughtful frown—"unless you know something you're not telling me." She sniffed derisively. "Of course you do! It would be just like you, wouldn't it? Oh yes, that's you all right, straight down to the ground. Sneaky and underhanded."

"How you do go on," Pierre drawled, resting his palm on her forehead and peering down at her assessingly. "Perhaps you have picked up a touch of fever. It isn't uncommon, I'm told, in people with delicate constitutions—and those who persist in trying to attack rocks with their heads. Why don't you get a good night's rest, and we can talk again in the morning."

"I don't want to talk in the morning—I want to talk *now!*" Caroline removed his hand from her brow with some force, ignoring the renewed slab of pain the impulsive movement caused her. "How did you know I hadn't regained my memory?"

Pierre thought quickly, searching his agile brain for some reasonably believable explanation that would fob her off—at least until he could come up with a more convincing fib. Then he sighed, letting her know he was giving in to her much the way a weary parent does when it can stand a child's whining no longer. "Very well, brat," he relented, "but you won't like it. You see, it was your eyes."

"My eyes? What have my eyes got to do with anything? You know, this is just like you, Pierre. You're not making any sense."

"On the contrary, I am making sense, or at least I do when I am allowed to speak more than two words without being interrupted by a mannerless infant."

"I'm so prodigiously sorry," Caroline spat, not sorry in the least. "Please go on with your explanation, I shan't interrupt."

"Yes, you will," Pierre contradicted, lightly flicking his index finger across the tip of her nose. "You live to interrupt me. I imagine, in fact, that it has become one of your premier pleasures in life. But as I said, it was your eyes that told me. When you opened them they were still quite blank."

"*Blank!* How dare you! As if it weren't enough to relegate me to the role of puling infant, now you must make me sound like some brainless ninny!"

Pierre tilted his head in her direction and pointed a finger at her, wordlessly reminding her that he had said she would interrupt him. "You are never stupid, Caroline," he corrected her. "But if the blow to your head had served to shake your memory loose, you would have awakened with your eyes filled with wonder, not blank with incomprehension. It's simple, really, with no mystery involved, no hidden secrets."

"And if I believe you, will you promise to let me jump Obtuse over a five-bar gate once I'm recovered?" she countered, letting him know she had not swallowed his obvious bag of moonshine. "However, I will allow myself to be satisfied with your explanation—for now. What really concerns me is the way the girth came loose the moment I put Lady into a gallop. I can't bring myself to believe that the groom was careless. He is too good at what he does.''

Pierre surprised her with a small bow. ''I make you my compliments, imp, and shall convey your high praise to the groom, who has been desolated by your tumble. Even with your brains addled from your latest injury you have been able to deduce the fact that your accident was—dare I say it?— no accident.''

All thoughts of her headache and painful back faded instantly as Caroline's attention narrowed to exclude everything except the digestion of this latest piece of information. ''No accident? But how—why?''

Pierre sat on the side of the bed, taking the hand she had impulsively held out to him. ''The how of it is very simple. Both sides of the leather strap had been shaved, not so much as to be noticed by the groom, but just enough so that the cinch was not a true fit and would begin to slide open once you put Lady into a gallop. It was not a matter of *if* you would fall, but *when*. The method was woefully unoriginal, not the sort of thing to inspire my awe, but it was effective just the same.''

''Whoever committed the deed would doubtless be forever cast down to learn that the great Pierre Standish was not overly impressed with his technique,'' Caroline pronounced in accents of disgust. ''You would have been much more prone to voice your appreciation of his efforts had I been killed, I'm sure.''

Pierre squeezed her hand, smiling. ''Poor little Caroline. Forgive me, brat. A disdain for mediocrity, even in villains, is my besetting sin. In truth, I should have been inconsolable had you died.''

''You say that with the same feeling you'd give to voicing your displeasure over the second remove at dinner,'' Caroline complained pettishly, tugging hard to free her hand from his grasp, but he wouldn't let her go.

"Think, my dear hothead. Don't let your anger with me distract you from the point," he warned quietly.

Her hand stilled in his, and she looked at him closely, her huge eyes opened wide. "Someone's trying to kill me, aren't they, Pierre?"

He nodded, his gaze not leaving hers. "Either one someone, or perhaps even two someones. It's not exactly a revelation though, is it, considering the first attempt in the gardens?"

"Then you really *do* believe someone wants me dead?" Although Caroline had considered just such an idea many times since the incident in the gardens, hearing it spoken out loud, and by Pierre Standish, who didn't seem to ever believe in *anything,* frightened her more than she thought possible. "But who—and why?"

Pierre took a deep breath, and let it out in a weary sigh. "We progress, I see, from how and why to who and why. Unfortunately, I have precious few answers for you. All I can say for now is that you obviously are a great deal of bother to someone—besides me, that is—and that someone would very much like to have you removed from the face of the earth. It's a terrible thing, isn't it, to have enemies?"

"You ought to know," Caroline groused, as his words had only served to sink her spirits lower than before. "You must have acquired dozens of them over the years with your winning ways. But that's nothing to the point, is it? What do we do now?"

"*We* don't do anything," he told her, ignoring her sarcasm. "You are to lie here until you feel completely recovered, and then you are to go about your business just as you have been doing, taking care not to outrun your groom or wander away from the house without Victoria in tow. That is why Father sent her here, you know, crafty devil that he is. I do not consider the so volatile Mrs. Merrydell sufficient protection no matter how ferocious her demeanor, so please do not consider yourself safe if you are alone with her. Leave it to Father and me to ferret out the bogeyman responsible for your 'accidents.'"

Caroline was livid. "Do you really believe I can know what I know now and just stand back and put my safety into your hands, without lifting a finger to save myself? Well, I refuse to be treated as if I were incapable of defending myself. You must be out of your mind, Pierre Standish! How can you possible expect me to—*oh!*"

Pierre's mouth swooped down on hers, effectively shutting off her tirade before, his lips still on hers, he lowered her gently onto the pillows by her shoulders, being careful not to touch her tender back before raising his hands to cup either side of her face. His thumbs worked gently against her soft cheeks, molding her to him and wordlessly urging her mouth to open beneath his so that he could deepen the kiss.

Against her will, if indeed she'd had any will left to summon, Caroline felt her arms sliding up around Pierre's neck and gloried in the warm solidity of him as his firm body pressed lightly against her tingling breasts. His tongue was foreign to her, but a welcome stranger, introducing itself by way of quick, teasing thrusts, its slightly raspy texture stroking the roof of her mouth. She reached out to meet it, the touch of warm, wet flesh against warm, wet flesh causing an extraordinary explosion deep inside her.

Pierre felt her daring exploration and shuddered convulsively, longing to crush her completely against him in order to convince himself that she was truly all right.

Only that afternoon he had thought he'd lost her, had thought that his arrogant manipulations had failed to protect her. The possibility of losing Caroline had nearly driven him mad as he had ridden out on Obtuse, not caring for the animal's safety as he urged the stallion to fly over the ground to where Caroline lay.

If there had been any questions, any lingering doubts in

his mind as to exactly how he felt toward his Good Deed, they had all been laid to rest during the terrible ride.

He loved her. He didn't know how, he didn't know when; he only knew that she had come into his life unwanted, un-looked for, and had become the most important, the most valuable part of it. And he'd die before he let anyone hurt her.

Even himself.

This last thought brought Pierre back to a realization of what he was doing. He pulled away from her slowly, regret-fully, looking deeply into her tear-washed eyes before closing his own for a sanity-restoring moment, shaking his head. He had said too much, frightening her, and now his ill-timed passion had frightened her even more.

"Pierre?" Caroline's voice was very small, very confused.

He smiled, deliberately lifting his left eyebrow in the mocking way she had told him infuriated her. "Sorry, dar-ling. I am a brute, but it's the only way I've ever known to silence a beautiful female when she's talking too much. I'll leave you now so that you can get some well-earned rest. Victoria will be tippy-toeing in here as early as is decent tomorrow morning, to plague you with a million or more questions of her own."

Caroline's tears spilled over to run down her pale cheeks, but he ignored them, turning for the door.

"But—but—" she began, reaching out to him. Suddenly, reason rushed back into her brain and she flushed with shame. "I detest you, Pierre Standish," she called after his departing back, knowing no other response except anger. "Do you hear me? I *detest* you!"

He didn't answer.

Once Susan had satisfied herself that her charge was settled comfortably for the night, and only moments before Caroline was pushed to the point of screaming by the maid's affec-tionate fussing, she was left to turn her head into her pillow and quietly cry herself to sleep while, downstairs, in the privacy of his father's study, Pierre drank his brandy slowly, far into the dark hours of the night.

THE SOUND OF THE SLAP, the sharp sting of flesh connecting with flesh, echoed through the small clearing, scattering a pair of birds who had been resting in the branches of a nearby tree.

"Ouch!" Ursley Merrydell exclaimed in a high, whining voice, his hand flying to his cheek to rub the tingling skin. "I knew you were going to do that, from the minute I found out that the stupid girl didn't die. You always do that. Why do you always do that?"

His mother, who was feeling only slightly mollified by her physical display of temper, shot back angrily, *"Why* do I always do that, Ursley? It's a wonder you should ask. I always do that because you always fail—*that's* why. I beg one simple favor of you, one simple little murder, but do you do it? No, you don't. 'As simple as falling off a horse,' that's what you said. Only it wasn't so simple, was it?" She slapped him again, on the shoulder, just for good measure. "I had such high hopes for you, Ursley, I really did. But you're just like your father. He could never get the straight of anything, either."

Panic invaded Ursley's stringy body, turning his bony knees to water. He didn't want to be compared to his father. His father had failed once too often—and his father had been eliminated. "No, Mother, don't say that!" he protested on a sob, dropping to his knees at her feet. "Didn't I do just as you said at the cobbler's?"

Amity softened, for Ursley was her son, and she loved him. Really she did—at least most of the time. It was just at times like these, when she was on the hunt, that she tended to conveniently misplace her motherly instincts.

She bent down to pat his cheek affectionately, ignoring his

involuntary wince. "Of course you did, my darling boy. You were just wonderful at the cobbler's. I was very proud of you. It's just that I had so hoped she would die when the saddle slipped. It was just an unfortunate accident; you couldn't have known she'd be able to throw herself clear of the horse's hooves, now could you?"

"No, Mama," Ursley agreed hurriedly, clambering to his feet, knowing from experience that the worst was over and they would be able to talk now. "I couldn't know that. But—but what do we do now? I won't be able to get near the stables again. Standish is sure to post guards."

But Amity wasn't listening. She was still suffering from one of her increasingly rare bouts of motherly affection. She inspected her son for signs of illness, turning his face this way and that as she held his cheeks painfully tight between thumb and forefinger. "Are you sleeping well, my dear boy? You look a mite pulled. You aren't letting that cheeky serving wench have her wicked way with you, are you, while Mama's not close by to watch out for you? You could catch something, you know, and a whopping dose of the pox wouldn't do either one of us a dram's worth of good."

Ursley hid his eyes, knowing they would reveal the fact that the ungrateful wench at the inn was still turning down his every offer. She'd even poured an entire pitcher of ale over his head the last time he had tried to win her favor with a well-placed pinch. "I wouldn't have anything to do with the slut, Mama. I'm a good boy. You know that. Besides, we're here on business."

They *were* in the middle of a piece of business, and Ursley's reminder brought Amity's mind back to the matter at hand. She released his face, leaving Ursley to gratefully massage his cheeks, and began to pace as she thought out loud. "Standish is getting suspicious. He'd have to be dumb as a redbrick not to be, I suppose, but I don't much like the way he's been looking at me. And he makes sure I'm never alone with her. I'm beginning to have a bad feeling about this. We have to move fast or lose everything.''

Ursley nodded, happy to step in and take charge now that his mother had admitted she had been feeling some qualms of her own. ''You'll have to do it yourself,'' he said, beginning to pace in step with her. ''Slip something nasty into her tea, or something. We can't count on her not remembering you sooner or later and setting up a hollering that will bring Pierre Standish on the double. Then there'll be the very devil to pay, and I won't be able to help you.''

Amity turned on her son, cold fury in her eyes. ''No, you wouldn't, would you? You'd be on a coach heading away from here just as fast as you could. You'd go to America, wouldn't you? Oh yes, I've seen your face when you talk about those golden streets over there. Well, let me tell you a thing or two, my fine young man. If I go to prison I won't go alone. You'll be right there beside me!''

Ursley frowned, for this was a sobering thought indeed. He was convinced he would not like prison above half, and a ride to prison shared with his free-swinging mother could prove to be an extremely painful journey. ''Nothing will go wrong,'' he assured her as he tried to reassure himself. ''The third time's the charm, as they say. You'll find the perfect thing to do and we'll be on our way to wealth and a life of ease. Just you wait, Mama. We'll have the best of everything, exactly like you always promised. It'll be grand!''

Amity Merrydell smiled and allowed herself to be mollified. Her son was right. She was forgetting that he was his father's son, a born bungler. It was her turn now. The girl was as good as below ground.

CHAPTER FIFTEEN

"En voila une affaire!"

"Jaw bangin' ter yerself in that froggie croak agin, are yer?" Jeremy commented, looking up from the boot he had been polishing with more energy than effect as the valet stormed into the workroom, slamming the door shut behind him in a show of temper. "Yer always gripin' 'bout somethin', like some ol' biddy leanin' over a washtub. Now wot's stickin' in yer craw?"

"I have not the cat in my throat," Duvall denied angrily, abruptly grabbing his master's favorite riding boot from the young boy's hands and taking up a clean polishing rag, intent on demonstrating the correct way to put a mirror finish on the costly leather. "And do not dare to speak to me so of my language, *mouffette*. Your language, it is of *la poubelle*, the garbage."

Jeremy eyed the valet narrowly, knowing he wanted to learn how to be a gentlman's gentleman, yet hating the fact that his beloved guv'nor had seen fit to place him under Duvall's tutelage. His short sojourn as a fledgling groom having come to a bad end—a circumstance having much to do with a certain, truly unlikable groom (who had endeavored to administer his instructions to the former chimney sweep with the toe of his boot) having discovered a prodigious amount of ripe manure in his cot—Jeremy knew his master's hopes were aimed a smidgeon too high, but he longed to make the man proud of him anyway.

Jeremy's loyalty to Pierre, always strong, had increased

tenfold with the rousting of Hawkins the sweep, and the thought of failing his guv'nor again distressed him mightily; so much so that he now said, "Oi'm sorry, Frenchie, truly Oi am. Oi'll do better, 'onest Oi will.''

"It is not of your miserable self that I speak,'' Duvall informed him, shoving the shined boot under Jeremy's nose and turning it this way and that, so that the leather would gleam in the sunlight. "It is this affair of the nameless lady, this Miss Addams. She will be the death of my master. I feel it here,''—he beat the polishing rag against his breast for emphasis—"in my heart.''

Jeremy, who had heard of Caroline's fall from a horse the day before, seemed to be of the opinion that, if the lady persisted in tumbling onto her head it would be *she* who would be carried to bed on six men's shoulders, not his beloved guv'nor. He said as much to Duvall, who immediately cuffed him across the top of his short, golden fuzz.

"Ow! Yer villain!'' the lad exclaimed, rubbing his head. "Wot yer do that fer? Yer always after m' 'ead, ain't yer, some ways or otter?''

"I only hope for to knock some sense into it,'' Duvall answered reasonably, pulling a short stool beside the boy and squatting down on it so that he could see Jeremy as well as talk to him. "I don't mean the master will die, you fool. And it won't be the girl who will perish, so much the pity. Didn't you listen with your fat cabbage ears when the master told us to watch with both eyes the Merrydell woman who is trying to harm her? No, it is not an end of life of which I speak. It is my master's heart I worry for.''

Jeremy's head snapped up, and he looked straight at the valet, grinning wickedly. "Billin' an' cooin' are they? Yer'd better watch yer steps, Frenchie, or she'll toss yer out on yer ear when she snags 'im. Guv'nor won't take kindly ter yer iffen yer bad-mouth 'is missus. Me, Oi like 'er fine, an' guv'nor knows it. *Oi'm* safe, Oi am. Yer won't find Jeremy 'Olloway back in Piccadilly!''

Duvall's sallow skin flushed an unhealthy orange. "I never said I did not like Miss Addams," he corrected rapidly. "It's just that we get along so well, the master and me, and I do not look forward to a petticoat household."

Jeremy nodded his understanding. "Nothin' worse than wimmen. Always wantin' ter be boss, an' all. But Miss Addams is straight up. Yer won't get no trouble from 'er, iffen yer can learn ter keep yer yapper shut."

Duvall hopped to his feet, not knowing if he was angry with Jeremy, who couldn't see the handwriting on the wall, or with himself, for being dull-witted enough to think the simpleton would understand his problems. He and Pierre made a good team, and had done so for years. A woman would ruin everything; probably even want a gaggle of children about, drooling on his master's spotless waistcoat. *"Va te faire cuire un oeuf!"* he spat in Gallic fury, turning away before he did Jeremy an injury.

"Huh?" the boy questioned blankly as he righted the stool Duvall had kicked over in his fury.

Duvall turned back to level Jeremy with a look that brooked no argument. "You know nothing, less than nothing! I said for you to go cook yourself an egg!" Then he stormed out of the workroom to nurse his present and anticipated wounds in the privacy of his small sanctum located behind Pierre's dressing room.

Jeremy scratched the side of his head. Cook himself an egg? He sighed, feeling slightly sad in spite of himself. It was obvious the valet was slipping round the bend. If he, Jeremy Holloway, wished to remain under the man's tutelage, and in the house—where there was not a bit of horse manure to be found, let alone shoveled into piles—he had better be extra nice to him, for the man's mind was about to snap. He set down the half-polished boot and headed for the kitchens, intent on boiling a fresh egg.

LADY WICKFORD KNOCKED softly on the door, then lifted the latch and poked her head inside the room, peeking toward the bed that stood in the shadows at the far side of the chamber. "Caroline?" she questioned in a loud whisper. "Are you awake?"

Caroline, who had been awake for hours, remained very still, hoping her visitor would take the hint and go away. She was not up to facing the countess. She was not up to facing anyone. She just wanted to lie there, in the darkness, until everyone forgot about her.

Her eyes tightly closed, she sensed rather than saw Victoria beside her bed. "Caroline? It's past noon. Surely you should be hungry?"

Sighing, Caroline turned her head in Victoria's direction, still refusing to open her eyes. "I am never going to eat again," she vowed quietly but firmly.

Victoria laughed, pulling up a small chair so that she could make herself comfortable. "Pierre does have that effect at times, doesn't he?" she remarked kindly. "It is Pierre you are hiding from, isn't it? He's a difficult man to understand, I know, but he cares very deeply for you, although I'm sure you don't believe me."

Caroline opened her eyes and looked up at Victoria. "You're right. I don't believe you."

Victoria settled back in her chair, arranging her skirts over her knees. "Then I imagine you wouldn't be interested in hearing how Pierre behaved when he was told that you had suffered an accident. Pity," she said, sighing. "It was quite a remarkable reaction from a man who has made it a rule never to react to anything. Ah, you're sitting up. Wonderful. Perhaps you will decide to have a small meal?"

Caroline ignored this second offer of food, her entire attention directed to Victoria's hint that Pierre had been worried about her. "What did he do?" she asked curiously, leaning toward her visitor. "Was he truly upset? I remember you saying something about it being Pierre who carried me here—and he held my hand, didn't he? I didn't dream it all, I'm convinced of that."

Victoria used the tip of her index finger to push her spectacles more firmly onto the bridge of her nose. She was enjoying herself, and only wished her dearest Patrick could be here as well, to share in the fun. "Pierre was distraught from the moment he heard the terrible news until you finally awoke, Caroline. He was totally unhinged. He bellowed at the doctor—at all of us—and threatened anyone who came close to you with bodily harm, caring for you himself." She lifted her chin, smiling at the memory. "It was wonderful to see. I always wondered if Pierre were human, and now I know that he is. I should have known it would take a woman to bring a man such as he fully to life."

Caroline reached out a hand, found Victoria's, and squeezed it hard. "Thank you, my friend," she said, blinking away tears. "I needed to hear that. He confuses me so, you understand," she admitted, "kissing me one moment and treating me as if I were an annoying rash the next. I never know where I stand with him, or what he wants of me."

"Kissing you?" Victoria repeated interestedly. "He hasn't—"

Caroline shook her head vehemently. "No, *no!* Of course not! Pierre would *never*—that is, I wouldn't *allow*—not that he *tried* to—"

Victoria waved her hands, signaling her understanding. "I didn't think so, my dear, but as a married woman, and supposedly conventional, I had to ask. I remember Patrick—" She hesitated, intent on a memory of her own courtship. "But Pierre is an honorable man," she ended firmly. "If he has kissed you, you and he are as good as affianced."

Now Caroline's tears came in earnest, for there was nothing she would love more than to be married to Pierre. She loved him, infuriating, secretive despot that he was, and she could almost believe he loved her, too, in his own way. But whom did he love? She was a nameless nobody, and as if that in itself were not enough, somebody was trying to kill her. What sort of future could the two of them have with such a terrible cloud hanging over their heads?

It was impossible, and so she told Victoria, who listened politely and then replied in her most officious tone: "Poppycock! Pierre would never let anyone hurt you, so that is one problem as good as solved, although I will admit you had a close call yesterday. I believe Pierre spent most of last night kicking himself for that, so he will be twice as protective from this point on, until the person or persons who wish you harm are unearthed and punished."

"And my memory?" Caroline questioned, Victoria's matter-of-fact solutions amazing her. "Can you solve that problem so easily as well?"

"Your memory will return any day now, as I have read extensively on just this sort of phenomenon, and your chances of a full recovery are extremely high. I am not one who puts much credence in prophecy, but I do believe I am in this case allowed to say with full conviction that you and Pierre will then marry and remove to London, where you will become the darling of Society and Pierre will astonish all who know him by doting on you night and day."

Caroline shook her head. "You make it all sound so simple. You've really read about cases like mine?" she asked, this part of Victoria's conversation completely penetrating her brain. She looked closely at the woman, noting once more the wire-rimmed spectacles and the sharp intelligence lurking behind them. "Are you a bluestocking, Victoria?"

"I was," she told her, winking. "I've retired from all that now, content to be a wife and, if my sudden aversion to my morning chocolate is any indication of my condition, soon to be a mother. If you don't mind my saying so, I believe you might be just a tad blue yourself, Caroline. You're certainly no featherheaded miss, even if Pierre tells me your education must have come at the hands of a person who didn't mind his speech in front of you.''

After congratulating Victoria most sincerely, and thanking her for traveling by coach to come to Pierre's aid while in her delicate condition, Caroline broached a subject she had been longing to discuss with someone. ''Last night, when everyone was talking above my head, I thought that they were as loud as the pieman calling outside my window. Piemen don't hawk their wares in the country, do they? It must mean that I have lived in London.''

Nodding, Victoria added, ''Or some other town of reasonable size. I told you that you were quick. Another young woman wouldn't have realized that the pieman was a valuable clue. Let me ring for a tray before you tell me what else you have discovered.''

PIERRE SAT BEHIND his father's desk, the fingertips of his right hand rhythmically drumming on the tabletop. It had been too close, this last attack. He had been cutting it too fine, trying to play his cards closely to his vest and not allowing anyone else in on his plans. His secrecy had cost him, and Caroline. He couldn't make another mistake.

He stopped his drumming to open the top drawer of the desk and remove the letter he had received from his father more than a week earlier. Unfolding the single sheet, he read over the missive, nodding his silent agreement with his father's conclusions, then shaking his head as he reread the last line.

''No, Father, I'm afraid I cannot do that any longer,'' he said aloud. ''I cannot wait for your return before putting an end to this nonsense. It has proved too dangerous.'' He refolded the paper and replaced it in the drawer, then rose to stare out the window overlooking the gardens.

How long he stood there he didn't know, but when he turned around once more it was to see his father standing before him, still dressed in his traveling cape and hat.

"Good afternoon, my son," André said by way of greeting, still in the process of stripping off his gloves. "You look like the very devil, if I might say so without fear of being tossed out of my own home on my ear."

"Good afternoon, Father," Pierre returned calmly, automatically concealing any shock André's sudden reappearance might have caused. He hadn't heard a carriage draw up, or been aware of any commotion in the foyer. "You've had a pleasant journey, I trust."

"Yes, indeed," André agreed. "I had quite forgotten the myriad joys of traveling about the countryside by coach, making do with post-horses, sleeping between damp linen, and picking at indifferent meals. You may kiss me if you wish, although I'd rather you didn't, as displays of affection can be so wearing. How fares our Miss Addams?"

Pierre averted his eyes from his father's penetrating stare, preferring to cross to the drinks table and pour them each a small glass of wine. "She had a small accident with her horse yesterday," he told him as he handed over one of the glasses. "The saddle cinch had been shaved." Lifting his own drink to his lips, he drained the liquid in one swallow and then hurled the glass into the cold fireplace. "Playtime's over, Father."

"She will recover." André stated, didn't question, for he already knew the answer. If any permanent harm had come to Caroline, Pierre would have had his head by now and not just contented himself with destroying a fine piece of French crystal. "Forgive me, my son. It now seems I sadly underestimated our adversaries, and led you to do likewise. They appear to be more than mere bumbling nuisances. We have no more time to hope for Caroline to recover her memory on her own.''

He stripped off his hat and cloak and flung them carelessly onto a nearby chair in preparation of getting down to business. ''May I presume that the Merrydell is still walking among us, or have you got her hanging by her thumbs in the cellars?''

Pierre shot his father a piercing look. ''She and the son met for a heated conference this morning among the trees at the bottom of the gardens, but she's back in the house now. I've given orders that she is to be watched at all times and is not allowed to see Caroline alone. I think she'll try poison next, if she listens to her son, whom she seems alternately to adore and detest. I only wish I could have overheard all of their conversation, as I cannot yet fathom how they plan to handle identifying Caroline's body and claiming the money. After all, Mrs. Merrydell certainly can't suddenly pretend she has recognized her ward, can she? I have to own it, Father, the woman is beginning to get on my nerves.''

''Yes. I had noticed that.'' André retired to the chair behind his desk and sat down, steepling his fingers as he leaned his elbows on the desktop. ''She's not suspicious?''

Pierre shook his head derisively. ''Our dear Mrs. Merrydell is too sure of herself, too single-minded in her mission, to be suspicious, although we cannot rely on her overweening stupidity for much longer.'' He walked over to the desk and perched on one corner. ''Must I beg, Father, or are you going to tell me who Caroline really is? Surely you know by now. You seem to know everything else.''

''Tsk, tsk, Pierre,'' André could not refrain from teasing. ''It isn't like you to be so precipitate. I do believe I like it. Your Good Deed has been all that I could have hoped. I think I'll just toddle upstairs to thank her personally. I wouldn't wish to be rude, you understand. And then there's dear Lady Wickford. I should be very shabby indeed if I didn't clean up my dirt and present her my compliments as soon as may be." He rose, placing his palms on the desktop. "You will excuse me, Pierre, won't you?"

"I'd have a lesser man's heart for a paperweight," Pierre returned cheerfully enough, "but I'll allow you to play out your string as long as it pleases you, Father, with only a word of caution. My patience grows thin."

André leaned across the desk to tap his son on the cheek. "Humility. That's the ticket, *mon fils*. You've come a long way. Now, what say we dispense with these melodramatic displays of affection so that I might retire to change before we visit the ladies. Victoria is with her, I imagine, standing guard?

Pierre bowed his head, silently counting to ten. He had earned this, he knew, all this and more, for having doubted his father, for having doubted his mother's constant love. But, oh, how it hurt to have to stand back and let the older man call all the moves. Yet, if it had been left to him he would have done much the same, right up until the moment he knew his heart to be committed.

Now, the moves, the strategies, the thrill of the hunt, seemed no more than childish games, and more than a little dangerous. At last he understood why Patrick Sherbourne had seen so little humor in Victoria's quest to find Quennel Quinton's murderer.

When love enters the picture, the thrill of the game flies directly out the window.

"Coming, Father," Pierre heard himself saying dutifully, just as Jeremy Holloway erupted into the room without bothering to knock.

"Guv'nor! Guv'nor! She put somethin' in the tea. Oi wuz boilin' an egg, jist like Frenchie said ter do—'es so tip-top, knowin' just wot Oi should do—an' Oi seen 'er plain wit m' daylights, that bracket-faced bubby, sneakin' sumthin' inter missy's teapot. Oi came right 'ere, jist like yer said ter do, ter tell yer. Yer coulda knocked me flat—that Frenchie is fly!'' Catching his breath, Jeremy turned to see André Standish in the room and quickly tugged at his nonexistent forelock. ''Oh, 'ello there, Whitey. Oi didn't 'ear yer wuz back.''

''My lapse entirely, young man,'' André confessed dryly. ''Henceforth I shall make it clear you are to be informed of all my arrivals and departures. But for now, with your kind permission and with heartfelt thanks for your keen eyesight and steadfast loyalty, I find that I have matters to which I must attend.''

Jeremy gave a negligent wave of his hand. ''Be m' guest, Whitey. Oi gots ter get back ter m' egg anyways.''

Pierre and his father exchanged gazes, then both walked rapidly toward the stairs.

CHAPTER SIXTEEN

THEY ENTERED the chamber without knocking, two perfectly dressed gentlemen whose physical presence displayed the best of their generations, from the understated elegance of their well-cut clothing, to the athletic healthfulness of their bodies, to the light of intelligence that burned so brightly in their dark eyes.

Once more Caroline was struck by their close physical resemblance: André, who proved that a gentleman can age without losing one iota of his attractiveness, and Pierre, who was enjoying the full flower of his manhood. But more than their physical likenesses, Caroline was once again aware of the uncanny, silent communication they shared.

Pierre had taken no more than three steps into the room before he saw Victoria standing to one side of Caroline's bed, neatly pouring the contents of a full china teapot into the base of a large potted plant. As he turned to André, who had also seen Victoria, the two men visibly relaxed, their bodies unknowingly mimicking each other in the way they immediately became more slack of shoulder, less aggressive in their step; their dark eyes became instantly shuttered, their entire posture changing from controlled haste to smiling congeniality, radiating a mood of ease and even slight boredom.

"Good day, ladies," André said, stopping just short of the bed where Caroline rested, a half-dozen pillows propped at her back. He bowed from the waist. "Please excuse our precipitate entrance, my dears, but I was so overcome with eagerness to see both you dear people again that I completely misplaced my good manners. Victoria, you are positively glowing. May I presume that you are planning to present dearest Patrick with a token of your affection, as we so politely phrase it? Caroline, you naughty puss, I hear you have taken a tumble. Shall we have to relegate you to using my late wife's dogcart?''

Caroline, recovering from her momentary awe, mumbled a curt welcome, then narrowed her eyes and looked past André to where Pierre stood, idly inspecting one lace shirtcuff, and announced baldly, "Mrs. Merrydell brought me tea and Victoria dumped it on a plant, which I do believe is already showing signs of wilting. I know that ladies in my new friend's delicate condition are at times prone to eccentricities, but I doubt this is one of them. Would you care to offer me an explanation, Pierre, or am I going to be forced to draw my own conclusions?''

"A flush hit, I'd say," André remarked, looking at his son.

"There's nothing wrong with her eyesight," Victoria slipped in, sitting down once more and replacing the empty teapot on the silver tray Mrs. Merrydell had delivered. "And hello to you, dearest André. You look fine as ninepence, even in your traveling clothes.''

Pierre stepped forward. "Ah, poor Father," he drawled, ignoring Caroline's demands. "You have just been reprimanded; quite gently, but reprimanded none the less. We will be happy to excuse you, of course, if you wish to go to your rooms and change out of your dirt.''

"No, we won't," Caroline piped up, quickly sitting up, as if ready to bound from the bed and physically restrain the man.

"We won't?" Pierre questioned, eyeing her warily. "Are you going to prove tiresome, brat?''

"We won't," she repeated firmly, ignoring his insult. "What you will do is gather round my bed like good little soldiers—as I am reluctant to leave it until my back feels less like Lady has stepped on it with all four feet—and tell me just what the devil is going on!''

"She seems a bit grumpy, my son," André commented kindly. "One can always tell, because her language slips a notch. Rather endearing, don't you think? Yet, all things considered, perhaps another visit from the good doctor is in order?"

"Yes, she does seem sadly out of coil," Pierre agreed. "I suggest we retire, you to change and me to summon Doctor Burgess, while Victoria fetches a cold cloth with which to bathe Caroline's fevered brow."

"Don't bother the doctor, Pierre," Caroline broke in, her voice rather strained. "I believe my agitation is easily diagnosed. As a matter of fact, I am convinced it is due to something I *almost* drank."

Victoria stood. "Oh, give it up, gentlemen," she told them, laughing. "The time has come to make a clean breast of things. Caroline wants some answers. As she has borne the brunt of the thing, being subjected to attempts on her life, I do believe she is not making an out-of-the-way demand. Besides, knowing only half the story thus far, I too am curious. André, have you been able to discover her identity since last we met?"

Caroline couldn't be sure, but she thought André hesitated for a moment, less than half a heartbeat actually, before shaking his head. "I am mortified to admit that I have not—at least not definitely." He brightened slightly as he looked directly at her and added, "I'm close, I am convinced of it. I lack only one last verifying communication from my man in Leicester, where I am fairly certain you lived. I would have traveled there myself, except for my strong desire to be back with you here at Standish Court."

"Leicester?" Victoria questioned, turning to Caroline. "That would explain the pieman." She turned to the older

Standish. "Your 'man,' André? He is on his way here now,
I trust?"

"On winged feet, my dear," André assured her, winking.

"Leicester. That is miles north of London, I'm sure, and
so far away from here," Caroline added, looking puzzled.
"Surely I could not have traveled from there barefoot. It must
be some mistake. I couldn't possibly have come from Leicester."

"You make it sound dreadful, imp. Leicester is a lovely
place," Pierre broke in smoothly, "although its history is
sometimes bloodthirsty. If I'm correct, Rich-ard III passed
the night before the Battle of Bosworth there, in the Blue
Boar Inn, and his body was buried in the Grey Friars' church.
Poor, abused man. Eventually his remains were exhumed and
tossed into the Soar from Bow Bridge and his stone coffin
turned into a horse trough, possibly for use at that same Blue
Boar Inn. Still, all things considered," he ended as Caroline's
steely stare threatened to skewer him where he stood, "it is,
as I said, a delightful city."

"Founded by King Lear, I believe, on the site of the Roman *Ratae*," André, barely containing his mirth, added helpfully, earning himself a steely stare of his own.

Pierre nodded. "Ah, yes, there is a wealth of history in
Leicester. But we digress. I believe I hear dearest Caroline
gnashing her teeth."

"I think you are both abominable!" Caroline declared vehemently, reaching behind her to toss a pillow in their general
direction. "*Ouch!* My back! Now see what you've made me
do! There are times when I think I have lost my memory,
and other times when I'm equally convinced I am only suffering from delusions, and that none of this is real. I'm not
in Sussex, surrounded by village idiots—save Victoria, who
has been the best of good friends to me. I'm actually in
Bedlam, *imagining* all of this!"

Victoria retrieved the pillow and placed it behind Caroline, gently pushing her against it while asking her to please not exert herself any further. She, Victoria promised in an undertone, would handle matters from here.

When she turned to face the Standishes, she was no longer Victoria Sherbourne, Countess of Wickford, but Victoria Quinton, master sleuth. "All right, gentlemen," she began, pulling herself up to her full height and glaring commandingly at them from behind her spectacles, "let's get down to cases, shall we? Restricting ourselves to only what is known for a fact, and not straying to conjecture or supposition—or even enlightening lessons in ancient history—just precisely what *do* you know?"

André made a great business of clutching at his chest and tottering to a nearby chair. "Good gracious!" he exclaimed wonderingly. "I do believe I am mortally wounded. Pierre, my only son, please, I beg you, take up the sword and defend your fallen sire."

Pierre lifted his hands to softly applaud his father. "Well done, sir," he complimented dryly. "Not that I am surprised you have chosen to retire to the fringes and leave me to make your explanations for you. My felicitations, Victoria, you remain as sharp as ever; even marriage to Patrick has not dulled your fire. Caroline," he continued, turning to face her. "I agree that you deserve some answers. However, before I tell you anything, I would ask that you promise you will listen very carefully to what I say, and then likewise promise to allow your friends to settle the situation for you while you remain out of harm's way."

Caroline very deliberately folded her arms across her stomach. "You'd have to be totally to let in the attic if you'd believe me, no matter if I swore those promises on a stack of Bibles piled high as the Tower of London," she pointed out reasonably. "Just get on with it, Pierre, please. Why don't you begin with Mrs. Merrydell, my dearest chaperone, if you need a place to start."

"All right, Caroline. I do begin to believe it would be performing a kindness to tell you something, so let me tell you what my father, through brilliant investigation, has learned—and then forwarded by way of discreet messengers almost daily to his son, who had been ruthlessly left behind here to act as resident nursemaid."

Pierre sat down familiarly at the bottom of the bed, as if the telling were going to take some time. "Mrs. Merrydell's meeting with you in the village was no accident," he began, much to Caroline's relief. "The entire incident was staged so that you would engage her services as chaperone, and the importuning dandy she beat heavily about the head and shoulders with her reticule was none other than her son, Ursley Merrydell. I had recognized them both a week earlier walking together outside the inn in the village, as Father—who had discovered their presence before leaving for London—had prudently warned me against them. I had been keeping them under observation ever since, long before Mrs. Merrydell so graciously helped me by imposing her way into this house."

"And you revealed *none* of this to poor Caroline," Victoria concluded quietly, shaking her head. "How infuriatingly typical of you, Pierre. At least André shared his knowledge of Mrs. Merrydell and Ursley with Patrick and me."

Pierre slanted her a smile. "Explanations are so tedious, Victoria," he explained softly, but without apology.

"*Ursley?*" Caroline exclaimed in disbelief, her mind whirling with this onslaught of information. "It is no wonder then that he grew up twisted, as if having Amity Merrydell for a mother were not inducement enough. Whoops!" She put a hand to her mouth as Pierre frowned. "Please," she urged, "forgive my interruption. Go on."

"Ursley was also the man Caroline first saw in the gardens—and the one who shaved the leather on her mount's cinch,'' Victoria interposed, her quick mind racing ahead to meet logical conclusions.

"One and the same, dear lady, I'm sure," André supplied from the corner. "We can only be thankful he is as incompetent as his mother is obnoxious—and that Caroline is an excellent rider who obviously knows how to take a fall."

Caroline frowned, then voiced a protest. "But—but he couldn't be! The man in the cobbler's was not very tall, and quite thin, although still rather strong, in a wiry sort of way. The man in the garden was *huge!*" Her frown deepened. "At least, I *thought* he was. Maybe it was his sack that was huge." She looked at Pierre. "And just maybe I was more frightened than I thought," she ended in a small voice.

"Now there's a revelation," Pierre told her, his smile taking any sting from his words.

Caroline immediately blushed to advantage, at least to Pierre's mind. "He's really such an unprepossessing little man. I feel foolish."

Pierre reached over to pat the hands that now lay in her lap. "We are all allowed to be foolish from time to time," he assured her.

She looked at him closely. "But not you," she said flatly. "You're always so composed."

She was amazed to see a slight hint of color invade his lean cheeks and immediately sensed he was thinking about his reaction to hearing that she had been hurt. Victoria had been correct; he must have been greatly overset. Caroline didn't know why, but it went a long way toward making her bruises less painful.

"We all have our moments, dear girl. Now," Pierre went on quickly, "to get back to the story as I know it. Father and I first became suspicious of the Merrydells when they installed themselves in the village a few days after you arrived at Standish Court. There was no reason for their presence, as the village is not exactly a social center, boasts no restorative waters, or can even be said to house an interesting historic ruin or two. So, armed with their names—as they signed the inn register with their true names, which was a mistake only dedicated bumblers could make—Father deserted us to set out for London, to conduct a small investigation."

"A very discreet yet intensive investigation," André amended carefully, "as I did not wish to expose my reasons for the questions I asked. I found no end of officials willing to speak to me about Mrs. Merrydell and her son, although I would beg Pierre not to soil your ears with all the details of the tales that I heard. I then traveled to dear Victoria and her Patrick, to enlist their aid as well."

"Do your best to appear flattered, Caroline," Pierre advised with a small smile. "Father doesn't go out of his way for people very often."

"Thank you, André," Caroline said dutifully. "Truly, I thank you all, for I have done nothing to deserve your interest in my dilemma. Now, with that out of the way, do you think, Pierre, that you could get on with it? I'm all but dying of curiosity."

Pierre obliged, for he knew that the explanation was rough ground and he'd rather get over it quickly. "Mrs. Amity Merrydell, although she is commonly known as Mrs. Amelia Chumley, Mrs. Agnes Forester, and Mrs. Agatha Terwilliger—there may be one other, although it escapes me for the moment—has made a moderately successful career of chaperoning less well-connected young ladies from the more remote regions of the country who wish to enter society. She inveigles herself into the unsuspecting family with false but glowing credentials, then introduces her son into the picture in the hopes of making a match with the young lady in question.

"When that ploy fails—and with Ursley cast in the role of hopeful swain, failure is all but a foregone conclusion—Mrs. Merrydell then steals what she can from her employer and departs for greener pastures. Bow Street has been looking for her for quite some time. Do I have it right thus far, Father?''

André rose from his chair to take up the story. ''As far as I can say for now, it would appear that you, Caroline, were to be her next victim, only this time with a twist. Your guardian died while Mrs. Merrydell was in residence, leaving you alone, but not penniless. Unfortunately, you were also left with Mrs. Merrydell as your legal guardian, an error in judgment I prefer to believe was caused by your previous guardian's failing health.''

''But that guardianship was to terminate with the arrival of your twenty-first birthday, when you would take control of your inheritance,'' Pierre added, watching her carefully for any signs of remembrance of the things they were telling her.

''Enter Ursley, the loving swain,'' Victoria concluded intelligently. ''Mrs. Merrydell would have to marry you off to her son before you reached your majority, or else lose everything. She must have been sorely tempted. A few pieces of pilfered silver were nothing compared to having your entire fortune for herself.''

Caroline raised her hands, wordlessly begging them to stop. ''I may not know my own name, but I do know one thing—I would rather die than be married to someone with the name of Ursley Merrydell. And if that weren't enough, the prospect of having Amity for a mother-in-law would be ample inducement to cheerfully slit my own throat.''

''Which, taking the thing a step further, leads us to the Merrydells' problem. If not marriage, then what?'' Pierre asked silkily.

Caroline's mouth opened, forming a silent ''Oh!''

''Yes, my dear girl; oh,'' André said kindly. ''We feel certain you were on the run from your prospective murderers when you stumbled into my son's life. It is no wonder you lost your memory, as your memories included the death of your guardian and the prospect of falling victim to the Merrydells' greed.''

Caroline shook her head, trying to take it all in. She knew she should be feeling sorry for the loss of her guardian, but she couldn't. She had no memory of any guardian. Instead, she concentrated on the question of her appearance in Sussex. ''But—but I still couldn't have gotten from Leicester to Sussex on my own. It's impossible.''

''You weren't in Leicester, my dear,'' André put in quickly. ''You were not thirty miles from here in a small, unpretentious town called Ockley, installed in a rented house to which the Merrydells had brought you, supposedly to recoup your strength after your guardian's death. After all, they could scarcely murder you in Leicester, could they? People would be too suspicious. If you refused to marry Ursley, they would simply arrange for you to have a fatal accident. It's all quite elementary, really, except that you must have discovered their plan and escaped, forcing the Merrydells to follow you here to finish the job.''

Pierre, André and Victoria exchanged glances while Caroline sat nervously plucking the bedcovers, deep in thought. Had they said too much, they asked each other silently. Had they said too little? Was this news too great a shock on top of her recent accident? Would they jolt her into remembrance, or block out her past forever?

At last, when the three thought they no longer could stand the silence, Caroline spoke. ''You *have* to know my name. You know too much *not* to know my name. Why won't you tell me?''

Pierre took her hand once more, squeezing it gently. ''Only André knows the whole of it, and it is a secret he seems to delight in keeping. I know my father, and it is useless to press him, as he can be as close as an oyster when he wishes. Besides, Caroline, the doctor feels it would be unwise to tell you too much at once. He'd rather you remembered your past on your own."

"Doctor Burgess said that?" she questioned in disbelief. "He didn't seem to know enough about memory loss to make a judgement."

"No," Pierre agreed readily enough, "but the doctors Father consulted in London do, and it is their orders we have followed, and will continue to follow. We have given you some answers, some reasons for the attempts on your life. The rest will come back to you, Caroline, I'm convinced of it. Why don't you lie back now, and get some rest? All in all, you've had a busy day."

Pierre's oblique reference to the goings-on in her chamber brought Caroline's mind back to Mrs. Merrydell, and her eyes narrowed in sudden anger. "You *knew*," she accused Pierre, her voice tight. "You knew who she was, and what she wanted, and you let her stay here anyway? You let the woman who wants me dead sleep under the same roof with me—*and never told me?* Didn't you think I would be vaguely *interested?*" Her voice rose shrilly. "Just who in bloody hell do you think you are, to use me this way?"

Victoria coughed discreetly, catching André's attention, and the two withdrew from the chamber, leaving Pierre to face Caroline's rightful wrath as best he could. It might not have been the right thing to do, or even the fair thing, but it was, they silently agreed, precisely what Pierre deserved. After all, *he* was the one who had been assigned to protect her.

"They've left you," Caroline informed him tersely, having been forced to look away from his clear, unblinking gaze. "Like rats deserting a sinking ship, as the saying goes." Her bravado left her, and her lower lip began to tremble. "Oh, Pierre, how could you? I know I have been a bother to you, but were you so uncaring that you could install a murderess under your roof just to watch the sport as she stalked her unknowing quarry? Victoria told me this morning how you teased her husband with what you knew about that poor, confused man—Quinton's murderer—watching as he and Victoria ran about willy-nilly trying to find out what you already knew. Were you doing it again? Was this a diversion for you, a bit of sport? I thought—I thought you cared for me, if just a little bit.''

Pierre shook his head, his all-seeing gaze never leaving her face. ''Just like a woman, aren't you, throwing my past in my teeth. As Victoria has told you, I can be a wicked, wicked man. But, Caroline—my dearest Caroline—can you really believe I'd let anyone harm you? I allowed Mrs. Merrydell in this house because it was the one way I could watch her, and because I had hoped her presence might somehow serve to bring back your memory. You've never been in any danger from her. My only error was in underestimating the son's ability to outwit my grooms, which led to your accident yesterday. For that I should be horsewhipped. But please, Caroline, don't think your welfare is no more than a game to me.''

Caroline drew a shaky breath, somehow knowing he was being more open with her than he had ever been with anyone in his life. He had not said he loved her, and she didn't really know if she was ready to hear those words from his lips. She only knew they had come a long way since their first meeting, that they had learned to trust each other at least a little bit, and that they were deeply attracted to each other. For now, with the cloud of her memory loss still hanging over her head, it was enough.

They had to take care of first things first.

She moved toward him a fraction. ''What do we do now, Pierre? Do we call the constable? It's obvious Mrs. Merrydell's presence isn't going to jog my memory, so I would think she has outlived her usefulness. I want that woman and her son out of my life just as soon as possible.''

Pierre leaned forward, placing a quick kiss on the tip of

her nose. "That's my girl, pluck to the backbone. There's only one small, nagging problem. Ursley has somehow slipped his leash, abandoning his room at the inn and eluding the bumbling man I sent to follow him after his meeting with his mother this morning. It's so hard to get good help these days, you understand, what with the war. We do still have Mrs. Merrydell where we want her, but I don't want the mother without the son. He's a loose end I'd rather see neatly tied. Can I count on your help to flush him out of hiding?"

The idea of turning the tables on the Merrydells filled her with delight. "What do I have to do?"

He kissed her again, on the lips this time, and she was suddenly aware that they were, yet again, alone in her chamber and in a most compromising position. His arms held her gently, though she could feel the leashed strength of him against her, and she longed to experience what it would be like really to be held by him, loved by him.

She broke from his kiss, flushed and breathless, and pushed against the pillow. "Pierre? What do you want from me?"

He lifted his left eyebrow a fraction, causing her blush to deepen. "You tempt me, Caroline," he teased, "but I have promised myself to be good, so I will answer the question you thought you asked. What I want from you now, dearest girl, is quite simple—I want you to die for me."

CHAPTER SEVENTEEN

IT WAS A ROOM rigged out for mourning the death of a beloved family member.

All the mirrors in the chamber had been shrouded with deepest black cloth, and the pictures denoting pleasant bucolic scenes or the smiling faces of various Standish forebears were all turned to face the wall.

The heavy, midnight-blue velvet draperies were pulled tightly across the wide windows, shutting out the light from the setting sun, and only a few softly flickering candles burned on either side of the black-crepe-hung bed that held the body of the late Caroline Addams—with two *D*'s.

All was quiet, hushed, until a high, piercing wail shattered the silence.

"Oh, my poor baby! My poor, poor baby!"

André came up behind the woman and took hold of her shoulders, his fastidiousness causing him to use only his fingertips in none-too-gently drawing her away from the doorway to Caroline's bedchamber. It wouldn't do to allow the harridan to enter and, most probably, cast her tall, angular body across the deceased in a distasteful display of grief.

"There, there, Mrs. Merrydell, attempt to get a grip on yourself, for all our sakes. Miss Addams was hardly your baby. It's not as if you knew her all that well, much as I am gratified to see your deep concern."

Mrs. Merrydell dabbed at her rouged cheeks with a lace-edged handkerchief, cruelly pushing a corner of the linen into one eye in order to manufacture a credible tear before she turned to face André. "It's not just that, dear sir. I was in charge of her welfare." She moaned disconsolately. "I should never have allowed her to go out for that ride yesterday. I knew, after all, that she was suffering some terrible scrambling of the brainbox—misplacing her memory, that is. She had no business on a horse, did she, sir? Oh, why did she have to die?"

"You mustn't blame yourself, my dear lady," he told her bracingly. "It was an accident, nothing more." André looked past the woman into the chamber, to where Caroline lay on top of the bedcovers, neatly dressed in a white lawn nightgown that covered her from neck to toes, her arms crossed gracefully over her breasts, a small sprig of wildflowers held in her clasped hands. Pierre had added that last bit, and André privately agreed it was a nice touch, although he much preferred roses.

"And just as we all thought she had rallied," he lamented sadly. "She was fine one moment this morning, sipping some of the lovely tea you made for her with your own hands and promising that she would even join us at table for dinner. And then—*pouf!*—she was gone, snatched from us in the first sweet flower of her youth, her last breath sighing from her body even as my son watched in horror. Ah, the pity of it, Mrs. Merrydell, the bleeding pity of it. And now we will bury her, hide her away in the cold, cold ground, without ever knowing her true name."

Mrs. Merrydell flung herself heavily into André's arms. "Oh no! *Dear* sir, no!" she cried in what might have been grief but could just as easily have been panic. "You cannot allow that to happen. Surely you must wait—in the chance someone may come to identify her! Surely someone will come!"

So that was it! "Someone" would come. That had been the part of the mother-to-son conversation Pierre had missed. André allowed himself a small smile. "It is a comforting thought, Mrs. Merrydell, and I *have* been placing advertisements in all the newspapers with just that hope in mind, since the very beginning. But in truth, madam, how long can we wait? After all, the weather is still warm. Excuse my indelicacy, but one cannot keep a dead body about indefinitely in the heat, can one? Of course," he added, as if thinking aloud, "there is always the icehouse, I suppose."

"Yes! That's it! Put her on ice!" Mrs. Merrydell exclaimed excitedly, then quickly lapsed once more into loud sobs of anguished grief.

André looked over the woman's shoulder and thought he could see Caroline's chest rising and falling slightly in silent mirth. "There, there, Mrs. Merrydell," he soothed, rolling his eyes in disgust at her blatant overacting. Disengaging himself from her convulsive grip, he hastened the weeping woman down the hallway to the stairs before a giggling corpse could give the game away.

"I'M BORED." Caroline pushed out her lower lip in a pout and crossed her arms over her chest as she sat in the middle of her bed, a deck of cards carelessly scattered across the satin coverlet. "And I'm hungry!"

Victoria, who had just entered the chamber, closed the door behind her and locked it securely. "*Shhh!*" she warned, a finger to her lips. "I'm supposedly the only person in this room who is capable of speech. For all our sakes, keep your voice down, Caroline."

She reached into her pocket to pull out an apple. "Will this do for now?" She tossed it to Caroline, who deftly caught it with one hand. "I'm only sorry I couldn't bring you my own uneaten dinner on a tray. I am convinced it was delicious, for everyone else ate their fill, even the grieving Mrs. Merrydell—who had two helpings of dessert—but I took one bite and thought I was going to disgrace myself by becoming ill right at the table."

"An apple, and not a big one at that. André brought me part of a nice meat pie from the kitchens when he stopped by earlier, but all you could find was an apple? Ursley had better show up soon to identify my remains or I'll starve to death." Caroline rubbed the apple against the satin coverlet, then bit into it, pushing the bite to one side of her mouth to add, "I'm sorry you're feeling ill, Victoria—it's the baby, isn't it? I know I'm being demanding, but Susan, my maid, is being less than useless."

"She seemed quite competent to me," Victoria said, frowning.

Caroline smiled. "That was before I died. She won't come anywhere near me since laying me out. She said I gave her the creeps, talking and laughing all the time she was putting this white powder on my face and hands to make me look bloodless." She turned her face this way and that. "What do you think, Victoria? Do I look properly dead?"

Victoria ignored this question, and sat down in the chair beside the bed, rapidly fanning herself with her handkerchief. "It's positively airless in here with all the windows shut. You may be enjoying yourself, Caroline, but I can tell you that— thanks to the unremittingly obnoxious Mrs. Merrydell—I have about reached the end of my tether. She insists on pestering us to be allowed to keep a vigil over your body, and breaks into hiccupping sobs every few minutes, just to let us all know how grievously she is suffering. I escaped up here just now because I was sure I would do her an injury if I had to remain in her encroaching company another moment."

Caroline was instantly contrite. She slid from the high bed to pour Victoria a cooling glass of water from the pitcher that stood on a stand in the corner. "Poor thing," she said sincerely, handing her friend the glass before crawling back onto the coverlet and recovering her apple. "The woman is dreadfully in the way, isn't she? Pierre should be forced to handle her, not you."

"Pierre?" Victoria laughed. "He's too busy arranging for the removal of your perishable mortal remains to the icehouse in the morning. Not that he plans to actually put you in storage, as it were, but only to hide you elsewhere in the house, as it is difficult to have you laid out here, where Mrs. Merrydell might be able to sneak in and see your supposed corpse gnawing on a chicken leg. Pierre is convinced that Ursley will appear tomorrow as if on cue to view the body—clutching one of André's advertisements in his hand, no doubt, and claiming you are his long-lost fiancée."

"No doubt," Caroline agreed coolly as she laid the apple core in a small dish on the nightstand. "Ursley Terwilliger is a toad, but he has always been an extremely punctual toad. As I recall, it is his single redeeming virtue."

The water glass dropped to the floor unheeded, to splinter into a hundred pieces. *"Caroline!"* Victoria exclaimed in sudden excitement, her fatigue, and even the slight queasiness she had been feeling lately whenever confronted by food, forgotten. "It's working, just as the doctors said! It's above everything marvelous! All you needed was a start, some gentle nudging. You're beginning to remember!"

Caroline put a trembling hand to her suddenly aching forehead and stared at her friend in wonder, not really seeing her but concentrating on a picture that was floating in the forefront of her mind. "I can see him, Victoria…sitting at the head of a long dining table…pushing food down his skinny throat as fast as he can. How dare he sit there? He doesn't belong there."

"Who does belong there?" Victoria prodded in a fierce whisper, leaning toward the bed. "Who belongs there, Caroline?"

"Caroline?" Caroline covered her eyes with her hands, trying to recapture the image that had splintered and disappeared. "Oh, it's gone. It's gone." She looked at Victoria, her huge eyes burning with tears in her powdered, too-white face. "I—I don't remember. Who—who is Caroline?"

"Oh, my dear Lord," Victoria breathed in horror, wishing she could kick herself for her loose tongue. "You've forgotten who you are *now!* This couldn't be what is supposed to happen. Just stay there, my dear, and try not to worry. I must get Pierre at once."

Caroline was looking at her strangely, just as if she had never seen her before that moment. "Pierre? Who is Pierre? I know no one by that name." She shook her head, then winced at the pain the movement caused.

Victoria's eyes opened wide behind her spectacles, and she knew she was gaping at Caroline, her mouth at half-mast. "You—you don't remember Pierre, either?"

"Pierre? No. Silly French name. And who are you? Did you tell me your name? Oh, my head. It hurts terribly. It's so strange. I never get the headache. Oh, well, I can't think about that now. What were we talking about? It hurts to think, just like that evening I tried champagne when I wasn't supposed to and could barely remember how to walk. I'll ask my questions again later. Would you mind if I were a poor hostess and lay down for a time? It helped enormously when I drank the champagne. Grandfather will surely be delighted to entertain you while I rest. We have so few visitors here at Abbey House, you know."

Her heart pounding with mingled dread and excitement, Victoria dared to try pushing Caroline a little further. "Yes, of course," she agreed swiftly. "I don't mind at all, Miss— oh, dear, what a scatterbrain I am! Please forgive me but, like you, I have always had such a difficult time with names. Now I seem to have forgotten yours."

Victoria held her breath as she waited for Caroline to answer.

The girl was already lying against the pillows, her knees drawn up high against her body, one hand tucked beneath her cheek. Her eyes closed, she murmured quietly, "Please don't apologize. My name is Catherine. Catherine Halliford. But dearest Grandfather, he always calls me Caro."

IT WAS AFTER MIDNIGHT.

Pierre paced the floor of his father's study like a caged animal, once more like the dark, brooding panther to which his father had once so aptly compared him.

Everything was wrong, he decided, pounding his fist into his palm. From start to finish he had bungled the affair, and bungled it badly.

It was his fault that Caroline—no, *Catherine;* he had to begin thinking of her as Catherine—was lying upstairs, deeply asleep or unconscious, he did not know.

He should have turned Amity Merrydell and her idiot son over to the constable the moment he had decided they were out to harm Catherine. Never mind that he had possessed no proof; never mind that all he could have told the constable was that the two were suspicious merely because of their presence. But no, he had been content to wait, believing himself superior to anything they might try, any rig they might run.

"Arrogant," he said aloud as he walked to the drinks table to pour himself three fingers of port. "You're so damned arrogant, Standish. I don't know how you stand yourself, you're so bloody perfect."

And if he couldn't have had the pair of them tossed into gaol, he should have taken greater care with Catherine. He had been placed in charge of protecting her, while his father had gone haring off in search of her true identity. It had been a simple job, elementary actually, something any moderately intelligent ape could have accomplished without undo effort.

But, no, he had to botch that as well, not once, but twice. "London society has dulled your wits, Standish," he told himself, tossing off the port. "You've degenerated into the very worst sort of man, becoming nothing but a toothless drawing-room ornament.''

Even Sir John Oakvale, that featherbrain who had more hair than wit, could have done better than he had, and with one badly manicured hand strapped behind his back! It was a disgrace, that's what it was, and Pierre knew that if he lived to be one hundred, he would never forgive himself.

Pouring another drink, he continued with his mental self-flagellation.

The day Ursley had accosted Catherine in the cobbler's shop—that should have been the day the man drew his last breath. He should have throttled the miserable little worm, choked him until his eyes bulged from their sockets, then tossed his carcass in the dirt and had his harridan mother transported in chains to the other side of the world.

But, no, he had been too smart to do that, too enthralled with the supposed brilliance of his own schemes to consider that he might be playing a dangerous game with Catherine's physical welfare.

Even when she fell from her horse, he had chosen not to act, but merely played the spy, watching Amity Merrydell and her son as they met at the bottom of the gardens to discuss strategy. Merely capturing them was too mundane, too expected. He was going to dazzle Catherine with his ingenuity, his fancy footwork, by tripping the Merrydells up at their own game.

The fine French crystal goblet hit the cold stones of the fireplace and exploded with an unsatisfying, splintering crash.

If he had been too thick, too impressed with his own brilliance to act before, why hadn't he called a halt to the game when his father had returned home with definite evidence that the Merrydells meant to kill Cath-erine? Yes, there had been the business about Ursley escaping the eye of the man sent to watch him, but how dangerous could that puppy be without his mother to direct him?

His reluctance had been only another excuse in an endless string of excuses that allowed him to continue playing the game.

Now Catherine's overburdened mind had snapped beneath the strain, sending her into a dark, confused world where she knew her name but had lost all recollection of him, the man who loved her beyond life itself. What an evil justice!

He hadn't been able to look at Victoria, meet that intelligent woman's eyes when she had come to tell him what had transpired in Catherine's bedchamber. He had fled from the room, leaving his father and Victoria to whisper between themselves, and had hidden here in this study, where his frustrated pacing was fast wearing a hole in his father's carpet.

The only thing worse than going back over his many mistakes was thinking about the young woman lying in the room above him. His supposed redeeming Good Deed. Would this sleep she had slipped into ease Catherine's confusion, so that when she awoke—if indeed she ever did awake—she would remember everything—her past, her present, and, he prayed with all his being, some slight knowledge that she may have planned for a future that had him in it?

Their future together. His heart squeezed with pain at the thought. How had he come to this—he, Pierre Claghorn Standish, who had been heart-whole for so long? When had it happened? When had his concern for Catherine turned to love; when had his very natural attraction to a beautiful young woman grown into passion?

He remembered her kiss, the feel of her soft warmth pressed against him, wordlessly telling him things he had no right to ask. Even in that he had behaved abominably, advancing on her when she was off balance, her mind confused, her body injured. He was a cad—worse than a cad. He didn't deserve her.

If only she would waken and look at him with recognition in her beautiful wide eyes. If only she would waken whole, with all her memories intact. He would let her go then, knowing she would be all right. He didn't deserve her love, and wouldn't press his suit anymore.

He stood sightlessly staring down into the fireplace at the second wanton destruction of his father's crystal in two days, then gave a short, self-mocking laugh. "Who do I think I'm kidding? I can't do that. I *won't* do that."

"Prattling to yourself, my son?" André said from the doorway. "Bad sign, that. Perhaps your time would be better spent in prayer."

Pierre turned to face his father, looking at him from beneath half-closed lids, his dark eyes unfathomable, his face an emotionless mask. "Prayer? You're becoming damned moral, Father. It doesn't suit you."

"Just as the sackcloth and ashes you're wearing fit you extremely ill," André responded, causing his son to wince. "I asked for a softening tint of humanness, a smidgeon of humility. I did not ask for maudlin self-pity. Poor Victoria has just stumbled off to her bed near tears, unable to reconcile herself to your lack of fighting spirit. You've been a bitter disappointment to her, you understand, as she had begun to think of you as unflappable."

A tic began to work in Pierre's cheek. "Enjoying yourself, Father?"

André sat down behind his desk, crossing his legs. "Oddly, Pierre, I'm not. I believe I like your deliberate arrogance much more than this uncharacteristic sentimental self-condemnation. It certainly isn't doing Catherine much good, and on top of everything else, it's dashed boring to watch."

Catherine. Mention of her name brought Pierre's head up, and he stared at his father, who was looking back at him levelly, a small smile on his lips, his brows raised a fraction, as if waiting for his son to speak. "Father, I—"

"Yes, *mon fils?*" the older man purred.

The corners of Pierre's mouth slowly curved upward as, with a deep, flourishing bow to his sire, he threw off his despondency. "My congratulations. You're still the master, *mon pére*. Now, if you'll be so kind as to excuse me, I have a pressing matter to attend to before our expected visitor descends on us."

"You're going to Catherine?" André questioned softly as his son walked toward the door. "I'm very pleased."

Pierre stopped, his hand on the latch, but did not face his father. "I don't give a tinker's curse for your pleasure, Father. Between us, *pleasing* ourselves has led to more heartache than happiness. It's my *salvation* I seek now."

CHAPTER EIGHTEEN

HE USED HIS KEY to enter Catherine's darkened bedchamber, locking the door behind him while consigning any thoughts of impropriety to the devil. This time was his, his and Catherine's. He would brook no intrusions from the outside world.

Walking over to the bed, he looked down at her sleeping form. She looked totally at peace, with the world and herself, a slight smile curving her lips as if she were dreaming of some fond memory.

Was it a memory of him? He doubted it.

Pierre frowned, noticing the white powder that still marred the perfection of her beloved features. It was another reminder of his stupidity, and he felt an overwhelming urge to have it gone. He extracted his handkerchief and sat down on the edge of the bed, using the clean linen to softly wipe away the traces of powder.

This was love. For the first time in his life he understood why his father had been so happy, and why he had retired from society when his beloved wife had died. He understood Patrick's desperation when confronted with Victoria's plan to ferret out Quennel Quinton's murderer, for the need to protect one's beloved was an all but overpowering emotion.

And how Pierre loved his Catherine. His love had stripped him of all arrogance, all confidence, and even, for a time, all common sense. His father had been wrong. Completing a good deed would not make Pierre human. Only love could do that.

So intent was he on the performance of his task, so involved was he with his thoughts, that Catherine took him completely by surprise when she opened her eyes and looked directly up into his tear-streaked face.

"Pierre," she whispered, her own eyes filling with tears. "Please don't cry."

"Catherine!" he breathed hoarsely as she reached to pull him down to her. "You remember me. Oh, thank God! My dearest love! You remember me."

"I love you, Pierre," she said simply, those four words, spoken so matter-of-factly, thawing once and forever all the ice that had for so long surrounded his heart.

IT WAS TEN o'clock in the morning, and they were all gathered around a heavily laden tea tray in the drawing room, Mrs. Merrydell having earlier been securely locked in a storage room by Pierre, who had kept his resolution not to play at conspirator any longer. Now he sat beside his beloved on the settee, dressed in his impeccable black and white, looking well rested and ready for action.

"Grandfather Halliford had been ill for a long time, not that I wasn't devastated by his death," Catherine told her interested audience. "It was his greatest wish that I have a Season in London, which is why he hired Mrs. Merrydell as my chaperone and mentor although, as we've already established, Grandfather and I knew her as Agatha Terwilliger.

"I disliked her on sight, and really didn't wish for a Season, but Grandfather was adamant. He may have been naught but a simple, successful manufacturer of shoes—a rich upstart with machine oil beneath his fingernails, as he described himself—but his granddaughter was a full two generations from the smell of the shop! He was quite a man, my grandfather, and the reason my language is, as you all have noticed, sometimes unladylike."

"Never unladylike," André interrupted from his position

against the mantelpiece. "Your grandfather's generation, male and female both, were much freer with their speech than people of polite upbringing are supposed to be today. For myself, I find your lapses honest and refreshing. But I must be quiet. Please continue with your story, Catherine, my dear."

Catherine thanked him for his kind words and went on, "You can imagine my distress when I learned Mrs. Ter— Mrs. *Merrydell* was to be my guardian. We had no living relatives and I suppose Grandfather, knowing I was soon to reach my majority, saw no harm in it."

Victoria set down her empty teacup and leaned forward slightly in her chair, the better to see Catherine, for she had purposely left her spectacles on her dresser that morning. "You must have been terribly overset. But your grandfather sounds to have been a wonderful man, and I am happy to hear you do not hold his ill judgment against him. How was he to know the Merrydells' dastardly plans for you?"

Catherine grimaced. "Marriage to Ursley had been their first intention, but I wasn't having it. I was walking in the gardens when I overheard them discussing the proper way to dispose of me," she told Victoria as Pierre reached over to squeeze her hand.

"I had removed my slippers so that I could creep closer and hear everything without giving myself away with my footsteps, when I stepped on a dry branch—and the race was on." She chuckled, remembering the way she had run barefoot into the forest, Ursley doing his best to follow her in his ridiculous high-heeled shoes. "I lost him easily enough, but I had no money, no shoes, no idea where I was, and no one to turn to for assistance. In the end, Ursley found me again, and I would have been well and truly caught if Pierre hadn't come along. Of course, I rather wish I hadn't been so clumsy as to trip over a rock and hit my head in my effort to capture his coachman's attention. All I could think about was getting back to Abbey House. Even now, it isn't a pleasant memory."

"Many a man would have broken under such strain," André assured her. "I don't wish to press you further, Catherine, but one thing still troubles me. How did you come by the cloak?"

Catherine turned to grin at Pierre, who grinned back, having already heard the story as the two of them, lying side by side on her bed, had talked through the night. "I stole it, of course," she quipped. "Somewhere there is a gentleman who will never again leave his cloak behind in his curricle when he visits a country inn for luncheon. The only thing I feel sorry for is stealing that lovely pie from some good farm wife's windowsill. But I did have to eat, didn't I?"

Victoria got up and went to squint through the window overlooking the drive at the front of the house, her third visit to the window in the past half hour. "I'm just happy it has all turned out so well, especially after that little scare you gave us last night, Catherine. First you lost your past, then you misplaced your present—it is good to have all of you with us this morning."

"Hear, hear!" André echoed, lifting his teacup in a toast. "Still looking for my man to return here from faraway Leicester, Victoria?" he asked as he replaced the cup on the mantel. "Perhaps if you sent a maid for your spectacles."

The young matron flushed becomingly and shot André a quelling look, just as the sound of a horse approaching the house at a rapid clip filled the room. She pushed aside the thin draperies to look out over the drive, gave a small girlish squeal, and ran for the foyer.

Catherine looked after her friend, frowning in confusion. "What on earth—"

Pierre gently pushed her against the settee. "My wits have been dulled, have they not, Father, that I haven't guessed before now? Your man, the one who was to make the final confirmation of Catherine's identity, is none other than my good friend, Patrick Sherbourne. I should have known he wouldn't allow estate business to keep his aristocratic nose out of my affairs. He's waited too long for some well-earned revenge.''

A few moments later, the Earl of Wickford and his countess entered the drawing room arm-in-arm, and Pierre and Catherine rose to greet them as André, looking pleased with himself, watched from a distance.

"Pierre, you sly old dog!" Patrick called, extending a hand to his friend. "What's this I hear about cupid's arrow having got you at last? It couldn't happen to a more deserving man. And this is Catherine," he continued as Pierre took his hand and shook it. "Such a little thing to cause such a great upheaval. You have my deepest thanks, Miss Halliford. I understand from my wife that you have succeeded in penetrating this fellow's dark soul and bringing it into the sunlight. Heaven knows I've tried and failed a dozen times or more.''

"Perhaps you didn't possess the correct tools, my lord," Catherine answered, coloring under Patrick's interested scrutiny.

Patrick threw back his head and laughed out loud. "She's witty as well as beautiful, Pierre," he told his friend. "The question remains, however—what are you, a confirmed bachelor, going to do about it?''

Slipping an arm around Catherine's shoulders so that he could pull her close to him, Pierre answered, "As I once told you, my friend, understanding the workings of a woman's mind is a lifelong study. I begin to believe that I shall enjoy that study, and all that goes with it, immensely.''

André, having heard another horse approaching up the drive, cleared his throat as he pushed himself away from the mantelpiece. "I hesitate to interrupt this heart-warming, truly affecting reunion, gentlemen, but it appears we are about to have another visitor.''

"Ursley," Catherine said at once, one hand involuntarily going to her throat. She looked up at Pierre, her eyes wide. "I can almost forgive him, for he was naught but his mother's tool, but do I have to see him, Pierre? It's silly, I know, but his face will bring back so many unpleasant memories."

Pierre's expression hardened, his dark eyes going strangely flat and colorless. He had promised her he would capture the man with as little fuss as possible and have him carted off to gaol with his murderous mother. He had promised, but now seeing the fear on Catherine's face, he regretted that promise.

Catherine saw the reluctance in his face, correctly interpreting how he felt. Pierre was unused to following orders, as he had been forced to do throughout most of this strange adventure, and his every instinct cried out for him to finish the project by marking its conclusion with his own, very individual stamp.

She bit her bottom lip, realizing that, although she loved him when he was open and vulnerable, as he had appeared to her a few moments last night when his tears had betrayed his deepest emotions, and she loved him excessively when he was being tender, as he had been with her all through the night, she loved him best of all when he was being arrogant, self-assured, and totally in control of a situation he had, in his own inimitable way, engineered.

She didn't say a word, but he knew what she was thinking. His left eyebrow, the one she alternately despised and adored, rose almost imperceptibly as he looked down on her and breathed quietly, "Caro?"

Catherine smiled brilliantly, then slipped from beneath his encircling arm to grab Victoria's hand and lead her toward the door to the morning room. "Come, my friend. We're dreadfully in the way right now, as the boys wish to play, and we wouldn't want to rob them of their sport."

"I like her, Pierre," Patrick declared, grinning. "I like that little girl more than I can say." He rubbed his palms together in anticipation of what he was sure to be some jolly good fun. "Now, what do you want me to do?"

Pierre turned toward the door to the foyer, absently adjusting his snowy cravat with one steady hand. "Just follow my lead, my friend, and I'm sure you'll pick it up in no time. Father? Are you with us?"

André spoke from the chair he had positioned himself in, his legs crossed negligently at the ankle, his handsome face looking as bright and lively as his son's. "Need you ask *mon fils?* Let the farce begin."

"MR. URSLEY TERWILLIGER, sir," the loyal Hartley announced as he stood, rolling his eyes, just inside the open door.

Ursley entered the room in a great rush, brandishing a copy of one of the London newspapers, just as Pierre had prophesied, only to collide with the butler as that unfortunate man turned smartly on his heel to return to his post before—from the fierce expression on his face—he gave Terwilliger a pop on the nose.

Ursley's mother, had she been present, would have cuffed her son on the ear for his clumsiness, and that lowering thought instantly filled him with a firm resolve not to blunder again. "Watch where you're walking, you dolt!" Ursley blustered, rudely pushing the old man to one side and thereby giving his audience one less reason to love him. "Where do you have her?" he demanded hotly—following the script his mother had written for him—while rushing up to where Pierre stood watching him, idly stroking the crescent-shaped scar on his left cheekbone. "Where do you have my darling Catherine?"

Pierre peered owlishly down at Ursley, his dark eyes raking the smaller man from head to toe and obviously concluding the man was lacking—something or other, exactly what Ursley couldn't be sure. He only knew he had been judged and found wanting.

"*Ter*-williger. Terwilli-*ger?* Ter-*will*-iger!" Pierre mused aloud, then shook his head sadly. "No, I'm afraid not. I can't say as I recall the name. But then, I meet so many people. Have we been introduced?"

"Yes...no!...that is..." Ursley floundered into silence. Where was his mother, damn her black soul to hell anyway! She promised she'd be here, to guide him through this. His shifty gaze shot around the large, sunlit room. She hadn't told him the father was going to be here as well. The only thing that could be worse than one Standish was *two* Standishes. And who was that grinning fellow over there, for crying out loud? *Mama!* he cried silently. He wanted his mama!

"Terwilliger," Patrick drawled silkily, walking up to stand beside Pierre, the two tall, handsome, immaculately dressed men making Ursley feel small and more unlovely than ever. "I once knew a Terwilliger on the Peninsula. Wellington had him hanged from a tree, for looting, I believe. He was a poor dresser, as I remember him, who always looked as if he had made his own trousers. Any relation, old man?"

Ursley ran a finger inside his suddenly too-tight collar. "No!" he exclaimed quickly, guiltily removing the finger. "No relation at all. I—I'm here because of this," he explained, holding out the newspaper that was folded back to expose André's advertisement. "Having read it most carefully, I believe your unknown young woman to be none other than dearest Catherine Halliford, my missing *fiancée*."

André, his quizzing glass stuck to his eye, rose to walk fully around Ursley's now noticeably trembling body. "He reads," he said, as if to assure himself he had heard aright. Turning to Patrick, he repeated, "He reads! I wouldn't have thought it. It must have been the waistcoat. I've always wondered about the mental profundity of gentlemen who prefer pink satin, haven't you, Patrick?''

The earl could barely suppress his mirth. Marriage was wonderful, but there was nothing like a bit of good fun with one's male friends to brighten a day. ''I'll reserve my answer until I've inspected my own wardrobe, sir, if you don't mind,'' he answered congenially. ''But I think we are being sidetracked by this discussion of Mr. Terwilliger's intellectual prowess. He seems to be inquiring about your houseguest, the woman you called Caroline Addams. I think he is convinced she is his long-lost love.''

Pierre raised a hand to his mouth, feigning shock. ''Oh, dear! Patrick, do you really think so? Now here's a dilemma. How can I do this tactfully?'' He turned to look at Ursley, who was perspiring quite freely in the cool room. ''Could you perhaps describe to us the young lady in question, Mr. Terwilliger?''

Describe her? Ursley was nonplussed. His mother said they had the dratted girl laid out upstairs. Why couldn't he just tippy-toe up there and take a quick peep in at her? Something was wrong; he could feel it in his bones. The bitter taste of failure was a familiar one, and it was stinging him now, deep in the back of his throat. ''Describe her, you say. Yes, well, *um*,'' he began hesitantly, ''she was short. Yes, that's it, short—and dark.''

''Dark skin?'' Pierre pressed him.

Ursley shook his head. ''Dark hair, light skin.'' He held out his hand at shoulder level. ''And—and short.''

''Pretty?'' Pierre asked, unearthing his enameled snuffbox and offering some of his personal sort to everyone save Ursley.

The smaller man frowned, trying to decide if Catherine was pretty. She was presentable enough when she kept her mouth shut, he supposed. ''Pretty,'' he answered, nervously clearing his throat. "Look—if I could view, I mean, if I could just *see* her—"

Pierre shut the snuffbox with a loud snap that instantly had Ursley thinking of the trapdoor falling open beneath the gibbet. "That's impossible, sir." He took hold of Ursley at the elbow. "Not that I don't believe you, you understand. Our Caroline Addams is most certainly your Catherine Halliford."

"So—so what's the problem?"

"Perhaps you should sit down," Pierre suggested, his voice tinged with sympathy. "I fear I have some bad news."

Well, it was about time! Suppressing a relieved smile, Ursley allowed himself to be led to a chair, looking over his shoulder at Pierre as that man walked round to stand behind him, almost as if guarding him. "Bad news? Your advertisement said she had lost her memory. Don't tell me it's even worse than that? You—you aren't going to tell me that she's *dead,* are you?"

And that, as Patrick was to tell Victoria later, was when the bottom fell out of Ursley Terwilliger-Merrydell's dreams of wealth.

"Dead? My good gracious, no. I shan't tell you anything of the kind, Mr. Terwilliger," Pierre assured him, laying one hand heavily on his shoulder as Ursley made to rise.

"She—she's not?" Ursley squeaked, twisting in the chair to look up at Pierre.

"No, she's not. She's in amazingly good health, as a matter of fact," Pierre assured him. "I will, however, tell you that your Miss Halliford is also the most fickle of women, and not worthy of your obvious devotion."

"Oh, don't dress it up in fine linen, my son," André broke in. "It won't make it any easier for the poor fellow in the long run."

Ursley's head whipped around to look at the older Standish. "It—it won't?"

"No," Pierre said, sighing. "It won't. I'm sorry to be the bearer of such sad tidings, Mr. Terwilliger, but your Miss Catherine Halliford eloped last night with my valet, Duvall. They will be well on their way to Gretna Green by now, I imagine. I shall miss him, for he did have the most wonderful way with a cravat."

Ursley Merrydell, looking as if he had been poleaxed, slumped in his chair as if all his bones had turned to mush. Patrick turned on his heel to head for the drinks table, fearing his expression would give the game away. Pierre was in top form this morning; he had to hand it to the man, especially as this was an impromptu performance. Patrick almost pitied Ursley, for even such a dolt as he must know now that the game was up.

Patrick had been half correct in his assessment. Ursley was a beaten man—yet he was also wiser. He looked over to where André Standish was lounging against the mantelpiece, and could read his fate in that man's dark eyes.

He didn't have to see Pierre Standish's face, for he could feel that man's heavy hand on his shoulder. He wondered randomly where they had put his mother, and how many of them it had taken to subdue her, and he wondered when Catherine Halliford would enter the room, very much alive, to point an accusing finger and confront him with the full gravity of his intended crime.

All in all, it was the most profound bit of wondering to which Ursley had ever subjected his brainbox in his lifetime, and he was beginning to feel the dull throb of a headache approaching behind his eyes.

He made another, albeit halfhearted, attempt to rise. "Yes, well, these things will happen, I guess. I'll go now, I think," he mumbled, then felt a renewed surge of hope as Pierre removed his hand, allowing him to get to his feet.

"You do that," Pierre purred, smiling at him in a way that made Ursley feel the man could have killed him without so much as blinking an eye. "I think you should go very far away, please, *Mr. Merrydell,* and never, ever return. Your mother will not follow you, if that news cheers you, as she'll be otherwise occupied for quite some time. Do they still have the women beat hemp at Bridewell, Father, do you suppose?"

Patrick whirled in astonishment. Was that compassion he heard in Pierre's voice? "You're letting him *go?*" he asked, incredulous. They had done all this, only to let the man go? "You've got to be kidding!"

But André, walking across the room to lay an arm across his son's shoulders, only smiled and said proudly, "Please, dearest Patrick, don't sound so amazed. My son is a very human sort. It becomes him, don't you think?"

EPILOGUE

LONDON WAS ANXIOUS for the start of the fall Little Season, with stragglers daily arriving back in the city from their house parties or hunting parties or periods of judicious retrenching after spending a poor spring season at the gaming tables.

If there was a little added fillip to the buzz of gossip that was once more making its rounds through the *haut ton,* it could be traced to the presence of André Standish in their midst after an absence of more than six years. Previously one of the darlings of the *ton,* it was already as if he had never been gone. No evening was complete without him, no hostess a success unless he graced her party.

Yet even more exciting, although at the same time depressing, at least to the eligible young ladies and hopeful mamas in their midst, was the appearance of Pierre Standish, his smiling bride on his arm. The town had been set on its collective ear with the news of the marriage of the unfathomable Pierre to his gorgeous young heiress, and everywhere they went necks craned so that people could observe the couple as they strolled through drawing rooms or went gracefully down the dance.

The Earl and Countess of Wickford were also in town, even though the dear countess was increasing, a fact that could be overlooked, as they were hosting André Standish at their mansion. As a matter of fact, as a show of support to the young countess, more than a few matrons were now sporting spectacles whether they needed them or nay.

Indeed, it was showing all the signs of being an extraordinarily festive Little Season.

André, out for a stroll in the park, his oddly endearing blond page skipping three paces behind him, couldn't have agreed with Society more. As he walked in the cool afternoon sunshine, his walking stick idly twirling between his agile fingers, he called over his shoulder without turning around: "Master Holloway, I implore you, although I appreciate your happiness at being once more in London, try not to whistle like that. You're unnerving the horses as they pass by."

"Yer gots it, Whitey, right an' right!" Jeremy Holloway responded gaily, with his usual disregard for André's consequence. He smoothed his hands down the front of his new jacket, wondering if they would be stopping at the guv'nor's house for dinner so that he could show this latest mass of beauty to Frenchie. He'd be that proud, Frenchie would, for the two of them had become bosom chums since they had helped to rout the Merrydells. It also helped the fledgling friendship considerably that they no longer resided beneath the same roof.

Jeremy looked down the path, his eyes brightening. "'Ey, Whitey, ain't that the guv'nor an' 'is missus comin' up on that rattle an' prad?"

André looked ahead, to see his son and his daughter-in-law approaching in a shiny midnight-black high-perch phaeton, Catherine handling the spirited greys between the shafts with an ease that marked the true whipster. He stopped on the path and planted his walking stick, waiting for them to draw up alongside.

"Good day to you, Father," Pierre called, tipping his hat. "I see you have gotten your Good Deed yet another new suit of clothes. You'll spoil him, you know."

"Master Holloway is completely unspoilable," André responded carelessly. "Besides, as I recall, he was to be *your* Good Deed. Catherine was mine, until you usurped her." He winked up at her, for she already had been informed as to the whole of the events that had led to Pierre's willingness to accept her and Jeremy as his responsibilities.

Putting her arm through her husband's, Catherine looked into his eyes and drawled cheekily, "Jeremy may be uncorruptible but I, on the other hand, simply *adore* being indulged. What do you have to say to that, my dearest husband?"

With a look so soft and loving in his dark eyes, a melting look that would have astonished anyone who had ever faced the not-yet-reformed Pierre Claghorn Standish across a green felt table or a dewy green dueling ground, he responded quietly, "I say I have every intention of indulging you shamelessly all the days of our lives."

And then, shocking and titillating the passersby, he leaned down quite deliberately and kissed his wife square on the lips.

André smiled, whether in memory of his own love or in celebration of his son's happiness only he knew. With a tip of his hat to the oblivious pair, he resumed his walk, calling over his shoulder, "Master Holloway! A whistle if you will—and damn the horses!"

MILLS & BOON®

Live the emotion

Historical
romance™

SPRING BRIDES

THREE BRIDES AND A WEDDING DRESS
by Judith Stacy

Mail-order bride Anna Kingsley journeys across country – only to find her groom has disappeared. Then his handsome cousin Cade Riker offers her a job as his housekeeper. Will she find her happy ending in his arms…?

THE WINTER HEART *by Cheryl Reavis*

Eleanor Hansen is eager for a fresh start in Wyoming. But she finds a lawless land where revenge rules. Can she convince ranch hand Dan Ingram that love is worth more than any vendetta?

McCORD'S DESTINY *by Pam Crooks*

Juliette Blanchard's future depends on buying rancher Tru McCord's land. But her old flame won't sell unless she meets his demands. Juliette must decide how far she'll go for the chance of a lifetime – and the man of her dreams…

THE GLADIATOR'S HONOUR
by Michelle Styles

A hardened survivor of many gladiatorial combats, Gaius Gracchus Valens's raw masculinity fuels many women's sexual fantasies. Roman noblewoman Julia Antonia knows she should have nothing to do with a man who is little more than a slave, but she is drawn inexorably towards the forbidden danger Valens represents…

On sale 5th May 2006

Available at WHSmith, Tesco, ASDA, Borders, Eason, Sainsbury's and most bookshops

www.millsandboon.co.uk

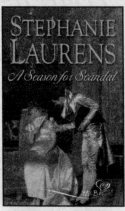